New Stories by

Southern Women

New Stories by

Southern Women

edited by

Mary Ellis Gibson

University of South Carolina Press

Copyright © University of South Carolina 1989

Published in Columbia, South Carolina, by the
University of South Carolina Press

Manufactured in the United States of America

Library of Congress Cataloging-in-Publication Data

New stories by southern women / edited by Mary Ellis Gibson.
    p.   cm.
  Bibliography: p.
  ISBN 0-87249-633-3. — ISBN 0-87249-634-1 (pbk.)
  1. Short stories, American—Southern States. 2. Short stories,
American—Women authors. 3. American fiction—20th century.
4. Southern States—Fiction. 5. Women—Fiction. I. Gibson, Mary
Ellis, 1952–
PS551.N48 1989
813′.01′089287—dc19   89-30840
                                                     CIP

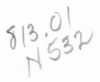

For my mother,

Lorene Meares Gibson

Contents

Acknowledgments

From *Return Trips* by Alice Adams. Copyright © 1984 by Alice Adams. Reprinted by permission of Alfred A. Knopf, Inc.

From *The Sea Birds Are Still Alive* by Toni Cade Bambara. Copyright © 1977 by Toni Cade Bambara. Reprinted by permission of Random House, Inc.

From *American Voice* (Spring 1986): 30–37. Reprinted by permission of Sallie Bingham.

From *Virginia Quarterly Review* (Autumn 1986): 695–705. Reprinted by permission of Jane Bradley.

From *Tongues of Flame* by Mary Ward Brown. Copyright © 1986 by Mary Ward Brown. Reprinted by permission of the publisher, E. P. Dutton/Seymour Lawrence, a division of NAL Penguin Inc.

From *Southern Review* (Winter 1984): 188–198. Reprinted by permission of Moira Crone.

From *All Set About with Fever Trees* by Pam Durban. Copyright © 1985. Reprinted by permission of David R. Godine, Publisher.

From *Victory Over Japan* by Ellen Gilchrist. Copyright © 1983, 1984. Reprinted by permission of Little, Brown and Company.

From *Carolina Quarterly* (Autumn 1977): 5–15. Reprinted by permission of Marianne Gingher.

From *Dream Children* by Gail Godwin. Copyright © 1976 by Gail Godwin. Reprinted by permission of Alfred A. Knopf, Inc.

From *Nine Women* by Shirley Ann Grau. Copyright © 1985 by Shirley Ann Grau. Reprinted by permission by Alfred A. Knopf, Inc.

From *How Far She Went*. Reprinted by permission of Candida Donadio & Associates. Copyright © 1984 by Mary Hood.

From *White Rat* by Gayl Jones. Copyright © 1977 by Gayl Jones. Reprinted by permission of Random House, Inc.

Pp. 165–178 from *Shiloh and Other Stories* by Bobbie Ann Mason. Copyright © 1982 by Bobbie Ann Mason. Reprinted by permission of Harper & Row, Publishers, Inc.

From *St. Andrew's Review* (Fall/Winter 1987): 1–10. Reprinted by permission of Jill McCorkle.

From *Virginia Quarterly* (Summer 1983): 491–97. Reprinted by permission of Naomi Shihab Nye.

From *Fast Lanes* by Jayne Anne Phillips. Copyright © 1987 by Jayne Anne Phillips. Reprinted by permission of the pubisher, E. P. Dutton/Seymour Lawrence, a division of NAL Penguin Inc.

"A Birthday Remembered" by Ann Allen Shockley, from *The Black and White of It*, Tallahassee, Naiad Press, 1980, 1987, is reprinted with the kind permission of the author and the publisher.

"Heat Lightning." Reprinted by permission of the Putnam Publishing Group from *Cakewalk* by Lee Smith. Copyright © 1981 by Lee Smith.

"Indian Summer" copyright © 1978 by Elizabeth Spencer. From *The Stories of Elizabeth Spencer*. Reprinted by permission of Doubleday, a division of Bantam, Doubleday, Dell Publishing Group, Inc.

"Kindred Spirits." Reprinted by permission of The Wendy Weil Agency, Inc. Copyright © 1985 by Alice Walker.

The editor gratefully acknowledges the assistance of Virginia Holman, Charles Davis, and Charles Orzech. Special thanks go to Mark Fleming, without whom this collection would not have been possible. Publication of this collection is supported by the Research Council of the University of North Carolina at Greensboro.

New Stories by

Southern Women

Introduction

This collection brings together twenty-one stories by women writers who grew up in the south and who have published distinguished and distinctive fiction in the last decade. The variety and quality of the stories from which I chose this selection in part results from a recent resurgence in publishing the short story by quarterlies and little magazines, by successful short story annuals, and by southern university and regional presses. The stories gathered here, nonetheless, represent more than a regional subset of a renewed national interest in the short story. This anthology is the first collection of fiction by southern women. It marks an important moment in literary culture—a moment when a definable tradition presents itself to editors and readers as a focus of critical interest and of writers' energies.

To bring together fiction by distinguished southern women writers need not imply a monolithic and coherent tradition. Both in general discussions of southern literature and in discussion of southern women writers too easy an assumption of coherence leads to empty and repetitive generalizations about the southern sense of place, of history, or of voice. Rather, like the categories of American literature and southern literature, the grouping of southern women writers has an adversative function. Just as American literature as a notion had its origin in opposition to English literature and southern literature as a category arose in antebellum sectionalism, so recent interest in the gender of southern authors can be understood as corrective to the canon of southern literature—notwithstanding the fact that for many years there have been prominent women writers from the south.

Like the notion "southern literature," the category "southern women writers" is defined by geography, race and gender, but it involves an interpretation of these factors rather different from the traditional definitions of southern literature. Southern literature

3

was originally defined in terms that were white and largely male and has taken the notion of southernness as its center; from this center it has accommodated work by white women, black men, and less often black women. The category "southern women writers" takes gender as a defining center, and in recent years as a category of legitimate value, it has not depended on exclusion by race. Consequently, one sees in this collection as elsewhere a principle of inclusion in which geography is subordinated to gender and especially to a desire to include black and white women on a more equal footing than literary histories have in the past. Though virtually all the authors represented here were born and brought up in the south, Toni Cade Bambara provides the significant exception.

Because the category "southern women writers" is necessarily adversative it allows us to perceive new similarities among the disparate works that it may include. It gives readers and critics a new purchase on old generalizations, new ways of understanding the power and effectiveness of art. To explore the blind spot created by the category like "southern women writers" will of course be to discuss the work of southern men and of writers outside the south in relationship to writing by southern women. At the same time, to examine the writing of southern women in itself suggests new ways for scholars and readers to approach the canon of southern literature and new ways of understanding how women writers have seen themselves in a southern and female tradition. It suggests generalizations about themes and form, about stylistic affinities, and about literary history.

Though any construction of a historical moment must be partial, I believe this collection and other similar efforts will mark a time when the center of gravity shifted in what is called southern literature. It may mark the moment when it became both possible and desirable for young women writers to see themselves in a tradition of writing by southern women.

In the past decade, as in the years between 1940 and 1955 when Eudora Welty, Flannery O'Connor, and Carson McCullers published much of their work, women writers have been prominent, but younger writers now have had an advantage their predecessors lacked. Writers coming to maturity in the seventies and eighties are the first generation of southern women behind whom lies a long and distinguished tradition of writing by southern women, writing which has won the respect of critics, of other writers, and of readers. To be sure, Welty, O'Connor and McCullers could look to Ellen Glasgow, the successful novels of Elizabeth Maddox Roberts and Marjorie Kinnan Rawlings, and especially to the work of Katherine Ann Porter. Porter's enthusiasm for Welty's stories and McCullers' sometimes embarrassing veneration of Porter are well known. Caroline Gordon, too, was an important presence in southern letters in the thirties. There was then in 1940 a fair number of distinguished southern women writers, enough to constitute something of a tradition for a slightly younger generation.

But how much richer the experience of writers whose first books began appearing in the late 1960's and in the 1970's or eighties. Most of the writers represented here, with the notable exceptions of Elizabeth Spencer and Shirley Ann Grau who are characterized by unusually long and productive careers, matured as writers during the fifteen years or so beginning in 1965. It is arguable that in this period more good fiction by southern women was published in a cumulative and easily accessible way than in any previous period. We might take as a beginning the 1965 publication of Katherine Ann Porter's _Collected Stories_. The same year saw the publication of O'Connor's _Everything That Rises Must Converge_, followed by _Ship Island and Other Stories_ by Elizabeth Spencer (1968); _Flannery O'Connor: Complete Stories_ (1971); Welty's _The Optimist's Daughter_ (1972) and _Collected Stories_ (1980); Elizabeth Spencer's _Collected Stories_ (1981) and Caroline Gordon's _Collected Stories_ (1981). At the same time the sixties saw the revival of Kate Chopin's _The Awakening_ and the republication of that novel and of Chopin's stories; and in 1978 Zora Neale Hurston's work was also revived when _Their Eyes Were Watching God_ was reprinted along with Hurston's autobiographical writings.

For a young woman reading new books, national book reviews, and the book pages of southern newspapers and attending colleges variously touched with a new emphasis on women writers, the 1960's and 1970's were rich with good writing by southern women. Indeed it is arguable that an unusual proportion of distinguished American short stories in twentieth-century have been written by southern women writers. And for young writers in the sixties and seventies the second wave of feminism came together with this rich moment in publishing.

For young southern women, then, precedents were many. A woman, at least a white woman, growing up in the south in the sixties and seventies could expect, as often as not, that her fiction would be taken seriously. And she inherited a strong tradition to live up to, to imitate, to rebel against.

Many contemporary southern women writers are conscious of inheriting their tradition from the preceding generation: Anne Tyler acknowledging Eudora Welty, Jill McCorkle studying with Lee Smith who herself owes much to the voices of Welty's first person narrators, Alice Walker tracing a lineage that includes Flannery O'Connor as well as Zora Neale Hurston, Elizabeth Spencer acknowledging from the first her respect for Welty whom she invited across the street to talk to her college literary society, Ellen Gilchrist making a television screenplay of Welty's stories.

Of course southern women writers find their literary forebears in many places and ages; the history of the short story is unimaginable without Chekov or Mansfield, the history of modern southern literature unimaginable without Faulkner or Allen Tate. Any significant literature is a mix of traditions and any significant writer achieves her or his own style. For all the variousness of writers' individual debts and achievements, however, I think the writers represented in this collection have demonstrably profited by, developed from, and been in differing ways empowered by the distinguished southern women who came before them.

The stories in this collection, taken together, are in some measure representative of contemporary writing by southern women; from them certain themes and narrative strategies emerge. Immediately striking is the emphasis on dailiness, on the nature of living within a social fabric, a fabric that may seem hopelessly torn but which it is always somebody's duty to repair. Ellen Glasgow's prescription for southern fiction, that it needed blood and irony, finds a concise new expression in Elizabeth Spencer's "Indian Summer." Spencer's narrator reflects, "I remembered that we are back in the bosom of the real family now—the blood one—and that blood is for spilling, among other things." Blood families and other families; their food and communal occasions; their disintegration and reconstitution in a changing culture; relationships between mothers and their children, between women, between classes; the illusory nature of maturity: these are themes central in the stories collected here, and they are explored, for the most part, through the experiences or consciousness of central female characters.

Resolutions come within the characters themselves or between them, though except for the cementing of friendships in Shirley Ann Grau's "Home," in Ann Allen Shockley's "A Birthday Remembered" and in Alice Walker's "Kindred Spirits," little is firmly resolved. There is less violence in these stories than one might find in the writing of O'Connor of McCullers or of Faulkner or Wright or in the fiction of contemporary writers like Madison Smartt Bell. Certainly in stories or novels not presented here Alice Walker and Gayl Jones and others explore racist or domestic violence, but in most of the collections from which these stories come the plots do not turn on violent culminations of action. In the stories I have chosen here an incident closes and the protagonists, most often women, are left to carry on in the texture of their everyday lives. Perhaps Lee Smith's "Heat Lightning" can stand for the group; the lightning which might portend a storm, a release, a sudden and unconditional in change Geneva's meager life never materializes; it's just "heat lightning." At the same time Smith's Geneva though stifled is not pitiable. She unwillingly reaffirms her ties to her family, including her son who is "different," and the story ends as she calls, "you all come on and eat." The emphasis on dailiness in most of these stories reminds one of Welty's fiction, of McCullers in her least extravagant mode. So too does the repeated emphasis on eating and on family events—holidays, funerals, weddings, occasions or visiting.

Food, family celebrations, feasts are remarkable features of many of these stories, as they are in the writing of women generally. Food comes to us with mimetic, symbolic, even humorous dimensions. In Sallie Bingham's "Pleyben" numb and grief stricken parents whose daughter has died order their dinner in a foreign language, barely able to understand the menu or each other's misery. In a much lighter vein, Jill McCorkle's "Dear Is a Greeting" brings us an elementary school teacher and her friend the school dietitian who reckon with the divorced and single life by labeling their ex-husbands and lovers for symptomatic dishes, "Tony Ravioli," "Beef Stew," "the Deviled Crab." Equally appealing is Bobbie Ann Mason's "Graveyard Day" in which food symbolizes the shift in details of southern life and the strains between generations.

In Mason's suburbanized south, chicken is still fried even if it's franchised, and the teenager who has discovered health food watches her unreformed mother eat. The graveyard picnic and tombstone cleaning promise the reconstitution of families despite serious obstacles.

Like Mason's "Graveyard Day" many of these stories examine the dynamics of family in a time of frequent divorce, and they explore, often from the mother's perspective, the relationships between parents and children. Alice Walker's "Kindred Spirits" touches on all these elements: the dislocation of unexpected divorce, the force of family for the protagonist who has missed her grandfather's funeral, the compounded distances of class and generations. In Jane Bradley's "Mistletoe" a mother wishes to protect in her daughter that imagination which she cannot protect in herself or in her marriage. A shotgun blast bringing mistletoe down from oak trees emblematically does equal violence to nature and to family. With concise and unrelenting power Mary Hood's "Solomon's Seal" explores the forces that disintegrate a marriage, forces symbolized in the opposition of the husband's hunting dogs to the wife's transplanted wildflowers. A more hopeful resolution comes in Ann Allen Shockley's "A Birthday Remembered," in which a young woman remembers and loves as family the woman whom her dead mother loved and lived with for many years. Many of these stories share with "A Birthday Remembered" indications that reconciliation or daily happiness, when it comes, cannot be measured by the conventions of romance or traditional marriage.

Indeed, reconciliation in these stories as often as not involves coming to terms with children or even the idea of children. The writers whose work is represented here allow us to understand motherhood with new and startling intimacy. Pam Durban's "This Heat" is a tour de force describing a mother's grief at her son's death. The most powerful story of Durban's extraordinary first collection, *All Set About With Fever Trees*, "This Heat" shows us the sorrow and the strength in Ruby Clinton's life. Ruby's mistaken marriage to Charles Clinton, her love for her son Beau, and her anger at Beau's congenital heart defect and at his behavior, her labor in the textile mill are inextricably connected: "she felt the whole dense web of love and grief descending, settling over her shoulders as it had before in the prison. 'This don't ever stop,' she said out loud. And she thought of how she had never loved Charles, not in the way that a woman loves a man, and how, still, he was part of the law that turned and turned and bound them all together, on each turn, more closely than before." While "This Heat" examines the end of a child's life, Jayne Anne Phillips's "Bluegill" is the monologue of a mother addressed to her unborn child, and Shirley Ann Grau's "Home" is a moving story about a young woman who wishes to have another woman's child. As the variety of these stories suggests, contemporary women writers in the south have begun to explore the nature of family and the relationships of parents and children in new ways. Often they sympathetically and carefully examine the mother's point of view.

Another interesting pattern in these stories is their common way of approaching the question of maturity. Instead of presenting growing up as moral or sexual initiation and the achievement of a stable and adult sense of self, these stories give us a richer and more complex understanding of maturity as a continuing and unresolved process. The story that comes closest to the common pattern of an initiation plot is Ellen Gilchrist's "Music." Her protagonist Rhoda, a much tougher version of McCullers' Mick Kelly, picks up a boy in a pool hall, smokes defiantly, flaunts her supposed independence; yet even thirty years later she wishes above all for her father to endorse her imaginative vision of herself. Moira Crone's "Recovery," like Gayl Jones's "Persona," explores issues of identity in a college setting, and Marianne Gingher's experimental "Variation on a Scream" juxtaposes childhood and college scenes with a fairy tale to examine the nature of sexual threat. Alice Adams' "Return Trips" is also about the complex meaning of maturity. With great compression Adams reveals how uneven is a relationship to the past; we see that maturity is not a progressive assimilation of experience toward a settled identity, but a process infinitely uneven and circular of coming to terms with all we had hoped to be. In refusing a linear understanding of psychological development, these stories realize a pattern often identified as common to female bildungsroman. One thinks, too, of characters like Welty's Laurel Hand or of Virgie Rainey suspended between going and staying, old definitions of self and new relationships. As they represent psychological realities these stories suggest a pattern of life that circles and recircles like Ruby Clinton's threads, a law that "don't ever stop."

Often in these stories the dynamics of maturity are presented in the context of suburbanization and of disrupted communal and family patterns. In contemporary fiction by southern women we continue to find the strong sense of place typically attributed to southern writing. But the local details in these stories go beyond the piling up of particulars for their own sake that seems to infect southern writing generally when it capitulates to conventionality. Instead, much of the work by the writers represented here resists over particularization and any nostalgia for a vanished south. In contemporary writing by southern women a sense of place is the background for studies of deracination, escape, and retreat. Nostalgic vision is subordinated to the sense that land without family or family without place can be equally miserable propositions. Sometimes even land with family is beyond bearing, as in "Solomon's Seal," or is bearable only through ironic detachment as in "Indian Summer." Of these stories Naomi Shihab Nye's "Pablo Tamayo" most explicitly examines deracination; an old man is made instantly rootless by his landlord's decision to build an office and parking lot.

Like Hood and Nye, Lee Smith, Bobbie Ann Mason, Jane Bradley, and Pam Durban, among others, fully realize a world of working class experience, not for the local color of collards and cornbread, but to make us feel the possibilities and limitations, and achievements and losses of women who live in house trailers or raise too many children on a shoestring or find their way of life mocked by the superior wisdom of a younger generation. Mary Ward Brown's "Barbecue," for instance, shows us the changes in the rural south where daughters can be friends at Vanderbilt while their parents are unable to bridge traditional class divisions. Stories by Sally Bingham, Shirley Ann Grau, and Alice Adams, on the other hand, focus on an upper middle class world and especially on the ways children delight and endanger the spirits of those who raise them. From house trailers to jets, from elegant town houses to country stores, we see the varieties of contemporary southern life and the conflicts among them.

In these stories, the specificities of place and class are of a piece with the pleasures of a writer's style. These stories have the resonance of locally typical yet individually specific speech. Moreover, many of them are amusing. Bobbie Ann Mason's wit, or the satiric delight of Gail Godwin's "An Intermediate Stop" or of Toni Cade Bambara's "Christmas Eve at Johnson's Drugs N Goods," surely accounts for much of the pleasure in reading these stories. Even Pam Durban's moving story has its moments of examined ambiguity, its preacher who is treated at once ironically and tenderly.

But perhaps the chief characteristic of most of these stories is their unassuming tone. They are not in the least narcissistic; they are technically accomplished, skillful, without as a rule calling attention to their own artistry. In fact, few of them are explicitly about art. Alice Walker's "Kindred Spirits" is the one obvious exception, and yet Walker shows us a writer who learns the price of changing life into art as she recognizes her real kinship with her sister.

Walker's story typifies this collection in yet another way. While the realities of racism are an important part of the story's texture, its focus is elsewhere. In fact as I read much of the writing by southern women in the last decade I found that surprisingly little deals directly with racial tension. Mary Ward Brown's collection, _Tongues of Flame_, includes several interesting stories that show a new arrangement of class and race in the small town south, but I found her "Barbecue" so completely evokes a way of southern life that I chose it instead. Ellen Gilchrist's Traceleen stories in _Victory Over Japan_ are less successfully about race than about upper class mores and manners; I have chosen "Music," one of the Rhoda stories from the same collection.

That integration marks no end to cultural separation is evident. White southern women have not as often as one might wish written well about race, racism, black women and men; the dangers of assuming knowledge of differences and the opposite danger of denying likenesses are perhaps only too clear. Black women writers, particularly southern black women, continue despite Alice Walker's fame to be under-represented by major presses and in major quarterlies and magazines. My own search for stories turned up fewer southern black writers of short fiction than I had anticipated.

I have chosen almost exclusively stories that have been published in the last decade. Even so, the list of wonderful writers who have necessarily been left out is at least as long as the list of those included. Some writers, like Caroline Gordon and Eudora Welty, have been omitted because they published most of their work before 1975. Other important writers like Josephine Humphreys and Anne Tyler are omitted because they work primarily in the novel. Even with these restrictions it is difficult to choose among the many talented young writers of short fiction, a number of whom are listed in suggestions for further reading appended to this volume. Most of the stories here have not been anthologized before; many have appeared only recently in magazines and quarterlies. As it includes many new voices and gives their proper place to established contemporary writers this collection is prospective rather than retrospective. These stories both represent a tradition in the making and provide their own particular pleasures. Best of all, they are a promise of things to come.

Mary Ellis Gibson
*University of North Carolina
at Greensboro*

Return Trips

Alice Adams

Some years ago I spent a hot and mostly miserable summer in an ugly yellow hotel on the steep and thickly wooded, rocky coast of northern Yugoslavia, not far from the island of Rab. I was with a man whom I entirely, wildly loved, and he, Paul, loved me, too, but together we suffered the most excruciating romantic agonies, along with the more ordinary daily discomforts of bad food, an uncomfortable, poorly ventilated room with a hard, unyielding bed, and not enough money to get away. Or enough strength: Paul's health was bad. Morosely we stared out over the lovely clear, cool blue water, from our pine forest, to enticing islands that were purplish-gray in the distance. Or else I swam and Paul looked out after me.

Paul's problem was a congenital heart condition, now correctable by surgery, but not so then; he hurt a lot, and the smallest walks could cause pain. Even love, I came to realize, was for Paul a form of torture, although we kept at it—for him suicidally, I guess—during those endless sultry yellow afternoons, on our awful bed, between our harsh, coarse sheets.

I wanted us to marry. I was very young, and very healthy, and my crazy, unreal idea of marriage seemed to include a sort of transfer of strength. I was not quite so silly as to consciously think that marrying me would "cure" Paul, nor did I imagine a lifelong nurse role for myself. It was, rather, a magic belief that if we did a normal thing, something other people did all the time, like getting married, Paul's heart would become normal, too, like other, ordinary hearts.

Paul believed that he would die young, and, nobly, he felt that our marriage would be unfair to me. He also pointed out that whereas he had enough money from a small inheritance for one person, himself, to live on very sparingly, there was really not enough for two, and I would do well to go back to America and to the years of graduate study to which my professor mother wanted to stake me. At that time, largely because of Paul, who was a poet,

13

I thought of studying literature; instead, after he died I turned to history, contemporary American. By now I have written several books; my particular interest is in the Trotskyite movement: its rich history of lonely, occasionally brilliant, contentious voices, its legacy of schisms—an odd choice, perhaps, but the books have been surprisingly popular. You might say, and I hope Paul would, that I have done very well professionally. In any case you could say that Paul won our argument. That fall I went back to graduate school, at Georgetown, and Paul died young, as he said he would, in a hospital in Trieste.

I have said that Paul loved me, and so he did, intensely—he loved me more, it has come to seem to me, than anyone since, although I have had my share, I guess. But Paul loved me with a meticulous attention that included every aspect. Not only my person: at that time I was just a skinny tall young girl with heavy dark hair that was fated to early gray, as my mother's had been. With an old-fashioned name—Emma. Paul loved my hair and my name and whatever I said to him, any odd old memory, or half-formed ambition; he took all my perceptions seriously. He laughed at all my jokes, although his were much funnier. He was even interested in my dreams, which I would sometimes wake and tell him, that summer, in the breathless pre-dawn cool, in the ugly hotel.

And so it is surprising that there was one particular dream that I did not tell him, especially since this dream was so painful and troubling that I remember it still. Much later I even arranged to reënact the dream, an expurgatory ritual of sorts—but that is to get far ahead of my story.

In the dream, then, that I dreamed as I slept with Paul, all those years ago in Yugoslavia, it was very hot, and I was walking down a long, intensely familiar hill, beside a winding white concrete highway. In the valley below was the rambling white house where (long before Yugoslavia) my parents and I had lived for almost five years, in a small Southern town called Hilton. I did not get as far as the house, in the dream; it was so hot, and I was burdened with the most terrific, heavy pain in my chest, a pain that must have come from Paul's actual pain, as the heat in the dream would have come from the actual heat of that summer.

"Oh, I had such an awful dream!" I cried out to Paul, as I burrowed against his sharp back, his fine damp skin.

"What about?" He kissed my hair.

"Oh, I don't know," I said. "I was in Hilton. You know, just before my parents' divorce. Where I had such a good time and my mother hated everything."

Against my hair he murmured, "Your poor mother."

"Yes, but she brings it on herself. She's so difficult. No wonder my father . . . really. And I don't want to go to graduate school."

And so I did not tell Paul my dream, in which I had painfully walked that downhill mile toward the scene of our family's dissolution, and the heady start of my own adolescence. Instead, in a familiar way, Paul and I argued about my future, and as usual I took a few stray shots at my mother.

And Paul died, and I did after all go to graduate school, and then my mother died—quite young, it now seems to me, and long before our war was in any way resolved.

A very wise woman who is considerably older than I am once told me that in her view relationships with people to whom we have been very close can continue to change even after the deaths of those people, and for me I think this has been quite true, with my mother, and in quite another way with Paul.

I am now going back to a very early time, long before my summer with Paul, in Yugoslavia. Before anyone had died. I am going back to Hilton.

When we arrived in Hilton I was eleven, and both my parents were in their early forties, and almost everything that went so darkly and irretrievably wrong among the three of us was implicit in our ages. Nearly adolescent, I was eager for initiation into romantic, sensual mysteries of which I had dim intimations from books. For my mother, the five years from forty-two or forty-three onward were a desolate march into middle age. My father, about ten months younger than my mother—and looking, always, ten years younger—saw his early forties as prime time; he had never felt better in his life. Like me, he found Hilton both romantic and exciting—he had a marvellous time there, as I did, mostly.

My first overtly sensual experience took place one April night on that very stretch of road, the gravelled walk up above the highway that wound down to our house, that I dreamed of in Yugoslavia. I must have been twelve, and a boy who was "walking me home" reached for and took and held my hand, and I felt an overwhelming hot excitement. Holding hands.

About hands:
These days, like most of my friends, I am involved in a marriage, my second, which seems problematical—even more problematical than most of the marriages I see—but then maybe everyone views his or her marriage in this way. Andreas is Greek, by way of Berkeley, to which his parents immigrated in the thirties and opened a student restaurant, becoming successful enough to send their promising son to college there, and later on to medical school. Andreas and I seem to go from friendliness or even love to rage, with a speed that leaves me dizzy, and scared. However, ambivalent as in many ways I am about Andreas, I do very much like—in fact, I love—his hands. They are just plain male hands, rather square in shape, usually callused and very competent. Warm. A doctor, he specializes in kidneys, unromantically enough, but his hands are more like a workman's, a carpenter's. And sometimes even now an accidental meeting of our hands can recall me to affection; his hands remind me of love.

I liked Paul's hands, too, and I remember them still. They were very smooth, and cool.

Back in Hilton, when I was twelve, my mother violently disapproved of my being out at night with boys. Probably sensing just how exciting I found those April nights that smelled of privet and lilacs, and those lean, tall, sweet-talking Southern boys, she wept and raged, despairing and helpless as she recognized the beginning of my life as a sensual woman, coinciding as it probably did with the end of her own.

My feckless father took my side, of course. "Things are different down here, my dear," he told her. "It's a scientific fact that girls, uh, mature much earlier in the South. And when in Rome, you know. I see no harm in Emma's going to a movie with some nice boy, if she promises to be home at a reasonable hour. Ten-thirty?"

"But Emma isn't Southern. She has got to be home by ten!"

My mother filled with a searing discomfort, a longing to be

away from her. Having no idea how much I pitied her, I believed that I hated her.

My father was not only younger than my mother, he was at least a full inch shorter—a small man, compactly built, and handsome. "Has anyone ever told you that you look like that writer fellow, that Scott Fitzgerald?" asked one of the local Hilton ladies, a small brunette, improbably named Popsie Hooker. "Why no, I don't believe anyone ever has," my father lied; he had been told at least a dozen times of that resemblance. "But of course I'm flattered to be compared to such a famous man. Rather a devil, though, I think I've heard," he said, with a wink at Popsie Hooker.

"Popsie Hooker, how remarkably redundant," hopelessly observed my academic mother, to my bored and restless father. They had chosen Hilton rather desperately, as a probably cheap place to live on my father's dwindling Mid-western inheritance; he was never exactly cut out for work, and after divorcing my mother he resolved his problems, or some of them, in a succession of marriages to very rich women.

Popsie Hooker, who was later to play a curious, strong role in my life, at that time interested me not at all; if I had a view of her, it was closer to my mother's than I would have admitted, and for not dissimilar reasons. She was ludicrous, so small and silly, and just a little cheap, with those girlish clothes, all ribbons and bows, and that tinny little laugh. And that accent: Popsie out-Southerned everyone around.

"It's rather like a speech defect," my mother observed, before she stopped mentioning Popsie altogether.

Aside from her smallness and blue-eyed prettiness, Popsie's local claim to fame was her lively correspondence with "famous people," to whom she wrote what were presumably letters of adulation, the puzzle being that these people so often wrote back to her. Popsie was fond of showing off her collection. She had a charming note from Mr. Fitzgerald, and letters from Eleanor Roosevelt, Norma Shearer, Willa Cather, Clare Boothe Luce. No one, least of all my mother, could understand why such people would write to dopey Popsie, nor could I, until many years later, when she began to write to me.

However, I was too busy at that time to pay much attention to my parents or their friends, their many parties at which everyone drank too much; my own burgeoning new life was much more absorbing.

My walks at night with various boys up and down that stretch of highway sometimes came to include a chaste but passionate kiss; this would take place, if at all, on the small secluded dirt road that led down from the highway to our house.

One winter, our fourth year in Hilton, when I was fifteen, in January we had an exceptionally heavy fall of snow, deep and shadowed in the valley where our house was, ladening boughs of pine and fir and entirely covering the privet and quince and boxwood that edged the highway. For several days most of the highway itself lay under snow. Cars labored up and down the hill, singly, at long intervals, wearing unaccustomed chains.

Those nights of snow were marvellous: so cold, the black sky broken with stars as white as snow. My friends and I went sledding; that winter I was strongly taken with a dark boy who looked rather like Paul, now that I try to see him: a thin, bony face, a certain Paul-like intensity. On a dare we sledded down the highway, so perilously exciting! We lay on the sled, I stretched along his back.

We went hurtling down past the back road to my house, past everything. At last on a level area we stopped; on either side of us fields of white seemed to billow and spread off into the shadows, in the cold. Standing there we kissed—and then we began the long slow ascent of the highway, toward my house. He was pulling the sled, and we stopped several times to kiss, to press our upright bodies warmly together.

As we neared and then reached the back road to my house, we saw a car stopped, its headlights on. Guiltily we dropped hands. Dazzled by the light, only as we were almost upon it could I recognize our family car, the only wood-panelled Chrysler in town. In it was my father, kissing someone; their bodies were blotted into one silhouette.

If he saw and recognized us, there was no sign. He could easily not have seen us, or, knowing my father, who was nothing if not observant, I would guess it's more likely he did see us but pretended to himself that he did not, as he pretended not to see that my mother was miserably unhappy, and that I was growing up given to emotional extremes, and to loneliness.

"Stricken" probably comes closest to how I felt: burning rage, a painful, seething shame—emotions that I took to be hatred. "I hate him" is what I thought. Oblivious of the tall boy at my side, I began to walk as fast as I could, clumping heavily through the snow; at the door of my house I muttered what must have been a puzzlingly abrupt good night. Without kissing.

By the time we left Hilton, the summer that I was sixteen, my parents were entirely fed up with Hilton, and with each other. My father thought he could get a job in the Pentagon, in Washington—he knew someone there; and my mother had decided on New York, on graduate school at Columbia; I would go to Barnard.

I was less upset about my parents' separation than I was about leaving Hilton, which was by now to me a magic, enchanted place. In the spring and summer just preceding our departure there were amazing white bursts of dogwood, incredible wisteria and roses.

I wept for my friends, whom I would always love and miss, I thought.

I hated New York. The city seemed violent and confusing, ugly and dirty, loud. Voices in the streets or on subways and busses grated against my ears; everyone spoke so stridently, so harshly. Until I met Paul I was lonely and miserable, and frightened.

I would not have told him of my unease right away, even though Paul and I began as friends. But he must have sensed some rural longings just beneath my New York veneer. He would have; almost from the start Paul felt whatever I felt—he came to inhabit my skin.

In any case, our friendship and then our love affair had a series of outdoor settings. Paul, melancholy and romantic, and even then not well, especially liked the sea, and he liked to look out to islands—which led us, eventually, to Yugoslavia, our desolate summer there.

Not having had an actual lover before, only boys who kissed me, who did not talk much, I was unprepared for the richness of love with Paul—or, rather, I assumed that that was how love was between true intimates. Paul's sensuality was acutely sensitive, and intense; with him I felt both beautiful and loved—indescribably so.

You could say that Paul spoiled me for other men, and in a way that is true—he did. But on the other hand Paul knew that he was dying, gradually, and that knowledge must have made him profligate with love. We talked and talked, we read poetry; Paul read Wallace Stevens and Eliot aloud to me, and his own poems, which I thought remarkable. We made jokes, we laughed, we made love.

Since Hilton was only twelve hours from New York by train, and we both liked travel, and trains, in a way it is odd that Paul and I did not go down to Hilton. I know he would have said yes had I suggested a trip. His curiosity about me was infinite; he would have wanted to see a place that I cared so much about. I suppose we would have stayed at the inn, as I was to do later on, when finally I did go back to Hilton. We could have taken a taxi out to what had been my house.

However, for whatever reasons, Paul and I did not go to Hilton. We went to upstate New York and to Connecticut, and out to Long Island.

And, eventually, to Yugoslavia.

Our unhappiness there in the ugly yellow hotel on the beautiful rockbound coast was due not only to Paul's declining health and my unreal but urgent wish to marry. Other problems lay in the sad old truth, well known to most adults but not at that time to us, that conducting a love affair while living apart is quite unlike taking up residence together, even for a summer. In domestic ways we were both quite impossible then—and of course Paul did not get time to change.

I could not cook, and our arrangement with the hotel included the use of a communal kitchen, an allotted space in the refrigerator and time at the stove; my cooking was supposed to save us money, which my burned disasters failed to do. Neither could I sew or iron. I even somehow failed at washing socks. None of this bothered Paul at all; his expectations of me did not run along such lines, but mine, which must have been plucked from the general culture rather than from my own freethinking mother, were strong, and tormenting.

Paul had terrible troubles with the car, a Peugeot that we had picked up in Paris, on our way, and that had functioned perfectly well all across the Italian Alps, until we got to Trieste, where it began to make inexplicable noises, and sometimes not to start. Paul was utterly incapable of dealing with these *crises*; he would shout and rant, even clutch melodramatically at his thin black hair. I dimly sensed that he was reacting to the car's infirmities instead of to his own, which of course I did not say; but I also felt that men were supposed to deal with cars, an insupportable view, I knew even then, and derived from my father, who possessed remarkable mechanical skills.

We were there in Yugoslavia for almost three months in all, from June to September. It was probably in August, near the end of our stay, that I had my dream of going back to Hilton, and walking down the highway to our house—in the heat, with the pain in my heart that must have been Paul's pain. The dream that I did not tell Paul.

And in the fall I went back to America, to Washington, D.C., to study at Georgetown.

And Paul moved up to Trieste, where shortly after Christmas he went into a hospital and died.

Sheer disbelief was my strongest reaction to the news of Paul's death, which came in the form of a garbled cablegram. I could not believe that such an acute and lively intelligence could simply be snuffed out. In a conventional way I wept and mourned his loss: I played music that he had liked—the Hummel trumpet concerto, of which he was especially fond—and I reread "Sunday Morning" and "Four Quarters." But at the same time I never believed that he was entirely gone (I still do not).

Two years after Paul's death, most unexpectedly my mother died, in a senseless automobile accident; she was driving to see friends in Connecticut and swerved on a wet highway to avoid an oncoming truck. I was more horrified, more devastated, really, than I could have believed possible. I went to an analyst. "I haven't even written her for a month!" I cried out, during one dark fifty-minute hour. "How many letters does it take to keep a mother alive?" was the gentle and at least mildly helpful answer. Still, I wrestled with my guilt and with the sheer irresolution of our connection for many, many years.

In my late twenties I married one of my former professors; Lewis—a large, blond, emphatically healthy, outgoing man, as much unlike Paul as anyone I could have found; this occurred to me at the time as an ironic twist that only Paul himself could have appreciated. We lived in New York, where we both now taught.

To sum up very complicated events in a short and simple way: my work prospered, while my marriage did not—and I present these as simultaneous conditions, not causally linked. A happier first marriage could have made for even better work on my part, I sometimes think.

During those years, I thought of my mother with increasing sympathy. This is another simplification, but that is what it came to. She did her best under very difficult, sometimes painful circumstances is one way of putting it.

And I thought of Paul. It was his good-friend aspect that I most missed, I found, in the loneliness of my marriage. I felt, too, always, the most vast regret for what seemed the waste of a life.

And Hilton was very much in my mind.

Sometimes I tried to imagine what my life would have been like if I had never left: I could have studied at the university there, and married one of those lean and sexy sweet-talking boys. And often that seemed a preferable way to have taken.

I divorced Lewis, and I had various "relationships." I wrote and published articles, several books—and I began getting letters from Popsie Hooker. Long, quite enthralling letters. They were often about her childhood, which had been spent on a farm in Illinois— southern Illinois, to be sure, but, still, I thought how my mother would have laughed to hear that Popsie, the near-professional Southerner, was really from Illinois. Popsie wrote to me often, and I answered, being compulsive in that way, and also because I so much enjoyed hearing from her.

Some of her letters were very funny, as when she wrote about the new "rest home" in Hilton, in which certain former enemies were housed in adjacent rooms: "Mary Lou and Henrietta haven't spoken for years and *years*, and there they are. Going over there to visit is like reading a novel, a real long one," Popsie wrote, and she added, "They couldn't get me into one of those places if they carried me there on a stretcher." I gathered that Popsie was fairly rich; several husbands had come and gone, all leaving her well endowed.

We wrote back and forth, Popsie and I, she writing more often than I did, often telling me how much my letters meant to her.

Her letters meant a great deal to me, too. I was especially moved when she talked about the seasons down there in Hilton—the weather and what was in bloom; I could remember all of it, so vividly. And I was grateful that she never mentioned my parents, and her own somewhat ambiguous connection with them.

During some of those years, I began an affair with Andreas, the doctor whom I eventually married: a turbulent, difficult, and sometimes rewarding marriage. Andreas is an exceptionally skilled doctor; he is also arrogant, quick-tempered, and inconsiderate, especially of other people's time—like all doctors, I have sometimes thought.

Our conflicts often have to do with schedules: his conference in Boston versus mine in Chicago; his need for a vacation in February versus mine for time to finish a book, just then. And more ordinary arguments: my dislike of being kept waiting, his wish that I do more cooking. Sometimes even now his hot, heavy body next to mine in bed seems alien, unknown, and I wonder what he is doing there, really. At other times, as I have said, I am deeply stirred by an accidental touching of our hands.

At some of our worst moments I think of leaving Andreas; this would be after an especially ugly quarrel, probably fuelled by too much wine, or simply after several weeks of non-communication.

In one such fantasy I do go back to Hilton, and I take up the rest of my life there as a single woman. I no longer teach, I only do research in the library, which is excellent. And I write more books. I imagine that I see a lot of Popsie Hooker; I might even become the sort of "good daughter" to her that I was so far from being to my own mother. And sometimes in this fantasy I buy the house that we used to live in, the rambling house down the highway, in the valley. I have imagined it as neglected, needing paint, new gutters, perhaps even falling apart, everything around it overgrown and gone to seed.

Last June, when I had agreed to give a series of lectures at Georgetown, Andreas and I made reservations in a small hotel where we had stayed before, not far from the university. We both like Washington; we looked forward to revisiting favorite galleries and restaurants. It was one of the many times when we needed a vacation

together, and so, as I might have known would happen, this became impossible: two sick patients got sicker, and although I argued, citing the brilliance and the exceptional competence of his
partners (an argument that did not go over very well), Andreas
said no, he had to stay in New York, with the kidneys of Mrs.
Howell and old Mr. Rosenthal.

I went to Georgetown and to our hotel alone. I called several
times, and Andreas and I "made up" what had been a too familiar
argument.

In Georgetown, the second day, as I walked alone past those ele-
gantly maintained houses, as I glanced into seductively cloistered,
luxuriantly ferned and flowered gardens, some stray scent of privet
or a glimpse of a yellow rosebush in full bloom—something reminded me strongly, compellingly of Hilton, and I thought, Well,
why not? I could take the train and just stay for a couple of days.
That much more time away from Andreas might be to the good,
just now. I could stay at the Hilton Inn. I could visit Popsie. I
could walk down the highway to our house.

And that is what I did, in more or less that order, except that I
saved the visit to Popsie for the last, which turned out to be just as
well. But right away I stopped at a travel agency on Wisconsin
Avenue, and I bought a ticket to Raleigh, treating myself to a
roomette for a five-hour trip; I felt that both ceremony and privacy
were required.

I had thought that on the train I would be struck by the deep
familiarity of the landscape; at last, that particular soil, that special
growth. But actually it was novelty that held me to my window:
the wide flat brown shining rivers that we crossed, with their
tacky little marinas, small boats, small boys on the banks. Flooded
swamps, overgrown with kudzu vines and honeysuckle. I had the
curious illusion that one sometimes gets on trains, of traversing an
exotic, hitherto untravelled land. I felt myself to be an explorer.

That night I had an unmemorable dinner alone at the inn—
which, having been redone, was all unfamiliar to me. I went to bed
early, slept well.

Sometime in the night, though, I did wake up with the strange
and slightly scary thought that in a few years I would be as old as
my mother was when she died, and I wondered what, if anything,

that fact had to do with my coming back to Hilton, after all these years.

The next morning's early air was light and delicate. Dew still shone on the heavy, dark-green shrubbery around the inn, on silver cobwebs, as I set out for my walk—at last! The sky was soft and pale, an eggshell blue. Walking along the still gravelled sidewalk, beside the tarred road that led from the inn out to the highway, I recognized houses; I knew who used to live in almost all of them, and I said those names to myself as I walked along: Hudson, Phipps, Zimmerman, Rogerson, Pittman. I noticed that the old Pittman place was now a fraternity house, with an added sun porch and bright new paint, bright gold Greek letters over the door. In fact, the look of all those houses was one of improvement, up-grading, with their trim lawns, abundant boxwood, their lavish flower beds.

I reached the highway, still on the gravelled walk, and I began the long descent toward my house. The air was still light, and barely warm, although the day to come would be hot. I thought of my dream in Yugoslavia, of this walk, and I smiled, inexplicably happy at just that moment—with no heat, no pain in my heart.

I recognized more houses, and said more names, and I observed that these houses, too, were in splendid shape, all bright and visibly cared for. There was much more green growth than I remembered, the trees were immense, and I thought, Well, of course; they've had time to grow.

No one seeing me as I walked there could know or guess that that was where I used to live, I thought. They would see—a tall thin woman, graying, in early middle age, in a striped gray cotton skirt, gray shirt. A woman looking intently at everything, and smiling to herself.

And then, there before me was our house. But not our house. It, too, had been repainted—all smartened up with bright white paint and long black louvred shutters, now closed against the coming heat and light. Four recent-model sports cars, all imported, were parked in the driveway, giving the place a recreational, non-familiar air. A group of students, I thought; perhaps some club? The surrounding trees were huge; what had been a small and murmurous pine grove at one side of the house now towered over it, thickly green and rustling slightly in a just-arisen morning breeze.

No one came out while I stood there, for not very long, but I was sure that there was not a family inside but some cluster of transients—young people, probably, who liked each other and liked the house, but without any deep or permanent attachment.

I continued on my walk, a circle of back roads on which I was pleased to find that I still knew my way, which led at last back to the highway, and up the hill, to the inn.

I had called Popsie Hooker from Washington, and again from the inn, when I got there. She arose from her nap about four in the afternoon, she said, and if I could come out to her house along about then she would be thrilled, just simply thrilled.

By midafternoon it was too hot for another walk, and so I took a taxi out to Popsie's house, in the direction opposite to mine. I arrived about four-thirty, which I assumed to be along about four in Southernese.

Popsie's house, the fruit of one of her later marriages, was by far the most splendid I had yet seen in town: a Georgian house, of ancient soft red brick smartly trimmed in black, with frequent accents of highly polished brass. Magnificent lawns, magnolias, rhododendrons. By the time I got to the door I half expected to be greeted by an array of uniformed retainers—all black, of course.

But it was Popsie herself who opened the door to me—a Popsie barely recognizable, so shrunken and wizened had she become: a small woman withered down to dwarf size, in a black silk dress with grosgrain at her throat, a cameo brooch. She smelled violently of gardenia perfume and of something else that at first I could not place.

"Emma! Emma!" she breathed up into my face, the old blue eyes filming over, and she caught at both my arms and held them in her weak tight grasp. I recognized the second scent, which was sherry.

"You're *late*," she next accused me. "Here I've been expecting you this whole long *afternoon*."

I murmured apologies, and together we proceeded down the hallway and into a small parlor, Popsie still clutching my arm, her small fierce weight almost tugging me over sideways.

We sat down. The surfaces in that room were all so cluttered with silver and ivory pieces, inlay, old glass, that it could have been an antique shop, or the parlor of a medium. I told Popsie how happy I was to be there, how wonderful Hilton looked.

"Well, you know, it's become a very fancy place to live. Very *expensive*. Lots of Yankees retiring down here, and fixing up the old houses."

"Uh, where do the poor people live?"

She laughed, a tiny rasp. "Oh, there you go, talking *liberal*, and you just got here. Well, the poor folks, what's left of them, have moved out to Robertsville."

Robertsville was the adjacent town, once predominantly black, and so I next asked, "What about the Negroes?"

"Well, I guess they've just sort of drifted back into the country-side, where they came from. But did you notice all the fancy new stores on Main Street? All the restaurants, and the *clothes*?"

We talked for a while about the new splendors of Hilton, and the rudeness of the new Yankees, who did not even go to church— as I thought, This could not be the woman who has been writing to me. Although of course she was—the same Popsie, half tipsy in the afternoon; she probably spent her sober mornings writing letters. This woman was more like the Popsie of my early years in Hilton, that silly little person, my mother's natural enemy.

Possibly to recall the Popsie of the wonderful letters, I asked about the local rest home. How were things out there?

"Well, I have to tell you. What gripes me the most about that place is that they don't pay any taxes" was Popsie's quick, unhelpful response. "Tax-*free*, and you would not believe the taxes I have to pay on this old place."

"But this place is so beautiful." I did not add, And you have so much money.

"Well, it is right pretty," she acknowledged, dipping her head. "But why must I go on and on paying for it? It's not fair."

Our small chairs were close together in that crowded, stuffy room, so that when Popsie leaned closer yet to me, her bleary eyes peering up into mine, the sherry fumes that came my way were very strong indeed. And Popsie said, "You know, I've always thought you were so beautiful, even if no one else ever thought you were." She peered again. "Where did you get that beauty, do you think? Your mother never was even one bit pretty."

More stiffly than I had meant to, I spoke the truth. "Actually I look quite a lot like my mother," I told her. And I am not beautiful.

Catching a little of my anger, which probably pleased her, Popsie raised her chin. "Well, one thing certain, you surely don't favor your daddy."

"No, I don't. I don't favor him at all." My father had recently moved to La Jolla, California, with another heiress, this one younger than I am, which would have seemed cruel news to give to Popsie.

After a pause, during which I suppose we both could have been said to be marshalling our forces, Popsie, and I continued our conversation, very politely, until I felt that I could decently leave.

I told her how much I liked her letters, and she said how she liked mine, and we both promised to write again, very soon—and I wondered if we would.

On the plane to New York, a smooth, clear, easy flight, I was aware of an unusual sense of well-being, which out of habit I questioned. I noted the sort of satisfaction that I might have been expected to feel on finishing a book, except that at the end of books I usually feel drained, exhausted. But now I simply felt well, at peace, and ready for whatever should come next.

Then Paul returned from nowhere to my mind, more strongly than for some time. In an affectionate way I remembered how impossible he was, in terms of daily life, and how much I had loved him—and how he had loved me.

Actually he and Andreas were even more unlike than he and Lewis were, I next thought, and a little wearily I noted my own tendency to extremes, and contrasts. Andreas likes to fix and mend things, including kidneys, of course. He is good with cars. "I come from strong Greek peasant stock" is a thing that he likes to say, and it is true; clearly he does, with his powerful black hair, his arrogant nose. His good strong heart.

We were planning a trip to Greece the following fall. Andreas had gone back as a boy to visit relatives, and later with both his first and second wives. And he and I had meant to go, and now we would.

We planned to fly to Rome, maybe spend a few days there; we both like Rome. But now another route suggested itself: we could fly to Vienna, where we have never been, and then take the train to Trieste, where we could pick up a car and drive down to Greece by way of Yugoslavia. We would drive past the ferry to the island of Rab, and past the road that led to our yellow hotel. I did not imagine driving down to see it; Andreas would be in a hurry, and my past does not interest him much. He would see no need to stop on such an errand.

Nor do I. And besides, that particular ugly, poorly built structure has probably been torn down. Still, I very much like the idea of just being in its vicinity.

Christmas Eve at Johnson's Drugs N Goods

Toni Cade Bambara

I was probably the first to spot them cause I'd been watching the entrance to the store on the lookout for my daddy, knowing that if he didn't show soon, he wouldn't be coming at all. His new family would be expecting him to spend the holidays with them. For the first half of my shift, I'd raced the cleaning cart down the aisles doing a slapdash job on the signs and glass cages, eager to stay in view of the doorway. And look like Johnson's kept getting bigger, swelling, sprawling itself all over the corner lot, just to keep me from the door, to wear me out in the marathon vigil.

In point of fact, Johnson's Drugs N Goods takes up less than one-third of the block. But it's laid out funny in crisscross aisles so you get to feeling like a rat in an endless maze. Plus the ceilings are high and the fluorescents a blazing white. And Mrs. Johnson's got these huge signs sectioning off the spaces—TOBACCO DRUGS HOUSEWARES, etc.—like it was some big-time department store. The thing is, till the two noisy women came in, it felt like a desert under a blazing sun. Piper in Tobacco even had on shades. The new dude in Drugs looked like he was at the end of a wrong-way telescope. I got to feeling like a nomad with the cleaning cart, trekking across the sands with no end in sight, wandering. The overhead lights creating mirages and racing up my heart till I'd realize that wasn't my daddy in the parking lot, just the poster-board Santa Claus. Or that wasn't my daddy in the entrance way, just the Burma Shave man in a frozen stance. Then I'd tried to make out pictures of Daddy getting off the bus at the terminal, or driving a rented car past the Chamber of Commerce building, or sitting jammed-leg in one of them DC point-o-nine brand X planes, coming to see me.

By the time the bus pulled into the lot and the two women in their big-city clothes hit the door, I'd decided Daddy was already at the house waiting for me, knowing that for a mirage too, since Johnson's is right across from the railroad and bus terminals and the house is a dollar-sixty cab away. And I know he wouldn't feature going to the house on the off chance of running into Mama. Or even if he escaped that fate, having to sit in the parlor with his hat in his lap while Aunt Harriet looks him up and down grunting, too busy with the latest crossword puzzle contest to offer the man some supper. And Uncle Henry talking a blue streak bout how he outfoxed the city council or somethin and nary a cold beer in sight for my daddy.

But then the two women came banging into the store and I felt better. Right away the store stopped sprawling, got fixed. And we all got pulled together from our various zones to one focal point—them. Changing up the whole atmosphere of the place fore they even got into the store proper. Before we knew it, we were all smiling, looking halfway like you supposed to on Christmas Eve, even if you do got to work for ole lady Johnson, who don't give you no slack whatever the holiday.

"What the hell does this mean, Ethel?" the one in the fur coat say, talking loud and fast, yanking on the rails that lead the way into the store. "What are we, cattle? Being herded into the blankety-blank store and in my fur coat," she grumbles, boosting herself up between the rails, swinging her body along like the kids do in the park.

Me and Piper look at each other and smile. Then Piper moves down to the edge of the counter right under the Tobacco sign so as not to miss nothing. Madeen over in Housewares waved to me to ask what's up and I just shrug. I'm fascinated by the women.

"Look here," the one called Ethel say, drawing the words out lazy slow. "Do you got a token for this sucker?" She's shoving hard against the turnstile folks supposed to exit through. Pushing past and grunting, the turnstile crank cranking like it gonna bust, her Christmas corsage of holly and bells just ajingling and hanging by a thread. Then she gets through and stumbles toward the cigar counter and leans back against it, studying the turnstile hard. It whips back around in place, making scrunching noises like it's been abused.

"You know one thing," she say, dropping her face onto her coat collar so Piper'd know he's being addressed.

"Ma'am?"

"That is one belligerent bad boy, that thing right there."

Piper laughs his prizewinning laugh and starts touching the stacks of gift-wrapped stuff, case the ladies in the market for pipe tobacco or something. Two or three of the customers who'd been falling asleep in the magazines coming to life now, inching forward. Phototropism, I'd call it, if somebody asked me for a word.

The one in the fur coat's coming around now the right way—if you don't count the stiff-elbow rail-walking she was doing—talking about "Oh, my God, I can walk, I can walk, Ethel, praise de lawd."

The two women watching Piper touch the cigars, the humidors, the gift-wrapped boxes. Mostly he's touching himself, cause George Lee Piper love him some George Lee Piper. Can't blame him. Piper be fine.

"You work on commissions, young man?" Fur Coat asking.

"No, ma'am."

The two women look at each other. They look over toward the folks inching forward. They look at me gliding by with the cleaning cart. They look back at each other and shrug.

"So what's his problem?" Ethel says in a stage whisper. "Why he so hot to sell us something?"

"Search me." Fur Coat starts flapping her coat and frisking herself. "You know?" she asking me.

"It's a mystery to me," I say, doing my best to run ole man Samson over. He sneaking around trying to jump Madeen in Housewares. And it is a mystery to me how come Piper always so eager to make a sale. You'd think he had half interest in the place. He says it's because it's his job, and after all, the Johnsons are Black folks. I guess so, I guess so. Me, I just clean the place and stay busy in case Mrs. J is in the prescription booth, peeking out over the top of the glass.

When I look around again, I see that the readers are suddenly very interested in cigars. They crowding around Ethel and Fur Coat. Piper kinda embarrassed by all the attention, though fine as he is, he oughta be used to it. His expression's cool but his hands give him away, sliding around the counter like he shuffling a deck of slippery cards. Fur Coat nudges Ethel and they bend over to watch the hands, doing these chicken-head jerkings. The readers take up positions just like a director was hollering "Places" at em.

Piper, never one to disappoint an audience, starts zipping around these invisible walnut shells. Right away Fur Coat whips out a little red change purse and slaps a dollar bill on the counter. Ethel dips deep into her coat pocket, bending her knees and being real comic, then plunks down some change. Ole man Sampson tries to boost up on my cleaning cart to see the shells that ain't there.

"Scuse me, Mr. Sampson," I say, speeding the cart up sudden so that quite naturally he falls off, the dirty dog.

Piper is snapping them imaginary shells around like nobody's business, one of the readers leaning over another's shoulder, staring pop-eyed.

"All right now, everybody step back," Ethel announces. She waves the crowd back and pushes up one coat sleeve, lifts her fist into the air and jerks out one stiff finger from the bunch, and damn if the readers don't lift their heads to behold in amazement this wondrous finger.

"That, folks," Fur Coat explains, "is what is known as the indicator finger. The indicator is about to indicate the indicatee."

"Say wha?" Dirty ole man Sampson decides he'd rather sneak up on Madeen than watch the show.

"What's going on over there?" Miz Della asks me. I spray the watch case and make a big thing of wiping it and ignoring her. But then the new dude in Drugs hollers over the same thing.

"Christmas cheer gone to the head. A coupla vaudevillians," I say. He smiles, and Miz Della says "Ohhh" like I was talking to her.

"This one," Ethel says, planting a finger exactly one-quarter of an inch from the countertop.

Piper dumb-shows a lift of the shell, turning his face away as though he can't bear to look and find the elusive pea ain't there and he's gonna have to take the ladies' money. Then his eyes swivel around and sneak a peek and widen, lighting up his whole face in a prizewinning grin.

"You got it," he shouts.

The women grab each other by the coat shoulders and jump each other up and down. And I look toward the back cause I know Mrs. J got to be hearing all this carrying-on, and on payday if Mr. J ain't handing out the checks, she's going to give us some long lecture about decorum and what it means to be on board at

Johnson's Drugs N Goods. I wheel over to the glass jars and punch
bowls, wanting alibi distance just in case. And also to warn
Madeen about Sampson gaining on her. He's ducking down behind
the coffeepots, walking squat and shameless.

"Pay us our money, young man," Fur Coat is demanding, rap-
ping her knuckles on the counter.

"Yeah, what kind of crooked shell game is you running here in
this joint?" say Ethel, finding a good foil character to play.

"We should hate to have to turn the place out, young man."

"It out," echoes Ethel.

The women nod to the crowd and a coupla folks giggle. And
Piper tap-taps on the cash register like he shonuff gonna give em
they money. I'd rather they turned the place out myself. I want to
call my daddy. Only way any of us are going to get home in time
to dress for the Christmas dance at the center is for the women to
turn it out. Like I say, Piper ain't too clear about the worker's interest versus management's, as the dude in Drugs would say it. So
he's light-tapping and quite naturally the cash drawer does not
come out. He's yanking some unseen dollar from the not-there
drawer and handing it over. Damn if Fur Coat don't snatch it, deal
out the bills to herself and her friend and then make a big production out of folding the money flat and jamming it in that little red
change purse.

"I wanna thank you," Ethel says, strolling off, swinging her
pocketbook so that the crowd got to back up and disperse. Fur
Coat spreads her coat and curtsies.

"A pleasure to do business with you ladies," Piper says, tipping
his hat, looking kinda disappointed that he didn't sell em something. Tipping his hat the way he tipped the shells, cause you
know Mrs. J don't allow no hats indoors. I came to work in slacks
one time and she sent me home to change and docked me too. I
wear a gele some times just to mess her around, and you can tell
she trying to figure out if she'll go for it or not. The woman is
crazy. Not Uncle Henry type crazy, but Black property owner type
crazy. She thinks this is a museum, which is why folks don't
hardly come in here to shop. That's okay cause we all get to know
each other well. It's not okay cause it's a drag to look busy. If you
look like you ain't buckling under a weight of work, Mrs. J will

have you count the Band-Aids in the boxes to make sure the company ain't pulling a fast one. The woman crazy.

Now Uncle Henry type crazy is my kind of crazy. The type crazy to get you a job. He march into the "saloon" as he calls it and tells Leon D that he is not an equal opportunity employer and that he, Alderman Henry Peoples, is going to put some fire to his ass. So soon's summer comes, me and Madeen got us a job at Leon D. Salon. One of them hushed, funeral type shops with skinny models parading around for customers corseted and strangling in their seats, huffin and puffin.

Madeen got fired right off on account of the pound of mascara she wears on each lash and them weird dresses she designs for herself (with less than a yard of cloth each if you ask me). I did my best to hang in there so's me and Madeen'd have hang-around money till Johnson started hiring again. But it was hard getting back and forth from the stockroom to this little kitchen to fix the espresso to the showroom. One minute up to your ass in carpet, the next skidding across white linoleum, the next making all this noise on ceramic tile and people looking around at you and all. Was there for two weeks and just about had it licked by stationing different kind of shoes at each place that I could slip into, but then Leon D stumbled over my bedroom slippers one afternoon.

But to hear Uncle Henry tell it, writing about it all to Daddy, I was working at a promising place making a name for myself. And Aunt Harriet listening to Uncle Henry read the letter, looking me up and down and grunting. She know what kind of name it must be, cause my name in the family is Miss Clumsy. Like if you got a glass-top coffee table with doodads on em, or a hurricane lamp sitting on a mantel anywhere near a door I got to come through, or an antique jar you brought all the way from Venice the time you won the crossword puzzle contest—you can rest assure I'll demolish them by and by. I ain't vicious, I'm just clumsy. It's my gawky stage, Mama says. Aunt Harriet cuts her eye at Mama and grunts.

My daddy advised me on the phone not to mention anything to the Johnsons about this gift of mine for disaster or the fact that I worked at Leon D. Salon. No sense the Johnson's calling up there to check on me and come to find I knocked over a perfume display two times in the same day. Like I say—it's a gift. So when I got to clean the glass jars and punch bowls at Johnson's, I take it slow and pay attention. Then I take up my station relaxed in Fabrics, where the worst that can happen is I upset a box of pins.

Mrs. J is in the prescription booth, and she clears her throat real loud. We all look to the back to read the smoke signals. She ain't paying Fur Coat and Ethel no attention. They over in Cosmetics messing with Miz Della's mind and her customers. Mrs. J got her eye on some young teen-agers browsing around Jewelry. The other eye on Piper. But this does not mean Piper is supposed to check the kids out. It means Madeen is. You got to know how to read Mrs. J to get along.

She always got one eye on Piper. Tries to make it seem like she don't trust him at the cash register. That may be part of the reason now, now that she's worked up this cover story so in her mind. But we all know why she watches Piper, same reason we all do. Cause Piper is so fine you just can't help yourself. Tall and built up, blue-black and smooth, got the nerve to have dimples, and wears this splayed-out push-broom mustache he's always raking in with three fingers. Got a big butt too that makes you wanna hug the customer that asks for the cartons Piper keeps behind him, two shelfs down. Mercy. And when it's slow, or when Mrs. J comes bustling over for the count, Piper steps from behind the counter and shows his self. You get to see the whole Piper from the shiny boots to the glistening fro and every inch of him fine. Enough to make you holler.

Miz Della in Cosmetics, a sister who's been passing for years but fooling nobody but herself, she always lolligagging over to To-bacco talking bout are there any new samples of those silver-tipped cigars for women. Piper don't even squander energy to bump her off any more. She mostly just ain't even there. At first he would get mad when she used to act hinkty and had these white men picking her up at the store. Then he got sorrowful about it all, saying she was a pitiful person. Now that she's going out with the blond chemist back there, he just wiped her off the map. She tries to mess with him, but Piper ain't heard the news she's been born. Sometimes his act slips, though, cause he does take a lot of unnec-essary energy to play up to Madeen whenever Miz Della's hanging around. He's not consistent in his attentions, and that spurs Madeen the dress designer to madness. And Piper really oughta

put brakes on that, cause Madeen subject to walk in one day in a
fishnet dress and no underwear and then what he goin do about
that?

Last year on my birthday my daddy got on us about dressing
like hussies to attract the boys. Madeen shrugged it off and went
about her business. It hurt my feelings. The onliest reason I was
wearing that tight sweater and that skimpy skirt was cause I'd
been to the roller rink and that's how we dress. But my daddy
didn't even listen and I was really hurt. But then later that night, I
come through the living room to make some cocoa and he apolo-
gized. He lift up from the couch where he always sleeps when he
comes to visit, lifted up and whispered it—"Sorry." I could just
make him out by the light from the refrigerator.

"Candy," he calls to make sure I heard him. And I don't want to
close the frig door cause I know I'll want to remember this scene,
figuring it's going to be the last birthday visit cause he fixin to get
married and move outta state.

"Sir?"

He pat the couch and I come on over and just leave the frig door
open so we can see each other. I forgot to put the milk down, so I
got this cold milk bottle in my lap, feeling stupid.

"I was a little rough on you earlier," he say, picking something I
can't see from my bathrobe. "But you're getting to be a woman
now and certain things have to be said. Certain things have to be
understood so you can decide what kind of woman you're going to
be, ya know?"

"Sir," I nod. I'm thinking Aunt Harriet ought to tell me, but
then Aunt Harriet prefers to grunt at folks, reserving words for
the damn crossword puzzles. And my mama stay on the road so
much with the band, when she do come home for a hot minute all
she has to tell me is "My slippers're in the back closet" or "Your
poor tired Ma'd like some coffee."

He takes my hand and don't even kid me about the milk bottle,
just holds my hand for a long time saying nothing, just squeezes it.
And I know he feeling bad about moving away and all, but what
can he do, he got a life to lead. Just like Mama got her life to lead.
Just like I got my life to lead and'll probably leave here myself one
day and become an actress or a director. And I know I should tell
him it's all right. Sitting there with that milk bottle chilling me

through my bathrobe, the light from the refrigerator throwing funny shadows on the wall, I know that years later when I'm in trouble or something, or hear that my daddy died or something like that, I'm going feel real bad that I didn't tell him—it's all right, Daddy, I understand. It ain't like he'd made any promises about making a home for me with him. So it ain't like he's gone back on his word. And if the new wife can't see taking in no half-grown new daughter, hell, I understand that. I can't get the words together, neither can he. So we just squeeze each other's hands. And that'll have to do.

"When I was a young man," he says after while, "there were girls who ran around all made up in sassy clothes. And they were okay to party with, but not the kind you cared for, ya know?" I nod and he pats my hand. But I'm thinking that ain't right, to party with a person you don't care for. How come you can't? I want to ask, but he's talking. And I was raised not to interrupt folk when they talking, especially my daddy. "You and Madeen cause quite a stir down at the barbershop." He tries to laugh it, but it comes out scary. "Got to make up your mind now what kind of woman you're going to be. You know what I'm saying?" I nod and he loosens his grip so I can go make my cocoa.

I'm messing around in the kitchenette feeling dishonest. Things I want to say, I haven't said. I look back over toward the couch and know this picture is going to haunt me later. Going to regret the things left unsaid. Like a coward, like a child maybe. I fix my cocoa and keep my silence, but I do remember to put the milk back and close the refrigerator door.

"Candy?"

"Sir?" I'm standing there in the dark, the frig door closed now and we can't even see each other.

"It's not about looks anyway," he says, and I hear him settling deep into the couch and pulling up the bedclothes. "And it ain't always about attracting some man either . . . not necessarily."

I'm waiting to hear what it is about, the cup shaking in the saucer and me wanting to ask him all over again how it was when he and Mama first met in Central Park, and how it used to be when they lived in Philly and had me and how it was when the two of them were no longer making any sense together but moved down here anyway and then split up. But I could hear that breathing he does just before the snoring starts. So I hustle on down the hall so I won't be listening for it and can't get to sleep.

All night I'm thinking about this woman I'm going to be. I'll look like Mama but don't wanna be no singer. Was named after Grandma Candestine but don't wanna be no fussy old woman with a bunch of kids. Can't see myself turning into Aunt Harriet either, doing crossword puzzles all day long. I look over at Madeen, all sprawled out in her bed, tangled up in the sheets looking like the alcoholic she trying to be these days, sneaking liquor from Uncle Henry's closet. And I know I don't wanna be stumbling down the street with my boobs out and my dress up and my heels cracking off and all. I write for a whole hour in my diary trying to connect with the future me and trying not to hear my daddy snoring.

Fur Coat and Ethel in Housewares talking with Madeen. I know they must be cracking on Miz Della, cause I hear Madeen saying something about equal opportunity. We used to say that Mrs. J was an equal opportunity employer for hiring Miz Della. But then she went and hired real white folks—a blond, crew-cut chemist and a pimply-face kid for the stockroom. If you ask me, that's running equal opportunity in the ground. And running the business underground cause don't nobody round here deal with no white chemist. They used to wrinkly old folks grinding up the herbs and bark and telling them very particular things to do and not to do working the roots. So they keep on going to Mama Drear down past the pond or Doc Jessup in back of the barbershop. Don't do a doctor one bit of good to write out a prescription talking about fill it at Johnson's, cause unless it's an emergency folk stay strictly away from a white root worker, especially if he don't tell you what he doing.

Aunt Harriet in here one day when Mama Drear was too sick to counsel and quite naturally she asks the chemist to explain what all he doing back there with the mortar and pestle and the scooper and the scales. And he say something about rules and regulations, the gist of which was mind your business, lady. Aunt Harriet dug down deep into her crossword-puzzle words and pitched a natural bitch. Called that man a bunch of choicest names. But the line that got me was—"Medication without explanation is obscene." And what she say that for, we ran that in the ground for days. Infatuation without fraternization is obscene. Insemination without obligation is tyranny. Fornication without contraception is obtuse, and so forth and so on. Madeen's best line came out the night we were watching a TV special about welfare. Sterilization without strangulation and hell's damnation is I-owe-you-one-crackers. Look like every situation called for a line like that, and even if it didn't, we made it fit.

Then one Saturday morning we were locked out and we standing around shivering in our sweaters and this old white dude jumps out a pickup truck hysterical, his truck still in gear and backing out the lot. His wife had given their child an overdose of medicine and the kid was out cold. Look like everything he said was grist for the mill.

"She just administered the medicine without even reading the label," he told the chemist, yanking on his jacket so the man couldn't even get out his keys. "She never even considered the fact it might be dangerous, the medicine so old and all." We follow the two down the aisle to the prescription booth, the old white dude talking a mile a minute, saying they tried to keep the kid awake, tried to walk him, but he wouldn't walk. Tried to give him an enema, but he wouldn't stay propped up. Could the chemist suggest something to empty his stomach out and sooth his inflamed ass and what all? And besides he was breathing funny and should he administer mouth-to-mouth resuscitation? The minute he tore out of there and ran down the street to catch up with his truck, we started in.

Administration without consideration is illiterate. Irrigation without resuscitation is evacuation without ambulation is inflammation without information is execution without restitution is. We got downright silly about the whole thing till Mrs. J threatened to fire us all. But we kept it up for a week.

Then the new dude in Drugs who don't never say much stopped the show one afternoon when we were trying to figure out what to call the street riots in the sixties and so forth. He say Revolution without Transformation is Half-assed. Took me a while to ponder that one, a whole day in fact just to work up to it. After while I would listen real hard whenever he opened his mouth, which wasn't often. And I jotted down the titles of the books I'd see him with. And soon's I finish up the stack that's by my bed, I'm hitting the library. He started giving me some of the newspapers he keeps stashed in that blue bag of his we all at first thought was full of funky jockstraps and sneakers. Come to find it's full of carrots and oranges and books and stuff. Madeen say he got a gun in there too. But then Madeen all the time saying something. Like she saying here lately that the chemist's jerking off there behind the poisons and the goopher dust.

The chemist's name is Hubert Tarrly. Madeen tagged him Herbert Tareyton. But the name that stuck was Nazi Youth. Every time I look at him I hear Hitler barking out over the loudspeaker urging the youth to measure up and take over the world. And I can see these stark-eyed gray kids in short pants and suspenders doing jump-ups and scissor kicks and turning they mamas in to the Gestapo for listening to the radio. Chemist looks like he grew up like that, eating knockwurst and beating on Jews, rounding up gypsies, saying *Sieg heil* and shit. Mrs. J said something to him one morning and damn if he didn't click his heels. I like to die. She blushing all over her simple self talking bout that's Southern cavalier style. I could smell the gas. I could see the flaming cross too. Nazi Youth and then some. The dude in Drugs started calling him that too, the dude whose name I can never remember. I always wanna say Ali Baba when I talk about him with my girl friends down at the skating rink or with the older sisters at the arts center. But that ain't right. Either you call a person a name that says what they about or you call em what they call themselves, one or the other.

Now take Fur Coat, for instance. She is clearly about the fur coat. She moving up and down the aisles talking while Ethel in the cloth coat is doing all the work, picking up teapots, checking the price on the dust mops, clicking a bracelet against the punch bowl to see if it ring crystal, hollering to somebody about whether the floor wax need buffing or not. And it's all on account of the fur coat. Her work is something other than that. Like when they were in Cosmetics messing with Miz Della, some white ladies come up talking about what's the latest in face masks. And every time Miz Della pull something out the box, Ethel shake her head and say that brand is crap. Then Fur Coat trots out the sure-fire recipe for the face mask. What she tells the old white ladies is to whip us some egg white to peaks, pour in some honey, some oil of wintergreen, some oil of eucalyptus, the juice of a lemon and a half a teaspoon of arsenic. Now any fool can figure out what lemon juice do to arsenic, or how honey going make the concoction stick, and what all else the oil of this and that'll do to your face. But Fur Coat in her fur coat make you stand still and listen to this madness. Fur Coat an authority in her fur coat. The fur coat is an act of alchemy in itself, as Aunt Harriet would put it.

Just like my mama in her fur coat, same kind too—Persian lamb, bought hot in some riot or other. Mama's coat was part of the Turn the School Out Outfit. Hardly ever came out of the quilted bag cept for that. Wasn't for window-shopping, wasn't for going to rehearsal, wasn't for church teas, was for working her show. She'd flip a flap of that coat back over her hip when she strolled into the classroom to get on the teacher's case bout saying something out of the way about Black folks. Then she'd pick out the exact plank, exact spot she'd take her stand on, then plant one of them black suede pumps from the I. Miller outlet she used to work at. Then she'd lift her chin arrogant proud to start the rap, and all us kids would lean forward and stare at the cameo brooch visible now on the wide-wale wine plush corduroy dress. Then she'd work her show in her outfit. Bam-bam that black suede pocketbook punctuating the points as Mama ticked off the teacher's offenses. And when she got to the good part, and all us kids would strain up off the benches to hear every word so we could play it out in the schoolyard, she'd take both fists and brush that fur coat way back past her hips and she'd challenge the teacher to either change up and apologize or meet her for a showdown at a schoolboard hearing. And of course ole teacher'd apologize to all us Black kids. Then Mama'd let the coat fall back into place and she'd whip around, the coat draping like queen robes, and march herself out. Mama was baad in her fur coat.

I don't know what-all Fur Coat do in her fur coat but I can tell it's hellafyin whatever it all is. They came into Fabrics and stood around a while trying to see what shit they could get into. All they had in their baskets was a teapot and some light bulbs and some doodads from the special gift department, perfume and whatnot. I waited on a few customers wanting braid and balls of macramé twine, nothing where I could show my stuff. Now if somebody wanted some of the silky, juicy cotton stuff I could get into something fancy, yanking off the yards, measuring it doing a shuffle-stick number, nicking it just so, then ripping the hell out the shit. But didn't nobody ask for that. Fur Coat and Ethel kinda finger some bolts and trade private jokes, then they moved onto Drugs.

"We'd like to see the latest in rubberized fashions for men, young man." Fur Coat is doing a super Lady Granville Whitmore the Third number. "If you would." She bows her head, fluttering her lashes.

Me and Madeen start messing around in the shoe-polish section so's not to miss nothing. I kind of favor Fur Coat, on account of she got my mama's coat on, I guess. On the other hand, I like the way Ethel drawl talk like she too tired and bored to go on. I guess I like em both cause they shopping the right way, having fun and all. And they got plenty of style. I wouldn't mind being like that when I am full-grown.

The dude in Drugs thinks on the request a while, sucking in his lips like he wanna talk to himself on the inside. He's looking up and down the counter, pauses at the plastic rain hats, rejects them, then squints hard at Ethel and Fur Coat. Fur Coat plants a well-heeled foot on the shelf with the tampons and pads and sighs. Something about that sigh I don't like. It's real rather than play snooty. The dude in Drugs always looks a little crumbled, a little rough dry, like he jumped straight out the hamper but not quite straight. But he got stuff to him if you listen rather than look. Seems to me ole Fur Coat is looking. She keeps looking while the dude moves down the aisle behind the counter, ducks down out of sight, reappears and comes back, dumping an armful of boxes on the counter.

"One box of Trojans and one box of Ramses," Ethel announces. "We want to do the comparison test."

"On the premises?" Lady G Fur says, planting a dignified hand on her collarbone.

"Egg-zack-lee."

"In your opinion, young man," Lady G Fur says, staying the arm of the brand tester, "which of the two is the best? Uhmm— the better of the two, that is. In your vast experience as lady-killer and cock hound, which passes the X test?" It's said kinda snotty. Me and Madeen exchange a look and dust around the cans of shoe polish.

"Well," the dude says, picking up a box in each hand, "in my opinion, Trojans have a snappier ring to em." He rattles the box against his ear, then lets Ethel listen. She nods approval. Fur Coat will not be swayed. "On the other hand, Ramses is a smoother smoke. Cooler on the throat. What do you say in your vast experience as—er—"

Ethel is banging down boxes of Kotex cracking up, screaming, "He gotcha. He gotcha that time. Old laundry bag got over on you, Helen."

Mrs. J comes out of the prescription booth and hustles her bulk to the counter. Me and Madeen clamp down hard on giggles and I damn near got to climb in with the neutral shoe polish to escape attention. Ethel and Fur Coat don't give a shit, they paying customers, so they just roar. Cept Fur Coat's roar is phony, like she really mad and gonna get even with the dude for not turning out to be a chump. Meanwhile, the dude is standing like a robot, arms out at exactly the same height, elbows crooked just so, boxes displayed between thumb and next finger, the gears in the wrist click, clicking, turning. And not even cracking a smile.

"What's the problem here?" Mrs. J trying not to sound breathless or angry and ain't doing too good a job. She got to say it twice to be heard.

"No problem, Mrs. Johnson," the dude says straight-face. "The customers are buying condoms, I am selling condoms. A sale is being conducted, as is customary in a store."

Mrs. J looks down at the jumble of boxes and covers her mouth. She don't know what to do. I duck down, cause when folks in authority caught in a trick, the first they look for is a scapegoat.

"Well, honey," Ethel says, giving a chummy shove to Mrs. J's shoulder, "what do you think? I've heard that Trojans are ultrasensitive. They use a baby lamb brain, I understand."

"Membrane, dear, membrane," Fur Coat says down her nose. "They remove the intestines of a four-week-old lamb and use the membrane. Tough, resilient, sheer."

"Gotcha," says Ethel. "On the other hand, it is said by folks who should know that Ramses has a better box score."

"Box score," echoes Mrs. J in a daze.

"Box score. You know, honey—no splits, breaks, leaks, seeps."

"Seepage, dear, seepage," says Fur Coat, all nasal.

"Gotcha."

"The solution," says the dude in an almost robot voice, "is to take one small box of each and do the comparison test as you say. A survey. A random sampling of your friends." He says this to Fur Coat, who is not enjoying it all nearly so much as Ethel, who is whooping and hollering.

Mrs. J backs off and trots to the prescription booth. Nazi Youth peeks over the glass and mumbles something soothing to Mrs. J. He waves me and Madeen away like he somebody we got to pay some mind.

"We will take one super-duper, jumbo family size of each."

"Family size?" Fur Coat is appalled. "And one more thing, young man," she orders. "Wrap up a petite size for a small-size smart-ass acquaintance of mine. Gift-wrapped, ribbons and all."

It occurs to me that Fur Coat's going to present this to the dude. Right then and there I decide I don't like her. She's not discriminating with her stuff. Up till then I was thinking how much I'd like to trade Aunt Harriet in for either of these two, hang out with them, sit up all night while they drink highballs and talk about men they've known and towns they've been in. I always did want to hang out with women like this and listen to their stories. But they beginning to reveal themselves as not nice people, just cause the dude is rough dry on Christmas Eve. My Uncle Henry all the time telling me they different kinds of folks in the community, but when you boil it right down there's just nice and not nice. Uncle Henry say they folks who'll throw they mamas to the wolves if the fish sandwich big enough. They folks who won't whatever the hot sauce. They folks that're scared, folks that are dumb; folks that have heart and some with heart to spare. That all boils down to nice and not nice if you ask me. It occurs to me that Fur Coat is not nice. Fun, dazzling, witty, but not nice.

"Do you accept Christmas gifts, young man?" Fur Coat asking in icy tones she ain't masking too well.

"No. But I do accept Kwanza presents at the feast."

"Quan . . . hmm . . ."

Fur Coat and Ethel go into a huddle with the stage whispers. "I bet he thinks we don't know beans about Quantas . . . Don't he know we are The Ebony Jet Set . . . We never travel to kangaroo land except by . . ."

Fur Coat straightens up and stares at the dude. "Will you accept a whatchamacallit gift from me even though we are not feasting, as it were?"

"If it is given with love and respect, my sister, of course." He was sounding so sincere, it kinda got to Fur Coat.

"In that case . . ." She scoops up her bundle and sweeps out the place. Ethel trotting behind hollering, "He gotcha, Helen. Give the boy credit. Maybe we should hire him and do a threesome act." She spun the turnstile round three times for she got into the spin and spun out the store.

"Characters," says Piper on tiptoe, so we all can hear him. He laughs and checks his watch. Madeen slinks over to Tobacco to be in asking distance in case he don't already have a date to the dance. Miz Della's patting some powder on. I'm staring at the door after Fur Coat and Ethel, coming to terms with the fact that my daddy ain't coming. It's gonna be just Uncle Henry and Aunt Harriet this year, with maybe Mama calling on the phone between sets to holler in my ear, asking have I been a good girl, it's been that long since she's taken a good look at me.

"You wanna go to the Kwanza celebrations with me sometime this week or next week, Candy?"

I turn and look at the dude. I can tell my face is falling and right now I don't feel up to doing anything about it. Holidays are depressing. Maybe there's something joyous about this celebration he's talking about. Cause Lord knows Christmas is a drag. The sister who taught me how to wrap a gele asked me was I coming to the celebration down at the Black Arts Center, but I didn't know nothing bout it.

"Look here," I finally say, "would you please get a pencil and paper and write your name down for me. And write that other word down too so I can look it up."

He writes his name down and spins the paper around for me to read.

"Obatale."

"Right," he says, spinning it back. "But you can call me Ali Baba if you want to." He was leaning over too far writing out Kwanza for me to see if that was a smile on his face or a smirk. I figure a smile, cause Obatale nice people.

Pleyben

Sallie Bingham

The woman in the hotel doorway seemed suspicious, almost hostile, as though she expected the two of them to force their way in under her arm; she was holding open the glass door, and the tiles in the entry, moss-green, gleamed in the first sun they'd seen all month. In crippled French, Lovett asked for a meal, and explained why they were so late: the road, the car breakdown, the sudden deluge of rain, which they had come to accept as part of the landscape of Brittany. The woman either understood or didn't. In any event, she stepped back and let them inside.

The entry was damp, with a smell of old cooking; they took off their soaked raincoats and hung them on a pair of hooks. Mrs. Lovett was afraid of the pools of water which began at once to gather beneath the coats; she drew the woman's attention to them in English, which was the only language she knew.

The woman shook her head and hurried away, presumably to find some rags.

"Shouldn't we wait and help her clean up?" Mrs. Lovett asked.

"Let's go ahead and sit down," her husband replied.

They went through another door into a small dining room, set against the outside wall of the large old building; the street was level with the windowsills, which were set with boxes of plastic geraniums. On the other side of the street, in an expansive flash of sun, the cathedral they had just visited turned its broad flank.

"I didn't like that bone place," Mrs. Lovett said as her husband pulled out her chair. "I wish we'd missed it, especially as damp as it's been."

"The ossuary," Mr. Lovett said, setting the word between them and what they'd seen. The smell of old bones had been as penetrating when they walked in as the steam from a bowl of chicken soup, magnified by the damp. There had been something matter-of-fact about the place, too, as though it was some kind of kitchen where Death cooked, then stored its fruits.

They were alone in the dining room, because of the hour; it was not a place, it appeared, for tourists, but perhaps for the businessmen of this small town. Several tables were still littered with crumbs and crushed white napkins, with empty wine bottles in the center, like shrines. Lovett consulted the menu, which looked entirely unfamiliar. They had been staying on the coast, and had learned the names of various seafood there, but this menu did not offer *fruits de mer*.

Mrs. Lovett was still thinking about the bone place. She had a habit of dwelling on a subject, like an oyster coating a grain of sand. "I can understand the logic of it," she said, placing her big purse on the table beside her fork. "In these old graveyards, there isn't room to let everybody lie forever. But why keep the bones at all, I wonder? Why not just throw them out or burn them, after the grave is opened?"

Lovett was still looking at the menu, searching for a familiar word. The dining room was as quiet as though it had been permanently vacated. He wished for their friends from the coastal hotel, a pair of touring Englishmen who had taught them about the local food and wine, taught them without a hint of condescension, too. "I think this is a kind of vegetable soup," he said, showing his wife the name on the menu. "Let's start with it."

"I'm chilled to the bone," she said, suddenly, her voice darkening, and he looked at her, uneasy as he always was when she changed her tone.

"You need some good hot soup, and a glass of wine," he said.

The woman who had let them in now reappeared, still dour, a dishcloth in her hand. She stood over Lovett, waiting for his order. Under her insistence, he broke down and simply pointed to several items on the menu. He realized how tired he was feeling, how the month of travel had worn away his resolve to enjoy himself. He wished they had just gone to the beach as they usually did in August, although he knew in the rainy Maine weather his wife would have continued to grieve.

"She'll have the same thing," he said, gesturing at his wife. The woman seemed to understand. She went away briskly, with a sense of mission.

"I hate it when you do that," Mrs. Lovett said. "You didn't even bother to ask me what I wanted."

"I can't cope with the menu. Half of it is handwritten, and I can't make it out."

"Sorry," she said, reaching across the table for his hand. "My, your hand is cold. Nobody warned us about all this mist and rain."

"We wouldn't have listened to them, anyway," he said, brightening at her change of mood. He wished there was some way to fix her as she was now, her face lightened from its obscure, shadowed look, which she wore when he drove her about, as though sitting beside him in the little rented car meant, for her, putting out her light.

The woman reappeared with a large white china tureen. She set it down on the table, and removed the cover; steam rose from its watery contents, in which several large pieces of bread floated, as well as a few carrots. Lovett seized the big tin spoon and began to serve his wife. "I imagine this is real local food," he said, and told the woman, this time in practical French, that they would have a bottle of red wine.

He watched his wife spoon the thin gruel, then take a sip of the almost black wine the woman had poured. Lovett thought he could see health and hope flooding back into his wife's face. She sighed, pushed her chair back a little, and he knew she was spreading her knees under her skirt.

"I feel better now," she said. "That bone place did get me down."

"Ossuary. I would have avoided it, but I didn't understand the sign."

"We've certainly seen enough graveyards, this trip," she said cheerily, "and they really don't bother me at all. But something about all those bones—"

"Don't think about it," he said.

That held them silent for the next ten minutes or so, while they finished the soup and their first glasses of wine. Lovett had never before felt such urgency for food and drink as he had these last weeks. It seemed that he and his wife traveled along a line slung between meals, a line that sagged badly midway. He did not think of himself as a glutton or a drunkard, yet on several evenings he had fallen into bed dead drunk, waking up to his own loud snores as, earlier in the summer, he had sometimes woken up to his wife's sobbing.

By the time the main course came—a sort of pot roast, with vegetables around it, succulent as a steak would have been at home—Mrs. Lovett could be put off no longer. She was determined from time to time to "talk it out," because she felt in that way she might stave off nightmares. It was the nightmares that left her sobbing.

"I wish now we'd had her cremated," she said, softly and carefully, cutting a bit of meat.

"Why do you say that?"

"Then I wouldn't have to imagine things. I'm sorry, Bert."

"Don't be sorry. What things?" He knew he had to ask.

"What's happening to her now, underground?"

"Nothing is happening," he said, taking a mouthful of wine.

"But it's bound to. They can't stop all that."

"You remember what the mortician said about the coffin," he said, nearly choking on a piece of dry bread. "He said that coffin is designed to hold out ground water for a hundred years."

"I think that's just talk," Mrs. Lovett said. "I bet it doesn't hold a month. Once wood is underground, it starts to rot—you know that."

"But it's treated," he croaked. "They explained that."

"I don't believe it," she said.

"Why think about it at all?"

"I can't help it. Sometimes I wake up with the clearest feeling, as though I'm in there with her, and I can see and feel what's happening to her."

"She's gone, she's not in there," he said.

"But then where is she, Bert? I only know her in that body," Mrs. Lovett said.

Mr. Lovett turned his head and looked at the broad side of the dark old cathedral. A cloud was passing over the sun, and as light drained from the stone walls, they darkened as with a stain. It would begin to rain soon, he realized, and wondered why he did not find the prospect daunting. Everything fit, this time, as it had never fit before: his wife's voice, the cathedral walls, the gathering clouds.

"Look, you can see the calvary from here," he said, almost exulting. "There's the thief who wasn't sorry, with his tongue stuck out. Did you notice, there's a little horned devil, like a toad, on his shoulder?"

Mrs. Lovett thought he was trying to distract her. "I try not to think this way, but it's so vivid," she said.

"How is it vivid?" he asked softly, not looking at her, knowing her thin, pale face would counter the effect of the words.

She leaned across the table. "I remember the way her little limbs used to feel when she was a baby, so smooth and pliable. Sometimes it seems to me they must be that way again, just so smooth and soft. It's terrible to talk this way."

"Tell me, if it helps," he said, but knew that was not his reason for listening. Since their daughter's death, six months before, he had been as numb as a nut.

"I'm ashamed," she said. "It's almost obscene."

"Yes, obscene," he wanted to shout with a great laugh, a belly laugh, his mouth full of red wine which would spray across the table, soaking her white blouse. Obscene as death. Not neat and dry, like his work, their habits, which had brought them to this gloomy town with the strange name—Pleyben, what did it mean?—and to this gruesome crossroads.

"Father Bill tried to get me to put it all out of my head," she continued, "to think about Katy's spiritual life. I don't think she had a spiritual life. I think she only had a life of the body. So now when I think of her, I think of the way her body is going on, underground, growing."

He got up and came around the table, then squatted awkwardly by her chair, as he had done on many other occasions when she had hastily burst into tears. This time she did not cry.

"I want to think about it from beginning to end," she said. "From her warm little body when she was first born and they laid her on my belly to her warm little arms and legs when she'd been playing in the sun, her warm round nakedness when she was still young enough to go in without a suit, and then all of a sudden her little round breasts and that time you said she was too old to wear a t-shirt without a bra."

"Forget that."

"And the time I felt her leg after she'd shaved it, and it was as smooth as glass, ankle to thigh."

"How does all that connect?" he asked, not looking at her for fear that she would see his avidity.

"I think she's still growing. Her hair and fingernails, of course. But something else, too. The cells. I think the cells are growing down there in the damp. The skin cells and the ones underneath that would have turned into babies."

The dining room was the wrong place; he knew it at once. They might be interrupted by the woman coming in with more food. "We're getting out of here," he said.

"But we haven't even had our dessert." She followed him when he went out into the entry, cornered the woman, and paid for their meal without waiting for the change. The same urgency that had filled his mouth with wine until he fell on his bed was driving him, again, driving him to hear his wife, take her words. He hurried her out to the car and packed her inside.

Then he wrenched the car into reverse, wheeled backwards down the cobblestones and turned to follow the menacing arrows that pointed toward the road to the coast. "Tell me some more," he said.

Now she was prim, almost angry. "I don't understand. It's very unpleasant. Why do you want to know more?"

"I can't feel anything about her," he said. "I've tried imagining the way it happened, the motorcycle, but I can't get anywhere. Maybe if I start where she is now and work backwards—"

"Why should you want to? You never wanted to before."

She seemed to see the face of greed or lust, like the face of the little horned devil perched on the shoulder of the unrepentant thief.

"It's terrible that it happened but somehow it's worse that I can't feel it," he said, and pulled over to the side of the road and rolled down his window. The smell of a crushed herb of some kind filled the car, and the sun, for a moment, glared down on the sodden grey-green hills. "Help me feel it," he said.

"I can't do that," she said, shrinking into the corner of the car.

He took her hand and kissed it, as though it was a relic of some kind. "Please."

She said carefully, "I think maybe all that matters is she died. Why don't we drive on? I know you want to get back to the hotel in time for drinks with those nice Englishmen."

He reached for her, reeling her in, and pressed her head against his lapel as though to comfort her, but she was dry and still now, there was no need for comfort. He wanted to put his face down inside the neck of her blouse, to feel her heart beating there under her thin, cool skin. Instead he put his hand on her shoulder and felt the synthetic sleekness of her blouse.

Mistletoe

—————————— Jane Bradley ——————————

I know I am not dead because I see her running toward me now. Her red hair fans out in this cold gray morning air, her green coat flaps open letting the breeze wrap around her chest, and her shoe laces fly untied slapping her ankles as she runs across this scrubby, frost-covered yard.

I stand by the truck here waiting with my baby, Darly, wrapped around my hip, and Mitch sits over there with the engine revving up, dying down, and revving again, he says to keep the engine turning, but I know it's to churn the quiet morning air into nothing but noise. To ease his pushing, I ran from the house with Darly bouncing, laughing on my hip, and I yelled to Marta, "Hurry, Daddy's waiting," and she comes fast now because even at six years old she knows not to make a man like him wait.

She runs, and I watch the white vapor float from her mouth, and I see she is so like me with my red hair, my dark green eyes, and my way of running with my mouth wide open, my arms flying, but my legs steady and fast. I'm afraid I've shaped her so like myself that she, too, will live a life underwater while others breathe the sharp real air.

I can see it has started. Already she loves old storybooks and pictures of the long dead who stare in a black and white trance. Already she collects dried weeds and rocks worn to odd shapes and colors rarely seen above ground. And she does odd things like the way each morning she picks a fairy tale to live by. She plays out the parts and pretends the world is just a story that's been written and has to be lived through to the end. Already her teachers call her deep. I never wanted a deep child. I just wanted a happy one who ran games and laughed like all the other giggling girls.

As she slips past me and climbs up into the truck now, I see the aluminum foil package hiding in her pocket, and I know she is Gretel today, and she will get safely lost in the woods. I smell the thick sweetness of the powdered doughnuts she has tucked under her arm for the ride. Darly smells the sweetness too, and she kicks

54

her legs and bounces as she watches Marta scoot across the seat and settle next to Mitch. "You want a doughnut, Darly?" Marta says, and before I can say no, Darly has the white cake crumbling in her fat hand. As she sucks the sugar, her feet kick and her eyes shine.

We are bouncing down the driveway now, and I am happy for a moment because I will finally have some of that mistletoe that grows in the oak trees. Only the scattered blast of buckshot can reach that high and bring those leaves down to your arms. I will finally have some of that mistletoe Dean once showed me, and I will hang it all through my little white house. I will see the lake again, the green-brown water where Dean taught me to hook a bass and clean it and eat it right there in the woods. He laughed to see me in big paint-splotched man's khaki pants, flannel shirt, and old brogans. Dean said he liked to see a woman in man's clothes because it made what was hid underneath a sweeter surprise.

"You know where you're going?" Mitch says, and all the sudden I smell his cigarette, the doughnuts, and the oily smell of old tools in his truck.

"Yes," I say. "You head up 58 Highway to Sparky's Bait Shop. Take a quick left. I'll know the dirt road when I see it."

"What makes you know so much about dirt roads," he says looking straight ahead and frowning out from under his cap.

"I grew up in this town too," I say. "I know all about dirt roads and mountains and streams."

"I bet you do," he says.

I tap Marta's shoulder. "There's a cave out near Sweetwater that's big enough to fly a plane around in. They call it Little Airplane Cave."

"Let's go" she says.

"One day," I say, and I look out the window at the stark brown trees whizzing by, and I think this ride will not be long enough. With Mitch there driving like a machine, Marta gazing out at the highway dreaming, and Darly's little mind drawn into the way her pink wet fingers can vanish in the white doughnut and come out full of crumbs, having them all with me locked into their own worlds, inside this black truck, I would like to listen to the sound of this old engine and watch forever the woods as they stand there so thick and straight. I see a dark bird swoop down in the branches, a flash of shadow, then it's gone as the truck pulls us toward that cold gray lake where mistletoe grows now with green leaves and white berries full of poison sap.

Seven years is a long time to love a man who isn't yours. He had Mildred with her dyed blue-black hair, her hips wide as a Christmas table, and I had, still have Mitch. And my girls. It's the girls who make this living something I can stand, and I know if Dean could have had a kid, he would have gone on living. I kept hoping he could have one with me with this body so rich I have to push Mitch away from me sometimes for fear he will plant another seed in me. I push because I know that sometimes life rushes through and takes hold in spite of all my efforts to make it stop. I still hurt for those two I wouldn't let come, but to let them come would have killed me for certain in a way nobody can see. So I went to the doctor who said things like "Terminate. Terminate the pregnancy." What words we find sometimes. But Marta was a wanted child. I wanted her when Mitch didn't because I had to invent something to stay in that house, to keep me from flying off this earth like a mist vanishing in the sun. So I pushed for my Marta, and she holds me here still.

Darly was his all-out effort to get a boy, a son to hand down a name. If you ask me, Mitchell Stone ain't a name worth saving. So when that baby pushed through my blood to be a girl, I laughed out loud and yelled, "That's my darlin'. That's my girl." The nurses all laughed at me so happy.

I wanted them to tie my tubes right then because I didn't want more chances, but they put me off saying it's a serious thing for a woman healthy and young as me.

"But I don't want no more," I said.

And they said, "But what if? What if?" And they got me thinking a child is all. And what if? What if, and my body was all tied up and dry as a rock. So I waited and I pushed Mitch off and I tried pills and they made me see spots, and I tried copper wires and they made me bleed like a pig, and I tried all those rubber things and creams. And I've pushed him off as much as I could.

But with Dean I opened all skin, bone, and muscle, and when I loved him I was so happy I wasn't tied up inside because I wanted his seed to grow. Dean moved in me like a warm river, and you'd have thought we'd grow a thousand babies.

Suddenly I see we've just passed the bait shop, and he is about to miss the turn. "Right here," I yell pointing, and he jerks the wheel bouncing me and Marta and Darly and the doughnuts go flying, but we make the turn, and bounce down this road toward the lake where Dean and I walked through the trees, where we slid his aluminum fishing boat in the water, cast our lures for a fat bright fish we could clean and cook on the spot with the bread and baloney and cheese we always brought along in case the fish didn't bite. We ate a lot of baloney, but we ate a lot of fish, too, fish cooked on his little Sterno stove, fried in the corn meal and lard and salt he kept packed in old peanut butter jars. He planned for everything, never forgot the napkins, forks, nothing. He always said, "It's got to be just right." And it was. It was until that little bit of blood pushed through the wrong place in his head and busted my life wide open.

Mitch looks out frowning. "Where is this place you claim mistletoe grows thick as trees?"

"On down a bit," I say.

"How do you know what's growing here?" He looks straight ahead the way he always looks when he asks me what might be a dangerous question.

"I hear things," I say, and I pat Marta's leg. "This is going to be so pretty."

He pulls a cigarette from his shirt pocket. "I don't know what's wrong with getting it where you always do. That ridge behind our house is full of the stuff waiting to be shot down."

"This place is pretty," I say. "The girls need a little trip, and there's not much else to do on a Sunday morning." He looks at his watch, and I know he's thinking he wants to be home in time to watch some football game. "Neighbors have shot down most of that mistletoe on the ridge," I say. "And we've got to have some in our house for Christmas."

"Yeah, I want kisses," Marta says laughing.

I pat her and say, "Shhhh," fearing her high happy voice will wake Darly who is now sleeping on my chest. I look at Mitch and say low and hard, "I don't want to have to buy it at the store."

He shakes his head. "Only thing crazier than shooting leaves off a tree is paying good money to buy a bunch of dead ones at the store."

"Who knows," I say, "Maybe you'll see something live you can kill."

He looks down at Marta and grins in a way he can't look at

anyone else. He loves her, and I know it. "You want rabbit stew for supper tonight?" he says.

Marta covers her mouth with her hand and stares up. "You won't kill a rabbit, Daddy," she says.

"Rabbit's good," he says. "Mmmm mmm."

"Momma, he won't," Marta says.

I say, "Hush, Darly's stirring." And he rubs Marta's red head, and she looks up at him and grins.

The truck slows, and I look up and see the road has ended in a wide patch of black dirt worn hard by so many cars and trucks parking, and tents standing, and kids playing, and boats going in and out of the water. It was early summer the last time with Dean, with the trees all green and breezy and the water warm and wavy full of bugs riding the surface, fish swimming under, and birds flying all around. "I'll bring you back Christmas," he said.

The truck squeaks to a stop, and before the wheels stop rolling, Mitch has pushed his door open and is heading for the trees. His gun is still here, so I know it's not that he's eager to shoot mistletoe. Marta has slipped out of the truck like a mouse, and now she stands by that icy dark water and looks out. Any other girl would be running and squealing and throwing rocks, but Marta stands there like she knows something has happened here more than camping and fishing and barbecue. And it did. I lived here awhile, lived more than in all my years growing and playing and working. Here I didn't live underwater. Here I heard and smelled and felt this world the way I should.

Mitch is back now, and he walks the edge of the water, looking out, waiting, knowing Marta likes her quiet and I'm not ready. He watches her from a distance as if she's a wild bird that will fly off if he moves. He shoves his hands in his pockets and squints against the cold wind off the water.

Sometimes I think he must know it was Dean who brought me here. It was Dean who would point out the high mistletoe with his sharp eyes. He could name a bird before I even saw it. He could spot a brown fish against a muddy lake bottom, and could name a tree by the smell of its leaves in a breeze. It was spring when he promised, "We'll come back in December and get mistletoe for you to hang all around and have kisses wherever you turn." But we never came back. He had his Mildred. He kept saying he'd leave her. He kept saying he loved me, but he had to stay a little longer. She had problems that held him hard: her momma died, her daddy died. She had operations, bad nerves, high sugar, low blood, something always, and he wouldn't leave her when she was sick or grieving, he couldn't leave her alone. He kept waiting, and he promised, he promised, but she kept slipping back somehow just when I thought he was ready to go. Then he had his stroke.

Stroke. A right word for it, like something rises up and slaps you down, and you don't even have the chance to ask, "How?" It just slams from the inside out. Stroke. He had it, then he couldn't move to fish or drive or hunt green leaves in tree tops. No. He could move just enough to get across his room. He could hardly talk with his mouth half frozen and his brain slowed, and his left arm and leg so weak, just moving on his bed would make him sweat. But he fought hard for living just long enough so he could finally move to hold his gun with one hand and blast his pain to nothing at all.

Dean had green eyes too, and green eyes always made me look long because they're kind of rare when you think of all the brown and blue eyes staring out at this world. Green eyes always make me stop and think, "Yes, I know how green eyes see." That's why when I watch Marta looking out, I can feel some living air move. She could have been Dean's with those eyes, but they are my green eyes no doubt. Dean didn't leave a mark in this world except for what he left pressed deep in my body, my heart, my tangled mind.

Darly stirs against my chest and suddenly opens her eyes wide as she looks at me. "Momma!" she says as if I've been gone for days.

"Let's see the trees," I say, and I step out of the truck and feel the leaves crunch under my feet, and I sigh out loud with the cold opening my head to the smells of dirt and water.

Mitch looks at me with a look so flat he might as well be looking at trees, and he turns back to squinting at the gray water. Marta is so busy poking sticks in the mud, she has no thought of what I might be doing now. A child, she just slides through living like it's a long truck ride. Darly whines, and I pull her bottle from my pocket and stick it in her mouth, and she sighs and sucks and closes her eyes.

I give her a squeeze and head toward that path along the syc-amores to where a stand of oaks grow so shady and full, squirrels run year round and people can lay back cool and hidden from the summer sun. But it's cold in these woods now, the ground hard as rock. Darly snuggles closer and peers out, but I don't mind the cold because if it were warm and green here now, I couldn't stand it. Five months isn't long enough to stop grieving, not five years, not five hundred years. So I'm cold and my arms ache from the weight of Darly, but the pain feels right to me. Now I see the spot where we cooked our fish and ate our bread and lay back on his old sleeping bag and stared up at the trees. I look up through those scraggly black branches that reach like dark veins across the sky, and I try to remember the way the smell of dirt fills your head when you're lying with your back on the ground. Looking close, I see that mistletoe creeping along the branches, drawing its own life from these giant trees.

I hear them rushing up behind me now, Marta with her feet stirring up as much noise as a child can make, and Mitch with those long smooth man's steps you can hardly hear. They are a hunter's steps, light but firm and sure. I look around and see his shot gun swinging low to the ground.

"Here," he says, gruff and flat as a cough.

"This is the place," I say staring up to where those leaves grow bunchy and green in the high sunlight. I say, "This is the place," but he can't know what I'm saying when he looks up and sees simple green leaves waving there in the breeze. All he has to do is pull that trigger and the buckshot will splatter into the trees, and he will be happy with himself for shutting me up about what I want, and he will drive us straight home. Mitch sees a thing up there, a thing he can have by simply knocking it down.

Even Marta sees this place is more than what she sees with her eyes. She has scattered the cornbread she hid wrapped in her pocket, and she has made a little trail of bread crumbs along the path while playing her game.

Even Darly sees more to this place than Mitch who walks around now squinting up seeing only where to shoot. Darly squirms against me, laughs, and points at things nobody can see. Babies do that, they live in a double world, and they talk and laugh and cry at things we'll never know. Old people do it too. And of course the crazy ones who wander the streets. I'd rather be a wild-eyed crazy woman who talks to fast voices and sees panthers in shadows or stars on her ceiling, fiery closets or jerky hands moving with a will of their own, I'd rather see madness than to see the world through the flat eyes of a man like Mitch who just lives to sleep and eat.

Marta is talking to me now, but I can't hear her for my thinking. I see she's walking in her private little paths through the trees and scattering crumbs as she speaks. I hate to miss a word she says because I know words are sometimes all we have to claim a little life, so when I miss something said, I want to cry. Sometimes I wish I could be all eyes, ears, hands holding all to see, but then I know it's easier and it don't hurt so if I can just shut down and stare at the world like it's all an old bad movie I've seen a hundred times.

We're all watching him now, walking in wide circles under these trees as he looks up, takes aim, walks a little more, takes aim again.

"Don't you shoot any birds, Daddy," Marta says.

Darly bounces and points. "Bird," she says in her thick baby voice that flattens any meaning to sweet simple sound.

Mitch aims then grins at Marta. "Don't you want bird soup? Witches eat bird soup," he says. She laughs with him but stares up at those trees with a warning on her face.

"He won't hurt nothing," I say, and he frowns at me.

Dean knew the meaning of mistletoe like most men don't. When we talked of hanging it all through my house, he'd laugh and say, "One man's kiss is another man's poison," because he knew Mitch was sure to dodge those green branches like they were hives full of bees.

He takes aim again now, and his quick nod tells me he's ready, so with one hand I pull Marta back, "Cover your ears," I say, and I squat on the ground with Darly squeezed against my thighs and I cover her eyes and hold her face to my chest and pull her in as best I can to keep her from hearing the blast that will shake these woods deeper than any storm. Marta stands there in front of me with her red chapped hands pressing her red hair against her ears. Her jeans are muddy at the cuffs and droop around her sneakers black from the lake's dirt, sad-looking and wet with shoelaces still untied and dragging in the leaves. But her red hair catches the light from the sun even down here in dark woods, and I see bright threads of gold sparkle as she tosses her head back to see up through the trees.

Mitch gives us a look to make sure we are ready, and he raises his gun. He squints up and his fingers reach.

"Fly birds!" Marta yells. "Fly away! Fly away!"

Mitch frowns at her just the way he looks at me, and I want to jump up and scream, but I just hold Darly close and give Marta a loving look she can't even see. And Mitch shoots.

My ears are humming and the woods are shaking and I hear the second shot ring. I look up and see a few scattered branches fall, but not much green hits the ground. Mitch reloads quick and shoots again so fast we haven't had time to move our hands from our ears. Again he reloads and shoots. He cusses walking in circles, and I can see he would kill these trees if he could for making him walk in the cold and shoot at the wind. He does it again, and again, and Marta has backed up to me now and she crouches against my arm and Darly is holding tight like she thinks the noise alone can rip her away. I look at Marta's green eyes so afraid, and I try to look loving, but my heart is so full of hate I can see she knows it because after looking at me her eyes blink, her mouth jerks, and she holds in a cry. Finally the blasting stops, and I look out and see branches scattered all around us like a storm tore around in a circle and sealed us at its center. I see Mitch mumbling something, and I yell, "What?"

He stares past me and yells, "Pick it up yourself!" as he heads back toward the truck.

We stand, and I try to pull Darly from me so I can see her face, but she presses into me and whimpers, so I hold her and rock her as I walk and look over the ground for my green leaves.

Marta runs ahead. She crouches, stares, runs again, crouches. "I don't see any dead birds," she yells.

"It's a wonder," I say. I bend to pick up my first small branch of this year's mistletoe. I hold it close and stare at those small green-yellow leaves, the white berries that make me think of tiny pearls, and I brush it against my cheek, hold the soft leathery leaves against my skin. I breathe its fresh winter smell, and I look out at Marta smiling at me just the way I know she sees me smiling at her when I catch her happy in the middle of some quiet thing she loves.

Darly feels my body ease up now, and she leans out and crushes a leaf in her hand and laughs. "Mmmm," she says, and I hug her and pull her hand free.

"Pick up all you can," I say to Marta, and we bend and stand filling our arms fast because we know if Mitch thinks he is missing his football game, he'll drive us out of these woods like runaway slaves. We want to take it all back. We want to fill that house with green. I'll wrap the branches in red yarn and let them dangle so thick with their outdoor smells that my closed little too warm house will feel as wild as these woods, and for little moments when I'm standing there folding clothes, mopping a floor, dusting a shelf, for a second anyway, I can think hard and remember this lake, these sweet rotting leaves, tall trees, and those winter birds who somehow fly fast enough to watch the woods shake and hear the air crash without dying in the noise.

The Barbecue

Mary Ward Brown

When Tom Moore saw Jeff Arrington come into his store and start back to the fireplace where he was, he braced himself. What does he want now? he wondered.

It was midmorning and Tom was sitting with a representative of the Power Company, there to negotiate a right-of-way across Tom's land. They were drinking Coca-Colas from sweating green bottles.

Since it was May there was no fire in the fireplace, but people sat around it all year. Smokers used it for an ashtray and chewers spat in it. Everyone used it as a wastepaper basket. Tom's black clerk, Willie, cleaned it out the first thing each morning when he swept the store. Over the mantel hung a wall clock in an oak case, its pendulum swinging back and forth hypnotically. The tick seemed to make babies stop crying and old people doze.

Jeff nodded to Tom's wife, Martha, busy behind the counter. The store was longer than wide, with groceries on one side and dry goods on the other. Martha was the main clerk and Willie her assistant. Tom helped out on Saturdays, and whenever he was free. He also had the farm to look after—plus business, as now.

At fifty-five Jeff still looked young. His hair was cut by a stylist, not a barber, and one side fell over his forehead in a boyish bang. He was over six feet tall and, except for a low stomach that pushed his belt down to hip level, had kept the rangy thinness of his youth. As usual, there was a half-smile on his face. At the fireplace, the smile expanded.

"How y'all today?" He held out his hand to the Power Company man, a stranger. "Jefferson Arrington," he said, and took a chair across from Tom's.

The chair was of unfinished wood with a cane bottom, like others for sale in the store, along with work clothes, patent medicine, nails, rattraps, and whatever else might save people in the surrounding area a ten-mile trip to town while making a profit for Tom.

64

"Nice weather," Jeff went on. "I hope it lasts through the weekend."

The Power Company man laughed. "You must not farm, then. The farmers need rain."

"No, I'm a lawyer. I've got a camp house down the road, but I live in town."

"Any kin to Dave Arrington, used to be in the legislature?"

"He was my father," Jeff said proudly. "I'm named for him. You knew him?"

"Just knew of him."

"Yes—he was the second, I'm the third, and my son Dave is the fourth."

"What can I do for you, Jeff?" Tom asked, to get it over.

"I'd like to use your phone, Tom, if you don't mind." Jeff lit a cigarette and threw the match in the fireplace. "I've got a pig and a lamb to barbecue Sunday night, and I need to call a few people."

Behind Tom's glasses one eye, of a somber blue, seemed locked in a different direction from that of the other eye, as if trying to see the bridge of his own nose. His good eye looked coldly at Jeff.

"Help yourself," he said.

Jeff had inherited money, securities, the antebellum house he lived in, and rental property all over town; but his renters told of falling plaster, leaking roofs, and dangerous gas heaters. Everything he owned was now mortgaged, sometimes more than once, according to people in the courthouse. He walked off to the office as if walking were a form of recreation.

Tom turned back to the Power Company man. This man had no authority. All he could do was repeat an offer already rejected. Time was money, Tom had learned long ago, and not to be wasted. From his pocket he took an inexpensive watch like the ones he kept in stock, looked at the time, then glanced up at the clock.

"You'll have to excuse me today, sir," he said. "That clock is slow, and I've got to get something in the mail."

The store had been built in 1890, the heart of a small community little changed except for paved roads, electricity, indoor plumbing, and new generations of the same families. The office, on the other side of the fireplace wall, was used for paying the help, bookkeeping, and business too complex to be transacted at the fireplace. On one side of the room was a stand-up desk with a square homemade stool that had come with the building when Tom bought it, thirty years ago. Jeff sat on the stool smiling into the telephone, inviting someone to his barbecue.

"Come early," he was saying, "in time for a drink."

At another, newer desk across the room, Tom uncovered an electric typewriter and inserted a sheet of stationery with the letterhead *Moore's Farm & General Store*. Using two fingers, he rapidly typed in the date.

Jeff turned with his hand over the mouthpiece. "Does this bother you?" he asked—a formality, Tom knew.

He shook his head as expected.

To his daughter, Laura, at Vanderbilt, he wrote, "My dear girl:– Kathy's Daddy using phone so I'll cut this short. Mother and I alright. No rain in three weeks. Nothing in the way of news. Call us Collect when you have time, and don't forget your old Dad. Allowance enclosed.

From the pocket of his shirt, he unclipped a pen and signed his name, Thomas J. Moore, as to anyone else.

Jeff was named for the southern hero Jefferson Davis. The first time someone told Tom his weekend neighbor was a collateral descendant of the president of the Confederacy, of the same blood and could trace it, Tom had laughed. "You mean they got the papers on him, like a bull?" Laura said there was an original portrait of President Davis's mother in one of the Arrington parlors. They prized it above everything else in the house, she said.

The *J* in Tom's name stood for Jefferson too. He was named for a hero even greater, the architect of American democracy, but he was no kin whatsoever. It was just a name his father had picked out, hoping it would help him amount to something, his mother said. His father had been a two-mule farmer in the poorest county of the state.

He wrote Laura's check and addressed an envelope.

"Better get that on in the box," Martha said, when he came out of the office. "It's time."

She was selling Minit-Rub to an old man in a felt hat, shapeless and faded from wear in all seasons. Willie was weighing bananas for a black woman with a baby. Outside a car, then a truck, pulled up for gas. While Tom filled the tanks, both drivers got out and went inside. The truck driver was eating sardines, hoop cheese, and crackers off the counter when Tom went back in. It was an ordinary busy morning.

Before the noon rush, Willie went next door to Tom's house, where the cook's job was to have a hot meal waiting. Tom and Martha would take turns going later.

No one was left in the store except Tom, Martha, and Jeff—still on the phone in the office. For the first time all day Martha sat down, on a stool behind the cash register. Tom walked up to stand in front of her while looking over the front page of the newspaper.

Jeff came out in an obvious hurry. When he glanced at the clock, he began to walk faster.

" 'Preciate it, Tom, Mrs. Moore." He lifted one hand in a gesture of farewell. "I've got to run now, but thank you!"

Martha smiled politely. Tom looked up from the paper with no change of expression. He watched Jeff hurry out the front double doors. A white Mercedes started up outside.

"How much does he owe?" Tom asked.

"Too much." Martha picked up a Popsicle wrapper and dropped it in a wire basket behind the counter. "I just looked it up."

"When you send his bill next month, I'll dun him."

She said nothing for a moment, then asked offhandedly, "He didn't invite us?"

"To his barbecue?" Tom looked at her in surprise. "Did you think he would?"

She made no reply.

"He didn't think of it, I guess," he said. "We don't belong with that crowd."

"But he used our phone to invite them."

After thirty-five years, he still didn't understand her. It had never entered his mind that Jeff would invite them. They wouldn't go if he did. They never went anywhere at night, except to bed. They had to get up and work the next day. What did she want—a chance to say no?

"You're just sensitive," he said. "He didn't mean to slight us. He just never thought of it, that's all."

"That's even worse," she said. "If he didn't think of it, we don't count at all to him. We're just nobody."

Like him, she had had few advantages growing up, but she was a remarkable woman. Everyone liked her, praised her. He could never have accumulated three thousand acres of prime Black Belt land without her. What did she care about a barbecue?

She did though. It was in her eyes.

He walked to the front door, looked out, and came back.

"I'm going to turn that bill over to Frayne," he said. Frayne was his lawyer. "He'll get some results."

She looked off into a blue-and-green landscape framed by the door. "They've always been nice to Laura . . ." she said. "Kathy has loved her since the first grade."

He said nothing.

"Laura's been exposed to a lot through Kathy," she went on. "She's stayed in their home, and they've taken her places. She's learned things."

He turned to look at her. "Are you telling me we have to *pay* for his daughter's friendship?"

She seemed not to hear. "And whatever he is, his wife's a real lady," she said.

"She is. That's a fact. Like you," he said.

She met his eyes directly. "You have to be born that kind of lady," she said.

A band of sunlight, teeming with dust motes, fell across the center aisle. Frowning, he stared at the dust motes. Silence seemed to build up in his ears like pressure. The ticking of the clock grew louder. He noticed the time.

"What's holding up Willie?" he burst out. "He's been gone thirty minutes! We ought to send him last, instead of first!"

Saturday was the biggest day of the week in the store. Martha got up at daylight and put on a pair of flat black shoes she called "old-lady comforts." The day before, trucks had brought in produce, dairy products, bread, and a supply of soft drinks. Their fresh meat was limited to chicken and pork chops, with less perishable wieners, bologna, sausage, and bacon. Hamburger, fish, pot pies, pizzas, and TV dinners were kept frozen. All day Friday, Martha and Willie had helped put up what the trucks had brought in, cleaning and straightening as they went.

Though it was still payday, Tom knew it had become more Martha's and Willie's day than his. He farmed with machinery

now. The bigger and better his machines, the fewer men he needed
Once it had taken him most of the day to pay the help. Now he
could do it in no time.

He was still the boss, however, and still there. He too got up
early and put on clean clothes, the khaki-colored pants and shirts
worn by middle-class farmers too old or too conservative for
jeans. Small farmers, who did their own work, wore overalls.
Tom's outfits were the same seven days a week, but he saved the
newest and best for Saturday and Sunday. On Sunday, and for trips
to town, he put on a tie. When Laura was a child she said he
looked funny in a suit, and he knew what she meant.

He suspected that most customers would rather be waited on by
Martha or Willie, that they hoped he would be back in his office
or out on the place. He waited on them anyway. There were also a
few, black and white, who preferred him, asked for him, waited
until he was free before coming forward with their lists. For them
he did his best, then waved aside the bag boy hired for Saturdays
and carried out the bags himself.

Today was as busy as ever. By ten o'clock Martha's wavy hair,
pulled back and pinned up, had lost its early-morning neatness.
Full-breasted and feminine, she looked more like a mother in the
kitchen than the manager of a store. Willie's face glistened and his
eyes were intent.

Helping his mechanic, Bud Howell, pick out a ventilated cap
with a visor, Tom glanced up to see a black man in white coveralls
hand a sheet of paper across the counter to Martha.

The man was called Pig and lived in town. He cooked for a living, and had a reputation for making the best barbecue, brunswick
stew, and gumbo in the county. People booked him months in ad-
vance for barbecues and fish fries. They took him on vacations and
trips to the coast. Everyone knew him.

"Excuse me a minute, Bud," Tom said. "I have to help my
wife."

At Martha's side, he smiled cordially. "How you, Pig?" he said.
"You down to cook for Mr. Jeff?"

"Yes, sir. That's right." Bowing slightly, Pig smiled back. "He
sont you his list."

On a yellow legal sheet, everything was listed in large quantity:
hard cabbages for slaw, bread and butter (good oleo, if no butter),

mayonnaise, Tabasco sauce, cases of Cokes, big bottles of ginger ale and club soda, tea bags and sugar, potato chips, sweet mixed pickles, lemons, vinegar, black pepper. Paper plates (best quality), big paper cups, dinner-sized napkins.

Tom's heart seemed to rise up in protest. Except for the meat and liquor, Jeff's whole barbecue was in his hand. He reread the items, calculating as he went, then turned toward the office.

"I'll be right back, Pig," he said.

Martha gave him an anxious, warning look. People were waiting, so she couldn't follow.

In the office he went straight to the ticket file and back to the *A*'s. Jeff's total, in Martha's careful figures, was even more than he had thought.

He placed a sheet of stationery on the stand-up desk and wrote, "Can't fill order until account is paid." Immediately he could see Martha's face, worried and vulnerable, loath to give offense for any reason. He knew what she would say. After staring briefly at the paper, he added: "In full, or substantial amount."

He attached his note to Jeff's list, folded both pages, and sealed them in an envelope.

"We can't get to Jeff's order right now, Pig," he said, handing him the envelope. "Give him this for me, will you?"

It was a while before Martha could talk to him.

"What did you do with that order?" she said, accusing not asking.

"What do you *think* I did with it?" he asked.

She looked at him and said nothing.

"Did you read it? Christ A'mighty! You want me to pay for a party you ain't even invited to?"

"But I didn't care. It was just—"

"What made you bring it up, then?" he flung at her, but her face was so bleak he wished he hadn't said it. "Don't worry. I'd have done it anyway. If I ever foot the bill for something like that, it won't be for a bunch of high-flyers better off than I am!"

"Always money . . ." she said.

"Damn right." As he turned away, he remembered something. "Did anybody help Bud find a cap?"

"I did," she said. "We found one."

"I went off and completely forgot him," he said.

Jeff and the barbecue were soon crowded out of mind, but Tom did not enjoy the rest of the morning. A vague sense of depression stayed with him. At noon he wasn't as hungry as usual. The iced tea tasted strong and bitter. There was too much salt pork in the vegetables, and too much cornstarch in the pie. He was sure the rutabagas, which he liked, would give him indigestion.

When he went back to relieve Martha, she was busy filling an order. Willie was out front selling gas. With a toothpick still in his mouth. Tom went to get fishhooks for two black boys who kept staring at his eyes.

The fishhooks were on the other side of the store, in the bottom of a showcase where he had to squat down to get them. When he stood up, Jeff's wife, Katherine, was already in the store, heading toward Martha.

Jeff was in and out of the store each week, charging, borrowing, killing time. His wife was never with him. If she came to the camp house more than once or twice a year, no one saw her.

Now as she hurried toward Martha, both of whose hands were full of Campbell's soups, Katherine Arrington was clearly upset. Tall and slender, in old slacks and a shirt, she had obviously rushed off without taking time to fix up. Even so, she had class, Tom thought.

"Mrs. Moore?" In the hush around her, Katherine's voice, high and urgent, could be heard throughout the store. "Oh, Mrs. Moore! I need to speak to your husband!"

Tom had left the black boys and fishhooks.

"Right here, Mrs. Arrington," he said, walking up beside her. "Let's step back to my office."

Country people, seated around the fireplace and standing in the aisle, stopped talking to look and listen. Grape and orange drinks, small cakes, and candy bars were forgotten in their hands.

Closing the door behind them, Tom took a seat on the stool. Too late he remembered he wasn't supposed to sit when a woman was standing. Getting up now would look worse, he decided, and stayed where he was.

From a worn leather bag on a shoulder strap, Jeff's wife took a handful of bills, unpaid, that Martha had sent months ago. As she held them out, her face was so flushed it looked swollen.

"I didn't know about this, Mr. Moore," she said. "I'm sorry. My husband—"

"Miss Katherine—please!" He lowered his voice to a near-whisper. "There's no hard feelings. It's just business."

"But it's not right! You look after your business and pay your bills."

"I come up the hard way," he said. "It was a case of have-to with me."

"You were better off, believe me."

Her hand was trembling as she opened a checkbook, to write out a check for the full amount.

"I appreciate your coming, Miss Katherine." His voice suddenly rasped, like a scratched phonograph record. He stood up and pushed the stool aside. "Now let's forget the whole thing—my wife will fill your order."

"Jeff took it on to town, Mr. Moore," she said. "But thank you, just the same."

On the way out she stopped to say good-bye to Martha, who looked as if she had a sudden fever, and to say that Kathy had heard from Laura not long ago.

When they finally closed the doors to the store, night had fallen. Quickly and efficiently, with few words, they emptied the cash register, locked the safe, and turned out the lights.

Outside, everyone had gone. The moon was new. There were few stars, and the sky seemed higher than usual. Their footsteps, loud on the hard dry ground, died without echoes.

With a flashlight, Tom led the way to the modest bungalow he had built conveniently near the store. Martha held the light while he opened the door.

At the flip of a switch the living room appeared, like a window display in a small-town furniture store. The sofa and chairs had been ordered sight unseen from a wholesale catalogue. Larger in scale than expected, they made the small room look crowded. Over the mantel a mirror, flanked by candlesticks without candles, reflected nothing but the opposite wall. Except for lamps, ash-trays, and framed pictures of Laura, the tables were bare.

Without a word, Martha went to the bedroom to take off her "old-lady comforts." She never talked much on Saturday night, so Tom did not consider her silence tonight unfriendly.

He did think she would ask what had happened in the office; but all she said before turning out the light was, "We forgot to feed the cats."

"They're supposed to catch rats," he said. "That's their business."

He was sure she had seen Katherine Arrington's check with the others.

The next day, as on every other Sunday, they slept later than usual, then went to Sunday School and church. Both were from generations of Baptists, but they attended the community church, which was Methodist.

Afterward Martha heated up a dinner the cook had prepared the day before, and washed the dishes. She seemed to enjoy working in the kitchen on Sunday. The cook was dirty, she said, and Tom had a hard time getting her to stop scrubbing pots, pans and surfaces. He did not help in the kitchen.

In the afternoon they read the paper and rode around the farm to look at the crops. As they rode, he outlined plans for the week ahead. Farming was one way to separate the men from the boys, he said. A few more days without rain, and the soybeans wouldn't have a chance this year.

"We'll get a rain," she said. "Don't worry. My corns hurt."

When they came back to sit on the porch and relax, the last thing in their Sunday routine, cars soon began to go by as if randomly spaced, one after the other.

"Oh." Tom sat up in his chair. "On their way to the barbecue. Wasn't that Judge Hixon?"

"I don't know." Martha got up. "I need to water the flowers."

"Somebody can do that in the morning," he said, but he knew she would go and not come back.

He sat alone and watched each car go by. Many people saw him and waved, since he was well known in the county. Some were busy talking and did not look to one side or the other, but everyone seemed to be happy and enjoying life. In the mild weather, windows were down and fragments of laughter flew out like discarded wrappings. The cars were all late models, clean and shining as in a parade.

When the last one had gone, Tom did not look with pride, as on other Sundays, at his store or the land he owned in all directions.

Taking a small, black-handled knife from his pocket, he opened a blade and began to trim and scrape his nails.

If someone had only had his eyes fixed, he thought, the rest wouldn't bother him the way it did Martha. He could get along without barbecues and pedigrees, even education, the worst drawback of all. But he did hate his eyes. As always in low moments, he saw them as they must look to the world—ugly and pathetic.

Hours later, when the cars came back, he and Martha were asleep. Martha did not wake up, and he didn't know why he should have. There was no loud laughter or honking horns such as sometimes disturbed them in the middle of the night—just cars going by in the darkness.

Unable to go back to sleep, he turned from one side to the other. His restlessness finally woke Martha.

"What's wrong?" she asked, with a hint of irritation, her words muffled by the pillow. For the day ahead of her, sleep was important. "Why don't you take an aspirin?"

After that he tried to lie still. But it was almost dawn before the blackboard of his mind, filled from one end to the other with questions he couldn't even understand, much less answer, was erased at last by sleep.

Recovery

Moira Crone

The spring I met Rae I wanted a single room. In the house where I spent my sophomore and freshman years, the glee club practiced every Wednesday in the parlor. The Whiffenpoofs would come up from New Haven. I applied to live in one of the original wooden houses overlooking the water. The view of Paradise Pond would be a curative.

I got my single but without a view. The building, originally a nineteenth-century boarding house, had been altered a little—firedoors and red extinguishers in the hall. There were six rooms on the floor. The carpet was low and striped. The stairs were covered with ribbed black rubber.

A freshman down the hall had an empty bed in the fall, and she complained she wanted a pal, a roomie. Beyond her was the bath, a room with the original high ceiling and a deep and old clawfooted tub.

In January, there was someone new in the living room downstairs. I was aware of her when I went to my mailbox. In it was a package from a friend, now in Alaska. She had run away her freshman year. Inside the package, a handthrown pot of dark silverish clay. There was an inscription and the sketch of a bark with two figures inside. Another figure leaned from the shore, almost touching the lip of the boat. I was holding it in the light, trying to make out the writing, when Rae walked up.

Her sandy hair went to her waist in a braid. She was wearing standard clothes, something I never did. A gray cableknit sweater, crisp worn jeans, mountain boots, and a navy cotton turtleneck. When we sat down on the couch near the fire, we took off our shoes and left them on the hearth as everybody did in the winter. Her legs stretched to the center of the coffee table. She was over six feet tall.

For several days, without much to do, we talked about being from the South. She quoted Willie Morris to me, about how he'd said Yankees assume you are an idiot the minute you open your mouth. Rae hadn't much of an accent.

It was winter midterm then. I'd come up early to settle in and get away from my family. She had very little luggage. There were a few pairs of pants and one black skirt in the closet. She complained her face was like a dinner plate lately. She used to be reed thin, she said, on account of some medicine she was taking. She showed me her photograph with a shorter dark-haired man. She was wearing a long white skirt, a gardenia in her hair, and an off-the-shoulder Mexican blouse. She looked much more sophisticated in the photo than she looked to me now. She said she didn't have any clothes since she was heavier.

She was assigned the room with the freshman. Four nights after I met her, she came in and reported to me that the girl had stuffed animals. She rolled her eyes in a way I can remember girls doing at a high school slumber party at the beach. It was pleasing to see. Like me, she had destroyed most of her mannerisms from her southern adolescence. They got us into trouble in New England. She was usually mannish and a little stiff, almost blank. Her eyes were large and slanted as two wings. They seemed impossible—decorative, oriental, too blue.

She was descended from Scots, and Scots are the tallest people in the world, disregard the Watusis. She told a story about her great-grandfather, an official in the South Carolina Confederacy. I told a story about my great-grandmother who took a promenade on Sherman's horse and dissuaded him from sacking my hometown. I wasn't a total southerner; my mother was from Chicago, but it went pretty far.

The day classes started, Rae mentioned she was twenty-five but she really didn't count four years. We were at breakfast with Lily, my only real friend in the house, who already knew all this. When Rae left, Lily told me with her mouth full of yogurt, "She didn't think she could handle an apartment, after everything, so she asked for a dorm room, just like a freshman, even though she's been through all this before."

I went upstairs and strapped on my uncomfortable boots.

The next afternoon, Rae came in and I offered her some tea from a hot pot. My room was inviting and mostly red, like a nest of scarves, she said. I had bought a decrepit daybed that served as a couch and the stuffing was so old that when it came out, it crumbled. I covered it with a pink throw. In the middle of the room was a glass terrarium with ferns and snails inside. There were papers and magazines, and racks, and a few boxes of souvenirs. The place gave me a kind of reputation.

"You remind me of someone I knew when I was here before," Rae said. "A nutty Irish Catholic. Always smoking something." She gave me a joint, wrapped in fuschia paper. "I am loosely attached, inherited from my mother's side," she said shortly after, after laughing. I had heard her mother was dead. Her father was a liberal lawyer. She was raised on a sea island out from Beaufort. Now a resort for people with boats, it was pretty empty then. She spoke the island dialect for me, and I realized she could do whatever accent the occasion required. From the time she was twelve, she said, she never knew anybody who could look her straight in the eye. Even her father was short, about five-ten, an anomaly in the family.

Again the delivery was plain as milk. No accent, a pursed smile. I liked her.

She was taking the equivalent of five courses. Daily elementary Greek, which counted for two, a practicum in piano, others. She said she registered for the load because she was so ignorant. Even though she'd learned a lot when she was here before, none of it had stuck.

The middle of February, there came a thaw. All the snow was gone, except for the gray, cold mounds in the center of the street in downtown Northampton. The pond was frigid green, littered with plates of ice. One afternoon, I couldn't get to class. I went to a movie with Spencer Tracy and Loretta Young at the Playhouse. Walking back up the soggy hill to campus, I was afraid that one afternoon would send me back to the way it had been a year before, when it had been so that I hadn't the will to do anything. I thought of the winter as a prolonged aberration, a disease the weather caught. The sky was like salt.

"I think I can tell *you*," Rae began. She came into my room ten minutes after passing me in the hall, her eyes very flashy. "Outside my window, this morning around two, I saw my mother. Her arms were stretched forward, and she was pregnant with me. I could see the veins in her hands." She had a dreamy expression, as if she were singing opera. She lit a joint and left me two in a pouch which I put in one of the three, narrow drawers at the top of my dresser.

It turned out to be four o'clock. Every day at four o'clock, Rae walked into my room without knocking and confessed what she had seen or thought that day. It had the same regularity as the meals and the classes and the weekends. I looked forward to it sometimes.

An ancient Oriental art professor gave me an "A" on an early paper about a large Buddhist monster painted on silk. It was from that time in Japanese history when the codified madness of tantrism was practiced, but it was too elaborate for Japan. It died out there. The silk icon was critically deteriorated. I had hitchhiked to Boston to see it: it was stained and worn from centuries of incense and intense attention. I had stared at it until the eight arms started to move and the swords and arms came forward. The professor, who walked with a limp, passed me in the Art Library one night at ten, just before it closed. He nodded at me and said something about the icon. He meant, you are a promising student. I thought he was an old bastard.

Six years before, Rae came as a music major. She played beautifully, but she was trying to do some new things this time. At the beginning of spring break that year she flew down to Columbia to see her piano teacher, a man she described as a saint. It was a few days after King was assassinated. Her teacher died accidentally at a gas station, caught in the crossfire, during the Black Bottom riots. Soon after she had to turn around and fly back, she had the first episode. She ended up at Northampton State, an institution those with a view could see out the west windows on the other side of Paradise Pond.

From the state hospital, she'd gone to a private one outside of Boston, and from a two-year stay there to psychotherapy in New York for three years. She'd worked and been somewhat independent and had a lover. She lived with a gang of friends from the institution, mostly men.

The old man with the cane was marvelous, according to her. I said she should finish the course for me. She was crazy about all the manifestations of the Buddha. She read my first paper as if it had a plot. She looked at me one night and announced, "When you die, you are what visions you have. All these monsters: this is hell, for instance," she said, holding up a print of an icon of a demon riding on a turtle. "That's what this religion is, an illustrated guide to monsters. When you are already dead, then there is no difference between them and you."

"No point in dying, then," I said. "You lose the advantage."

"What advantage?" she asked seriously.

My friend Lily was getting married to a man in architecture at Yale as soon as she graduated. She was away a lot, training down to New Haven. She was one of those people who look exactly right. She was rich. Her hair was a Breck ad. The wedding was complicated. He had a father and a stepfather: her parents were balking here and there. The more she talked about getting married, the less time we spent together. She was often with two girls I thought were too straight who lived directly across the hall from me. It hurt: I liked her a lot. All of them were taking sociology and that involved a practicum in Chicopee, a small town near Springfield, where they were counseling wayward girls in a halfway house.

Four weeks into the semester, Rae told me she had dropped out of intensive Greek. She said she had taken it because her New York analyst was Jungian trained, and she wanted to know the myths. She tried to transfer into a classics-in-translation course, but the registrar required permission. She told me she was going to get it, then she didn't.

Rae played piano daily in the ballet classroom over the boathouse at the edge of the pond. That room near the water was bright and aesthetic—brilliant gymnasium wax on the hardwood floors. Sometimes I would see her leaving, after someone had just finished playing very good Chopin. She denied practicing as much as she did.

She liked to talk to me about how I was sane. She was convinced I was like her but all right. It was not necessarily considered a compliment then. Everybody knew about the romance of the mad. We all had our copies of Plath, and except for the girls who were abnormally practical, we all courted craziness. The two across the hall were the only ones in the house who consciously avoided Rae once they knew she had been in an asylum. I heard them complaining that Rae didn't like to send out for pizzas at two a.m. And she didn't sleep, they swore. Rae was a pressure at the end of the hall, a permanent storm. Sometimes I would find her sitting up on the edge of the bathtub with a Benson & Hedges at five in the morning, looking at the bare trees, and the pond past them.

A year before, in the glee club house, I had worried a few people. Lily said it was a combination of Dexedrine and the fumes from all the silk-screaning I was doing. I had two wild friends who were a scandal. But they both dropped out in April, left for New Hampshire and Alaska. Finally there was a small fire in my studio. Somebody I really liked screamed at me—"You are too conscious, Jean, to be crazy. You don't talk yourself into being crazy." I went to the studio and scrubbed the smoke off the walls. I put everything into stacks. I began to feel numb. That was better.

In March, Lily and the ones across the hall had the girls from the Chicopee halfway house for dinner. Our dining hall was bright and delicate. Federal style mantel with a beveled mirror. The girls popped gum at the table, but you could tell they were acting politely. Afterwards, they went into Lily's room and sat around until ten, listening to Ry Cooder.

In the morning, there were three pairs of shoes missing on the hearth downstairs. Leather clogs, and the riding boots lined in lambskin that belonged to a horsey girl on the fourth floor.

Rae woke me at seven-thirty. "The Misses Dogoods got ripped off," she cracked. "They are in the living room right now, with security, revamping their liberal consciousnesses."

I was annoyed at being awakened, but it was nothing new for Rae to do it. I had to laugh. I hoped Lily hadn't called the cops. I learned she had tried to stop them, and my faith in her came back. We were at breakfast when she asked me, "Where's your shadow?" hoping I'd forget about the stolen shoes. She meant Rae, of course. I was afraid she was coming in any minute, that she would interrupt my time alone with Lily. "I never see you anymore," she went on. "Is she that interesting?"

Her little bit of jealousy was exciting—the way she sniffed, tilting her chin. I knew all of a sudden how much I missed her. She was always getting ready to get on the train, and besides, Rae had me. Every meal, every hour of conversation, whole Sundays over the *Times*. And Rae wasn't really with us; that had been five years ago when she was one of us. She was doing college this time a few feet off the ground, like someone on stilts, or a wading bird stalking back. She had started going to Oriental art with me. I didn't like it.

At first, I really wanted to know what it was like to go ahead and break down. When she felt me receptive, she told me the things she saw. I knew the whole catalog. At Northampton State, it had been angels. I had already suggested perhaps she was just a visionary or a saint. Like William Blake, she had vertical access, as my religious poetry professor put it. She gave me a look as if I were an alien. I had no idea what she was talking about. I had missed the point, let her down. These impasses were occasional. We kept up the four o'clocks. We constructed boundaries in our conversations. I had bad moods, and was arty, but I hadn't been over the edge. She was older and ten inches taller and much much sadder than me. She was so much the taller I could disappear behind her.

I learned, in the middle of March, that Rae had given up on most of her classes. "Why is she here if she isn't going to school?" the blonde across the hall asked me at dinner, as if I were responsible, or as if I lived in some quite other world where such things can be explained.

I began retreating, using a paper as an excuse. I decided I wanted to see a three-hundred-year-old book of prints at the Museum of Fine Arts. The old man would have to write me a letter of introduction, the museum told me. The paper prints were kept in a special vault. Exposure to the museum air and too many patrons would destroy them.

Lily came back from New Haven on a Saturday with a pack of Kents and two knapsacks of clothes and junk. Her hair was a little dirty. She had been irritable since the shoes were stolen. She had started to doubt she could be a social worker. Yet she already had a counseling job set up in New Haven which would begin after her honeymoon. Now the bottom had fallen out. Her fiancé had told her, without much preparation, that he really didn't feel like getting married in May.

April Fool's Day, Rae came in at four. I felt a little panicky when I saw her. She did not exactly look at me when she talked. She was going to kill herself, she said. It was not new, it was not hysterical. She was somber, as if she were talking about a job she had to finish. The time before, in 1968, she had seen an image of her mother outside the window of the room, and she'd dived through the glass to meet her. Rae already had shown me the scars on her legs.

And Lily stopped eating, I noticed. At breakfast, it was tea and toast. No butter, no milk in the tea. The same at lunch. Maybe a brownish apple. She chain-smoked. Her mother told her on the phone from Florida that the boyfriend had never been any good. Her ex-fiancé was crude, a snake, vile, no one she had ever wanted for a son-in-law. "Such luck she told me now," Lily kept repeating. "What if I'd married him and she never said she despised him? What then? Such luck."

But nothing was the same as it had been a week before. I could hear Lily all night in the next room, clicking things, turning the radio on and off. I listened to her for hours. I couldn't sleep either.

It was still winter even though it was April. I was sorry about Rae, and now there was Lily. It didn't do any good to talk. We talked all night, we, the three of us; we were good talkers. Their afflictions were either temporary or permanent, and mine were mine—that I was always falling back, discovering that what I had just said was precisely wrong, exactly false. It was why I was a good student, too. I was capable of imparting enthusiasm I didn't possess. Rae was infectiously sad and Lily was broken-hearted. I would strip us all down until five a.m., amazed to discover how much I could say to console or repair that I didn't believe. Rae's morose enthusiasm was boundless: whenever I looked up, her unnatural eyes still seemed hungry; they still looked hurt. I had the idea to tell her something on one of those nights, but I put it off. Eventually the sky would turn a cold blue. Then we could go downstairs in our bathrobes for soft-boiled eggs. The light and the glass in the dining room were shimmering, perfect. Nothing got better.

I told my parents I was staying over during the spring break to write the second paper. I had to go see the old professor to get the letter. His office was in the Art Library. It was a building in the late nineteenth-century mock Gothic style. His desk faced high-leaded windows and was surrounded by original Japanese prints. Someone had told me he'd had tenure for thirty-five years. He was a snob this time, worse than before. He had forgotten my name since I made a B-plus on the midterm. I had missed a slide of one of the most important Kwannons of the Heian period. Quite suddenly as I sat down, he made a horrible face, as if I gave him a pain. I wanted terribly to leave. Actually, I thought he might hit me with the cane if I made the wrong move. When I left the office, I saw Rae below me on the library stairs. I hadn't wanted to see her. She said she would drive me to Boston. I had no choice.

The day we set off, it was that time in New England spring when you can look forward to removing your coat if you walk a few blocks in the sun. We saw the book, which was as big as a table top. An encyclopedic collection of woodcuts of birds, some distorted as caricatures. But I couldn't enjoy it. It visibly disturbed Rae. The whole Oriental wing was empty and cool and dim: she was sullen all afternoon.

I wanted to remain in the city, go to Cambridge, but Rae seemed to think something terrible would happen if we stayed. She said she was feeling very depressed. Then she started a story she'd told me before.

In South Carolina, in 1968, she'd been caught in an airport limo on the way to see her old teacher, and she could not roll down the windows, and she could not open the door because the driver had them automatically locked. He was scared to death. Rae was the only passenger. There were roadblocks, policemen, fires. All this time, Rae was seeing the kinds of things she was susceptible to outside the tinted glass windows. She described this to me as we went through the outskirts of Boston, past White Coffee Pot Juniors, Friendly's Days Inns, green signs for Route 128 and Wellesley and Milton, Lexington and Waltham. She recounted the entire breakdown while she drove. I have always liked detail, but almost suddenly I was exhausted; there was no way I could respond, finally, to her memory. A murky, seawater gray overcame us both around Worcester. Then she said again that she wanted to die. It wasn't for the same reason I wanted to—my reason was that I never got anything perfect. She had concluded she was too sad to live.

It was a speech I had already practiced. I hadn't expected to say it. I had discussed it already with Lily who said it would be cruel and how could I be that way.

"If you want to talk about you and your death, Rae," I think I said, "then it really isn't between you and me. We are alive, in this. Your death is just about you. I have nothing to do with it. You undermine everything. I can't help."

I enunciated everything clearly, like an actress. It sounded artificial. I was almost shouting, as if the distance between us were very wide, as if I were shouting from the shore while she drifted out. I said it over and over to myself and I felt pleasure, exhilaration, something I could almost touch.

I could feel Rae freezing over, but I couldn't come back. Her eyes lowered and she stared at the road, like someone sleeping. Then I fell asleep. When Rae woke me we were in front of the house. I remember her face, looking injured, mouthing something to me through the window on my side. Then she used the key to unlock the door. I was out of the car.

Lily was doing well, considering the circumstances. She still had trouble at bedtime but the infirmary gave her something. She'd worked up a hatred for her ex-fiancé, and she had a huge party in her room one night, all women. It amazed me that Lily had the range of friends she had. I was one of many. Her long, competent fingers were wrapped around a plastic glass of sherry; raga music was playing on the stereo; she wore a caftan. She announced that she was moving to Florida to be a law student and be near her parents, who had bought a new place in Palm Beach. Her fiancé, who didn't deserve her anyway, would be exiled forever in dank Connecticut. Without contradiction, looking fierce, and whole and golden, she took my wrist. "I'm back," she told me, "and this is really what I want to do." I had the feeling I'd lost her. Some of the women started to dance, and I felt a surprising pleasance, a soft warmth in my brain that came to me like a prize.

Later, Lily asked if I had seen Rae. I wondered if she knew I was a traitor, but then I thought she didn't care too much. She was "back." The noise of the party disappeared in the hall. The other doors were tightly closed.

Rae was sitting in the window. The opposite bed was already stripped.

I once walked up on a heron by mistake on a South Carolina marsh. It was standing about a foot away, eating a fish. All around us were the silence of the saltwater creek and a million fiddler crabs who spread out of the way like sentient waters as I lowered my step. I realized there was something wrong with him, that he hadn't fled at my approach. He looked at me with indignance. Finding him had been a profound intrusion. Rae looked the other way, out the window, and I left.

In the morning, I learned there would be no art history lecture because the old man had had a serious stroke. A professor from Amherst would wrap up the course.

At breakfast Rae sat at the end of the table near the mantel, facing Lily and me. She said nothing. Finally, with coffee, I asked her when she was going home for the break. Her face was puffy; she looked horrible. "I'm going back to Boston," she said, meaning the hospital. Shortly, she left the table.

"It was inevitable, wasn't it?" Lily asked me too soon. "I mean, didn't it have nothing to do with us?" She lit a cigarette. I noticed her smooth pageboy was back. "Wasn't it inevitable that she would come here and do the same thing all over again? Didn't we have nothing to do with it?" She seemed almost angry.

I told her I thought it was silly for us to blame ourselves, but I didn't believe it. Lily said, "She's disturbed. She's ill, she's disturbed. She's not like us."

About four, Rae came into my room. We talked of the professor. She insisted he was going to die, that he was dead already. I said I had always thought he was awful, so pompous and frightening. I confessed I hated all old men with authority, and she said she had fallen in love, particularly with the way he pointed at the slides from the podium with his cane. We did not listen to each other very well. She did not talk about her decision to leave. It was territory she had reclaimed. Now I knew her much less well. I heard her accent for the first time in a long time, and I heard my own voice leaving me and going into the air in the room. I thought of hugging her before she went through the door, but she was too stiff. My arms could hurt her.

I stayed on campus during the break. The house finally emptied and there were no meals. I lived in my room, on crackers and tomato soup from cans. For almost a week, I could hardly rise from bed, and at night, I felt as if a shadowy sister of myself ran all around the room, over to the library, out to the pond: she was taking over where I had given up. I cried some, for muddled reasons. It would start out one thing, then shift to something else. I kept looking for the reason I was so low, and there wasn't one, except that there was an infinite regression, that nothing was the reason. Rae was not the reason: I was over Rae. It was very easy to be over her.

I would look into mirrors, even plan my day, wash my hair, spend an hour in the tub at the end of the hall where she used to sit, but it would be four in the afternoon before I was ready to leave and walk into town for some coffee. When I got there, the shops were beginning to close. There was a big-flaked snow the first afternoon I actually ventured out, in a cotton sweater and thin slacks. The cold was the first visceral experience I had in months. I finally got to the library and took out a book on Shiraku. My excuse for staying was the paper, and I hadn't started it yet. Then, in one night, I wrote the whole thing, starting with Rae's interpretation of the prints. The book was a compendium of prey. Big wading killers, with talons, claws, beaks. Hungry, harsh, and beautiful.

When the snow melted, I took a walk around the pond. The grass was newly lush, thick as a woman's hair. The trees were budding. It was the middle of April, and spring was finally inevitable: nothing could be done to stop it. I felt more solid, somehow more alive. But I still cannot say even now if I was worse or better.

This Heat

Pam Durban

In August, Beau Clinton died. He was playing basketball in the high-school gym and when his bad heart set him free he staggered and fell, he blew one bloody bubble that lingered, shimmering, until it burst, sprinkling blood like rust spots, all over his pale face. The school phoned Ruby Clinton but they wouldn't say what the trouble was, just that Beau was sick, in trouble, something—it was all the same trouble—and could Ruby or Mr. Clinton come right down. "Isn't any Mr. Clinton," Ruby snapped, but the woman had already hung up the phone. So she figured she'd best go down to see what he'd done this time, her son who looked so much like his sorry father, Charles Clinton, it was all she could do sometimes to keep from tearing into him.

Ruby walked down the hall working herself up for the next showdown with Beau or the principal or whoever crossed her. No one made her angrier than Beau. She could get so angry that bright points of light danced in front of her eyes. Of course it didn't matter, not at all; she might as well rave at the kudzu, tell it to stop climbing on everything and choking it, hauling it down under those deadly green vines. A woman with a worried face directed Ruby to the clinic room and Ruby quickened her step. But when she got there, a man blocked the doorway. "You can't go in there," he said. Ruby didn't answer and she didn't stop. She was used to plowing past men such as he, and she knew her strength in these matters. There were things in this life that wouldn't give, that was a fact, but you put your shoulder against them and you shoved anyway.

"The hell you say," Ruby said. "If he's having one of his spells I know what to do."

"He's not having one of his spells," the man said. "I'm afraid he's dead."

She squinted and watched while the man collapsed into a tiny man and then grew life-size again. She had a steady mannish face, and when something stunned her that face turned smooth and still,

87

as if everything had been hoarded and boarded up back of her eyes somewhere. Younger, she'd had a bold way of memorizing people, but that look had narrowed until she looked as if she were squinting to find something off in the distance. She'd been what they call *hot-blooded*, a fighter, all her people were fierce and strong, good people to have on your side. There was once something of the gypsy about her—a lancing eye and tongue and the gypsy darkness shot through with a ruby light. But that seemed like a long time ago. Now, at the time of Beau's death, Ruby was thirty-two, but she looked worn and strong. Her face had settled into a thick heavy grain like wood left lying outside since the day it was first split from the tree.

She'd gone there ready to scream at Beau, to smack him good for whatever he'd done, to drag him away from a fight one more time—he'd sat right there and heard what the judge had said—or from playing ball—he'd heard the doctor say that he was not to move faster than a walk if he wanted to live through the summer. She'd gone there ready to smack him, breathing harshly through her nose. She still had faith in the habit of hitting him—it roused him for a second or two, raised him out of the daze where he lived most of the time—a numb sort of habit that began as pressure behind her eyes and ended with the blunt impact and the sound of the flat of her hand landing hard against his skull.

The words she would have said and the sound of the blow she'd gone ready to deliver echoed and died in her head. Words rushed up and died in her throat—panicked words, words to soothe, to tame, to call him back—they rushed on her, but she forgot them halfway to her mouth and he lay so still. And that's how she learned that Beau Clinton, her only son and the son of Charles Clinton, was dead.

From then on it was just one amazement after another. She was amazed to find the day just as hot and close as it had been when she'd gone inside the school building. Everything should have been as new and strange as what had just happened. But the dusty trees stood silent against the tin sky, and below, in the distance, Atlanta's mirrored buildings still captured the sun and burned. Then the word *dead* amazed her, the way it came out of her mouth as though she said it every day of her life. "Well, that's what they tell me," she said to Mae Ruth as her sister sat there, hands gripping the steering wheel, exactly the way she'd been caught when Ruby dropped the word onto her upturned face. Then she was surprised by her sister's voice, how it boiled on and on shaped like questions, while Ruby breathed easily, lightheaded as a little seed carried on the wind. It was the most natural thing in the world that Beau should be dead; it had never been any other way. She patted her sister's hand: "That sneaky little thing just slipped right out on me," she said, chuckling to herself and wiping her eyes with the backs of both hands. And her heart gave a surge and pushed the next wave of words out, as though she were speaking to Beau himself, come back from the dead to taunt her: "That sneaky little bastard," she said, "goddamn him."

Mae Ruth drove like a crazy woman—running red lights, laying on the horn, heading back toward Cotton Bottom at sixty miles an hour, gripping Ruby's wrist with one hand. "We got to get you home," she said.

"You do that," Ruby said. It would be nice to be back there among the skinny houses that bunched so close together you could hear your neighbor drop a spoon. She could slip in there like somebody's ghost and nobody'd find her again. That was the comfort of the village—the tight fit made people invisible. Too many people with too much trouble lived here, and everybody had gotten in the habit of going around deaf and blind just so they could have some peace now and again. She could hide there and never come out again, the way Old Lady Steel did after her kid got run over by a drunk: rocking on her porch day and night, cringing anytime tires squealed, and crying out at the sight of children in the street. That was a good use for life, she thought. She just might take it up like so many of the rest of her neighbors. They saw something once, something horrible, and it stuck to their eyes and the look of it never left them.

When they turned onto Rhineheart Street, Ruby sat up. "This ain't right, Mae Ruth, you took a wrong turn somewhere," she said anxiously. Her gaze never left the road that ran into a lake of white light, a mirage. In the glare, her street looked like a familiar place that had been warped. Then there was her house and the neighbors three deep on the narrow porch because somehow the news had gotten loose and run home before her. And she saw that the glare, the mirage, was a trick of the light on the windshield and she sat back and said, "Oh, now I get it. Fools you, don't it?" And she chuckled to herself. Someone had played a fine joke and now it was revealed.

The place where Ruby lives is called Cotton Bottom because of the cotton mill and because it's set in a low spot, a slump in the earth. The streets there run straight between the mill on one end of the place and the vacated company store on the other. In February when the weather settles in and the rain falls straight down, the air turns gray and thin, and there's silence as though the air had all been sucked into the big whistle on top of the mill and scattered again to the four corners of the earth. But in the summer, this place comes alive: the kids all go around beating on garbage-can lids, the air is so full of their noise you couldn't lose them if you tried, and the heat is so heavy you drag it with you from place to place.

The other border of this place is an old city cemetery with a pauper's field of unmarked graves on a low hill. Ruby used to go there between shifts or after work if it was still light and sit and listen to the wind roughing up the tops of the trees. They were the biggest trees she'd ever seen—oaks, some with crowns as wide as rooftops. Sometimes she thought of the roots of the trees, and it gave her a funny cold knot in the pit of her stomach to think of the roots and the bodies down there all mixed up together, the bones in among the roots, feeding the trees. She sat very quietly then, listening, as if she might catch that long story as it begins below the ground, as it rises and ends in the wind, in the tossing crowns of the oaks, in the way they sigh and bend and rise and lash the air again.

By eight o'clock the morning after Beau's death the sun looked brassy, as though it had burned all day. You had to breathe in small sips for fear you'd suck in too much heat and choke on it. Everybody was busy mopping at themselves, blotting their upper lips, women reaching back, lifting their hair and fanning their necks. Ruby didn't question how the night had passed; she watched while the sweating men struggled and pushed Beau's coffin up the narrow steps. And as she watched them coming closer she had one of her thoughts that seemed to come out of nowhere: Who is that stranger coming here?

She must have mumbled it to herself, because Dan Malvern and Mae Ruth both leaned over at the same time to catch what she'd said. "You'd think that'd be the easy part," she said, nodding toward the men with the coffin. Her arms hung at her sides; her face was slack, red and chafed-looking; her feet were planted wide to keep her upright. When they passed with Beau's coffin, her mouth went dry and her knees gave a little and Dan squeezed her arm and whispered: "Ruby, you hold on now." His warm breath on her ear annoyed her.

She tried not to listen to the rustling of the undertakers, the way they whispered as they fussed with the casket. They opened the casket and draped an organdy net from the lid to the floor and arranged it in a pool around the legs of the coffin stand and it all seemed to be happening beyond glass somewhere. The open lid was lined with shirred white satin—the richest cloth she'd ever been close to, that was for sure—gathered into a sunburst. Below it her son rested on his cushions with that stubborn look stuck to his face as though he were about to say _No_ the way he did: jutting out his chin and freezing his eyes and defying the world to say him _Yes_. "I never believed it," she said, and the words were cold drops in her ears, "not for a minute, and now look." And with that, a heaviness in her chest dragged on her, she turned on the people close by and said: "What was the way he should've come, tell me that? What other road could he have gone, why doesn't somebody tell me?" She grabbed Mae Ruth's arm.

"Be strong, darlin'," Mae Ruth said, from somewhere close beside her ear. "You got to be strong now."

She sank into the chair they had guided her to. It seemed that she'd been strong forever and in everything. Just after Beau was born sick she'd been strong in her faith. It had leapt on her one day like something that had been lying in wait getting ready. Afterwards, she'd gone about preaching the Word to anyone who'd stand still long enough to hear. That's when Charles Clinton had left for the first time. But the Lord had stayed, yes He had. He sent His mighty spirit down to fill her where she stood inside the Holiness Lighthouse Tabernacle over on Gaskill Street. He slung her onto the floor and filled her some more till she was so full of His spirit it pressed out against the walls of her chest, the walls of her skull, till she thought it might tear her open, trying to get free.

She'd swooped down on her neighbor's houses after that night—praying, singing, weeping for all who lived there sunk in the sin and error of their ways, their sin a pressure building inside her as if it were her sin too. On Sunday, she sang the hymns with the force and flatness of a hammer hitting a rock, and on Wednesday evenings at prayer meeting, she beat the tambourine so hard that no one could stand close to her.

Then she'd been strong at work in the mill. First, she wielded the sharp razor, slashed open the bails so the cotton tumbled out. She roughed up the cotton and set it going toward the other room to be wooed and combed straight into fiber. They took note of how she worked and she was promoted to spooler. She stood beside the machines until she thought the veins in her legs might burst. She worked there yanking levers, guiding the threads as they sped along from one spool to the next. You had to yank the levers because the machines were old and balky, but the habit of it became the same as its action and the habit felt like fury after awhile. The threads flew by, never slowing, drawing tighter, flying from one spool to the next, the separate strands twisting, making miles of continuous threads for the big looms in the room beyond. The noise could deafen a person. The machines reared up and fell forward in unison and grabbed the fiber with metal claws and twisted the strands and rose and grabbed and fell again in rhythm all day and all night. The machines crashed like sacks full of silver being dropped again and again until she couldn't think, she could only watch the threads as they came flying out of the dark door and caught and flashed around the spools and flew out the other door.

For years she went to work during the day and at night she went to prayer meetings or to church singings. Later, when the Lord had eased up on her, she'd been with a bunch of women praying together one night when something ugly had come into their midst, something that smelled like burnt hair, and she'd stepped to the front like she knew just what to do. She'd been strong for them all and she'd led them in raising their voices louder in God's praise, every fiber set against the thing that had entered and filled the room right in the middle of prayer. She'd known right away that whatever it might be, it was between this thing and Beau that she needed to stand. "Don't be afraid," she said. She made *quiet down* motions with her hands and she said: "You know, it comes to me to say there isn't nothing strange under the sun, not good and not bad either one. There is this thing we call the Devil and that old Devil turns things inside out and upside-down just that quick. Why, he spins you around and turns you around and scares you into thinking that he's stronger than anything you can call on, ain't that right?" And that, she told them, was the work this Devil was appointed to do on this earth.

But the work didn't stop there, oh no. The work went on working and people began to call themselves shameful and ugly before God. You could see it all the time, she told them, in the sad empty eyes around you. And the end of the work came when people turned into living tombstones over their own lives, when people hid their faces from one another; then the work was finished, she told them. "Now you've all seen it happen," she said. "Every single one of us in this room's seen it happen. But the way I figure it, we got to go one better than that. We got to stand up and say 'All right then, I got something for you better than what you got for me.' That's what we're all put here to do on this earth, and we can't ever let each other forget."

But that all seemed to have happened in another lifetime, in another country, a long time ago. Now there was this: the undertakers finished their business and left the house. Ruby dragged the reclining chair right next to the steel-gray coffin and eased herself down, feeling like a bag of flesh with a cold stone at the center. The coffin looked cold and shiny as coins, and her mind wandered there, counting the coins.

The green vinyl of the chair arms stuck to the back of her arms, and she saw the looks go around the room from Mae Ruth to her aunts, to Granny Brassler and the rest of them. Looks and sighs that flew around the room, passing from one to another, but she didn't care. She knew what they were thinking; she'd thought the same herself many a time about someone else: they were worrying that all the fight had gone out of her and wondering what they would do with another one to feed and wipe clean. In the village, that's the worst that can happen. "I'm here to stay," she said, "don't want no bath, don't want no supper, so don't start on me about it, just tend to your business and let me tend to mine."

She thought of that business and how she'd learned it well. To work, to live you had to be angry, you had to fight—that much she remembered. Her father had fought for his life, for all their lives, the time half the mill walked out, and the mill police came muscling into their house on fat horses. She could still see the door frame give, see her father's arm raised, all the veins standing up, before he brought the stick of stove wood down hard across the horse's nose. That was what life was for—fighting to keep it. That's how she'd been raised. All the good sweet passion and flavor of life soured if you just let it sit. Like milk left out, it could spoil. You had to be strong.

She smelled her own exhausted smell, like old iron, leaving her. Someone had drawn the curtains across the front window. Someone wiped her face with a cloth. They bent over her one after the other. "Ruby, trust in the Lord," someone said. The thought rolled over her.

"I do," she said automatically, because the Lord was still a fact, more or less. "But it's got nothing to do with him." She nodded toward her son. There. She was afraid to say it, but that was the truth. She snapped up straight, defying any of them to say differently. And just then she was taken by grief that pushed up in waves from the dead center of her. Each wave lifted her out of the chair and wrenched her voice from her throat, and that voice warned them: "I can't bear it." She couldn't open her eyes and inside the darkness there was a darker darkness, a weight like a ball, rolling against the back of her eyes. "I can't support it," she said and everything obliged inside her and fell in, and there was a quick glimpse of Beau the way he'd come home one time after a fight—tatters of blood in the sink, too much blood to be coming out of his nose and no way to stop it—and she was falling, tumbling over and over. Someone shouted her name; hands held her face, her hands. They bobbed all around her, corks on a dark water.

And when finally she opened her eyes, she glared at them as if they'd waked her from a deep sleep. She looked at Beau's face: they had messed with it somehow till it looked almost rosy, and chalky too, dusted with powder. His hair was washed straight back as though a wave had combed it, so silky and fine. He'd taken to dyeing his hair—the roots were dark and a soapy cloying smell rose through the organdy—and she said on the last receding wave of grief: "Lord, don't I wonder what's keeping him company right now."

"Now don't you go wandering off there all by yourself," Mae Ruth said. Her eyes were inches from Ruby's own. Ruby looked at her sister and almost laughed in spite of herself at the funny veiny nose, more like a beak than a nose, the eyes like her own, two flat dark buttons. Now Mae Ruth's life was hard too, but it didn't fit her so tight. She made room in it. She could tell funny stories, then turn around and tell somebody off just as neat and they'd stay told off. Once they'd both gone to a palm reader out by Doraville and the woman had scared Ruby, and Mae Ruth had said, "Lady, far's I'm concerned you get your jollies out of scaring people half to death." That was Mae Ruth for you. Just then her face looked like she was about to imitate the way the woman had looked. Mae Ruth could pull her face down long as a hound's and say "Doom" in this deep funny voice and you'd have to laugh.

Someone new had come into the room. She felt it in the stirring among the crowd around her chair, the way they coughed and got quiet. "Dan?" she said. He'd left the room after the coffin was carried inside and had gone to stand outside with the men on the porch. She looked up, expecting to find Dan's narrow brown face, and there stood Charles Clinton and his new wife, looking cool in spite of the heat. "Well, look who's here," she said, "look who's showing his face around here again." The welcome in her voice would have chilled you to the bone, "Look who's come back to the well," she said. "Well's dried up, Charles Clinton," she said. Her breathing turned down like a low gas flame. His new wife tried to get in her line of vision, but Ruby kept ducking around her in order to keep an eye fixed on Charles. And doesn't it always happen this way? When she was most in need of the mercy of forgetfulness—just then, she remembered everything.

She was sixteen, up from Atlanta to Gainesville for the Chicopee Mill picnic. He stood apart from everybody, working a stick of gum, his eyes all over her every time she moved. The lights inside the mill had come winging out through the hundreds of small windows. Like stars, they'd winked on the water of the millpond. And the roaring of the mill barely reached them across the mild night, and it was no longer noise that could make you deaf. The air was

clean of cotton lint and clear, and the mill glittered. Everything
glittered that way. Oh yes, she remembered that glittering very
well. He had eyes like dry ice. She should have known; she should
have turned and run with what she knew instead of thinking she
could sass and sharp-tongue her way out of everything. He said:
"You're Ruby Nelson from Atlanta, aren't you?"

"How'd you know?" she said.

"I have my ways," he said. And thinking about those ways had
made her shiver.

She should have bolted for sure. She was supposed to have married Hudger Collins, and she had no business forgetting that. But
Hudger was dull next to this one who had hair like corn silk, a
sloped and angled face that reminded her of an Indian, and slanted
eyes that watched and watched.

"I take you for a soldier," she said. And he smiled that smile that
rippled out across his face and was gone so fast you couldn't catch
it.

"Now you're a right smart girl," he said, wrapping one hand
around the top of her arm. "It just so happens that I was in the
Navy. You're real smart."

Later that night as they lay over near the edge of the woods
where the grass was dry and patchy, he said her name again and
again as if he wanted to drive it into her. Now when she saw him
again a pit opened inside her and all the fiends let fly. She looked
at Beau jealously, as if he might rise up and join his father and
together they'd waltz away into the night. She said: "Charles
Clinton, why don't you come over here and look at your boy. He's
dead, he isn't going to get up and worry you now. You don't have
nothing to be ashamed of anymore." She hated her voice when it
got quavery like that. She heard a dry crackling sob burst out of
Charles's throat and nose and she leaned her head back and smiled
at the ceiling. "Why don't you come closer," she said. "You know
me and him both." She patted the edge of the coffin.

"Ruby," Mae Ruth rasped in her ear, "everyone's suffering, let
him be."

Ruby hooted and smacked the arm of the chair. "Who's suffering?"
she said. "How can you tell when Charles Clinton's suffering?"

"Oh Lord," someone said from the corner of the room, "there's
just no end to it."

He stepped closer, and for the first time she looked directly into his eyes. She was afraid to do it because she believed in what she saw in people's eyes. Halfway into another bitter word she saw his eyes and bit her lip. His eyes were washed out, drained, the color broken. His mouth turned down, and something elastic was gone from under his skin. He'd lost a tooth, and though his powder-blue leisure suit was clean, the backs of his knuckles looked grimy, like soot had been rubbed in under his skin. And those were the very eyes I searched and searched, she thought, the ones where I tried to see myself for so long. And those eyes stared at her, void of anything but a steady pain that threatened to break from him. It scared her so much she couldn't speak, and she leaned over and fussed with the net over Beau's coffin.

She didn't love Charles, never had, she'd known that from the start. But it acted like love, like a horse colt kicking inside her whenever he laid her down. And it was time—Ruby saw that in men's eyes when she passed them by on the street, and she saw it in her mother's eyes—time to start that kind of living and hope that she came to love him down the road. Hope that they'd come to be like Pappy and Mama had been before they'd moved to Atlanta to work in the mill, standing together in the field with their long burlap cotton sacks trailing behind them, picking cotton together and filling those sacks till the whole length of them was stuffed with their time together. That's what she'd seen could come of a married life. That's what she'd believed.

She wore a tight dress of lilac-colored imitation linen all the way to Jacksonville on the bus. It was their honeymoon trip, but all the while she had the sense that she was riding along beside herself. Away over there was the girl who was wild crazy in love, but she, Ruby, couldn't get to her. All the while she waited for the special feeling to come up in her throat, the way a spring starts up out of the ground. She wanted that feeling, but it didn't come. She didn't love him, but she shut that knowledge away. That was her secret. She always believed it would be different, and that was her secret. And her faith, and her shame.

So, love or no love, and faithful to another law, Beau was born barely moving, hardly breathing. His lips stayed blue for the longest time. And both times—after the birth when the doctor had come in peeling off his rubber gloves, talking about some little

something in Beau's heart that wouldn't close right, and now—
Charles had stood there looking like something broken, his face
taking on no more expression than the dead boy's. Only his eyes
still spoke, and his hand trembled like an old man's hand as he
lifted it to wipe his mouth. Why, I'm better off than he is, she
thought. For all this, I'm better off. It was cold, proud comfort.
The sweet vengeful cry she'd hoped for, the bass string she'd hoped
to hear singing inside her at the sight of him broken by the death
of his only son, wouldn't sound. She grabbed for Mae Ruth's hand
because the falling sensation was creeping in behind her eyes again.

The fact of the boy had stuck in Charles like a bone in his throat.
She spent her days sitting in the Grady Hospital clinics with Beau's
heavy head lolling over one arm, because there had to be an answer. You'd have thought the boy was contaminated the way
Charles's hands had stiffened when he picked up the baby. You'd
have thought the boy was permanently crippled or contagious the
way he held him away from his body. "Lots and lots of people's
born with something just a little off," she said. "Lord, some of
them never even know it," she told Charles pointedly. Of course,
as things had gone on, the depth of the damage had been revealed,
as it always is. By the time Beau had surgery on his heart at the
age of five, Charles wouldn't even come up to sit with him. He
said it was too humiliating to sit in the charity ward, where people
treated you like you were something to be mopped off the floor.

And after Beau had managed to grow up and after he started
coming home with pockets full of dollar bills, Charles could only
say "What's going on?" She could almost see the words forming
on his lips as he looked at his son in the coffin. Charles never understood a thing; that was his sorrow. She didn't want him near
her.

She remembered her own sorrow, how it had struck so deep it
had seemed to disappear inside her the first time Beau got caught
in Grant Park in a car with a rich man from the north side of
town. He was nothing but a baby, twelve years old. The police
cruiser brought him home because the other man was not only
rich, he was also important, and he didn't want trouble on account
of Beau. Her son smelled like baby powder and dirty clothes. He
was growing a face to hide behind. His lips were swollen as
though someone had been kissing them too hard, and she stared

and wondered whether that brand was put on his mouth by love or by hate or by some other force too strange to be named. She had to drag Charles into the room. "It ain't the money," Charles had shrieked at his son. "I know it ain't just for money." That was as much of the discovery as he could force out of his mouth; the rest was too terrifying.

"Why?" she asked her son. Her voice bored into him. She held onto his skinny arm and watched the skin blanch under her fingers.

"They talk nice to me," Beau said.

"Honey, those men don't care about you," she said, watching Charles turn away, watching Beau watch him turn away.

When Charles left, he said their life wasn't fit for human beings, and he moved out to Chamblee. He'd never lifted a hand against her. By Cotton Bottom standards that made him a good man. But she felt that violence had been done to her; there was a hardness and a deadness inside that made her swerve away from people as though she might catch something from them.

During that time, she went to Dan Malvern. It was right: he was her pastor as well as her friend, and together they'd puzzled over that deadness and prayed endlessly for forgiveness for her. She was never quite sure for what sin she needed to be forgiven, but she'd kept quiet and prayed anyway.

Now, sitting beside Beau's coffin, she'd come a whole revolution: she felt like asking for forgiveness about as much as she felt like getting up and walking to New York City. Forgiveness belonged to another lifetime, to people like Dan who had a vision left to guide them. Once, Dan had seen armies of souls pouring toward heaven and hell while he stood at the crossroads, frantically directing traffic. From that day on, he said, his cross and burden was to stand there until the Lord called him home. Now Dan stood just outside the door with his big black shoes sticking out of his too-short pants. You had to be gentle with Dan; he always had to be invited, so she said: "Dan'l, you're always welcome here." He crossed the room with one long country stride and grabbed her hand and rubbed it and said: "Are you holding up all right in the care of the Lord?"

"Getting by," she said. His eyes looked old. She took his hand more warmly and said: "Dan, bless you." But when she took her hand away it hung in front of her, bare and powerless. And there was Beau, dead, his life full of violence in spite of that hand, and she said "Oh," and bit her knuckle. Dan hauled her up, pulled her into the kitchen, and shut the door behind him. He rested a hand on her shoulder and threw back his head, and the tears squeezed out through the lashes like beads. She moved to embrace him but he stopped her. He was maneuvering into the current, setting his back to the wind. He shifted and hunched his shoulders: "Kneel down with me, sister," he said.

"Oh, all right, Dan," she said, sighing. She knew this part of the ritual, when they had to forget each other's names in order that God might hear their prayers. She knelt down facing him. She had to endure this because when Dan wasn't busy acting like God's own special riding-mule, he was one who shed a steady light onto her life, a light in which she could stand holding her shame and be loved, shame and all. Mae Ruth was another, only her light was barer and warmer. Dan remembered her and could remind her sometimes of ways she'd been that she could hardly recall. He knew her practically all the way back. She could go to him feeling small and cold, the way lights look in winter, and come away after talking about nothing for a few hours, with her feet set squarely on this earth again.

But something happened when he talked about God, when he started to pray. They didn't have much in common then. He became hard, he saw things in black and white and spoke of them harshly through his gritted teeth. His jawbone tried to pop through the skin, and his black hair began to tremble with indignation, and he jerked at the words as if he were chewing stringy meat. He strained after the words as though he could pull them from the air: "Lord, help her to see that sin is there," he began, "that sin has taken away her son. Help her to see the sin, to look on the *wages* of sin and to ask forgiveness, and help this woman, your servant, to know in her HEART the sin and to call OUT to the lord in her hour of need."

She would have laughed had she not felt so lonely. Dan could let himself down into it anytime and drink of the stern comfort there. She envied him that plunge. She imagined that the relief must taste hard and clean as water from a deep well sunk through rock. She closed her eyes and tried to pray, to sink into that place. It would be so good to believe again in the laws, she thought, because those laws named the exile and the means of coming home in such clear ringing tones. First there was sin, a person drifting in some foreign land, then confessing the sin, then redemption, then hallelujah, sister, and welcome home. She felt for her heart, for its secret shame, and found only a sort of homesickness, a notion that there was some place that she'd forgotten, a place where there were no such people as foreigners, a place big enough to hold sin, grief, ugliness, all of it.

But forgetfulness, that was the sickness, the worm in the heart. Words like *good* and *evil* and *death* simplified things and rocked you and lulled you and split things apart. There was something else moving back there; she could barely feel it but it was there.

She watched his face move through the prayer, laboring against a current, and when he came back to himself with a great bass "Amen" she said "Amen" too, and a sob broke from her at the sound of that blank word. Her shoulders shook and her head wagged from side to side and she said: "Dan, I'm gonna tell you something. It must tire out the Lord himself to listen to all that talk about sin all the time. There must be some wages due to you for that, wouldn't you say?"

"Ruby," he said, "don't blaspheme now, don't go piling sin on sin."

At that, she labored to her feet and shook herself. "The way I understand it," she said, "we're all born fools, ain't that right? Nothing we can do about that. What's the sin in that? Seems like everything we do has got wages." The man of God with thunder and sword faded, and his face was restored to him, and the Daniel she knew came back, looking sheepish, pulling on his bottom lip. "So where are you going to look for better wages is what I want to know?"

"I know you're under a terrible strain," he said, "but I don't know where you get such talk." But by then she was halfway into the other room. And seeing her son in his coffin again, she felt she was coming on him fresh, and she saw how much Beau's face looked like her own—much more like her own than like Charles's face—and it scared her. The life he'd led showed in the set defiance of the chin, in the squint-marks around the eyes that the morti-

cian's powder puff couldn't erase. That look was stuck there for all
eternity, and he was only sixteen years old.

It was the same look he'd given her anytime she'd asked him
about those men and why he went with them. She'd fought for
him for so long and the fatigue of that fight caught up with her
again and she was tossed up on a fresh wave of grief. She began to
sob and twist, turning this way and that, trying to escape from the
people who pressed in from all sides, suffocating her. Strong hands
gripped her and shook her, and she recognized Dan and Mae Ruth,
though neither of them spoke and her eyes were squeezed tight.
"Get it out," Mae Ruth said. "You go on and get it all out, then
you come on back here with us."

"I think I want to sleep for awhile now," she said, opening her
eyes.

"You want a nerve pill?" Mae Ruth asked. She shook her head.
She stopped beside the coffin.

"Well now," she said softly, "don't he look sweeter without that
harsh light on him?" During the minute that she'd had her spell of
grief, the light had shifted, softened to gray, pressing in at the windows. As the light softened in the room, her son's face softened
too; he looked younger and not so angry at the air. He hadn't
looked that way since he was a baby, and she loved him with a
sweetness so sharp she felt she might be opened by it.

And what became of that sweetness, she wondered, as she
pushed through the curtains into her bedroom. By what devilish
sly paths did it run away, leaving the harsh light that never ceased
burning on him? It took too much effort to remember that he was
not just that strange being who'd thrashed his way through her life
and out, leaving wreckage in his path. He was also another thing,
but it made her head hurt to think of it. She pulled off her slippers
and unhooked her slacks at the waist. It was easier to think that the
march he'd made straight to his grave was the sin, to call that life
ugly and be done with it. But the changing of the sweet to the
ugly was the most obvious trick in the book. Anyone with eyes
could see through that one. There was a better trick. She thought
how much she wished she could still believe that the Devil
dreamed up the tricks. That would explain the ashes around her
heart.

But never mind: the better trick was that the soft curtains of forgetfulness dropped so quietly you did not hear them fall. It was forgetfulness that made things and people seem strange: that was sin if ever there was sin. Still, remembering things made you so tired. Better to live blind, she thought.

Once she'd begged Beau to remember who he was. She'd meant *her* people, the Nelson side, dignity and decency deep enough to last through two or three lifetimes. But they were as strange to him as the whole rest of the wide world. "Sure," he'd said, "I know who I am. I'm a Nelson from the cotton patch and a Clinton straight from hell." Seeing her shocked, with her hand pressed to her throat, he'd laughed and said: "Well ain't I? You're always saying 'Goddamn your daddy to hell.'" The way he'd imitated her, his mouth drawn back like a wild animal's, had terrified her. "That means I come from hell, don't it, Mama?"

She shook her head in frustration and eased herself down onto her bed. She wished that he were there, given back to her for just one minute, so that she could collect, finally, all she'd needed to tell him, so that she could tell him in words he'd have to understand, that if one person loved you, you were not a chunk of dead rock spinning in space. That was what she'd tried to tell him all during the long winter just past.

That was the winter when the mill had stepped up production again and had taken on everyone they'd laid off. She'd gotten a job in the sewing room. All day she sat there sewing, while her mind worked to find an end to the business with Beau. It was quieter there than in the weave room and she could forget about everything but one seam running under her needle, one train of thought going through her mind. Last winter he was gone more than he was home, and his face was pale and sunken around the cheekbones. Every so often she'd start way back at the beginning and come forward with him step by step, puzzling out the way and ending always in the same spot: the place she'd seen him staring into. She turned it over and over like the piece-work in front of her, looking for the bunched thread, the too-long stitch that would give, the place where her mind had wandered and the machine had wandered off the seam.

Once she'd taken half a sick-day and had gone home to find him staring at nothing. She'd barely been able to rouse him, and when she'd bent over him she'd been repelled by his sweet sick odor. But it was the way he'd looked that stuck in her mind: tight blue jeans, a black shirt, a red bandanna wound tightly around his neck. And his face, when he'd finally turned it up to her and smiled dreamily into her screaming, was sly and serene as the face of a wrecked angel. It was the smile that made her blood shut off. When he smiled that way, there was a shudder in the room like the sound that lingered in the air if the looms shut down, and she knew that he was bound to die, that he was already looking into that place. She saw it in his eyes all winter.

The cotton came in bailed through enormous doors and was pulped, twisted, spun, woven, mixed with polyester and squeezed and pressed and dyed and made into sheets and blouses and printed with tulips, irises, gardens of blowing green.

It wasn't right that she should worry herself the way she did all winter. She was up all hours of the night waiting for him, but half the time he never came home. Then one day she just went into his room and nailed the window shut, and when he went into his room that night, she locked him in and sat in the living room with arms folded, crying, as he bumped and crashed around and screamed awful names at her. It was for his own good and because she loved him. And if you loved somebody, she told herself, you had to make a stand and this was her stand. In the morning she'd explain to him, in words he'd have to understand, that she did it out of love.

Afterwards she was ashamed, and she never told anyone, not even Mae Ruth. She felt that she'd been in a dream, a fever dream, where crazy things made perfect sense and everything hung suspended way up high in clear air. But it didn't matter anyway because when she unlocked the door to set him free in the morning, he was gone. Glass all over the floor and the window kicked out.

She woke up after dark, groping around with one hand, looking for something on the bedspread. She'd been dreaming of black rocks looming over her, and at the base of the rocks, hundreds of people scrambling around, picking up busted-off pieces of the largest rock and holding them up in the moonlight. She groped her way out into the living room, and people patted her and helped her ease down into her chair again.

All night she slept and woke. Whenever she woke, one pair of hands or another reached for her, and once she tried to say: "I want to thank you all for being so good." But her voice broke when she said "good," and someone said: "Hush, you'd do the same."

The voices went round and round her, a soothing drone that filled the room. Then the sun was up, the day was up bright and blazing. She looked at her son beside her in his coffin, and the thought of his going broke over her like a wave. And as the day rushed back at her, so did her memories of Beau, which were as sharp as if he were still alive. In fact, they were hardly memories at all, they were more like the small sightings we keep of someone's day-to-day life.

This is how he came in: her body had threshed with him for two days and a night. Then his sickness: she walked him day and night, while over on Tye Street Granny Brassler and the others went down almost to their knees, taken by the spirit, shouting: "Devil, take your hands off that baby."

He was never full of milk and quiet: he was long and gangly and he never fleshed out. And all the while he was growing a man's mind. By the time he was twelve, right after Charles left, he'd stay gone for days, nobody knew where. Then, last June, he and his friends had started sticking closer to home, robbing the men in the park nearby. That's when she'd set herself against him in earnest. The last time she'd smacked him good had been right there in the kitchen just as she was setting supper down on the table, when he'd come busting through the door yelling how someone was a nigger motherfucker. She'd grabbed his face and squeezed and said: "Don't you never let me hear you talking like trash again. You are not and never will be trash, and don't you forget it."

"Everybody calls me trash," he said. "What makes you any different?"

"Cause I'm your people," she said. "Cause you're mine."

"Ain't that funny?" he said. "That's what they say too."

Every time, somebody else was holding the gun, but the next time, or the time after that, she knew it would be Beau, and then he would be tried as an adult and sent away to the real prison up at Alto, and that would be that. Last June they'd only taken him as far as the jumping-off place, the _juvenile evaluation center_ they called

it. But it was a prison as surely as Alto where he'd end up someday, looking out with the others at the blue mountains beyond the
high wire fence.

She wasn't like the other mothers, the ones who wept or pleaded
or shouted. That time was long gone, and she knew it. She was
there for another reason but it had no name, only a glare, like the
harsh sunlight on the white white walls of his room. She listened.
He beat time on his thigh with the heel of one hand and talked,
and sometimes he looked up and said: "Ain't that right?" And
with knees spread, elbows resting on her knees, hands loosely
knotted and fallen between her knees, she looked back at him and
said: "No, that isn't right Beau, not as I see it," in the strongest
voice she could muster.

Staying, listening and staying, was a habit she'd had to learn.
The first visit to the evaluation center had ended with her reeling
out of the room, driven back by his words that were so ugly they
seemed to coil like tar snakes out of his mouth. But she went back,
she did go back, and she knew she must never let herself forget that.
She went back and she listened to every word, and she had never
felt so empty, so silent. The city, the room turned strange around
her, and the only familiar face was the one just in front of her, the
one with the mouth that opened and said: "You ought to see their
faces when Roy shows them the gun."

She looked up quickly, hearing that voice again just as clear as if
it were still ringing off the walls of the jail. She looked at his dead
face, and her head began to tug with it, and she stood and bore
down on him while all around her the dark closed in as it does
when a person's about to faint. Only she was far from fainting.
The dark narrowed around her until she stood inside a dark egg
looking down at her son, the stranger made up for his grave, who
rested in a wash of light that lingered at the core of the outer dark
shell. And as she watched and listened—watching and listening
with every cell—the stranger's face dropped away and the whole
harsh chorus of his life tangled in her and sang again, and she remembered what she'd seen in the jail, what she'd seen a long time
before the jail and had forgotten and carried with her the whole
stubborn way and had never wanted to believe, and had believed:
he was lost, and he had always been lost. His hands were folded,
his face eternally still. Whatever he had been, he was now, forever.

She gripped the coffin's edge while the fury rose up her legs and belly and chest and gathered inside her skull, a familiar pressure, and she wanted to strike or curse someone over what had become of this child. From the moment he was born, he was lost, *her own child*, lost. For a long time she'd believed that he was two children: one hers, the other possessed by another power. All his life, she'd worked to pull or wrestle *her* child free from the hold of his lost brother, to love the one, rage against the other and drive him out. She touched the wing of his nose where it flared out so pretty, then pulled her fingers away quickly and slipped her hand into the pocket of her dress. But it was too late. When she touched his skin, everything collapsed and ran together again, and there was no such thing as love apart from rage or this child freed from his own lost self. Nothing could be untangled, nothing pulled apart. Not then. Not now. Not ever. The roots all went down deep—the root of love, the root of fury, the root of the child—like the roots of the oaks that grew on the hill in the old cemetery on the border of this place. Down they went, and down, and mixed with the bones until the bones were roots and the roots, bones, and the trees grew tall over everything.

She stood very still, looking at his pinched white face. For the first time, she understood a Bible verse that people had always quoted at her. Dan had used it, everybody used it to tell her how to feel about trouble but she, Ruby, understood it for herself now, and no one could take it from her. *I will lift up mine eyes to the hills*, she thought. She looked and she saw the crowns of the oaks brushing the sky, and below the trees she saw the tangled maze of roots running through the hill of the dead. That was all the comfort there was.

She sat down in her chair with a moan and began to rock herself and to pat the edge of the coffin in time with her rocking. She saw the panic start up on every face, and she pressed a hand to her chest to quiet herself. "Things should slow down," she said, "so that a person can have time to study them."

As though they'd been held back, people crowded into the room again. The air got sticky and close, and the smell of flowers and sweat and not quite clean clothes and the soapy smell that hung over Beau's coffin began to make her dizzy. So she focused on Charles and a prickly rash began to spread over her neck and arms and her vision began to clear. Finally she said, in a lazy kind of voice—lazy like a cottonmouth moccasin stirring the water—"Charles, you and your wife's taking up more than your share of the air in here. Why don't you just step out onto the porch?" They ignored her. But Mae Ruth clucked her tongue.

"Ruby, shame, he's still the boy's father; you can't deny him that," she said.

"I know that," Ruby snapped. "Don't I wish I didn't."

She closed her eyes and wished for the old way, the old law that said *the ones that give, get back in kind.* She wished that the weight of that law might lie in her hand like a rock. She wished for some revenge sweet enough to fit his crimes, the kind of revenge that came from a time before people were condemned to stand linked to one another. She could make him order the tombstone and have Beau's name drilled there, yes, and be gone before the funeral started. She tried it out on herself but the little cold thrill the thought gave her wasn't enough to satisfy. Oh me, she said to herself, there isn't no country far enough away where I could send him. She opened her eyes and searched the room for a single unfamiliar face on which to rest her eyes, and found not a one. And she felt the whole dense web of love and grief descending, settling over her shoulders as it had before, in the prison. "This don't ever stop," she said out loud. And she thought of how she had never loved Charles, not in the way that a woman loves a man, and how, still, he was part of the law that turned and turned and bound them all together, on each turn, more closely than before.

Then there was the vault out under the strong sun without a tent to cover it, and the flowers were wilting under the sun, and Mae Ruth's strong voice led off a song. Then Daniel spoke of dust, and of heaven and the Redeemer for a long time. They were in a new cemetery and the lots were parceled out of a flat field. Through the thin soles of her shoes, Ruby could feel the rucks and ripples of once-plowed ground. She wore a dress of hard black cloth that trapped the heat inside and made the sweat trickle down her sides. Charles stood on the edge of the crowd, his chin sunk onto his chest, and he looked faded under the light that seemed to gather into a center that was made of even whiter and hotter light.

Ruby barely listened to the resurrection and the life. She saw her son's face: surrounded by darkness now, closed in darkness forever.

Those words Dan said, they weren't the prayers, she thought, not the real prayers. The prayer rested in the coffin, in the dark there. Her eyes followed its deaf, dumb lines. The prayer was his life that she couldn't save, and the prayer was her own life and how it continued. And the prayer never stopped; lives began and ended, but the prayer never stopped. She looked at the ground and had the sensation that she'd been standing there for a very long time, trying to memorize each one of the scrappy weeds that had begun to grow again out of the plowed-over land. Those weeds were like the threads; she watched them in the same way. The threads flew toward her like slender rays of light and twisted spool to spool and disappeared through another door toward the looms beyond. The sound of their coming and going made one continuous roar.

Because she wanted it that way, they all stayed as the coffin was lowered into the hole. She stepped up to the side of the grave and saw her own shadow, thrown huge, on the lid of the vault. It startled her so much she stepped forward instead of back and the edges crumbled under her shoes. Then there were hands on her arms, and she looked down again and saw Mae Ruth's shadow and Dan's beside her. It was as though they were in a boat together, looking over the side. And the sun beat down on them all: on the living, and into the grave, and on those who had lived and died.

Music

Rhoda was fourteen years old the summer her father dragged her off to Clay County, Kentucky, to make her stop smoking and acting like a movie star. She was fourteen years old, a holy and terrible age, and her desire for beauty and romance drove her all day long and pursued her if she slept.

"Te amo," she whispered to herself in Latin class. "Te amo, Bob Rosen," sending the heat of her passions across the classroom and out through the window and across two states to a hospital room in Saint Louis, where a college boy lay recovering from a series of operations Rhoda had decided would be fatal.

"And you as well must die, beloved dust," she quoted to herself. "Oh, sleep forever in your Latmian cave, Mortal Endymion, darling of the moon," she whispered, and sometimes it was Bob Rosen's lanky body stretched out in the cave beside his saxophone that she envisioned and sometimes it was her own lush, apricot-colored skin growing cold against the rocks in the moonlight.

Rhoda was fourteen years old that spring and her true love had been cruelly taken from her and she had started smoking because there was nothing left to do now but be a writer.

She was fourteen years old and she would sit on the porch at night looking down the hill that led through the small town of Franklin, Kentucky, and think about the stars, wondering where heaven could be in all that vastness, feeling betrayed by her mother's pale Episcopalianism and the fate that had brought her to this small town right in the middle of her sophomore year in high school. She would sit on the porch stuffing chocolate chip cookies into her mouth, drinking endless homemade chocolate milkshakes, smoking endless Lucky Strike cigarettes, watching her mother's transplanted roses move steadily across the trellis, taking Bob Rosen's thin letters in and out of their envelopes, holding them against her face, then going up to the new bedroom, to the soft, blue sheets, stuffed with cookies and ice cream and cigarettes and rage.

110

"Is that you, Rhoda?" her father would call out as she passed his bedroom. "Is that you, sweetie? Come tell us goodnight." And she would go into their bedroom and lean over and kiss him.

"You just ought to smell yourself," he would say, sitting up, pushing her away. "You just ought to smell those nasty cigarettes." And as soon as she went into her room he would go downstairs and empty all the ashtrays to make sure the house wouldn't burn down while he was sleeping.

"I've got to make her stop that goddamn smoking," he would say, climbing back into the bed. "I'm goddamned if I'm going to put up with that."

"I'd like to know how you're going to stop it," Rhoda's mother said. "I'd like to see anyone make Rhoda do anything she doesn't want to do. Not to mention that you're hardly ever here."

"Goddammit, Ariane, don't start that this time of night." And he rolled over on his side of the bed and began to plot his campaign against Rhoda's cigarettes.

Dudley Manning wasn't afraid of Rhoda, even if she was as stubborn as a goat. Dudley Manning wasn't afraid of anything. He had gotten up at dawn every day for years and believed in himself and followed his luck wherever it led him, dragging his sweet southern wife and his children behind him, and now, in his fortieth year, he was about to become a millionaire.

He was about to become a millionaire and he was in love with a beautiful woman who was not his wife and it was the strangest spring he had ever known. When he added up the figures in his account books he was filled with awe at his own achievements, amazed at what he had made of himself, and to make up for it he talked a lot about luck and pretended to be humble but deep down inside he believed there was nothing he couldn't do, even love two women at once, even make Rhoda stop smoking.

Both Dudley and Rhoda were early risers. If he was in town he would be waiting in the kitchen when she came down to breakfast, dressed in his khakis, his pens in his pocket, his glasses on his nose, sitting at the table going over his papers, his head full of the clean new ideas of morning.

"How many more days of school do you have?" he said to her one morning, watching her light the first of her cigarettes without saying anything about it.

"Just this week," she said. "Just until Friday. I'm making A's, Daddy. This is the easiest school I've ever been to."

"Well, don't be smart-alecky about it, Rhoda," he said. "If you've got a good mind it's only because God gave it to you."

"God didn't give me anything," she said. "Because there isn't any God."

"Well, let's don't get into an argument about that this morning," Dudley said. "As soon as you finish school I want you to drive up to the mines with me for a few days."

"For how long?" she said.

"We won't be gone long," he said. "I just want to take you to the mines to look things over."

Rhoda french-inhaled, blowing the smoke out into the sunlight coming through the kitchen windows, imagining herself on a tour of her father's mines, the workers with their caps in their hands smiling at her as she walked politely among them. Rhoda liked that idea. She dropped two saccharin tablets into her coffee and sat down at the table, enjoying her fantasy.

"Is that what you're having for breakfast?" he said.

"I'm on a diet," Rhoda said. "I'm on a black coffee diet."

He looked down at his poached eggs, cutting into the yellow with his knife. I can wait, he said to himself. As God is my witness I can wait until Sunday.

Rhoda poured herself another cup of coffee and went upstairs to write Bob Rosen before she left for school.

Dear Bob [the letter began],

School is almost over. I made straight A's, of course, as per your instructions. This school is so easy it's crazy.

They read one of my newspaper columns on the radio in Nashville. Everyone in Franklin goes around saying my mother writes my columns. Can you believe that? Allison Hotchkiss, that's my editor, say she's going to write an editorial about it saying I really write them.

I turned my bedroom into an office and took out the tacky dressing table mother made me and got a desk and put my typewriter on it and made striped drapes, green and black and white. I think you would approve.

Sunday Daddy is taking me to Manchester, Kentucky, to look over the coal mines. He's going to let me drive. He lets me drive **all the time**. I live for your letters.

Te amo,
Rhoda

She put the letter in a pale blue envelope, sealed it, dripped some Toujours Moi lavishly onto it in several places and threw herself down on her bed.

She pressed her face deep down into her comforter pretending it was Bob Rosen's smooth cool skin. "Oh, Bob, Bob," she whispered to the comforter. "Oh, honey, don't die, don't die, please don't die." She could feel the tears coming. She reached out and caressed the seam of the comforter, pretending it was the scar on Bob Rosen's neck.

The last night she had been with him he had just come home from an operation for a mysterious tumor that he didn't want to talk about. It would be better soon, was all he would say about it. Before long he would be as good as new.

They had driven out of town and parked the old Pontiac underneath a tree beside a pasture. It was September and Rhoda had lain in his arms smelling the clean smell of his new sweater, touching the fresh red scars on his neck, looking out the window to memorize every detail of the scene, the black tree, the September pasture, the white horse leaning against the fence, the palms of his hands, the taste of their cigarettes, the night breeze, the exact temperature of the air, saying to herself over and over, I must remember everything. This will have to last me forever and ever and ever.

"I want you to do it to me," she said. "Whatever it is they do."

"I can't," he said. "I couldn't do that now. It's too much trouble to make love to a virgin." He was laughing. "Besides, it's hard to do it in a car."

"But I'm leaving," she said. "I might not ever see you again."

"Not tonight," he said. "I still don't feel very good, Rhoda."

"What if I come back and visit," she said. "Will you do it then? When you feel better."

"If you still want me to I will," he said. "If you come back to visit and we both want to, I will."

"Do you promise?" she said, hugging him fiercely.

"I promise," he said. "On my honor I promise to do it when you come to visit."

But Rhoda was not allowed to go to Saint Louis to visit. Either her mother guessed her intentions or else she seized the opportunity to do what she had been wanting to do all along and stop her daughter from seeing a boy with a Jewish last name.

There were weeks of pleadings and threats. It all ended one Sunday night when Mrs. Manning lost her temper and made the statement that Jews were little peddlers who went through the Delta selling needles and pins.

"You don't know what you're talking about," Rhoda screamed. "He's not a peddler, and I love him and I'm going to love him until I die." Rhoda pulled her arms away from her mother's hands.

"I'm going up there this weekend to see him," she screamed. "Daddy promised me I could and you're not going to stop me and if you try to stop me I'll kill you and I'll run away and I'll never come back."

"You are not going to Saint Louis and that's the end of this conversation and if you don't calm down I'll call a doctor and have you locked up. I think you're crazy, Rhoda. I really do."

"I'm not crazy," Rhoda screamed. "You're the one that's crazy."

"You and your father think you're so smart," her mother said. She was shaking but she held her ground, moving around behind a Queen Anne chair. "Well, I don't care how smart you are, you're not going to get on a train and go off to Saint Louis, Missouri to see a man when you're only fourteen years old, and that, Miss Rhoda K. Manning, is that."

"I'm going to kill you," Rhoda said. "I really am. I'm going to kill you," and she thought for a moment that she would kill her, but then she noticed her grandmother's Limoges hot chocolate pot sitting on top of the piano holding a spray of yellow jasmine, and she walked over to the piano and picked it up and threw it all the way across the room and smashed it into a wall beside a framed print of "The Blue Boy."

"I hate you," Rhoda said. "I wish you were dead." And while her mother stared in disbelief at the wreck of the sainted hot chocolate pot, Rhoda walked out of the house and got in the car and drove off down the steep driveway. I hate her guts, she said to herself. I hope she cries herself to death.

She shifted into second gear and drove off toward her father's office, quoting to herself from Edna Millay. "Now by this moon, before this moon shall wane, I shall be dead or I shall be with you."

But in the end Rhoda didn't die. Neither did she kill her mother. Neither did she go to Saint Louis to give her virginity to her reluctant lover.

The Sunday of the trip Rhoda woke at dawn feeling very excited and changed clothes four or fives times trying to decide how she wanted to look for her inspection of the mines.

Rhoda had never even seen a picture of a strip mine. In her imagination she and her father would be riding an elevator down into the heart of a mountain where obsequious masked miners were lined up to shake her hand. Later that evening the captain of the football team would be coming over to the hotel to meet her and take her somewhere for a drive.

She pulled on a pair of pink pedal pushers and a long navy blue sweat shirt, threw every single thing she could possibly imagine wearing into a large suitcase, and started down the stairs to where her father was calling for her to hurry up.

Her mother followed her out of the house holding a buttered biscuit on a linen napkin. "Please eat something before you leave," she said. "There isn't a decent restaurant after you leave Bowling Green."

"I told you I don't want anything to eat," Rhoda said. "I'm on a diet." She stared at the biscuit as though it were a coral snake.

"One biscuit isn't going to hurt you," her mother said. "I made you a lunch, chicken and carrot sticks and apples."

"I don't want it," Rhoda said "Don't put any food in this car, Mother."

"Just because you never eat doesn't mean your father won't get hungry. You don't have to eat any of it unless you want to." Their eyes met. Then they sighed and looked away.

Her father appeared at the door and climbed in behind the wheel of the secondhand Cadillac.

"Let's go, Sweet Sister," he said, cruising down the driveway, turning onto the road leading to Bowling Green and due east into the hill country. Usually this was his favorite moment of the week, starting the long drive into the rich Kentucky hills where his energy and intelligence had created the long black rows of figures in the account books, figures that meant Rhoda would never know what it was to be really afraid or uncertain or powerless.

"How long will it take?" Rhoda asked.

"Don't worry about that," he said. "Just look out the window and enjoy the ride. This is beautiful country we're driving through."

"I can't right now," Rhoda said. "I want to read the new book Allison gave me. It's a book of poems."

She settled down into the seat and opened the book.

> *Oh, gallant was the first love, and glittering and fine;*
> *The second love was water, in a clear blue cup;*
> *The third love was his, and the fourth was mine.*
> *And after that, I always get them all mixed up.*

Oh, God, this is good, she thought. She sat up straighter, wanting to kiss the book. Oh, God, this is really good. She turned the book over to look at the picture of the author. It was a photograph of a small bright face in full profile staring off into the mysterious brightly lit world of a poet's life.

Dorothy Parker, she read. What a wonderful name. Maybe I'll change my name to Dorothy, Dorothy Louise Manning. Dot Manning. Dottie, Dottie Leigh, Dot.

Rhoda pulled a pack of Lucky Strikes out of her purse, tamped it on the dashboard, opened it, extracted a cigarette and lit it with a gold Ronson lighter. She inhaled deeply and went back to the book.

Her father gripped the wheel, trying to concentrate on the beauty of the morning, the green fields, the small, neat farmhouses, the red barns, the cattle and horses. He moved his eyes from all that order to his fourteen-year-old daughter slumped beside him with her nose buried in a book, her plump fingers languishing in the air, holding a cigarette. He slowed down, pulled the car onto the side of the road and killed the motor.

"What's wrong?" Rhoda said. "Why are you stopping?"

"Because you are going to put out that goddamn cigarette this very minute and you're going to give me the package and you're not going to smoke another cigarette around me as long as you live," he said.

"I will not do any such thing," Rhoda said. "It's a free country."

"Give me the cigarette, Rhoda," he said. "Hand it here."

"Give me one good reason why I should," she said. But her voice let her down. She knew there wasn't any use in arguing. This was not her soft little mother she was dealing with. This was Dudley Manning, who had been a famous baseball player until he quit when she was born. Who before that had gone to the Olympics on a relay team. There were scrapbooks full of his clippings in Rhoda's house. No matter where the Mannings went those scrapbooks sat on a table in the den. *Manning Hits One Over The Fence*, the headlines read. *Manning Saves The Day. Manning Does It Again.* And he was not the only one. His cousin, Philip Manning, down in Jackson, Mississippi, was famous too. Who was the father of the famous Crystal Manning, Rhoda's cousin who had a fur coat when she was ten. And Leland Manning, who was her cousin Lele's daddy. Leland had been the captain of the Tulane football team before he drank himself to death in the Delta.

Rhoda sighed, thinking of all that, and gave in for the moment. "Give me one good reason and I might," she repeated.

"I don't have to give you a reason for a goddamn thing," he said. "Give the cigarette here, Rhoda. Right this minute." He reached out and took it and she didn't resist. "Goddamn, these things smell awful," he said, crushing it in the ashtray. He reached in her pocketbook and got the package and threw it out the window.

"Only white trash throw things out on the road," Rhoda said. "You'd kill me if I did that."

"Well, let's just be quiet and get to where we're going." He started the motor and drove back out onto the highway. Rhoda crunched down lower in the seat, pretending to read her book. Who cares, she thought. I'll get some as soon as we stop for gas.

Getting cigarettes at filling stations was not as easy as Rhoda thought it was going to be. This was God's country they were driving into now, the hills rising up higher and higher, strange, silent little houses back off the road. Rhoda could feel the eyes looking out at her from behind the silent windows. Poor white trash, Rhoda's mother would have called them. The salt of the earth, her father would have said.

This was God's country and these people took things like children smoking cigarettes seriously. At both places where they stopped there was a sign by the cash register, *No Cigarettes Sold To Minors.*

Rhoda had moved to the back seat of the Cadillac and was stretched out on the seat reading her book. She had found another poem she liked and she was memorizing it.

> *Four be the things I'd be better without,*
> *Love, curiosity, freckles and doubt.*
> *Three be the things I shall never attain,*
> *Envy, content and sufficient champagne.*

Oh, God, I love this book, she thought. *This Dorothy Parker is just like me.* Rhoda was remembering a night when she got drunk in Clarkesville, Mississippi with her cousin, Baby Gwen Barksdale. They got drunk on tequila LaGrande Conroy brought back from Mexico, and Rhoda had slept all night in the bathtub so she would be near the toilet when she vomited.

She put her head down on her arm and giggled, thinking about waking up in the bathtub. Then a plan occurred to her.

"Stop and let me go the the bathroom," she said to her father. "I think I'm going to throw up."

"Oh, Lord," he said. "I knew you shouldn't have gotten in the back seat. Well, hold on. I'll stop the first place I see." He pushed his hat back off his forehead and began looking for a place to stop, glancing back over his shoulder every now and then to see if she was all right. Rhoda had a long history of throwing up on car trips so he was taking this seriously. Finally he saw a combination store and filling station at a bend in the road and pulled up beside the front door.

"I'll be all right." Rhoda said, jumping out of the car. "You stay here. I'll be right back."

She walked dramatically up the wooden steps and pushed open the screen door. It was so quiet and dark inside she thought for a moment the store was closed. She looked around. She was in a rough, high-ceilinged room with saddles and pieces of farm equipment hanging from the rafters and a sparse array of canned goods on wooden shelves behind a counter. On the counter were five or six large glass jars filled with different kinds of Nabisco cookies. Rhoda stared at the cookie jars, wanting to stick her hand down inside and take out great fistfuls of Lorna Doones and Oreos. She fought off her hunger and raised her eyes to the display of chewing tobacco and cigarettes.

The smells of the store rose up to meet her, fecund and rich, moist and cool, as if the store was an extension of the earth outside. Rhoda looked down at the board floors. She felt she could have dropped a sunflower seed on the floor and it would instantly sprout and take bloom, growing quick, moving down into the earth and upwards toward the rafters.

"Is anybody here?" she said softly, then louder. "Is anybody here?"

A woman in a cotton dress appeared in a door, staring at Rhoda out of very intense, very blue eyes.

"Can I buy a pack of cigarettes from you?" Rhoda said. "My dad's in the car. He sent me to get them."

"What kind of cigarettes you looking for?" the woman said, moving to the space between the cash register and the cookie jars.

"Some Luckies if you have them," Rhoda said. "He said to just get anything you had if you didn't have that."

"They're a quarter," the woman said, reaching behind herself to take the package down and lay it on the counter, not smiling, but not being unkind either.

"Thank you," Rhoda said, laying the quarter down on the counter. "Do you have any matches?"

"Sure," the woman said, holding out a box of kitchen matches. Rhoda took a few, letting her eyes leave the woman's face and come to rest on the jars of Oreos. They looked wonderful and light, as though they had been there a long time and grown soft around the edges.

The woman was smiling now. "You want one of those cookies?"

she said. "You want one, you go on and have one. It's free."

"Oh, no thank you," Rhoda said. "I'm on a diet. Look, do you have a ladies' room I can use?"

"It's out back," the woman said. "You can have one of them cookies if you want it. Like I said, it won't cost you nothing."

"I guess I'd better get going," Rhoda said. "My dad's in a hurry. But thank you anyway. And thanks for the matches." Rhoda hurried down the aisle, slipped out the back door and leaned up against the back of the store, tearing the paper off the cigarettes. She pulled one out, lit it, and inhaled deeply, blowing the smoke out in front of her, watching it rise up into the air, casting a veil over the hills that rose up behind and to the left of her. She had never been in such a strange country. It looked as though no one ever did anything to their yards or roads or fences. It looked as though there might not be a clock for miles.

She inhaled again, feeling dizzy and full. She had just taken the cigarette out of her mouth when her father came bursting out of the door and grabbed both of her wrists in his hands.

"Let go of me," she said. "Let go of me this minute." She struggled to free herself, ready to kick or claw or bite, ready for a real fight, but he held her off. "Drop the cigarette, Rhoda," he said. "Drop it on the ground."

"I'll kill you," she said. "As soon as I get away I'm running away to Florida. Let go of me, Daddy. Do you hear me?"

"I hear you," he said. The veins were standing out on his forehead. His face was so close Rhoda could see his freckles and the line where his false front tooth was joined to what was left of the real one. He had lost the tooth in a baseball game the day Rhoda was born. That was how he told the story. "I lost that tooth the day Rhoda was born," he would say. "I was playing left field against Memphis in the old Crump Stadium. I slid into second and the second baseman got me with his shoe."

"You can smoke all you want to when you get down to Florida," he was saying now. "But you're not smoking on this trip. So you might as well calm down before I drive off and leave you here."

"I don't care," she said. "Go on and leave. I'll just call up Mother and she'll come and get me." She was struggling to free her wrists but she could not move them inside his hands. "Let go of me, you big bully," she added.

"Will you calm down and give me the cigarettes?"

"All right," she said, but the minute he let go of her hands she turned and began to hit him on the shoulders, pounding her fists up and down on his back, not daring to put any real force behind the blows. He pretended to cower under the assault. She caught his eye and saw that he was laughing at her and she had to fight the desire to laugh with him.

"I'm getting in the car," she said. "I'm sick of this place." She walked grandly around to the front of the store, got into the car, tore open the lunch and began to devour it, tearing the chicken off the bones with her teeth, swallowing great hunks without even bothering to chew them. "I'm never speaking to you again as long as I live," she said, her mouth full of chicken breast. "You are not my father."

"Suits me, Miss Smart-alecky Movie Star," he said, putting his hat back on his head. "Soon as we get home you can head on out for Florida. You just let me know when you're leaving so I can give you some money for the bus."

"I hate you," Rhoda mumbled to herself, starting in on the homemade raisin cookies. I hate your guts. I hope you go to hell forever, she thought, breaking a cookie into pieces so she could pick out the raisins.

It was late afternoon when the Cadillac picked its way up a rocky red clay driveway to a housetrailer nestled in the curve of a hill beside a stand of pine trees.

"Where are we going?" Rhoda said. "Would you just tell me that?"

"We're going to see Maud and Joe Samples," he said. "Joe's an old hand around here. He's my right-hand man in Clay County. Now you just be polite and try to learn something, Sister. These are real folks you're about to meet."

"Why are we going here first?" Rhoda said. "Aren't we going to a hotel?"

"There isn't any hotel," her father said. "Does this look like someplace they'd have hotels? Maud and Joe are going to put you up for me while I'm off working."

"I'm going to stay here?" Rhoda said. "In this trailer?"

"Just wait until you see the inside," her father said. "It's like the inside of a boat, everything all planned out and just the right amount of space for things. I wish your mother'd let me live in a trailer."

They were almost to the door now. A plump smiling woman came out onto the wooden platform and waited for them with her hands on her hips, smiling wider and wider as they got nearer.

"There's Maud," Dudley said. "She's the sweetest woman in the world and the best cook in Kentucky. Hey there, Miss Maud," he called out.

"Mr. D," she said, opening the car door for them. "Joe Samples' been waiting on you all day and here you show up bringing this beautiful girl just like you promised. I've made you some blackberry pies. Come on inside this trailer." Maud smiled deep into Rhoda's face. Her eyes were as blue as the ones on the woman in the store. Rhoda's mother had blue eyes, but not this brilliant and not this blue. These eyes were from another world, another century.

"Come on in and see Joe," Maud said. "He's been having a fit for you to get here."

They went inside and Dudley showed Rhoda all around the trailer, praising the design of trailers. Maud turned on the tiny oven and they had blackberry pie and bread and butter sandwiches and Rhoda abandoned her diet and ate two pieces of the pie, covering it with thick whipped cream.

The men went off to talk business and Maud took Rhoda to a small room at the back of the trailer decorated to match a handmade quilt of the sunrise.

There were yellow ruffled curtains at the windows and a tiny dressing table with a yellow ruffled skirt around the edges. Rhoda was enchanted by the smallness of everything and the way the windows looked out onto layers of green trees and bushes.

Lying on the dresser was a white leather Bible and a display of small white pamphlets, *Alcohol And You, When Jesus Reaches For A Drink, You Are Not Alone, Sorry Isn't Enough, Taking No For An Answer.*

It embarrassed Rhoda even to read the titles of anything as tacky as the pamphlets, but she didn't let on she thought it was tacky, not with Maud sitting on the bed telling her how pretty she was every other second and asking her questions about herself and saying how wonderful her father was.

"We love Mr. D to death," she said. "It's like he was one of our own."

He appeared in the door. "Rhoda, if you're settled in I'll be leaving now," he said. "I've got to drive to Knoxville to do some business but I'll be back here Tuesday morning to take you to the mines." He handed her three twenty-dollar bills. "Here," he said. "In case you need anything."

He left then and hurried out to the car, trying to figure out how long it would take him to get to Knoxville, to where Valerie sat alone in a hotel room waiting for this night they had planned for so long. He felt the sweet hot guilt rise up in his face and the sweet hot longing in his legs and hands.

I'm sorry, Jesus, he thought, pulling out onto the highway. I know it's wrong and I know we're doing wrong. So go on and punish me if you have to but just let me make it there and back before you start in on me.

He set the cruising speed at exactly fifty-five miles an hour and began to sing to himself as he drove.

> _"Oh, sure as the vine grows around the stump_
> _You're my darling sugar lump,"_ he sang, and;
>
> _"Froggy went a-courting and he did ride,_
> _Huhhrummp, Huhhrummp,_
> _Froggy went a-courting and he did ride, Huhhrummp,_
>
> _What you gonna have for the wedding supper?_
> _Black-eyed peas and bread and butter, Huhhrummp,_
> _huhhrummp . . . "_

Rhoda was up and dressed when her father came to get her on Tuesday morning. It was still dark outside but a rooster had begun to crow in the distance. Maud bustled all about the little kitchen making much of them, filling their plates with biscuits and fried eggs and ham and gravy.

Then they got into the Cadillac and began to drive toward the mine. Dudley was driving slowly, pointing out everything to her as they rode along.

"Up on that knoll," he said, "that's where the Traylors live. Rooster Traylor's a man about my age. Last year his mother shot one of the Galtney women for breaking up Rooster's marriage and now the Galtneys have got to shoot someone in the Traylor family."

"That's terrible," Rhoda said.

"No it isn't, Sister," he said, warming into the argument. "These people take care of their own problems."

"They actually shoot each other?" she said. "And you think that's okay? You think that's funny?"

"I think it's just as good as waiting around for some judge and jury to do it for you."

"Then you're just crazy," Rhoda said. "You're as crazy as you can be."

"Well, let's don't argue about it this morning. Come on. I've got something to show you." He pulled the car off the road and they walked into the woods, following a set of bulldozer tracks that made a crude path into the trees. It was quiet in the woods and smelled of pine and sassafras. Rhoda watched her father's strong body moving in front of her, striding along, inspecting everything, noticing everything, commenting on everything.

"Look at this," he said. "Look at all this beauty, honey. Look at how beautiful all this is. This is the real world. Not those goddamn movies and beauty parlors and magazines. This is the world that God made. This is where people are really happy."

"There isn't any God," she said. "Nobody that knows anything believes in God, Daddy. That's just a lot of old stuff . . . "

"I'm telling you, Rhoda," he said. "It breaks my heart to see the way you're growing up." He stopped underneath a tree, took a seat on a log and turned his face to hers. Tears were forming in his eyes. He was famous in the family for being able to cry on cue. "You've just got to learn to listen to someone. You've got to get some common sense in your head. I swear to God, I worry about you all the time." The tears were falling now. "I just can't stand to see the way you're growing up. I don't know where you get all those crazy ideas you come up with."

Rhoda looked down, caught off guard by the tears. No matter how many times he pulled that with the tears she fell for it for a moment. The summer forest was all around them, soft deep earth beneath their feet, morning light falling through the leaves, and the things that passed between them were too hard to understand. Their brown eyes met and locked and after that they were bound to start an argument for no one can bear to be that happy or that close to another human being.

"Well, I'll tell you one thing," Rhoda said. "It's a free country and I can smoke if I want to and you can't keep me from doing it by locking me up in a trailer with some poor white trash."

"What did you say?" he said, getting a look on his face that would have scared a grown man to death. "What did you just say, Rhoda?"

"I said I'm sick and tired of being locked up in that damned old trailer with those corny people and nothing to read but religious magazines. I want to get some cigarettes and I want you to take me home so I can see my friends and get my column written for next week."

"Oh, God, Sister." he said. "Haven't I taught you anything? Maud Samples is the salt of the earth. That woman raised seven children. She knows things you and I will never know as long as we live."

"Well, no she doesn't," Rhoda said. "She's just an old white trash country woman and if Momma knew where I was she'd have a fit."

"Your momma is a very stupid person," he said. "And I'm sorry I ever let her raise you." He turned his back to her then and stalked on out of the woods to a road that ran like a red scar up the side of the mountain. "Come on," he said. "I'm going to take you up there and show you where coal comes from. Maybe you can learn one thing this week."

"I learn things all the time," she said. "I already know more than half the people I know . . . I know . . . "

"Please don't talk anymore this morning," he said. "I'm burned out talking to you."

He put her into a jeep and began driving up the steep unpaved road. In a minute he was feeling better, cheered up by the sight of the big Caterpillar tractors moving dirt. If there was one thing that always cheered him up it was the sight of a big shovel moving dirt. "This is Blue Gem coal," he said. "The hardest in the area. See the layers. Topsoil, then gravel and dirt or clay, then slate, then thirteen feet of pure coal. Some people think it was made by dinosaurs. Other people think God put it there."

"This is it?" she said. "This is the mine?" It looked like one of his road construction projects. Same yellow tractors, same disorderly activity. The only difference seemed to be the huge piles of coal and a conveyor belt going down the mountain to a train.

"This is it," he said. "This is where they stored the old dinosaurs."

"Well, it is made out of dinosaurs," she said. "There were a lot of leaves and trees and dinosaurs and then they died and the coal and oil is made out of them."

"All right," he said. "Let's say I'll go along with the coal. But tell me this, who made the slate then? Who put the slate right on top of the coal everywhere it's found in the world? Who laid the slate down on top of the dinosaurs?"

"I don't know who put the slate there," she said. "We haven't got that far yet."

"You haven't got that far?" he said. "You mean the scientists haven't got as far as the slate yet? Well, Sister, that's the problem with you folks that evolved out of monkeys. You're still half-baked. You aren't finished like us old dumb ones that God made."

"I didn't say the scientists hadn't got that far," she said. "I just said I hadn't got that far."

"It's a funny thing to me how all those dinosaurs came up here to die in the mountains and none of them died in the farmland," he said. "It sure would have made it a lot easier on us miners if they'd died down there on the flat."

While she was groping around for an answer he went right on. "Tell me this, Sister," he said. "Are any of your monkey ancestors in there with the dinosaurs, or is it just plain dinosaurs? I'd like to know who all I'm digging up . . . I'd like to give credit . . . "

The jeep had come to a stop and Joe was coming towards them, hurrying out of the small tin-roofed office with a worried look on his face. "Mr. D, you better call up to Jellico. Beb's been looking everywhere for you. They had a run-in with a teamster organizer. You got to call him right away."

"What's wrong?" Rhoda said. "What happened?"

"Nothing you need to worry about, Sister," her father said. He turned to Joe. "Go find Preacher and tell him to drive Rhoda back to your house. You go on now, honey. I've got work to do." He gave her a kiss on the cheek and disappeared into the office. A small shriveled-looking man came limping out of a building and climbed into the driver's seat. "I'm Preacher," he said. "Mr. Joe tole me to drive you up to his place."

"All right," Rhoda said "I guess that's okay with me." Preacher put the jeep in gear and drove it slowly down the winding rutted road. By the time they got to the bottom Rhoda had thought of a better plan. "I'll drive now," she said. "I'll drive myself to Maud's. It's all right with my father. He lets me drive all the time. You can walk back, can't you?" Preacher didn't know what to say to that. He was an old drunk that Dudley and Joe kept around to run errands. He was so used to taking orders that finally he climbed down out of the jeep and did as he was told. "Show me the way to town," Rhoda said. "Draw me a map. I have to go by town on my way to Maud's." Preacher scratched his head, then bent over and drew her a little map in the dust on the hood. Rhoda studied the map, put the jeep into the first forward gear she could find and drove off down the road to the little town of Manchester, Kentucky, studying the diagram on the gearshift as she drove.

She parked beside a boardwalk that led through the main street of town and started off looking for a store that sold cigarettes. One of the stores had dresses in the window. In the center was a red strapless sundress with a white jacket. $6.95, the price tag said. I hate the way I look, she decided. I hate these tacky pants. I've got sixty dollars. I don't have to look like this if I don't want to. I can buy anything I want.

She went inside, asked the clerk to take the dress out of the window and in a few minutes she emerged from the store wearing the dress and a pair of leather sandals with two-inch heels. The jacket was thrown carelessly over her shoulder like Gene Tierney in *Leave Her to Heaven*. I look great in red, she was thinking, catching a glimpse of herself in a store window. It isn't true that redheaded people can't wear red. She walked on down the boardwalk, admiring herself in every window.

She walked for two blocks looking for a place to try her luck getting cigarettes. She was almost to the end of the boardwalk when she came to a pool hall. She stood in the door looking in, smelling the dark smell of tobacco and beer. The room was deserted except for a man leaning on a cue stick beside a table and a boy with black hair seated behind a cash register reading a book. The boy's name was Johnny Hazard and he was sixteen years old. The book he was reading was *U.S.A.* by John Dos Passos. A woman who came to Manchester to teach poetry writing had given him the book. She had made a dust jacket for it out of brown paper so he could read it in public. On the spine of the jacket she had written, *American History.*

"I'd like a package of Lucky Strikes," Rhoda said, holding out a twenty-dollar bill in his direction.

"We don't sell cigarettes to minors," he said. "It's against the law."

"I'm not a minor," Rhoda said. "I'm eighteen. I'm Rhoda Manning. My daddy owns the mine."

"Which mine?" he said. He was watching her breasts as she talked, getting caught up in the apricot skin against the soft red dress.

"The mine," she said. "The Manning mine. I just got here the other day. I haven't been downtown before."

"So, how do you like our town?"

"Please sell me some cigarettes," she said. "I'm about to have a fit for a Lucky."

"I can't sell you cigarettes," he said. "You're not any more eighteen years old than my dog."

"Yes, I am," she said. "I drove here in a jeep, doesn't that prove anything?" She was looking at his wide shoulders and the tough flat chest beneath his plaid shirt.

"Are you a football player?" she said.

"When I have time," he said. "When I don't have to work on the nights they have games."

"I'm a cheerleader where I live," Rhoda said. "I just got elected again for next year."

"What kind of a jeep?" he said.

"An old one," she said. "It's filthy dirty. They use it at the mine." She had just noticed the package of Camels in his breast pocket.

"If you won't sell me a whole package, how about selling me

one," she said. "I'll give you a dollar for a cigarette." She raised
the twenty-dollar bill and laid it down on the glass counter.

He ignored the twenty-dollar bill, opened the cash register, removed a quarter and walked over to the jukebox. He walked with
a precise, balanced sort of cockiness, as if he knew he could walk
any way he wanted but had carefully chosen this particular walk as
his own. He walked across the room through the rectangle of light
coming in the door, walking as though he were the first boy ever
to be in the world, the first boy ever to walk across a room and
put a quarter into a jukebox. He pushed a button and music filled
the room.

> *Kaw-Liga was a wooden Indian a-standing by the door,*
> *He fell in love with an Indian maid*
> *Over in the antique store.*

"My uncle wrote that song," he said, coming back to her. "But
it got ripped off by some promoters in Nashville. I'll make you a
deal," he said. "I'll give you a cigarette if you'll give me a ride
somewhere I have to go." "All right," Rhoda said. "Where do you
want to go?"

"Out to my cousin's," he said. "It isn't far."

"Fine," Rhoda said. Johnny told the lone pool player to keep an
eye on things and the two of them walked out into the sunlight,
walking together very formally down the street to where the jeep
was parked.

"Why don't you let me drive," he said. "It might be easier." She
agreed and he drove on up the mountain to a house that looked
deserted. He went in and returned carrying a guitar in a case, a
blanket, and a quart bottle with a piece of wax paper tied around
the top with a rubber band.

"What's in the bottle?" Rhoda said.

"Lemonade, with a little sweetening in it."

"Like whiskey?"

"Yeah. Like whiskey. Do you ever drink it?"

"Sure," she said. "I drink a lot. In Saint Louis we had this club
called The Four Roses that met every Monday at Donna Duston's
house to get drunk. I thought it up, the club I mean."

"Well, here's your cigarette," he said. He took the package from his pocket and offered her one, holding it near his chest so she had to get in close to take it.

"Oh, God," she said. "Oh, thank you so much. I'm about to die for a ciggie. I haven't had one in days. Because my father dragged me up here to make me stop smoking. He's always trying to make me do something I don't want to do. But it never works. I'm very hard-headed, like him." She took the light Johnny offered her and blew out the smoke in a small controlled stream. "God, I love to smoke," she said.

"I'm glad I could help you out," he said. "Anytime you want one when you're here you just come on over. Look," he said. "I'm going somewhere you might want to see, if you're not in a hurry to get back. You got time to go and see something with me?"

"What is it?" she asked.

"Something worth seeing," he said. "The best thing in Clay County there is to see."

"Sure," she said. "I'll go. I never turn down an adventure. Why not, that's what my cousins in the Delta always say. Whyyyyyyy not." They drove up the mountain and parked and began to walk into the woods along a path. The woods were deeper here than where Rhoda had been that morning, dense and green and cool. She felt silly walking in the woods in the little high-heeled sandals, but she held on to Johnny's hand and followed him deeper and deeper into the trees, feeling grown up and brave and romantic. I'll bet he thinks I'm the bravest girl he ever met, she thought. I'll bet he thinks at last he's met a girl who's not afraid of anything. Rhoda was walking along imagining tearing off a piece of her dress for a tourniquet in case Johnny was bit by a poisonous snake. She was pulling the tourniquet tighter and tighter when the trees opened onto a small brilliant blue pond. The water was so blue Rhoda thought for a moment it must be some sort of trick. He stood there watching her while she took it in.

"What do you think?" he said at last.

"My God," she said. "What is it?"

"It's Blue Pond," he said. "People come from all over the world to see it."

"Who made it?" Rhoda said. "Where did it come from?"

"Springs. Rock springs. No one knows how deep down it goes,

but more than a hundred feet because divers have been that far."

"I wish I could swim in it," Rhoda said. "I'd like to jump in there and swim all day."

"Come over here, cheerleader," he said. "Come sit over here by me and we'll watch the light on it. I brought this teacher from New York here last year. She said it was the best thing she'd ever seen in her life. She's a writer. Anyway, the thing she likes about Blue Pond is watching the light change on the water. She taught me a lot when she was here. About things like that."

Rhoda moved nearer to him, trying to hold in her stomach.

"My father really likes this part of the country," she said. "He says people up here are the salt of the earth. "He says all the people up here are direct descendants from England and Scotland and Wales. I think he wants us to move up here and stay, but my mother won't let us. It's all because the unions keep messing with his mine that he has to be up here all the time. If it wasn't for the unions everything would be going fine. You aren't for the unions, are you?"

"I'm for myself," Johnny said. "And for my kinfolks." He was tired of her talking then and reached for her and pulled her into his arms, paying no attention to her small resistances, until finally she was stretched out under him on the earth and he moved the dress from her breasts and held them in his hands. He could smell the wild smell of her craziness and after a while he took the dress off and the soft white cotton underpants and touched her over and over again. Then he entered her with the way he had of doing things, gently and with a good sense of the natural rhythms of the earth.

I'm doing it, Rhoda thought. I'm doing it. This is doing it. This is what it feels like to be doing it.

"This doesn't hurt a bit," she said out loud. "I think I love you, Johnny. I love, love, love you. I've been waiting all my life for you."

"Don't talk so much," he said. "It's better if you stop talking."

And Rhoda was quiet and he made love to her as the sun was leaving the earth and the afternoon breeze moved in the trees. Here was every possible tree, hickory and white oak and redwood and sumac and maple, all in thick foliage now, and he made love to

her with great tenderness, forgetting he had set out to fuck the
boss's daughter, and he kept on making love to her until she began
to tighten around him, not knowing what she was doing, or where
she was going, or even that there was any place to be going to.

Dudley was waiting outside the trailer when she drove up.
There was a sky full of cold stars behind him, and he was pacing
up and down and talking to himself like a crazy man. Maud was
inside the trailer crying her heart out and only Joe had kept his
head and was going back and forth from one to the other telling
them everything would be all right.

Dudley was pacing up and down talking to Jesus. I know I had it
coming, he was saying. I know goddamn well I had it coming. But
not her. Where in the hell is she? You get her back in one piece and
I'll call Valerie and break it off. I won't see Valerie ever again as
long as I live. *But you've got to get me back my little girl. Goddammit,
you get me back my girl.*

Then he was crying, his head thrown back and raised up to the
stars as the jeep came banging up the hill in third gear. Rhoda
parked it and got out and started walking toward him, all bravado
and disdain.

Dudley smelled it on her before he even touched her. Smelled it
all over her and began to shake her, screaming at her to tell him
who it had been. Then Joe came running out from the trailer and
threw his hundred and fifty pounds between them, and Maud was
right behind him. She led Rhoda into the trailer and put her into
bed and sat beside her, bathing her head with a damp towel until
she fell asleep.

"I'll find out who it was," Dudley said, shaking his fist. "I'll
find out who it was."

"You don't know it was anybody," Joe said. "You don't even
know what happened, Mr. D. Now you got to calm down and in
the morning we'll find out what happened. More than likely she's
just been holed up somewhere trying to scare you."

"I know what happened," Dudley said. "I already know what
happened."

"Well, you can find out who it was and you can kill him if you
have to," Joe said. "If it's true and you still want to in the morning, you can kill him."

But there would be no killing. By the time the moon was high, Johnny Hazard was halfway between Lexington, Kentucky and Cincinnati, Ohio, with a bus ticket he bought with the fifty dollars he'd taken from Rhoda's pocket. He had called the poetry teacher and told her he was coming. Johnny had decided it was time to see the world. After all, that very afternoon a rich cheerleader had cried in his arms and given him her cherry. There was no telling what might happen next.

Much later that night Rhoda woke up in the small room, hearing the wind come up in the trees. The window was open and the moon, now low in the sky and covered with mist, poured a diffused light upon the bed. Rhoda sat up in the bed and shivered. Why did I do that with him? she thought. Why in the world did I do that? But I couldn't help it, she decided. He's so sophisticated and he's so good-looking and he's a wonderful driver and he plays a guitar. She moved her hands along her thighs, trying to remember exactly what it was they had done, trying to remember the details, wondering where she could find him in the morning.

But Dudley had other plans for Rhoda in the morning. By noon she was on her way home in a chartered plane. Rhoda had never been on an airplane of any kind before, but she didn't let on.

"I'm thinking of starting a diary," she was saying to the pilot, arranging her skirt so her knees would show. "A lot of unusual things have been happening to me lately. The boy I love is dying of cancer in Saint Louis. It's very sad, but I have to put up with it. He wants me to write a lot of books and dedicate them to his memory."

The pilot didn't seem to be paying much attention, so Rhoda gave up on him and went back into her own head.

In her head Bob Rosen was alive after all. He was walking along a street in Greenwich Village and passed a bookstore with a window full of her books, many copies stacked in a pyramid with her picture on every cover. He recognized the photograph, ran into the bookstore, grabbed a book, opened it and saw the dedication. _To Bob Rosen, Te Amo Forever, Rhoda._

Then Bob Rosen, or maybe it was Johnny Hazard, or maybe this unfriendly pilot, stood there on that city street, looking up at the sky, holding the book against his chest, crying and broken-hearted because Rhoda was lost to him forever, this famous author, who could have been his, lost to him forever.

Thirty years later Rhoda woke up in a hotel room in New York City. There was a letter lying on the floor where she had thrown it when she went to bed. She picked it up and read it again. *Take my name off that book*, the letter said. *Imagine a girl with your advantages writing a book like that. You mother is so ashamed of you.*

Goddamn you, Rhoda thought. Goddamn you to hell. She climbed back into the bed and pulled the pillows over her head. She lay there for a while feeling sorry for herself. Then she got up and walked across the room and pulled a legal pad out of a brief-case and started writing.

Dear Father,

You take my name off those checks you send those television preachers and those goddamn right-wing politicians. That name has come to me from a hundred generations of men and women . . . also, in the future let my mother speak for herself about my work.

Love,
Rhoda

P.S. The slate was put there by the second law of thermodynamics. Some folks call it gravity. Other folks call it God.

I guess it was the second law, she thought. It was the second law or the third law or something like that. She leaned back in the chair, looking at the ceiling. Maybe I'd better find out before I mail it.

Variation on a Scream

Marianne Gingher

In happier, less violent times lived a beautiful princess with skin as fragrantly soft as gardenia and hair the envy of Gold. Some said her heart was pure and sweet as valentine candy with I LOVE YOU written across it by the good faeries at her birth. Indeed, she was a very kind and generous princess, receiving lambs and tigers in the same company who, in her gentle presence, lay in peace with one another. Truly, each morning when she arose, the birds of the forest braided her hair with flowers and the shyest fawns trustingly nibbled fern seed from her palm.

She adored her father, the King, who was a wise old white-haired man and governed his people with the same compassion his daughter showed for her animal friends. So dearly did the princess love her father that when the time came for her to be married, she wept pathetically at the thought of having to part from him.

"Be not sad, my daughter," the kind King consoled her. "Prince Brightenbold is a handsome and noble lad, tender and true-hearted, wealthy and witty, and the two of you will be exceedingly happy."

Indeed, the princess loved Prince Brightenbold with half of her sugarcoated heart. But the other half remained loyally pledged to her father. She had fond memories of her courtship with the prince: riding their silver-and-gold saddled roebucks through the enchanted forests, discovering together a pot of gold at the end of last summer's rainbow, picnicking on fillet of mushroom (they were both vegetarians) and unicorn milk in the shade of the giant daffodil groves. Yet often, as her wedding day approached, the lovely princess thought how perfect her life might be if her father could accompany her to the Kingdom of Brightenbold where the three of them would live happily everafter. That was the way it always turned out in the story books, she complained, sweetly.

"Ah, but you must learn to accept reality, Daughter," the King sagaciously chided. "All beautiful princesses grow up to marry handsome princes. It is the natural order of things. Besides, I shall

135

come to visit you often, bearing gifts, of course, for all my flaxen-haired grandbabies: plum-colored ponies and baskets of pomegranates and kumquats, ostrich plumes to tickle their tummies, chocolates, bright-feathered toucans in ivory cages, visards made from butterfly wings. Such fun we shall have! Ours shall not be a permanent separation by any means." And thus he convinced the princess.

Now on the morning of her wedding day, the princess set forth for the Kingdom of Brightenbold. Ordinarilly, as was the custom according to the Rites of Royal Marriage, the father of the bride accompanied the wedding coach; however, on that special and particular morning the goodly King found mandatory the need to attend to important affairs of the kingdom which could not wait. Thus, he bade his daughter farewell at the castle gate and promised to follow as soon as his royal business had been completed. And so, wearing her exquisite lace and ribbon wedding gown, her lap filled with roses pink enough to break your heart, the princess rode into the forest. Her carriage, gingerbreaded with gold, was drawn by four fleet cream-colored stallions, their jewelled harnesses twinkling and jingling as they galloped.

Now the journey to Brightenbold was not hazardous except for a brief passing through the marshes of the Squint-Eyed Teufel who rode an equally terrifying flesh-colored dragon. The Teufel, however, had not been sighted for nearly two hundred years, and so the princess felt safe enough and settled back on her velvety cushion to pass the time, idly gazing out at the ferny and flowered countryside and reading the story books she had taken along.

It was not long, though, before the driver, an eager young lad in handsome livery, called out to the princess that he had sighted a fellow traveller ahead. And from the carriage window the princess joyously perceived the elderly gentleman of whom the boy spoke to be the King himself. "How merry!" she exclaimed, her face sweetening with a blush as delicate as the roses in her lap. "It is Papa come to join us."

"Yes! I shall stop," the coachboy cried from above, slowing the horses. But as the carriage approached the man, the princess clearly saw that he was not her father; rather, a strange yet dapper nobleman. Now the princess had often heard tales of rogues and bandits who roamed the highways: dashing young spitfires who donned feathered caps and eyepatches and brandished jewelled daggers stolen from the bodies of slain knights. Such men, her father warned, would toss a princess over their saddles like a sack of gold, riding far away to where the shadows of the moon catch up to those of the sun. The princess shuddered at the recollection of such stories, gazing out her carriage window at the stranger. Yet she could plainly see that he bore her no malice: a tender-faced, white-haired old man with laugh-wrinkles crisscrossing the flesh round his eyes like her father.

"My horse has gone lame," he told the driver courteously. "And I am on my way to my daughter's wedding and must not be late."

"Well, then, you shall certainly share my carriage!" cried the princess, for she had overheard. Compassion for his plight and the similarities of their circumstances overwhelmed her heart. And she was most desirous of fatherly company anyway.

So the old nobleman, steadying himself with a cane that bore the head of a ruby-eyed lizard, hoisted himself into the carriage and sat down beside the princess. "I shouldn't want you to catch a thorn," said she, graciously removing the roses from her lap and, to make room, placing them gingerly on the seat across.

"Why thank you," said the gentleman. "You are truly thoughtful, and so beautiful in your wedding gown."

For a while they talked of weddings, and then the princess, feeling travel-weary, settled back against her seat and went to sleep. She usually slept ever so peacefully and enjoyed a splendid treacle of dreams. But during this particular nap she dreamt of terrors that strove to turn her heart cold as stone: yellow-fanged bats, hordes of glossy, dark-bulbed spiders, mice and ticks and untameable tigers, red with the blood of slaughter, rampaged in her mind. She awoke with a cry to find the carriage lurching wildly through the bleak swamplands of the Squint-Eyed Teufel.

"What is happening!" she cried with alarm.

"The driver seems to have lost control of the horses," said the old nobleman, calmly.

"But I don't see the driver!" And, truly, as she leaned out the window, she saw he had vanished.

"Perhaps he has fallen off," said the nobleman. And then quite tenderly and fatherly, he comforted her: "Do not worry, these things happen. The horses know their way. We will simply ride this out." The eyes of the lizard on his cane glimmered, fiercely scarlet, as he reached for her trembling hand.

"But I'm afraid," wept the princess, suddenly aware of him leaning heavily against her as the carriage jolted along its madcap course. "I am afraid," she whimpered as she realized it was not an accident that, now, his weight was crushing her and his breath was hot and wheezing against her cheek. "Oh, please, I am so afraid." But he only grinned and she saw he had no teeth and his eyes were rolled back in his head, white and sightless.

"We shall be there soon. Bear with me," he groaned hoarsely. But the words seemed borne on a rotten-smelling wind and beneath the cloak that covered his lap rose the cane which he gripped with one hand.

As horrible as it may seem, the poor princess might have resigned herself to the ride, pressing herself to the side of the coach, had her eyes not caught sight of the quivering roses on the other seat. For *there* lay the cane, tossing and tumbling among them. At once she gave a tiny shriek and her fingers found the carriage door handle. Out she rolled, crown over slippers, into the swamp where she landed, quite unharmed, so they say, the hunting parties who still search for her, following the little shreds of wedding gown she has ripped and tied to the trees to mark her way.

* * *

Mama says I should rely on her memory, spoonfeeding me in my dark. And so, my past plays invalid for her. She is forty-six, and forty-six remembers more of its twenty-eight than twenty-two could ever recall of its four.

Her talk of it is well-worn and familiar as a hand-me-down. And I recall some parts she speaks of: Gramps and Nanny and Uncle Seymore and the cousins with funny names like Ludeen and Georgia June who had fat legs and ankles. Another one we called Smiles because her knees were full of them. And the thick Savannah heat despite shade that crawled like lava ash beneath the gasping trees. Shade hotter than sun because you expected the sun to be. We played in the lawn sprinkler to keep cool and ate huge hunks of watermelon, careful not to swallow the seeds So's a new one won't sprout and bust through yo gut, Aunt Teeter always laughed wetly, patting her monumental stomach as if in testimony. And Uncle Nard would take off his thumbs with no blood and grinning and pull quarters out of our ears.

Mama told me once: the kind of pervert that nigger was is the kind who can read just enough to find out when a kindergarten is having a picnic. A different kind is the one in the Sears parkinglot she saw once, loitering around the cars, who waved and smiled rottenly at her and when she returned to her car there was you-know-what glistening in the seat. I said: How did you *know* it was that? And she said: Honey, you grow up and get *married* and you'll know. There are always two kinds of perverts: the child kind and the woman kind, the wanna-stick-of-chew-gums and the actions-speak-louders.

She said the first mistake was the write-up about our family re-union in the Savannah newspaper. Just enough to whet his appetite. And him an old man, too: a respectable molasses color, stringy-limbed so that he looked as if the heat was slowly melting him down like a Sugar Daddy. White-headed with two dozen grand-children last time he checked, he told the policeman. Kindly cocky, Aunt Teeter liked to tell it. But the worst part, Mama said, was the one arm; the other, clipped off at the elbow, dangling shiny-dark and firm as an eggplant. It was the one he used to hoist me up with, and right between the legs, Ludeen or Georgia said later, giggly in their adolescent wisdom. And him, proud as a stunt man, to hear them tell it.

But it was not chewing gum he offered me. It was a ride on an albino mule. Scarce as hen's teeth, mules like that, the policeman said. And it made Mama mad: him wanting to buy that man's mule right that minute on the very spot of the crime. A cut of her lean mean eyes and he did business: Your name, boa.

It was Willard Testermount and he had a good alibi except he was colored with an albino mule on Columbus Drive which is practically downtown in Savannah. Plus the one stump arm that looked hard enough to be a weapon. Ludeen was supposed to be watching me, but no, it was Georgia June whose charge I was only she didn't know. But one or both of them had seen me down by the road looking after the man and the mule who were on their way to till up somebody's garden in the next block. And it was me who did the tempting, they decided in the end, which was the reason I got a paddling with Nanny's brush after we got home from the hospital. Me, hollering that man down for a ride so that he turned and came back. And that's when Ludeen or Georgia June or both of them saw him hoist me up with that arm and got scared when he led me out of sight. Mama said the thing that made her maddest was Uncle Nard slipping him a five dollar bill for the trouble we had made him so he wouldn't hold a grudge. Two years later she gets a letter from Nanny with a clipping enclosed about a Winslow Testermount dangling himself out in a park. Just goes to show, Mama snorts, and Uncle Nard putting him in business. Eighteen years ago and she can still get blistery about it. That's a vivid memory for you. But you don't know for *sure*, I have said. I mean, Winslow and Willard are only *similar*. Oldest trick in the book, Mama huffs. So old it should give a person's brain arthritis just thinking it up.

* * *

"I just don't feel like talking about it," my roommate tells the Dean. "Not now, in a little while, maybe, but not now." The confetti of a dozen wet kleenexes lies in her lap. Her face looks five pounds heavier, swollen with tears, checkered red and black with fury and mascara. Aimlessly her fingers knead the shredded kleenex.

"I'll be in the lobby with the officers when you feel like it," the Dean says kindly. She opens the door and, in the hallway, there is the whispery buzz of the entire dormitory. A sound almost reverent. Chipper slips in as the Dean goes out, with a finger at her lips, nods to the others, and closes the door. I'm glad Chipper has come. She is a worldly sophomore who plans to become a Playboy Bunny upon graduation. Three weeks ago she was the first to encounter Superman.

There is the smell of pre-storm ozone in the room, and Chipper briskly slams the window down. "I'd of thought that would be the first thing they do. Anybody want a cigarette."

The offer is for me since my roommate does not smoke. My roommate does not drink or curse either, and once she asked me didn't I think French kissing was perverted. Which of course makes this all the harder for her.

"I guess we ought to thank our lucky stars that he gets his jollies with a pane of glass between him and you." Jauntily Chipper sits down on the bed with the pink coverlet. So much in the room is pink: silk flowers in a KA Old South Ball goblet, a curly stuffed poodle, a remnant of shag carpet. You don't mahnd if I do the room? my roommate had asked in September. Pink is mah passion.

Chipper's skin is dark against the delicate color: ruddy with sun and rust-colored freckles. She is merely voluptuous but she looks heavy and almost overripe, summerlike with her bounty. Her hair is rich and lion-colored; she sucks her cigarettes down in three drags. "At least you got to admit the guy has style," she says to me.

He has appeared on campus twice. A pattern is being established, the police say. Twice he has been whistling. Songs from the thirties? Love ballads? Blues? *Who can remember. Maybe he was calling a dog.* Twice he shows up in a Superman mask. How do you know it was a Superman mask? *Because it was so steely-faced and conquering-eyed with the shiny, blue-black hair.* That could be a lot of guys: James Bond, Elvis Presley. *But don't forget about the S on his chest when he flung off the trenchcoat.* That's right. Lipstick. Some of it on the window glass where he pressed himself. But what about the tennis shoes. *Yellow. Both of them yellow, and no socks.* Are you positive they were yellow, it being dark and all. *Definitely a brilliant, shocking yellow. Like the yellow of tennis balls.* Tennis balls are white. *Tretorn makes yellow ones, sunny as dandelions.*

"The good thing that's going to come out of all this," says Chipper, "is Buck Mansfield. And I've heard he's really a hunk."

"Yeah," I say, "Dean Koontz was telling us about him and those self-defense courses."

"So look out Superman!"

"Yeah, look out, buddy."

We laugh. Tough. And light new cigarettes. My roommate smiles weakly. Her fingers leave the kleenex in her lap and reach out, timid and trembling, toward my cigarette. "You mahnd?"

I feel like hugging her, but it would be like touching a flower that the slightest brushing browns. Her eyes wander sadly across the room, to the window, back, slowly, over the room and rest on the cigarette she holds with all her fingers. "It . . . was so horribly pink," she says.

* * *

In chunky disciplined letters, the sign above the door read: CHARMIAN KOOTNZ, DEAN OF WOMEN. She looked back at the sign and it gave her courage. Reading it, her lips silently sculpting the words, she was at once fortified with a peculiar, self-aggrandizing gravity that sought to quell the loop-the-loop of her stomach. The sign alone, underneath which students—homesick or lovesick, frightened or furious—trembled for attention, shed its austerity and bolstered her sense of purpose. The rest—with the President, the fusty trustees, the mostly male faculty—was eye-winking diplomacy: her mini skirts and knee boots, the Peter Pan collars and pearls, her chic Sasoon were tokens outwardly offered to confirm in their minds her relevance to femininity. (Well, she was prone to rationalize, an ex-gym teacher needs all the reinforce-ments she can muster.) Yet now, as she hastened down the dark, wood-fragrant, Friday afternoon-deserted corridor toward the President's office, she was annoyed by those exterior flauntings as if they betrayed her, acknowledged the most intimate weaknesses of her sex: the whine of her nylons as her thighs rubbed one an-other, the tinkling of her bracelet, even the perfume seemed fla-grant denials of any toughness, silent admissions of vulnerability.

She had gotten the crying over with, and that was good. _That_ was a necessity. In the quiet of her office she had hung up the phone and bawled from the great blue convoluted depths of her heart, glad for the privacy of Friday afternoon when most of the students would be leaving for the weekend or curling their hair for a date. And once she had begun to cry for an immediate reason, the tears came for any and all: the fate of her mother who had been living in a nursing home for five years was a sudden epiphany, rubbing her heart as raw as the current crisis. Likewise the cat she had run over weeks before, the forgotten luncheon engagement with a dear old friend. All were interwoven somehow; all contrib-uted to the soggy fabric of her misery.

But she had pulled herself together, CHARMIAN KOONTZ, DEAN OF WOMEN. Like Mother Nature after a storm. The en-tire affair was her baby and she, herself, would abort it and clean up the mess. That is why she had, at first, considered not telling the President, the seed of an idea that tendriled its way through her imagination until the vision of herself flowered into the apotheosis of unflappable self-reliance, a do-it-your-selfer of Thoreauvian magnitude. All this in anger, drunk on adrenalin. Considering the police inquiries, her confidence had dwindled.

It had seemed a sound move, she reflected: the course in self-defense. When Mr. Mansfield, as a representative of whatever it was, approached her on the subject, the campus was ripe for such a project. She could see him even now: his brow kneaded with concern, his eyes, the icy penetrating blue of dedication. And oh, those pearly teeth that studded his smile after she had delivered the six hundred females of Sampson College into his karate-calloused hands.

He had won their hearts all right: him and his wholesome, spangled ski sweaters, his close-shaved cheeks, cherried by all-outdoors. The manly, hard-edged angles of his face demanded a trust reserved for comic book heroes, Kirk Douglas, Captain James T. Kirk of the Starship Enterprise. Charmian laughed, thinking how she almost deserved it: a kick in the seat of her frilly bikinis.

She had been out with him. _That_ was the worst part, if she were feeling selfish and self-pitying. Once to the campus dairy bar (the students turning green as lime sherbert, or was that her ego?) and once to dinner at the Tea Pot Dome where they had split a full bottle of Chianti and smoked two boxes of Tiperillos. Talking. And of what? Certainly about nothing incriminating. Although now, looking back, she might peel the layers of his character like an onion, each of his words redolent with innuendo. His younger sister had been raped. That was what had inspired his work. _Inspired_. Aha! Such an evangelical ring to the word: beware of the fire and brimstone. And his hand, handsome and bronze as an autumn leaf resting on the tablecloth except to touch hers briefly as if to physically punctuate the conversation, had been cold and wet. She could remember that, imagining now that there had been great rings of sweat under the arms of his suit jacket, underwear sticking to his chest and groin like sandwich wrap. And outside it had just stopped snowing.

He had wanted to come in with her, but she had said no. She wasn't sure about what the college would say. Not about that. She knew perfectly well about that. There was the question of whether she should be seeing him at all now that he was classified Visiting

Faculty. The college had its reasons. She had her job. And image. And so she had watched him crunching out to his car. Had turned off the porch and hall lights as soon as he reached it. The chilly part was that he reached it and nothing more. Behind the darkened glass she had watched him stop and light a Tiperillo, leaning against the hood of the car to look back at the house. To stare and stare, smoking mechanically every minute or so. And when the first Tiperillo had been crushed, hissing into the snow, he had lit another. Staring. Then, he had unzipped his pants and urinated, small and white there, like a part of the snow, the ground steaming and he blowing smoke from his mouth.

She had watched him, fascinated, waiting as if it were all arranged, waiting as if on the verge of some profound commitment, a part of her recoiling and fearful, yet another part, darkly, redly mesmerized. This was the memory that taunted her now. Not of him, but of herself. And she shrank from it as if from an obscene phone call.

And what would she tell the President about him? That he had failed to report to his Thursday night lecture and so she had called the number he had given but, according to his landlady he had checked out, bill unpaid? That the university from which he had presented a letter of recommendation had never heard of him? That a week ago she should have reported him for pissing in her yard? _A week ago makes you practically an accomplice, Dean Koontz._ Yes, well, sir, you see it has its roots. I have this thing, this little quirk, this numbing inability to act before I'm sure. Once when I was sixteen, a friend of mine and I drove by our high school one night and there, on the corner, was a young boy holding a red jacket in front of himself. When we passed him, well, he moved it, the jacket, and we screamed because we had never seen, you know. And we must have driven back by him five or six times before we went home to call the police.

Behind his desk, as she entered the office, the President donned his patronizing grin without even knowing.

* * *

And so why am I afraid at the bus station? Why do I pretend to be reading a story while the man beside me heaves and groans over a spittoon and the boy across from me, with his shirt unbuttoned, picks at the hairs on his chest and stares? I have read this story at least three times. It has made me laugh, it has made me shudder to sense a great unhealthiness that riddles illusion as much as reality. My eyes glance furtively above the pages I turn. How many steps to the policeman down the corridor? Who here has an honest face, as if that mattered. It is ten p.m. and the bus is late. I am afraid to reach in my purse for a cigarette, aware of the motion that catches eyes, anticipating the clatter of my keys and comb as I rummage, eyes listening. I watch the policeman joking with the Trailways ticket man. Something about Saturday night and hell. He touches his gun, chucks the holster tenderly as a baby's chin, rolls his head back and laughs. His face is round and flabby as dough. He is young and bored, here at the bus station on Saturday night. Better a raid on the Paradise Massage Parlor. (Better, a massage.) He yawns. Skews me? He yawns again and strolls, watery-eyed, into the bus station restaurant where the custards have been ripening under glass all day: the vanilla, pus-yellow; the chocolate, tar-skinned. Somehow he has ordered something, because I watch and he doesn't come out.

Chipper has said whatever I do not to use the bathroom but wait for the john on the bus. And so I've been waiting, crossing my legs tight the way Mama used to say to do on long car trips. But it isn't working. I know it's bad in the bathroom, so I won't be shocked. Just breathe through my mouth and drape the seat with toilet paper. The one confining thought is that if I get up to go (and I'll have to take my suitcase and purse and my dress in a plastic bag), the man next to me, still spitting, will think it is him. So I sit until it is too painful to be selfless and then, quickly, I get up, embracing my paraphernalia, and hurry, affecting the pose and stride of one preoccupied with deadly purpose.

It is as bad as I had imagined. After eating my only dime, the first stall remains barricaded. I have no choice but to enter the one marked: FREE. I am still sitting, reading the sad-scrawled graffiti when my bus is announced.

Waiting to board, a man behind me touched my shoulder. It is as if part of my skin has ripped itself from me. "Hey lady, you draggin some paper on you shoe." I should laugh, but I can't. First the fingers, dribbling, clumsily probing my attention, chilling, like ice down my back. But then the voice that touches my loneliness.

* * *

Alone, in the dormitory lobby, the woman is waiting. She sits,
uncomfortably in an overstuffed chair, picking imaginary lint from
her skirt, crossing and uncrossing her long, thin, runned-
stockinged legs. She wears a puckered, dark cardigan sweater over
a skimpy dress of tired blue flowers. Close-up, the sweater is pale
at the elbows with wear. She has replaced two missing buttons
with safety pins. She is plain and chinless, thin, with brassy yellow
hair that needs combing. The hair color and seedy angularity of
her body distort her age. I am thinking she is the woman who has
waited on me a hundred times in cheap ill-lit cafes. She is the
woman you don't tip well because she doesn't joke or smile because she is so sad or serious, you can't tell which.

We have stood watching her behind the small glass window of a
door. I have been thinking she will comb her hair or light a cigarette or unpeel a stick of gum to chew. But she simply sits on the
edge of her chair, fidgets with her skirt, stares at the floor. We
approach her quietly with a mixed reverence for something both
hated and admired. "*Three?*" she says, incredulous, her eyes bolt-
ing from one of us to another, red and small and hot in her face.

"I'm not one. I'm, just with . . . them." I turn to leave but she
says:

"It don't matter."

And so we sit down in chairs opposite hers, and everyone looks
at the floor. She is wearing scuffed loafers, curled at the toes,
paint-spattered. Beside them is her purse: enormous black patent-
leather, cracked and calloused with wear, the kind women who
ride buses with lots of babies carry along, stuffed with bottles and
diapers. Her hand delves into it, bony and blue-veined, and I think:
now a cigarette. She takes out a kleenex.

Chipper says, "I'm so sorry about all this, Mrs. Thorn." The
words cling, somehow superfluous, to the silence and rustle of
kleenex.

"I ain't gonna *cry*," the woman says, mostly to herself. "My
mama said, Ruthie, you get over to that college with them girls
that Sammy done his crime to and you be bawling your head off.
But I ain't yet, see? This here kleenex is just for safe-keeping." She
smiles, wanly.

We smile, desperately.

"Officer Cox, he said, Miz Thorn, why you want to make it hard on yourself? But I said, who's gonna know the other side less I say it. So I just come tell you the good, that's all. You know the bad. Everybody's crying about the bad. But there's plenty of good, I swear it."

"Would you like some coffee or a Coke?" Chipper asks. "I can run down to the snack room and get you something real quick."

Mrs. Thorn shakes her head, twisting the kleenex with very white fingers. "Mama, she's been such a comfort about it, just like he was her own flesh and blood. She said, Ruthie, he done wrong but he's still your Sammy. He's still the Sammy you said for better or worse till death us do part. He's got him a little problem, that's all. Like a belly ache or a hurt tooth. Something a doctor needs to fix."

Slowly, as I listen, I am feeling Willard Testermount's hard, shiny arms lifting me up on the back of that mule eighteen years ago in Savannah. I think I remember the smell of the mule, richly animal, stuffing my nose like sweet-sour fingers. No, they would say, that was *him,* and awful. Like Savannah as you cross the river near Union Bag. But I am remembering the way the sun beat happily hot on my head and how it was damp where I sat, my legs pressing the sides of the mule. And after I was down, I felt squashed low to the ground, and there were swirls of white hairs from the mule on the insides of my calves and thighs in a beautiful, delicate pattern they washed off with Ivory Soap and me, screaming.

An Intermediate Stop

———————————— *Gail Godwin* ————————————

The vicar, just turned thirty-one, had moved quietly through his twenties engrossed in the somewhat awesome implications of his calling. In the last year of what he now referred to nostalgically as his decade of contemplation, he had stumbled upon a vision in the same natural way he'd often taken walks in the gentle mist of his countryside and come suddenly upon the form of another person and greeted him. He was astonished, then grateful. He had actually wept. Afterward he was exhausted. Days went by before he could bring himself to record it, warily and wonderingly, first for himself and then to bear witness to others. Even as he wrote, he felt the memory of it, the way the pure thing had been, slipping away. Nevertheless, he felt he must preserve what he could.

Somewhere between the final scribbled word of the original manuscript and the dismay with which he now (aboard a Dixie Airways turboprop flying above red flatlands in the southern United States) regarded the picture of himself on the religion page of *Time* magazine, his tenuous visitor had fled him altogether. The vicar was left with a much-altered life, hopping around an international circuit of lecture tours (the bishop was more than pleased) that took him further and further from the auspicious state of mind which had generated that important breakthrough.

Exhibiting for his benefit a set of flawless American teeth, the stewardess now told him to be sure and fasten his seat belt. "Bayult," she pronounced it. Seat bayult. The trembly old turbo-prop nosed down toward a country airfield shimmering in the heat, and the captain's disembodied voice welcomed them all to Tri-City Airport, naming the cities and towns that it served, including one called Amity where the vicar was to address a small Episcopal college for women. "Present temperature is ninety-six degrees," said the captain mischievously, as though he himself might be responsible. A groan went up across the aisle, from several businessmen traveling together, wearing transparent short-sleeved shirts and carrying jackets made of a weightless-looking

148

material. It was the middle of September and Lewis had brought only one suit for his three-week lecture tour: a dark flannel worsted, perfect for English Septembers.

He thanked his hostess and, still vibrating to the thrum of the rickety flight, descended shaky metal stairs into the handshake of a fat gentleman who shook his hand with prolonged zest.

"Reverend Lewis, sir, it's an honor, a real honor. I'm Baxter Stikeleather, president of Earle College. How was the weather down there in New Orleans—hotter than here, I'll bet."

"How do you do, Doctor. No actually it seemed . . . not quite so hot."

"Aw, that's 'cause they've got the Gulf Coast sitting right there under their noses, that's why," said the other. Having thus contributed to the defense of his state's climate, he whipped out a huge white handkerchief and beat at his large and genial face, which was slick with perspiration.

They proceeded to the airport terminal, where Stikeleather pounced on Lewis's suitcase as though it contained the Grail and led the way to the parking lot. "The girls sure have looked forward to you coming, Reverend."

"Thank you." Lewis climbed into a roomy estate wagon whose doors bore in hand-lettered Gothic script "_Earle College for Women, founded 1889_." Stikeleather arranged his sphere of a belly comfortably behind the steering wheel. The vicar was going over in his mind what he'd lost just this morning in the New Orleans lecture: ("Getting further is not leaving the world. It is discarding assumptions, thus seeing for the first time what is already there. . . . ") _What_ was already there? What could he have meant? Once these words had connected him to an image, but that image was gone. He had continued glibly on this morning, as though he assumed everyone else knew what was already there, even if he didn't anymore. Perhaps they did know; they seemed to know. Discussing his book with people these past few weeks, he'd had the distinct feeling that they'd tapped a dimension in it that was denied to him, its author.

". . . I haven't read it yet," Stikeleather was saying, "but I sure have read a lot about it. I've got my copy, though. I'm looking forward to really immersing myself in it once the semester gets started. What a catchy title. _My Interview with God_. And from what I've heard, it was, wasn't it? Did you think up the title yourself?"

"No," Lewis said uncomfortably. "No, I shan't claim that little accomplishment."

"Oh, well," Stikeleather reassured him, "you wrote the book. That's what counts." He struck the vicar amiably between his shoulder blades and the estate wagon belched from the parking lot in a flourish of flying gravel. "Do you like music?"

"Yes, very much," replied Lewis, puzzled.

"Coming up," the president said, fiddling with knobs on the dashboard. The moving vehicle resounded at once with a sportive melody that made Stikeleather tap his foot on the carpeted floorboard. "Total Sound," he said.

"It's very nice," said Lewis. ("Matthew's familiar Chapter 6 seems at first to deal with separate subjects. It begins by talking about men who pray loudly in public rather than shut up in their own rooms, and goes on to discuss the impossibility of serving both God and Mammon. But if we look at God as Cause, or Source, and Mammon as certain outward effects, we begin to see a relation. Effects are but the reflection of something that emanates from one's own relationship with the Source. If that relationship is good—'If thine eye be single'—the effect will be full of light; if evil, full of darkness. But any deliberate intention of an effect, casting first towards Mammon with no relevance to the Source, will destroy the possibility of producing a worthwhile one. 'Every circle has its centre/Where the truth is made and meant,' and no good effect can come from focusing on peripheries.") He'd preached that sermon once, in the quiet days before the Illumination and the wretched fame that followed from his poor attempt to deter its passing.

"I went uptown," Stikeleather said, "and bought up all the copies I could find. What I was thinking, after your talk tomorrow morning, you might autograph them. I'll give each trustee one and keep two in our library. I hope you'll write a little something in mine, as well."

"I'd be delighted," Lewis said, charmed by his host's refreshing simplicity. Pale Dr. Harkins, two weeks ago at Yale: walking Lewis down the path to the Divinity School among first fallen leaves, he said, "You seem to be the first person inside organized religion—

that is, with the exception of Teilhard (naturally)—to reconcile with success the old symbols and the needs of our present ontology. I have often thought our situation today, theologically, is what the *I Ching* would call Ming I (the darkening of the light); we needed your sort of Glossary to light the way again." A Jewish boy at Columbia wedged his way under Lewis's big black umbrella and, biting his nails, hurried out with him to the taxi waiting to speed the vicar to LaGuardia for the Chicago flight. (What was his major? Something wild, eclectic, like Serbo-Croatian poetry.) He said, "But listen, Father, haven't you in an extremely subtle way, acceptable to modern intellectuals, simply reaffirmed the Bible stories?" "I . . . I intended to *affirm,* by way of modern myths, the same truths cloaked in the ancient myths, many of which we can no longer find acceptable. I hoped to contain that Truth which remains always the same within the parallels of the old and new myths . . . if you see what I mean." "Sure, Father. God between the lines." In San Francisco, he dined one night atop the city with a Unitarian minister his own age who had published an article on the six stages of LSD. The minister found Lewis's famous Interview directly comparable to stage 3 of the Trip "during which there's a sudden meaningful convergence of conceptual ideas and especially meaningful combinations in the world are seen for the first time." Over brandy, the minister offered to assist Lewis in reaching stage 6, "uniform white light," if he would care to accompany him back to his home. But Lewis had a morning lecture at Berkeley and declined the offer.

"I declare, I feel a whole lot better now, Reverend. There is nothing more necessary, to my way of thinking, than air-conditioning in your automobile. The trustees hemmed and hawed till I finally told them point-blank: I personally cannot drive the school station wagon until it is air-conditioned. I can't go picking up people in the name of the college and be sweating all over the place."

"It's jolly nice," agreed Lewis, feeling better himself. He looked out of the closed window at a baked clay landscape. A group of prisoners whose striped uniforms were covered with reddish dust labored desultorily in the terrible heat, monitored by a man carrying a gun. He remembered the quiet rainy garden in Sussex, outside the vicarage study window—how, looking out at this scene one totally relaxed moment after many hours of thought, he had seen suddenly beyond it into a larger, bolder kingdom. He had seen . . . He tried now to see it again, focusing intently on a memory of wet green grass, a tree, the sky as it had been, soft pearl, unblemished; he pushed hard at grass, tree, sky, so hard they fell away, leaving him with his own frowning reflection upon the closed window of the air-conditioned station wagon.

" . . . Unfortunate thing. My wife has the flu; she comes down with it every fall. I thought it would be risky to put you up at our house, so I asked Mrs. Grimes, our school nurse, to fix up a private room in the infirmary for you. Parents of our girls often stay there when the hotel uptown is full. I hope you aren't offended."

"Not at all," said Lewis, "It will be a change from those motels with the huge TVs and the paper seals over the lavatories."

Strikeleather whooped with appreciation over this description until Lewis began to find it rather funny and started laughing himself.

At dinner he soon became quite sure that no faculty member had actually read his book. Nevertheless, he was the undisputed focus of solicitude. Wedged between Miss Lillian Bell, who taught history and social sciences, and Miss Evangeline Lacy (American literature, English literature, and needlework), he was plied from either side with compliments, respect, and much affectionate passing back and forth of crusty fried chicken and buttermilk biscuits. He felt like a young nephew who has succeeded in the outside world and comes home to coast for a time in the undemanding company of doting maiden aunts to whom his stomach is more important than his achievements.

Miss Bell was the aggressor of the two women. Fast-talking and flirtatious, with leathery, crinkled skin and pierced ears, she played self-consciously with a tiny ceramic tomato bobbling from her earlobe. "We've all looked forward to this so much, Reverend," she said. "Most of our girls have never met an Englishman, let alone an English vicar."

"It is such a pleasure listening to your accent," crooned Miss Lacy, who had possibly been a raving beauty in her youth. Her enormous storm-gray eyes, lashed and lustrous, peered out of her old face from another era and seemed fascinated by all they saw.

"I'm going to tell you something that will surprise you, Reverend," said Lillian Bell. "Both my father and my grandfather were Episcopal ministers. You're not just saying in your book, like some are today, that God is just energy, are you?"

"Certainly not just energy," he assured her, biting into a second chicken leg and munching busily while framing his words for further explication. He was tired beyond thought. His eyes ached when he swiveled them to note that tables full of girls openly studied him. Dr. Stikeleather had gone home to make dinner for the sick wife, leaving him the only man in the dining room. He felt suddenly exhausted by explanations of something he no longer called his own. The darkening of *his* light, he felt, had reached its winter solstice. He clutched at a straw, the only thing left to him in explaining himself to this good woman: a quote from one of his reviewers. He said, "The book is, well, notes towards a new consciousness which reaches beyond known systems of theology."

Miss Bell's face closed down on him. "Are you a God-is-dead man?" she asked coldly.

"No, no!" he shouted, without meaning to. All conversation stopped. All eyes were riveted on the vicar. In a near whisper, he amended, "In my book, I try to offer a series of concepts through which persons without your fortunate religious upbringing, Miss Bell, might also have God."

"Oh, of course," said she, relieved. "I've been saying the same thing myself for years. It's our duty to share with the less fortunate. Will you have another buttermilk biscuit, Reverend?"

After dinner there was, it seemed, a coffee hour to be held in his honor. "You'll have a chance to meet our girls," said Miss Lacy, "some of them from the finest families in the state. Marguerite Earle is in her second year here."

"The Earle of the college's name?" he inquired politely. A tiny throb had set up a regular rhythm just behind his left temple.

"Dabney Littleton Earle was Marguerite's great-great-great grandfather," explained Miss Lacy. "He was a wealthy planter and built this place as his home in the late seventeen-hundreds. During the War Between the States, it was given over as a hospital for our wounded. After the war was over, unfortunately, it fell into the hands of the Freedman's Bureau, who used it for their headquarters." Here she sighed sadly and her friend Miss Bell shook her earrings furiously at the outrage. "But in 1889, the Episcopal diocese bought the property and established the college. As a matter of fact, I went here myself, but that was an awfully long time ago."

The coffee hour was in the drawing room. He stood, with a whopping great headache now, backed against a faded brocade curtain, facing a semicircle of avid ladies; holding his cup and saucer close against his chest like a tiny shield, he accepted their admiration. President Stikeleather entered suddenly. En route to Lewis, he plunged briefly into a cluster of girls long enough to pluck from it the flower of them all. Steering this elegant creature by her elbow, he cruised beaming toward the vicar.

"Reverend Lewis, may I present Miss Marguerite Earle, president of the Earle Student Body," he announced, his voice breaking with pride.

"How do you do?" said Lewis, marveling at the sheer aesthetic value of her. The flaunted English complexion paled beside this girl's pellucid sheen in which morning colors dominated. He counted five such colors in her face: honey, rose, gold, pearl, and Mediterranean blue.

She took Lewis's hand in her cool one and looked up at him with deference. "I have really looked forward to this," she said. "All of us have. Won't you sit down? Let me get you another cup of coffee."

At this gentleness within such beauty, Lewis felt close to tears. Gratefully, he let himself be led to a beige settee. Stikeleather, overflowing with pleasure, stepped over to compensate the semicircle of ladies abandoned by the vicar.

Marguerite returned with his coffee and sat down. "I think it would be wonderful to live in England. Especially the English countryside. When I graduate, if I ever do, and take my trip abroad, I'm going straight to England. I love those people in Jane Austen. So relaxed and witty and tactful with one another. You know something funny, Reverend Lewis? I felt more at home reading her than I sometimes feel in real surroundings."

"I can understand that," he said. "Yours is rather a Jane Austen style. I'm a fan of hers, myself. *Emma* has always been my favorite, however, and you know one can't honestly say she was always tactful. The thing with Miss Bates, for instance, was—Have I said something to upset you?"

"Oh, dear, I've only read _Pride and Prejudice_. We had it in Miss Lacy's class last spring. You must think I'm an idiot." The girl flushed, laced her long fingers together in confusion, and looked perfectly charming.

"Not to worry," he said. "All the better, to have _Emma_ ahead of you. You can go back into that world you love without waiting to graduate. But look—a favor for me: remember when you come to Reverend—Reverend—oh, blast, what is his name. You know, Miss Earle, I have forgotten everything but my own name these past few weeks. Well, anyway, when you come to that pompous reverend somebody in _Emma,_ don't believe all vicars are like him."

"Oh, whenever I think of an English vicar, I certainly won't think of _him,_" she said. She wore some delicate woodsy scent that opened up long-neglected channels in his dry bachelor existence. "Will you tell us about the country homes tomorrow, and the English nobility?"

"Well, certainly if there's time. I mean—if there's time. I've been invited to give my, you know, lecture on the b-book." He paused, amazed. He had not stuttered since his Oxford days, when he'd never quite mastered the knack of smooth conversation with lovely women.

"Oh, I hope there'll be time," she said. "The girls have loads of questions. Where exactly do you live?"

"In a s-small village in Sussex, near the Downs—"

"I declare I hate to disturb you-all, looking so relaxed." Stikeleather stood before the settee. "But there are some who haven't met you yet, Reverend. May I borrow him for just a minute, Marguerite? I want you to meet Miss Julia Bonham, who teaches modern dance, Reverend." He led Lewis away, toward a fulsome lady awaiting them beside the silver service.

Having finally achieved his bed in the infirmary, he couldn't sleep. He fingered the choice of bedside reading left for him by Mrs. Grimes. There was a mint-green _Treasury of Religious Verse,_ brand new, with the price $8.95 written in pencil just inside the cover; a choice of Bibles (RSV or King James); and back issues of an inspirational pamphlet called *Forward: Day by Day*. There was a paperback book of very easy crossword puzzles, most of which had been worked in pencil, then erased. Book thoughts led inevitably to consideration of his own 124-page effort, out there in the world, an object in its own right now, separate even from the thing that had inspired it, which was gone. What was that vile vicar's name in the Emma book? Pelham? Stockton? The wife with the brother-in-law in Bristol with his everlasting barouche-landau . . . When you began forgetting the villains of literature, you were definitely losing your grip.

He tried different positions: board-straight, scissors-legs, fetal. He clanked around the hospital bed like a lorry full of scrap metal. His bones strummed with phantom vibrations from the turboprop and under the bottom sheet was a waterproof pad that caused his feet to slide. "What a catchy title; did you think it up yourself?" ("What were you thinking of calling it, Mr. Lewis?" over a pint of bitter at the publisher's lunch. "Oh, I don't know. It's difficult to call it anything. It was what it was, simply: a very fleeting glimpse of God on His own terms, quite apart from all my previous notions of Him. I've said all I was able to say about this, er, glimpse, in my book. Why not just *View from a Sussex Vicarage,* something of the sort?" "Ah, come, Mr. Lewis, let us put our heads together over another pint and see if we can't come up with something more provocative. After all, 'Feed my Lambs' has become today a matter of first winning their appetites, has it not?") 'Every circle has its centre/Where the truth is made and meant,' and no good effects will come from focusing upon peripheries. "We needed your sort of Glossary to light the way again." Going out to La-Guardia in the speeding taxi, through sheets of rain, he saw the most appalling cemetery, miles and miles of dingy graves, chock-a-block. . . . "Sure, Father, God between the lines." "When You're Out of Schlitz, You're Out of Beer," he was warned again and again on the turnpike. Blessed are the pure in heart, for they shall see . . . uniform white light? And then darkness, darkness, darkness, plenty of it. What was that damn vicar's name? Parkins, Sheldon; force it. Can a fleeting vision be seized by the tail, made to perform again and again to circus music? That perfume she was wearing . . . The Blessed Henry Suso, after seeing God, was tormented by a deep depression that lasted ten years. . . . The scent reminded one of spicy green woods, hidden fresh-water springs; he knew so little of women's lore, how they created their effects, yet he was not even old, thirty-one. Was this to be his dry and barren decade, his Dark Night of the Soul? (Mr. Knightley was thirty-seven when he proposed to Emma Woodhouse.) He had been so immersed in his commitment: representative of Christ on earth. Vicar, vicarius: God's deputy. No light matter. He had trod over-carefully, unsure of his right to be there at all. Had his most un-sound days, then, been his most profound? Parnham, Parker, Pelton, Felpham, Farnhart, Rockwell, Brockton? Hell. Was there to be no Second Coming? He slept, then, dreamed he and Stike-leather sat under a tree in the vicarage garden, discussing how much it would cost to air-condition the vicarage. Marguerite and her friends, wearing flowing afternoon dresses to their ankles, played a lively game of croquet. Marguerite smashed a red ball CRASH! through his dusty study window, and he was alarmed, but then Stikeleather began laughing, his large belly jiggling up and down, and Lewis, infected, began to laugh, as well, until tears came into his eyes.

At breakfast, there were more of the buttermilk biscuits, which one soaked in a spicy ham gravy called "red-eye." Anxious about giving a lecture that had dried up on him in New Orleans, he ate too many. He signed Miss Bell's copy of *My Interview with God* feeling an imposter.

When he mounted the speaker's platform in the little chapel, ev-eryone applauded him. Eight biscuits soaked in red-eye clumped stubbornly together and refused to digest. He shuffled his pile of note cards, dog-eared from fourteen other lectures, and cleared his throat. He addressed Dr. Stikeleather, who was perspiring lightly in seersucker in the front row, and called every faculty member by name (there were only six). This caused another flurry of delighted clapping. He wished he might repeat the stunt with the girls, but there were too many of them; "charming young ladies" would have to suffice.

"Well, now," he began, flushing, and looking down at the first 4 x 6 note card. One more time, he must give this lecture. He thought of the VC–10 that would depart tonight, with him aboard, for London.

The first note card read:

a. Unitive life, df. state of transcendent vitality (Underhill)
b. Luke 14:10
c. things *seen*

He failed utterly in seeing how these puzzling fragments had ever arranged themselves into an effortless, meaningful opening. Yet here he was; here they were. What, in his totally depleted hour, could he tell them? His feet, it seemed, touched down on the abyss; the light that had been darkening steadily for a year and a half now switched off. And they were waiting, with upturned faces. What to say?

Then he saw Marguerite Earle, his croquet girl, sitting by the window, her bright hair aflame like a burning bush from the morning sun, and he remembered. His Amity muse, a veritable earthly vision, shone before him in her raiments of color with the promise of a rainbow and gave him his topic. Hands folded neatly on her lap, she smiled at him, waiting to hear.

He squared his note cards with a final clack, turned them face down on the rostrum, and said, "The reason I am here with you this morning is because nearly two years ago I was sitting calmly in my vicarage study, looking out on a peaceful rainy afternoon, and, being more or less at one with myself, was admitted—very temporarily—to the presence of God. Afterwards I thought I should preserve the experience by, ah, minting it, in printed words, rather like—well, your Treasury Department distributing the late President Kennedy on silver half-dollars. Only they never for a moment, I am sure, fooled themselves into thinking they were giving away with that coin the essence of the man. It was only a tribute, don't you see, in the same way that my book can only be a tribute to a very special happening. St. Thomas Aquinas once said, long after he'd completed his ponderous *Summa,* 'There are some things that simply cannot be uttered,' after which he serenely folded his hands over his great stomach and spent his last days elevated, they say, in rapturous prayer. Can you not see it, that great portly body floating like a thistle by the Grace of God?"

(There was a short hush during which his audience teetered between respect for a dead saint and amusement at the spectacle of a floating fat one. . . . Then Stikeleather broke the tie by laughing heartily and they all followed suit.)

"Well, then," Lewis said, a bit breathless, standing naked before them now, a man like any other, no vision standing between them, "rather than try and give you a third-hand rendition of a faded illumination, or to go over material which is there for better or for worse in a little green-and-white volume which my publishers call *My Interview with God,* I'd like to return your hospitality to me by taking you briefly into my own world. What shall I show you first? Shall we start with where I live, my vicarage in Sussex, which is five hundred years old?"

Their enthusiastic answer rang out. Marguerite Earle began clapping and they joined her. So he took them first into his study, lined with over four thousand books, many belonging to past vicars dead several hundred years, and warmed even in summer by a fireplace. He led them up narrow circular stairs to his *pièce de résistance,* the loft under the eaves where, in the sixteen-forties, it was rumored that a Royalist vicar had once hidden Charles II from his murderous pursuers. They adored this. He took them to his garden, blushing when he said, "Large enough f-for, um, a game of croquet." In summer, he told them, the Queen's orange-braceleted swans swim upriver and come waddling boldly in the garden at teatime. . . .

He took them on a Cook's tour of London; then, for the benefit of Marguerite, who loved the countryside, he returned them to Sussex Downs for a ramble. It was while lingering there, relaxed and at one with his happy group, in this dreamy country air that he remembered his old friend Mr. Elton, petty vicar of Highbury. Elton, Elton, Elton, of course! He lightened, began the upward trip from his abyss, as though St. Thomas the old dog himself had loaned him a bit of divine buoyancy. Eight buttermilk biscuits melted like hosts in his stomach. Elton! Spouse of Augusta Hawkins for the sum of ten thousand. Hypocrite, flatterer, pompous ass. Lewis had never been so glad to see anyone in his life. His universe expanded as the dark began to fade. He chuckled aloud in the midst of his guided tour. Agreeably, in a body, Earle College chuckled, too, for they were with him.

Home

—————— Shirley Ann Grau ——————

At five-fifteen when Angela Taylor got back to her office, there were six telephone messages waiting for her.

Dinny, who worked afternoons at the reception desk, said, "Mrs. Marshall called twice. She was getting impatient."

"*The* Mrs. Marshall? *My* Mrs. Marshall? God."

Dinny giggled. Mrs. Marshall was old, rich, difficult, and fond of buying and selling houses. Of the fifteen agents at Peerless Realty, only Angela Taylor dealt with her successfully.

"Well," Angela twirled the note in small circles, "she pays my commission, so I don't care. How long has she been in her present house, Dinny?"

"A couple of years," Dinny said.

"A year to remodel, a year to live in it. And now she's getting restless. Maybe I can talk her into selling this house and moving into a hotel while we look for another. That would make it easier on me." She flicked through the other messages, began whistling quietly through her front teeth. It was a childhood habit she had never corrected, and it meant that she was extremely pleased.

Dinny said, "Good news?"

"If this is what I think it is, I have just sold that monster of a Boudreaux place. I'll get on this right now."

In her glass-walled office cubicle, she kicked off her shoes, wiggled her toes against the soft carpeting. Her back was aching—wrong shoes again. She'd just have to start wearing sensible laced oxfords. They looked dreadful, but she was on her feet too much and the days were just too long. . . . She dropped into her chair and fought off the desire to put her feet on the desk—hardly proper office behavior. She rubbed her face briskly; her makeup had worn off, leaving the skin slightly rough to the touch. It was time to go back to Monsieur Raoul for another series of treatments.

She tossed a half pack of cigarettes into the wastebasket; she would take a fresh one tomorrow morning. She always did. She'd

160

discovered that no matter how annoying or stupid a client was, how devious, uncertain, and utterly exhausting, she needed only to light a cigarette, slowly, slowly, and after the first puff consider the burning tip as if it were the most interesting thing in the world—her annoyance would vanish, her calm return. (Even clients seemed impressed by her solemn ponderous movements.) In all this time—and she'd been a successful agent for twenty years—she'd never grown to like tobacco. She needed it, and it became part of her working day, like the pale pastel suits she wore all year round, very smooth, very well-tailored, with never a pleat or a ruffle on them.

She arranged her telephone messages carefully in order of importance. Took a deep breath and began. It was then five-thirty.

"Miss Prescott, please." A pause. "Look, Vicky, just wait for me. I think I'm finally getting rid of the Boudreaux house and I've got to close before they change their mind. I'm running late, I just got back here, and I've got a list of other calls—a good half hour before I can leave. Okay?"

She scarcely waited for Vicky's answer, she was so eager to get on with the business of the Boudreaux property. The old uptown Victorian house had been on the market for two years, it was way overpriced—and now she had a buyer.

It wasn't until she'd finished—all calls answered, details for the Boudreaux transaction settled, Mrs. Marshall put off until the end of the week—that she remembered the edge in Vicky's voice.

Angela paused, hand holding the phone halfway to the cradle. Dear lord, not one of Vicky's moods. Not when things were going so well and she was feeling so very pleased with herself. . . . She remembered that cool edgy voice. . . . Another mood, probably made worse by that hasty phone call.

She shrugged away her annoyance. Vicky was like that—constantly demanding assurance as if she were a child and not a nearly middle-aged woman.

And that, Angela thought, never would change.

She put her shoes back on, grimacing. She was the last in the office; she switched off the lights and set the burglar alarm as she left.

In the parking lot the summer air was still and hot, the fading light an uncertain pale yellow. She hurried to her car, turned on air conditioner and radio, and took her place in the slow-moving lines of traffic.

Vicky was waiting just outside the shop. Over her head, across the entire second-floor facade, a five-foot signature announced *Victoria*.

Angela looked with approval at the large flowing white script. My idea, she thought, and a damn good one. Flash without trash, she chuckled to herself.

There were still people in the shop: late afternoon was always busy. The last customers often didn't finish until nearly seven, crossing paths with the incoming night security guard.

She'd been right about the location: Angela gave herself another little pat on the back. She didn't usually handle commercial property, but that didn't mean she didn't know a good thing when she saw it. And this location was perfect for an expensive shopping area. She knew it and she worked hard to see that it developed correctly. She even put a lot of her own money into the area—at the start when things needed a push. Eventually she sold out very profitably, so that now the only thing she owned, with Vicky, was the handsome two-story building that housed the dress shop.

Angela brought the car to a stop. Vicky, small, trim, dark, wearing a lavender dress, slipped quickly inside. Bal á Versailles filled the car.

Ever so much the trim businesswoman, Angela thought with a glint of amusement, except for that perfume. Too heavy a scent, too many flowers had died to produce it.

"I thought you'd never come," Vicky snapped. "Another half hour and I'd have called a cab."

"And be deprived of my charming company?" Yes, Vicky was in one of her moods; the only thing was to pretend not to see it, to be flip and casual. "A good day?"

"Average." Vicky wiped an invisible speck of dust from the dashboard. "The shipment from Arnold didn't arrive, of course."

"They're always late," Angela said. "Don't I remember some terrible confusion with last fall's line?"

"You do." Vicky slumped back in her seat and stared straight ahead. "I don't know why I keep dealing with them. They are so impossible."

"Because, luv, you like their clothes, and your customers like
their clothes and they pay ridiculous prices for them and you turn
a tidy little profit. Which is why you put up with all the nonsense
from Arnold."

"Huum," Vicky said. And fell silent.

The flowers of Bal á Versailles were as suffocating as smoke.

Except for a single lamp in the entrance foyer, their apartment was
dark. "Well now," Angela said as she flipped the wall switches
that filled the rooms with soft irregular patterns of light, "home at
last, far from the madding crowd, the bustle of commerce. Now
we discover what Madame Papa has left for us to have with our
cocktails."

"Angela, why do you call her that? If she hears, she's going to
quit and she is such a good housekeeper."

Angela raised her eyebrows. So the silence is over, she thought.
How nice of you to make your first words criticism. . . . I was
really getting used to the quiet. I really enjoyed whistling and
humming to the radio all that long drive home.

But she said nothing aloud. In their fifteen years together she
had learned that nothing she could do would alter Vicky's moods.
Sometimes she wondered if Vicky herself controlled them. Sometimes she knew she did not, that they were seizures or spasms
quite independent of the body they inhabited.

Ignoring the neatly stacked mail, Angela crossed the living
room. "I'm having a drink. You want one?" The curtains were
closed, and she wondered if she should open them—there was still
a bit of soft twilight in the park outside their windows. No, she
thought, drink first. "A drink, Vicky?"

"You're not going to open the curtains?"

She reads my thoughts. Angela gave a mental shrug. . . . "Later.
I need my drink to celebrate. This was a very good day."

In the small bar the glasses and bottles and ice were waiting.
God bless Madame Papa, Angela thought fervently. She filled the
largest glass with ice and poured the gin, not bothering to measure. The feel of the bottle in her hand cheered her immensely, as
did the small dish of lemon peel. Madame Papa, whose name was
Papadopoulous, was a most efficient housekeeper. And, Angela

thought, taking the first long taste of her martini, she makes the most marvelous baklava; why didn't I ever have baklava when I was a child . . .

She stopped abruptly and laughed out loud. The thought was so silly, so utterly silly. The kitchen in her mother's house had been staffed by large black women who presided over greasy black stoves that were never cleaned and large black pots whose outsides were crinkled with grease and age until they resembled an alligator's skin. The pots rattled, half-burned wood spoons thumped against their sides, and the kitchen filled with steam and loud voices and laughter. The food was greasy and heavy and delicious. But, she thought, it wasn't baklava.

She waved her glass and laughed again.

"What did you say?" Vicky called.

"Nothing."

"You were laughing."

So shoot me, Angela thought. But she only said calmly, "I was thinking of the kitchen when I was a child." She added more gin and ice to her glass and turned back to the living room, where Vicky was thumbing through the mail.

"Here," Vicky said. "A fund-raiser for Hart."

"For who?"

"Gary Hart. You know, the next President of the United States."

"Ah," Angela said. "Didn't we just go to something for him? Cocktails in the park with little zoo animals wandering around underfoot."

"That was cocktails and only twenty-five dollars." Vicky was studying the heavy card carefully. "This one is two hundred and fifty."

"Good lord," Angela said, "he must really be serious."

"Look at the list of sponsors." Vicky's practiced eye scanned the long list. "At least ten are customers. We'll have to go."

"I suppose," Angela said to the ice cubes, "you are going to sell them dresses for that event and you are going to make a lot more than the five hundred dollars it's going to cost us."

Vicky said, "I'll put it in the book. The twenty-second."

"I suppose," Angela went on ruminatively to her martini, "your Hart-inclined customers see you there and think you are one of them. And your Reagan customers aren't there to see that you are not one of _them_."

"What?" Vicky frowned slightly. "We are going to a Reagan lunch, I forget the exact date, but it's in the book."

"Behold the devious mind of a retailer." The alcohol was filtering into her blood now. A pleasant warmth began in the pit of her stomach and spread upward, washing over her ears like some soft tropical sea. She sat down and kicked off her shoes.

Vicky went on thumbing through the mail, opening and sorting quickly. For a fraction of a second she hesitated over one letter, then with an impatient gesture tossed all remaining ones aside.

Oh, oh . . . Angela watched the quick flip of the small hand, the flash of rings . . . what's this? That letter annoyed her very much. What do we have here?

"Angela, I asked you about the curtains."

"Open them if you like," Angela said, wiggling her toes.

"I was asking if _you_ wanted them. I don't. I don't like this time of day at all. The way the light hits the windows and they shine back like blank eyes, like eyes with cataracts. You know that."

"No, I didn't know that. I don't think you ever said that before."

"I hate this time of day."

"A martini?" Angela suggested again.

"I'll get it," Vicky said. "You put in too much vermouth."

"Ah well." Angela lifted her glass and toasted the ceiling. Things were going to be very difficult, but at least Vicky was talking. Once last year she had not said a word for three days. The absolute silence had eaten into Angela's nerves, though she'd managed to maintain her calm indifferent exterior. She'd even considered some kind of record keeping, some sort of cryptic numbers on a calendar. But Vicky might have found it, might have guessed. And that would have hurt her—she thought of herself as even-tempered and easygoing.

Angela whistled at the ceiling, a bit of the Colonel Bogie march. I wonder if I could stand another one of those, she thought, another record-breaking tantrum.

Vicky tossed herself into the opposite chair. She'd made her drink carelessly. Her lavender dress showed a broad pattern of splash marks.

Angela waited for the liquor to soften her mood. Patient, un-moving, almost not breathing . . .

Vicky drank very fast, and at the end gave a little sigh, a tiny sound like an echo.

Angela said, "I had one fantastic sale today. The old Boudreaux place."

Vicky stared directly at her, round blue eyes registering no com-prehension, no acknowledgment.

"Just about everybody in the office had tried with it and no luck. Then I remembered that couple from Clarksdale—we met them somewhere about a year ago—they talked about wanting to move to town, and they said they wanted a big old house to do over. A period piece, I remember them saying. So I called them and because they have far more money than sense, they bought that ghastly monster."

Vicky's eyes didn't change.

This is going to be quite an evening, Angela thought. And then, aloud, "We have tickets for that experimental theater tonight. Do you want to go?"

Vicky's eyes snapped suddenly into focus. "No."

"It probably isn't very good." Angela kept her voice even and toneless. "Let's have dinner downstairs at Paul's and then come home."

"I have been to Paul's so often I know that menu by heart. I know how every single thing is going to taste before I taste it."

"When you live in a building, you tend to eat downstairs fairly often because it is so convenient."

"I hate it."

"Well now"—the smallest trace of anger appeared in Angela's voice—"I certainly don't feel like fixing supper here. I think I'll go to dinner and then have a look at that foolish play or multimedia presentation or whatever they call it."

Vicky's eyes glittered and changed, sparkles like tinsel appeared in the blue irises.

Her eyes were so damned expressive, Angela thought. They showed hurt too clearly, you could see the blood of invisible wounds. Faced by their pain, Angela retreated to the pantry for another drink. Deliberately, measuring carefully, she fixed the martini, tossed both lemon and olive on top the ice. Still elaborately casual, she sauntered back, stopping to pick up the mail Vicky had tossed aside. On top, with its clear printing, its elaborately scrolled capitals, was a letter from Angela's daughter, Louise. Why had that upset Vicky?

The paper crackled loudly in the silence as she smoothed the folded sheets. "Your glass is empty, Vicky. Why don't you have another drink while I read this."

Angela was not sure how she felt about her daughter, that beautiful young woman who seemed capable of endless understanding without a hint of malice or anger. She'd adjusted to her parents' divorce, had lived happily with her father, had grown to love her stepmother. With Vicky, she'd been quietly friendly, relaxed, and quite free of embarrassment. Cool, disciplined, well organized, a model student in college, now working on an MFA, she was married to an associate professor of economics who looked like a young John Wayne.

Perfection, Angela thought. How could I have produced anything so damn perfect. . . . And where was Vicky?

She was standing at the refrigerator, one finger rubbing a small circle on the door. Carefully Angela put her arms around her. In the softness of that body and the muskiness of that hair, Angela felt again the familiar rush of pain and love and tenderness. And something else, something darker and stronger. Something she could not name, something she refused to think about, a force that gave a restless desperation to her life.

Wearily, for the uncounted thousandth time, Angela pushed back the thing that crouched waiting in the shadows. She heard the crackling of its voice and the swishing of its tail. Not yet, she told it, not yet. Not this time.

And softly into Vicky's ear, pink curves under wisps of black hair, "We're both tired, honey. Come on, let's finish our drinks now. I saw some kind of dip in the refrigerator. And after a while we'll go and have dinner at Paul's, but we won't try the theater. Not tonight, when we're both so tired."

Vicky nodded silently, eyes closed, anger lines fading from her small face—the wistful, heart-shaped face that had haunted Angela ever since they first met, years ago, when Vicky was a college student, Angela a young matron with a husband and child.

Now again, as always, seeing Vicky's face close up, seeing the perfect porcelain skin, the lash-fringed eyes, naturally shadowed as some Irish eyes are, the thin-lipped and very small mouth—the face of a mannequin—Angela was reminded again of the toys of her childhood, the dolls whose china heads she had smashed open against rocks just to see the glass eyes spring out and roll away.

Dinner was pleasant. They knew a dozen people in the restaurant, they waved to them. The Bartons, their neighbors down the hall, joined them in the bar for an after-dinner brandy. It was the sort of evening Angela liked best—lively, amusing, time filled with people who were not close to you. Nice people, people you liked, people who were gone before they became tiresome.

Vicky's moodiness vanished. She talked gaily with the Bartons, laughing at their long stories of misfortune and confusion during a trip to Hong Kong.

By eleven they were home. "Huuuu." Angela closed the door and leaned against it. "I am tired!" She stretched, rubbed her eyes. "Bed is going to feel so good."

They had separate bedrooms now that the first frenzy of love had passed and they no longer required a presence within arm's reach all night. Angela shook her head, still puzzled by the lust of those early years, the rhythmic beating of blood that silenced everything else. They had been, she thought, more than a little crazy.

Eventually balance and control had come back. Or was it weariness? Angela yawned. Age and habit finally muffled everything, that was sure.

She ran her bath, poured in oil, and eased herself into the slippery tub, sighing with comfort. These pleasures were becoming more and more important to her—the perfumed hot tub, the wide bed all to herself, the smooth cool sheets with their embroidered edges.

She soaked, half asleep, remembering the first time she met Vicky, fifteen years ago. It seemed even longer than that, all the figures were fuzzy and out of focus, softened by time and distance.

It was a Thursday. Angela and Neal always went out to dinner on Thursday. Their ten-year-old daughter stayed with the housekeeper, Felicia, a thin pious spinster who left the house only for early Sunday mass, who never touched the television, and who turned on the radio only for the evening rosary in Spanish. All her salary went into a savings account. One day she would return to Guatemala and start a shop, a fabric shop that also sold candies and baked goods, she told Angela. But years passed and Felicia did not go home. She seemed to have forgotten her plans. After the divorce she stayed with John and the child. When they moved, she went with them. She was still there; Louise's letters mentioned her occasionally: "Felicia, dour as ever."

On that Thursday night fifteen years ago, the night her life changed, Angela and her husband had dinner early and went to the University Theater for a production of _The Glass Menagerie,_ directed by Neal's sister. Angela was bored: the actors were painfully amateur, the staging was awkward. Still, remembering Neal's sister, she applauded dutifully and smiled and tried very hard to be encouraging. Afterwards they went to the cast party in the student center, where they hugged and kissed everybody and laughed loudly and made silly toasts in beer. And Angela met Vicky.

She remembered the exact moment she first saw her—a jolt, a shock. Too violent to be pleasant. (Vicky remembered it differently: "I didn't notice you until you spoke to me, Angela. And then I thought you had a lovely voice.")

Angela remembered it all—the way the room smelled: beer, dust, sweat, the sourish odor of makeup, the sweet smell of cold cream. Somebody broke a confetti egg against the roof and bits of colored paper whirled in the air like bright midges. Neal and his sister were at the bar filling their mugs, laughing and talking as they worked their way through the crowd. A group of student stagehands in T-shirts and blue jeans gathered in one corner, fifteen or twenty of them, stretched on the dusty floor, perched on the windowsills. Vicky was there. She was standing in the bewildered way that was so characteristic of her, hands limply at her sides, a small frail figure in large overalls, dark hair cut short in fashionable imitation of Mia Farrow. She seemed utterly alone in the midst of the crowd.

Angela walked briskly across the room and touched Vicky's sleeve. "I feel that I know you," she said. "Isn't your name Vicky?"

"No," Vicky said.

"It should be. Vicky Prescott."

"It's not."

"It is now," Angela said. "I just gave you a new name."

Three months later they moved into a small apartment near the campus. Angela took four suitcases of clothes—nothing else—with her.

When she told Neal, he said nothing, absolutely nothing. His face froze, then gradually drained of color until the bones showed as dark shadows. His lips turned white and then a clear pale blue. Without a word he went upstairs into the bedroom and locked the door.

Felicia said he stayed in the room all that day, and there hadn't been a sound. The morning of the second day he appeared at breakfast, he read the paper and talked with his daughter; he asked Felicia formally to stay on as housekeeper, and he drove the child to school. She was delighted; usually she took the bus.

A year later, to the day, Neal sued for divorce. Angela did not contest child custody, finding that weekend afternoons with her daughter were quite enough. She and Neal met occasionally at lunch to agree on the details of the dissolution of their marriage. "You know I have quite enough income of my own," she told him. "I do not think I should ask you for anything."

He nodded gravely. (He seemed to have become very ponderous and solemn, she thought.) "When will you come to the house to select the things you want to keep?"

She shook her head.

"Things of sentimental value? Things from your family?"

"There is nothing," she said. "Nothing at all."

Three years later Neal moved to the West Coast, to begin his own consulting firm. Angela supervised the packing and the moving. And declined again the offer of furniture. Neal kissed her good-bye on one cheek, her daughter on the other. (Vicky had not come, she had always refused to meet Neal.) Then they were gone, astonished at how very simple and easy it all had been.

Six months later there was a formal announcement of Neal's marriage. After that, from a distance, Angela saw her daughter through the rituals of growing up—birthday presents, summer visits, graduation presents, wedding presents. All conducted quietly and factually and coolly, like the business transactions they really were.

Drowsy and comforted by the warm perfumed waters, Angela left the tub, toweled carelessly, reached for a nightgown without looking at it. She patted the heavy embroidery on the edge of the sheet once or twice and fell into a deep black sleep.

When Vicky slipped into her bed next to her, she scarcely stirred. "Tomorrow." She pulled away. "Vicky, it's late and I'm tired."

"I don't want to make love," Vicky whispered so close to her ear that her breath tickled unpleasantly.

"You can't be this spoiled," Angela muttered. "Go away."

"I have to talk to you." There was that rasping note of decision in the soft voice.

Oh, oh, oh, Angela thought in her comfortable sleepy haze, I hope this isn't going to be one of Vicky's long rambling middle-of-the-night talks. "I'm dead tired, Vicky. You can't be this selfish."

"I have to talk to you now." The small voice was cool and steady.

Well, Angela thought, maybe it won't be such a long talk. . . . She rolled over, reaching for the lamp switch. Vicky's hand closed over hers, stopping it.

"No, I want to talk in the dark," Vicky said. "I always talk better in the dark."

"You always talk longer in the dark." Angela squinted at the green dial on the clock: three-fifteen. "I've got a nine-fifteen appointment, and just look at the time."

"Now," Vicky repeated.

Angela sighed deeply, pulled the pillows up behind her, and settled back against them. For a moment she dozed—then shook herself awake. Vicky remained curled in the middle of the bed.

"My dear," Angela said, stifling a yawn, "this had better be important or I am going to be perfectly furious with you."

"I want a child," Vicky said. "I want to get pregnant."

In the silence a far-off clock ticked steadily. A police siren waved a thin finger of sound down a distant street.

"That is important," Angela said dryly.

Vicky was silent, unmoving.

"Is there anything more you want?"

A small despairing hiss, like air from a balloon. "I knew you'd misunderstand."

"You must give me a moment," Angela said, "to catch up with you." (Is this how Neal felt when I told him—when the unthinkable happens?)

"I knew you'd be angry . . . and I knew you'd misunderstand. I've been dreading this so much that I've been putting it off and putting it off. For months. I just couldn't tell you."

"You have lost your mind."

The bed moved slightly. Vicky was shaking her head. "I don't want to want a child, you see. I know it would be trouble, and I thought you might even leave."

Did you? Angela thought. I don't believe that.

"It got so bad, I even began going to a psychiatrist."

"I didn't know."

"I thought at first it would go away, so I waited. But it didn't. I thought about a tranquilizer or an energizer or lithium if I was really crazy."

"A strange pharmacopoeia," Angela said into the dark. "Was the shrink any help?"

"No drugs," Vicky said sadly, raising her head slightly so that she showed briefly as a silhouette against the pale yellow wallpaper. "He said it would be months or years before anything could change. If then."

"No help from him."

"No," Vicky said.

The clock was still ticking, but the siren had vanished. The room was filled with a faint humming, the building's air-conditioning system. Like the far-off hum of bees, Angela thought. There'd been hives on her family's summer place in Maine.

Vicky was talking again, rapidly, slurring her words. Angela noticed the heavy smell of brandy. She'd been drinking, and she probably hadn't been to bed at all.

"I didn't want you to be angry. I tried every way I knew. But nothing helped. It's even getting worse."

"The urge to procreate."

Vicky sobbed softly.

Dear God, Angela thought, if I still believed in you, I would think that you are punishing me for my sins. But I left Sunday school too long ago for that. . . .

"You've got to understand," Vicky said. "You've always helped before. Even when my parents died. You were so kind then."

They'd been killed in a highway accident and Vicky, wild with grief, neither ate nor slept. Finally Angela took her, dizzy with Librium, for a six months' trip through Europe. They worked their way page by page through the points of interest listed in their Baedekers. They climbed mountains, hiked through forests, they exhausted themselves in the thin Jura air and staggered through the smells of Naples.

"Listen to me now." Vicky spoke clearly and slowly, as if she were instructing a child. "I am thirty-six. How much longer can I have children. One child. I feel, I don't know, I feel hollow and empty and useless. Sometimes I feel so light I think the wind will blow me away."

"It won't," Angela said.

"You have a child." The harsh accusation startled Angela. "You have a child. Every time a letter comes from her, every time she telephones and talks to us, I want to die. Because I have nothing."

Nothing, Angela thought dully, sadly. You have me. And your career. You are the owner of a very successful shop. You have friends. You have a lovely apartment. And just today I saw a carriage house uptown, not too large, early nineteenth century, with lovely cypress woodwork, and a garden that is completely enclosed by a high brick wall, a perfect house for us. And you have love.

"Nothing," Vicky repeated as if she had heard.

"I'm going to get a drink."

"Take mine." Vicky put her glass carefully into Angela's hand. "I want you to understand, but I'm not saying it very well."

"I understand," Angela said.

"No," Vicky said. "I love my life. I love you and I love my work. There isn't anybody else, you know that. I make more money every year. So it isn't any of the things it's supposed to be—not sex, not money, not boredom."

"That what the psychiatrist said?" Angela drained the glass, almost choking on the straight brandy. She hated drinking like this, in a race for comfort.

"Not exactly, but I guess so, really."

"Look, Vicky." Angela tried to put the glass on the night table, missed in the dark, and heard the glass roll across the rug. "It's late, we have to work tomorrow. Why don't we both come home early and have a sensible discussion."

"No," Vicky said. "I know what I'm going to do."

"Get pregnant?"

"Yes." The darkness and the small voice and the absolute determination.

I am angry, Angela thought, I am white hot and frozen with anger. "You seem to have thought it out. Have you decided how? I mean, you are an attractive woman, you can certainly find a man. You could even shop around until you found a man whose face you'd like to have repeated in a child."

A small sigh. And silence. Vicky was not going to be lured into an argument.

"I suppose," Angela went on, "you could always have it done artificially. Like a cow."

This time Vicky was silent so long that Angela thought that she had fallen into a drunken sleep. Her own eyelids strained in the confining dark, dry and aching.

Eventually Vicky said, "At least then my bones and blood will be quiet."

"Just what I always wanted: quiet blood." Angela bounced out of bed, went to the pantry. She poured a large brandy, noticing that the bottle was almost empty. I ought to get out, she thought, I ought to take the car and go for a long drive and just keep driving around until things make more sense to me.

But she didn't. She went back into the bedroom. "Time's winged chariot."

"It's like being thirsty," Vicky said. "You have to have water."

"Brandy. Do you know how much brandy you've drunk? The bottle is almost empty."

"To give me courage," Vicky said simply.

And there it was, the tone, the motion, the gesture that ended all discussion, all argument. Why am I like this, Angela thought, why can she always do this to me. . . . Why does she turn me around? Why can't I leave, even for a drive. Is there so much of my life invested here?

"You are proposing that you and I raise this child together?"

"Yes," Vicky said. "At first I thought you might want to leave, but now I don't think so. I think it will be all right and you will love the child because it's half me."

"Jesus Christ." Angela made another trip to the pantry to empty the bottle of brandy into her glass and top it with soda and the bits of ice that remained in the bucket. The clock there said four-thirty.

Vicky uncurled and lay stretched crosswise on the foot of the bed. Angela sat down Indian-fashion to keep from touching her. "All right, Vicky, we'll raise the child together. If that's what you want."

Vicky's voice was thick with sleep and alcohol. "I knew you would."

"How the hell could you know that?"

Vicky stretched and prepared to fall asleep where she was. "I knew."

Do you know how much of my life I have invested in you? Do you? You, a small arrangement of bones and skin and flesh and blood that I would kill if it would free me. But it wouldn't.

Vicky lay so still Angela thought she had fallen asleep. She got up slowly, carefully, not to disturb her, and began tiptoeing toward the door.

Vicky said clearly, without the slur of alcohol, "You're going to love the child. And I'm going to come to hate it."

"Go to sleep, Vicky." And stop talking, let me alone for a while anyway. Before something I can't imagine or control happens . . .

"You're going to love the part that's me, and I'm going to hate the part that isn't you."

"Vicky, you are terribly drunk. You're not making sense."

"I want your child," Vicky said. "A child that's you and me. Now tell me why that's so stupid."

And with a slight movement and a small sigh, she turned face down and fell asleep. The mattress moved softly with her sudden increase in weight.

Angela went into the living room. She felt strange and detached and very calm. She opened the curtains and stared at the city that stretched beyond the pale reflection of herself. She raised an arm, saluting herself in the imperfect mirror. She was breathing regularly and slowly, all anger and fear were gone. But the moving arm didn't belong to her, nor did that figure reflected distantly back to her.

Traffic flickered slowly through the leaf-obscured streets, lights were beginning to show in some of the distant hill houses, it would not be long until daylight.

She sat at her desk and began a note to Mrs. Papadopoulous, saying that Vicky was not to be disturbed, no matter how long she slept. She herself would call the shop to tell them that Miss Prescott would be late, if indeed she came in at all today, please do not call, any decisions can wait until tomorrow.

She watched the sky. Despite the brandy, she was not drunk, she wasn't even tired. Her mind moved lightly, decisively, thoughts clicking like high heels on marble.

When the first gray morning streaks showed, she would make coffee and scramble a couple of eggs. She would shower and dress, and go to her office earlier than usual. She would finish the paperwork there and then she would make an offer for that uptown carriage house, whose small walled garden would be a lovely safe place for a child to play.

Solomon's Seal

Mary Hood

When they were courting, her people warned her, but she knew better. Who had kept them in meat through the Hoover years? With his rabbit boxes and early mornings, he was a man already, guarding a man's politics and notions, and like a mountain, wearing his own moody climate, one she prospered in. He brought the rabbits to her mother's kitchen window and held them up by the hind legs, swinging them like bells. When he skinned them and dressed them, she watched his quick knife as though learning. But she never did.

How they started out, that was how they wound up: on the same half-acre, in the same patched cabin. He was no farmer. Anything that grew on that red clay was *her* doing. After a few years she had cleared the stones from the sunny higher ground, piling them in a terrace, backfilling with woods dirt she gathered in flour sacks on her walks. She planted strawberries there. In the red clay of the garden she grew beans in the corn, peas, tomatoes, and bunching onions an uncle had given her as a wedding present. Some years, when the rains favored, she grew squash and mushmelons, the sweet little ones like baby heads.

They never had children. They never lacked dogs. He kept a pen full of coon dogs and spent the nights with them in the moonlight, running them, drinking with his friends, unmending the darns she had applied to his overalls. He was a careless man. He had a way of waiting out her angers, a way of postponing things by doing something else just as necessary. So she postponed a few things too. She didn't even unpack her trunk filled with linens and good dishes her mama and aunts had assembled for her. They had practically blinded themselves sewing white on white, making that coverlet, but it was yellowed now, in its original folds, deep in the napthaed heart of her hope chest. What was the use of being house-proud in a house like that? She decided it was good enough for him to eat off oilcloth. She decided he didn't care if his cup-

matched his saucer, and if he didn't care, why should she? She decided after a time to give as good as she got, which wasn't much. The scarcity of it, and her continuous mental bookkeeping, set her face in a mask and left her lips narrowed. She used to sing to him, before they could afford a radio. Now he had the TV on, to any program, it didn't matter which, and watched it like a baby watches the rustling leaves of a tree, to kill a little time between feedings. She didn't sing to him anymore. She didn't sing at all. But she talked to her plants like they were people.

Sometimes he thought maybe there was company in the yard, and he'd move to the window to see if a man had come to buy one of his dogs. But it was only her. He'd give the wall a knock with the side of his fist, just to let her know he was listening.

"I'm praying," she'd say, without looking up from where she was pouring well water from a lard pail onto the newest seedlings.

"Witch," he'd mutter, and go back to his TV.

She had the whole place covered by now; she was always bringing in new plants, little bothersome herbs she warned him against stepping on in his splayed boots as he stumbled along the trails she had outlined in fieldstones. The paths narrowed as she took more and more room for her pretties. It was like a child's game, where he could or could not step. And what were they anyway but weeds? Not real flowers, like his mama had grown. He told her that often enough. He'd been all over that lot and had never seen one rose. Sometimes he stopped at the hardware store and lifted a flat of petunias to his nose, but they weren't like the ones he remembered, they didn't smell like anything. He asked her about it, asked if she reckoned it was the rockets and satellites. She knew better. She blamed it on the dogs.

She blamed his dogs for stinking so you couldn't smell cabbage cooking. The health department ought to run him in, she said. He said if she called them she'd wind up in hell faster than corn popping. She said if he cut across the lower terrace one more time he'd be eating through a vein in his arm till his jaw healed, if ever. When he asked what she was so mad about, she couldn't for the life of her remember, it was a rage so old.

The madder she got, the greener everything grew, helped along, in the later years, by the rabbit manure. He was too old now to run rabbits in the field. And the land had changed, built up all around, not like it used to be. So he rigged up cages at home and raised rabbits right there. Then it was rabbits and dogs and TV and his meals and that was his whole life. That and not stepping on her plants.

He removed the spare tire from the trunk of the Dodge and fastened it to the roof of the car. In the extra space, and after taking off the trunk lid, he built a dog box. He started carrying his better hounds to the field trials and she went along too, for the ride. Everywhere they went she managed to find a new plant or two. She kept a shovel in the back seat, and potato-chip bags or cut-off milk jugs to bring the loot home in. They'd ride along, not speaking, or speaking both at once, her about the trees, him about the dogs, not hearing the one thing they were each listening their whole life for.

Sometimes she drank too. Sometimes, bottle-mellowed, they turned to each other in that shored-up bed, but afterward things were worse somehow, and he'd go off the whole next day to visit with other cooners, and she'd walk for miles in the woods, seeking wake-robin or Solomon's seal. She always dug at the wrong time, or too shallow, or something. For a few hours it would stand tall as it had grown, but the color would slowly fade, and with it her hopes. She'd be out there beside it, kneeling, talking to it softly, when he'd drive in, red-faced, beery. He'd see her turned back and head on up to the kennel to stand a few minutes, dangling his hands over the fence at the leaping dogs.

Forty years like that. It surprised her very much when he told her he wanted a divorce. He had been in the hospital a week and was home again. While he was in the hospital they told her not to upset him, so she held back the news. When he got home he found out that three of his whelps were sick and two more had already died. It was Parvo virus, locally epidemic, but the vet couldn't persuade him it wasn't somehow _her_ fault. He spent the nights, sick as he still was, sitting up with the dogs, feeding them chicken soup from one of her saucepans. That was how the final argument started, her resenting that. If she really wanted to help him, he said, she'd just leave him alone. We'll see how you like that, she said, and took some clothes and went to her sister's. While she was there, a man came and served her with papers. He's crazy, is what he is, she said to the ferns; consider the source, she said to the laurel. He didn't want her? She knew better.

She used the rabbit's foot to rouge her cheeks, to add a little color. It surprised her, tying on her scarf to go to court, how much her face looked like his. The likeness was so sudden it startled her into a shiver. "Rabbit running over your grave," she said, thinking she was saying it to him.

There wasn't anything to the divorce. Uncontested, it was all over with very soon. But there was some heat over the division of property. He wound up with the house and she got the lot. He had custody of the dogs. He had six months to remove them and any-thing he wanted from the property, and after that he must stay away forever. He had the house moved in one piece. He hired a mover to come and load it onto a truck and haul it away. He set it up on a lot north of the river, among the pines, and in a few months he had pens for the dogs built alongside so he didn't have to walk far.

She bought a secondhand mobile home and moved it onto her lot when his six months were up. He had left things pretty well torn up; the housemovers had crushed and toppled her trellises and walls. She had weeks of work to right that. Even though it was all final, she was still afraid. She painted pieces of board with KEEP OUT and DO NOT DIG and nailed them to the trees. She tied scraps of rag to wires she ran from tree to tree, setting apart the not-to-be-trod-upon areas. She listened sharp, kept her radio tuned low, in case he was out there, coming back, like he used to, knock-ing over trash cans, beating on the door, crying, "It's me . . . Carl . . . let me in?"

But he didn't come back. She had no word of him at all, though she knew well enough where he was living, like some wild thing, deep in the woods with his hounds. Sometimes she saw his car going down the main road, it couldn't be missed, with that funny dog crate nailed in the trunk and the spare tire on the roof. She could watch the road from the hilltop as she stood at her clothes-line. He drove as slow as always. It maddened her to see him go by so slow, as though he were waiting for her to fling herself down the hill headlong, to run after him crying, "Carl! Come back!" She wouldn't. She went on with her laundry. The old towel she picked up from the basket next was so bleach-burned it split in two when she snapped it. She hung the pieces on the line between her and the road, turned her back, picked up her basket, and headed for her trailer, down the hill, where he couldn't see her, though she knew how he drove, never looking left or right, even when she rode along with him, not turning his head one inch in her direction as he went on and on about the dogs. No more neck than a whale.

She was at the post office buying a money order when she heard he had remarried. She knew that couldn't be true. It wasn't a reliable source. She asked around. Nobody knew. She let it get to her, she couldn't rest just thinking of it. She didn't care; if she just knew for *sure,* that was it. "He's seventy-two years old," she said. Meaning: who could stand him but his dogs? She was out raking leaves from the main path when she decided to go see for herself. She finished up in her garden and changed to a clean shirt. She walked out to the store and phoned Yubo to come take her. Yubo was planting Miss Hamilton's garden, always did plant beans on Good Friday, and he wouldn't be there right away. She said as soon as possible, and stood at the store waiting. It gave her time to think over what she was going to say when she got there. She knew where it was; she'd been by there once, just to see how it looked, had held her pocketbook up to shield her face in case he happened to be there and noticing anybody going by. Not that he was a noticer. She drank Coca-Cola while she waited, and when Yubo came she almost said take me home, because the long wait and the walk in the sun and the whole project was making her dizzy. But she had come this far, and so had Yubo.

The house looked about the same as when it had been hers, except it stood on concrete blocks now instead of those shimmed-up rocks from the river. She told Yubo to wait. She walked down the drive to the door, which was open, unscreened, and she called, before she could think better, "I'm home," but of course she meant, "I'm here." Confused, she didn't say anything when the woman came out to see who it was. An old woman as big and solid as Carl, bare-armed, bright-eyed. One of the dogs was out of the pen, two of the dogs, and they were following right at her heels. They had the run of the house! The old woman sat on the steps and the dogs lay beside her, close enough so she could pet them as they panted against her bare feet. "Carl's not here," the old woman said.

"I was just passing by," she said, and turned to go to Yubo, who had the taxi backed around and waiting. It wasn't a real taxi, not a proper taxi, and it was considerably run down. Still, she slammed the door harder than necessary. The wind of its closing made the just-set-out petunias in the circle around the mailbox post shiver and nod.

At home, among her borders and beds, she worked all afternoon carrying buckets of water up the hill to slop onto her tomato seedlings, her pepper sets, her potato slips. She worked till she was so weary she whimpered, on her sofa, unable to rest. She fell asleep and had a bad dream. Someone had come and taken things. She woke herself up to go check. She locked the door and moved the piled papers and canned goods off her hope chest and raised the lid. Everything she had held out against him all those years was there. She took the coverlet out and looked it over, as though someone might have stolen the French knots off it. Then she unwrapped the dishes, fine gold-rimmed plates. They weren't china, but they were good. She thought she heard someone. Startled, she turned quickly, knocking the plate against the trunk. The dish broke in two, exactly in two. She took up a piece in each hand and knelt there a long time, but the tears never came. Finally she said, "That's one he won't get," and the thought gave her peace. She broke all the others, one by one, and laid them back in the trunk. She kept the coverlet out. It would do to spread over her tomato plants; the almanac said there would be no more frost, but she knew better. There was always one last frost.

After staking the coverlet above her young plants, weighting it at the corners with rocks, she stooped to see how the Solomon's seal was doing. She had located it by its first furled shoots, like green straws, sticking up through the oak-leaf duff on one of her walks; had marked the place, going home for a bucket and pail, digging deep, replanting so it faced the same way to the sun. It had not dried out. It had good soil. But already it was dying. There was some little trick to it. "You'd think I could learn," she said. But she never did.

Persona

Gayl Jones

I heard the young girls talk. I heard what they said of me.
"It seems as if some man would marry Miss King. She's a nice
woman."
They were freshmen. Nice girls. They were walking into town
and I picked them up. The pretty one rode beside me, the other
one near the door. The one beside me was not talking. The other
one was asking me question after question about the school. And
other things.
"I'm reading a book on women in prisons. Tonight they're
showing a movie about it."
"That's for Professor Gant's class?" I asked.
"Yes. I find social psychology really interesting. I think I might
major in it. . . . My mother wouldn't understand."
"Why wouldn't she want you to major in social psychology?"
"Oh, I don't mean that. I mean in my mother's day they didn't
have classes like that. Professor Gant talks so openly. Doesn't she,
Gretta?"
Gretta nodded, but said nothing. I looked at her a moment, then
back at the road. I smiled a bit.
"If she knew what we talked about, she'd take me out of
school."
I said nothing. I looked over at Gretta. She was looking straight
ahead.
"It isn't anything *bad,* but she speaks so openly."
When they were where they wanted to go, I said goodbye. It
was Gretta I looked at, the large dark eyes. I wanted to know if I
would see her again. Yes, of course I'd see her again. But I wanted
to invite her home to talk, to have dinner with me. I wanted to *see*
her again. They got out of the car and were running somewhere.
Her thick dark straightened hair. Her thin waist. I pulled off. I
should have asked if I could pick them up, how long they'd be in
town.

At the freshman lecture the psychiatrist told them they would experience sexual ambiguity here—that they would be uncertain about their womanhood. But it was natural, she said, they should not worry, most would feel it, attachments to each other, the process of growing up. They'd break away. Many young girls thought they were . . . worried about their sexuality but . . . they should not worry. Things would even out.

Did you like her?

Yes.

It is nothing to worry about. Many young women have doubts that way.

What do you mean?

It's a perfectly natural thing. You shouldn't feel like there's something wrong. You'll grow out of it.

Then I told him: I went to a woman doctor. She felt my breasts. I didn't want her to examine me there. She felt my breasts. And under my armpits. And . . . I couldn't help the way I felt when she put her hands there. A dark-haired lovely woman. She was pregnant. That made me feel tender toward her. She was very gentle and I . . . It was so strange. Then I went back to her. I kept going back to her.

They were going up the walk to the assembly building for the convocation. I kept behind them, watching the back of her head, then her waist, her broad hips.

"Do you believe in segregated schools?" her friend asked.

"What?" she said quickly. I could feel her jump.

"The separation of men and women?"

"Oh. I thought you meant. Where I come from it means something else."

"Oh, no! I didn't mean that."

They were silent.

"I like Miss King," she said. Not Gretta. "She's nice, don't you think? I can't understand why some man hasn't married her. She's really pretty too. In her own way."

I cut across the lawn to go in from another door, afraid one of them would turn and see me, afraid of our embarrassment, afraid it might be Gretta.

Gretta? That's a strange name for a girl from the South. She's a violet. Or a sunflower. Or a chinaberry. I sat in the back row of the auditorium where I could see everyone.

"The lecture she gave those girls. I just stood there and smiled."
I sat in the booth, saying nothing, looking at the small woman with the short hair and handsome eyes. Jean Gant. I stirred my coffee and set the spoon down.
"You'd think by now they'd do away with that lecture."
I said nothing.
"What do you think?"
"What?"
"What do you think about it?"
"Oh, I don't know."

I invited the girls to dinner. The pretty one stood behind her friend and then they entered. The pretty one, Gretta, was silent, uncomfortable. I wanted to say something, to get her talking, but . . .
"You have a lot of old books," her friend said. "Are you a collector?"
"No. Most of them were given to me. Most of the really nice ones."
"You know I didn't want to come here. To the school, I mean. I didn't want to come to an all-girls school but my parents made me. They're supposed to be the best schools." She laughed. "When I said 'segregated school' to Gretta she thought I meant like the ones they have down South."
"Gretta, have you ever been to this part of the country before?"
"No."
"Would you like more mushrooms?"
"Thank you."
She handed me her plate. I spooned on mushrooms, gave it back.
"I can't understand Eliot," her friend was saying. "I can understand Frost. I have Mrs. Justice for the poetry class. She's a good teacher, but . . . "
I looked at Gretta. She was saying nothing.
"What?" I asked her friend.
"He's so neutral . . . sexually, I mean. Even his love poems are neutral. How can anyone write intellectual love poems? Neuter love poems. That's what they are. . . . I've still got to get used to this place."
"Would you like some wine, Gretta?"
"No, I don't drink."

She kept her hands in her lap. Her knees were tight together. She looked at me, at the piano, at the pictures on the wall, the fireplace.

"I'd like some."

"What?"

"Some wine."

"Oh, I'm sorry." I got the wine, poured her and myself a drink.

"You have a fireplace," she said.

"Yes."

"It's nice to have a fireplace. We have one, but it's artificial."

"It's a luxury," I said. "One of the few I allow myself."

Why did I say that? I got up and went into the kitchen for dishes of ice cream. The one who followed me back was not Gretta.

She stood near me as I scooped ice cream out.

"You have a really nice place," she said. "It's really nice."

"Thank you."

"I'd like to have an apartment. It's a pain living in a dorm."

"I thought it was good when I was a student—meeting so many different people."

"But the upperclassmen think freshmen are fools. Women, I should say."

"What?"

"Upperclasswomen."

"Oh."

"I didn't want to come here."

"What about the classes? You said you liked Professor Gant's class."

"Yeah, the classes are okay. Hers is anyway. Academically I don't have any complaints, but . . . "

"Maybe you'll learn to like it here. The first year anyplace takes adjustments. Even if you were at a coeducational college there'd be a lot of adjustments to make."

"Yeah."

I lifted the tray. She took if from me and carried it to the living room. I got a plate of cookies. As I came in she was saying, "I don't think you act like a child." What had Gretta asked? She saw me and frowned. I set the cookies on the coffee table, and sat down, watching her.

"When I first saw you you acted very reserved and serious, but I liked you. . . . You don't think Gretta acts like a child, do you, Miss King?"

"No."

She put her arm around Gretta. Gretta looked away from her and me. She was frowning. I wanted to say, "You're making her uncomfortable," but that would have sounded . . . patronizing?

"Gretta and I went over to one of the mixers."

"How was it?"

"It makes you feel like cattle. It's so unnatural. Men and women shouldn't have to meet like that. It's not like that in the real world."

I smiled. I started to say something, but didn't. I looked at Gretta. She was staring down at her bowl of ice cream. I felt like going over and taking her friend's arm away, pushing her away.

"Gretta handles herself real cool though. This man came over and started talking to her. Finally he looked real funny and then left. What did you say to him?"

"Nothing. He said he had to speak to somebody and just left."

"You probably said something to him you just don't want to tell."

Gretta said nothing.

"Let Gretta eat her ice cream."

"Oh."

She patted Gretta's shoulder, pushed away and picked up her bowl. When we finished, I watched her take Gretta's bowl and then mine and go out. I sat for a moment watching Gretta act uncomfortable, starting to say, "This must be a new world for you." I said nothing. Then I heard water running and went back to the kitchen.

"I'll do the dishes," she said smiling.

"No, leave them."

"I won't feel right if I don't."

I stared at the side of her face, then her back, then the dishcloths.

"You go sit down," she said. "I'll do them."

I went back into the living room. Gretta was in the same place. I'd expected her to be standing, looking at the books or pictures. I wanted to say something. I still did not know what. Her knees were so close together.

"I haven't really talked with you tonight," I said.

She looked at me. She smiled a little.

"It's always hard the first year," I said. "Every new experience is hard, and then you get used to it."

I waited. She didn't speak. I stood. "Excuse me," I said.

She looked at me, confused. I went into the kitchen. Her friend, Susan, turned to me and smiled. I took a dishtowel to dry.

"I have to do a critical paper on him," she said after a moment. She'd said something before that I hadn't heard.

"Who?"

"Eliot."

"I'm going to call it 'An Alternative to Loneliness.' "

"What?"

"The paper."

"Yes, I know. But what do you mean?"

"When I read him I have the feeling he doesn't know what to do with women."

"Who?"

She turned. I looked at her.

"I just get the feeling he wouldn't know what to do with a woman."

I stared at her invisible bosom. She was tall and straight-legged, her hair short and curly, long in the front.

"I just don't get the feeling he would know what to do. He might sleep with a woman, but just sleep."

"Has she spoken to you about persona?"

"What?"

"Has your teacher talked to you about persona?"

"Oh, yes."

I looked at her. I didn't know how my eyes were. I didn't know if she saw my look.

"I like your wooden table," she said.

I said, "Thank you."

Then I looked away from her. I started drying the pans.

"Why don't you go and sit with your friend?" I asked.

"Oh, Gretta. She's just like that. At first I thought she didn't like me. I liked her, but I thought she didn't like me. But that's just her way. She's just like that."

I took another dishtowel down from the rack, hung up the soggy one.

"She's all right when you get to know her," she said.

I started to dry the skillet but put it down.

"I'll leave these," I said. I turned back to her.

She brushed her hair back from her forehead. Her eyes were bright.

"I'll take the two of you home," I said.

"The dorms aren't far."

"But it's not good this time of night."

She shrugged, then she said, "Gretta and I were coming home last night. We went to get a pizza. There were these men at this filling station. They thought we were whores. Even Gretta doesn't look like a whore."

"Why did you say 'even'?" I stared at her.

"Well, you know . . . " She looked embarrassed, turned aside.

"Well, you shouldn't go out too much at night," I said. "The men . . . they didn't bother you, did they?" I said it like an afterthought.

"No, they just said some things. But I can't see why a woman shouldn't go ahead and do what she wants to do. I mean, you shouldn't keep yourself from doing things, going places. Nobody should take *risks*. But you shouldn't *not* do things just because you're a woman."

I said nothing. She looked at me a moment, smiling. She told me I looked tired. I smiled but still said nothing.

I let Susan off first, and then I drove Gretta back to her dorm. Gretta turned to me. "Thank you for the dinner," she said.

"When will I see you again?" I asked. My voice was almost too low to hear.

"Whenever you want to," she said. Her voice too was quiet. I couldn't see her eyes. She turned away from me. I stared at the back of her head.

I held her shoulders, then both her hands.

"You're nice," she said. "You still hide yourself too much though. . . . When I first met you you'd be sitting there, you'd be talking and friendly but you'd never really say anything personal and it was like you'd disappeared. But other times, I was mesmerized."

She held the small of my back.

"Do you remember that lecture Dr. Hunt gave my freshman year?"

"Yes, of course."

I waited for her to say something.

"I was just thinking about it," she said.

I touched the back of her head.

"Have you seen Gretta?" she asked.

"No."

I took my hand away.

"I saw her yesterday. She acted like she didn't know me. She's started wearing her hair all over her head, like a revolutionary. They say some of the students wanted to take over one of the dorms to turn it into a black house. The chaplain spoke to them about their missing out on all the other people they have things in common with. That they shouldn't restrict their own humanity that way. One of them said the church always was the enemy. . . . I can't understand why they give so much shit about it. I can understand it, but . . . "

"Was she one of them?" I asked too quickly.

She stared at me.

"Were you in love with her? Did she ever come here?"

I didn't answer. I felt far away.

"I used to be shaped like her," she said. "And then I had gallstones taken out, and I lost my hips." She took her arms from me, holding herself.

I stared at her. She looked as if she didn't see me. I put my hand in her short hair and made her look at me.

Graveyard Day

———————— Bobbie Ann Mason ————————

Waldeen's daughter Holly, swinging her legs from the kitchen stool, lectures her mother on natural foods. Holly is ten and too skinny.

Waldeen says, "I'll have to give your teacher a talking-to. She's put notions in your head. You've got to have meat to grow."

Waldeen is tenderizing liver, beating it with the edge of a saucer. Her daughter insists that she is a vegetarian. If Holly had said Rosicrucian, it would have sounded just as strange to Waldeen. Holly wants to eat peanuts, soyburgers, and yogurt. Waldeen is sure this new fixation has something to do with Holly's father, Joe Murdock, although Holly rarely mentions him. After Waldeen and Joe were divorced last September, Joe moved to Arizona and got a construction job. Joe sends Holly letters occasionally, but Holly won't let Waldeen see them. At Christmas he sent her a copper Indian bracelet with unusual marks on it. It is Indian language, Holly tells her. Waldeen sees Holly polishing the bracelet while she is watching TV.

Waldeen shudders when she thinks of Joe Murdock. If he weren't Holly's father, she might be able to forget him. Waldeen was too young when she married him, and he had a reputation for being wild. Now she could marry Joe McClain, who comes over for supper almost every night, always bringing something special, such as a roast or dessert. He seems to be oblivious to what things cost, and he frequently brings Holly presents. If Waldeen married Joe, then Holly would have a stepfather—something like a sugar substitute, Waldeen imagines. Shifting relationships confuse her. She tells Joe they must wait. Her ex-husband is still on her mind, like the lingering aftereffects of an illness.

Joe McClain is punctual, considerate. Tonight he brings fudge ripple ice cream and a half gallon of Coke in a plastic jug. He kisses Waldeen and hugs Holly.

Waldeen says, "We're having liver and onions, but Holly's mad 'cause I won't make Soybean Supreme."

191

"Soybean *Delight*," says Holly.

"Oh, excuse me!"

"Liver is full of poison. Poisons in the feed settle in the liver."

"Do you want to stunt your growth?" Joe asks, patting Holly on the head. He winks at Waldeen and waves his walking stick at her playfully, like a conductor. Joe collects walking sticks, and he has an antique one that belonged to Jefferson Davis. On a gold band, in italics, it says *Jefferson Davis*. Joe doesn't go anywhere without a walking stick, although he is only thirty. It embarrasses Waldeen to be seen with him.

"Sometimes a cow's liver just explodes from the poison," says Holly. "Poisons are *oozing* out."

"Oh, Holly, hush, that's disgusting." Waldeen plops the pieces of liver onto a plate of flour.

"There's this restaurant at the lake that has Liver Lovers' Night," Joe says to Holly. "Every Tuesday is Liver Lovers' Night."

"Really?" Holly is wide-eyed, as if Joe is about to tell a long story, but Waldeen suspects Joe is bringing up the restaurant— Bob's Cove at Kentucky Lake—to remind her that it was the scene of his proposal. Waldeen, not accustomed to eating out, studied the menu carefully, wavering between pork chops and T-bone steak, and then suddenly, without thinking, ordering catfish. She was disappointed to learn that the catfish was not even local, but frozen ocean cat. "Why would they do that," she kept saying, interrupting Joe, "when they've got all the fresh channel cat in the world right here at Kentucky Lake?"

During supper, Waldeen snaps at Holly for sneaking liver to the cat, but with Joe gently persuading her, Holly manages to eat three bites of liver without gagging. Holly is trying to please him, as though he were some TV game-show host who happened to live in the neighborhood. In Waldeen's opinion, families shouldn't shift membership, like clubs. But here they are, trying to be a family. Holly, Waldeen, Joe McClain. Sometimes Joe spends the weekends, but Holly prefers weekends at Joe's house because of his shiny wood floors and his parrot that tries to sing "Inka-Dinka-Doo." Holly likes the idea of packing an overnight bag.

Waldeen dishes out the ice cream. Suddenly inspired, she suggests a picnic Saturday. "The weather's fairing up," she says.

"I can't," says Joe. "Saturday's graveyard day."

"Graveyard day?" Holly and Waldeen say together.

"It's my turn to clean off the graveyard. Every spring and fall somebody has to rake it off." Joe explains that he is responsible for taking geraniums to his grandparents' graves. His grandmother always kept them in her basement during the winter, and in the spring she took them to her husband's grave, but she had died in November.

"Couldn't we have a picnic at the graveyard?" asks Waldeen.

"That's gruesome."

"We never get to go on picnics," says Holly. "Or anywhere." She gives Waldeen a look.

"Well, O.K.," Joe says. "But remember, it's serious. No fooling around."

"We'll be real quiet," says Holly.

"Far be it from me to disturb the dead," Waldeen says, wondering why she is speaking in a mocking tone.

After supper, Joe plays rummy with Holly while Waldeen cracks pecans for a cake. Pecan shells fly across the floor, and the cat pounces on them. Holly and Joe are laughing together, whooping loudly over the cards. They sound like contestants on *Let's Make a Deal*. Joe Murdock had wanted desperately to be on a game show and strike it rich. He wanted to go to California so he would have a chance to be on TV and so he could travel the freeways. He drove in the stock car races, and he had been drag racing since he learned to drive. Evel Knievel was his hero. Waldeen couldn't look when the TV showed Evel Knievel leaping over canyons. She told Joe many times, "He's nothing but a show-off. But if you want to break your fool neck, then go right ahead. Nobody's stopping you." She is better off without Joe Murdock. If he were still in town, he would do something to make her look foolish, such as paint her name on his car door. He once had WALDEEN painted in large red letters on the door of his LTD. It was like a tattoo. It is probably a good thing he is in Arizona. Still, she cannot really understand why he had to move so far away from home.

After Holly goes upstairs, carrying the cat, whose name is Mr. Spock, Waldeen says to Joe, "In China they have a law that the men have to help keep house." She is washing the dishes.

Joe grins. "That's in China. This is *here*."

Waldeen slaps at him with the dish towel, and Joe jumps up and grabs her. "I'll do all the housework if you marry me," he says. "You can get the Chinese to arrest me if I don't."

"You sound just like my ex-husband. Full of promises."

"Guys named Joe are good at making promises." Joe laughs and hugs her.

"All the important men in my life were named Joe," says Waldeen, with pretended seriousness. "My first real boyfriend was named Joe. I was fourteen."

"You always bring that up," says Joe. "I wish you'd forget about them. You love *me*, don't you?"

"Of course, you idiot."

"Then why don't you marry me?"

"I just said I was going to think twice is all."

"But if you love me, what are you waiting for?"

"That's the easy part. Love is easy."

In the middle of *The Waltons*, C. W. Redmon and Betty Mathis drop by. Betty, Waldeen's best friend, lives with C. W., who works with Joe on a construction crew. Waldeen turns off the TV and clears magazines from the couch. C. W. and Betty have just returned from Florida and they are full of news about Sea World. Betty shows Waldeen her new tote bag with a killer whale pictured on it.

"Guess who we saw at the Louisville airport," Betty says.

"I give up," says Waldeen.

"Colonel Sanders!"

"He's eighty-four if he's a day," adds C. W.

"You couldn't miss him in that white suit," Betty says. "I'm sure it was him. Oh, Joe! He had a walking stick. He went strutting along—"

"No kidding!"

"He probably beats chickens to death with it," says Holly, who is standing around.

"That would be something to have," says Joe. "Wow, one of the Colonel's walking sticks."

"Do you know what I read in a magazine?" says Betty. "That the Colonel Sanders outfit is trying to grow a three-legged chicken."

"No, a four-legged chicken," says C. W.

"Well, whatever."

Waldeen is startled by the conversation. She is rattling ice cubes, looking for glasses. She finds an opened Coke in the refrigerator, but it may have lost its fizz. Before she can decide whether to open the new one Joe brought, C. W. and Betty grab glasses of ice from her and hold them out. Waldeen pours the Coke. There is a little fizz.

"We went first class the whole way," says C. W. "I always say, what's a vacation for if you don't splurge?"

"We spent a fortune," says Betty. "Plus, I gained a ton."

"Man, those big jets are really nice," says C. W.

C. W. and Betty seem changed, exactly like all the people Waldeen has known who come back from Florida with tales of adventure and glowing tans, except that C. W. and Betty did not get tans. It rained. Waldeen cannot imagine flying, or spending that much money. Her ex-husband tried to get her to go up in an airplane with him once—a seven-fifty ride in a Cessna—but she refused. If Holly goes to Arizona to visit him, she will have to fly. Arizona is probably as far away as Florida.

When C. W. says he is going fishing on Saturday, Holly demands to go along. Waldeen reminds her about the picnic. "You're full of wants," she says.

"I just wanted to go somewhere."

"I'll take you fishing one of these days soon," says Joe.

"Joe's got to clean off his graveyard," says Waldeen. Before she realizes what she is saying, she has invited C. W. and Betty to come along on the picnic. She turns to Joe. "Is that O.K.?"

"I'll bring some beer," says C. W. "To hell with fishing."

"I never heard of a picnic in a graveyard," says Betty. "But it sounds neat."

Joe seems embarrassed. "I'll put you to work," he warns.

Later, in the kitchen, Waldeen pours more Coke for Betty. Holly is playing solitaire on the kitchen table. As Betty takes the Coke, she says, "Let C. W. take Holly fishing if he wants a kid so bad." She has told Waldeen that she wants to marry C. W., but she does not want to ruin her figure by getting pregnant. Betty pets the cat. "Is this cat going to have kittens?"

Mr. Spock, sitting with his legs tucked under his stomach, is shaped somewhat like a turtle.

"Heavens, no," says Waldeen. "He's just fat because I had him nurtured."

"The word is *neutered!*" cries Holly, jumping up. She grabs Mr. Spock and marches up the stairs.

"That youngun," Waldeen says. She feels suddenly afraid. Once, Holly's father, unemployed and drunk on tequila, snatched Holly from the school playground and took her on a wild ride around town, buying her ice cream at the Tastee-Freez, and stopping at Newberry's to buy her an *All in the Family* Joey doll, with correct private parts. Holly was eight. When Joe brought her home, both were tearful and quiet. The excitement had worn off, but Waldeen had vividly imagined how it was. She wouldn't be surprised if Joe tried the same trick again, this time carrying Holly off to Arizona. She has heard of divorced parents who kidnap their own children.

The next day Joe McClain brings a pizza at noon. He is working nearby and has a chance to eat lunch with Waldeen. The pizza is large enough for four people. Waldeen is not hungry.

"I'm afraid we'll end up horsing around and won't get the graveyard cleaned off," Joe says. "It's really a lot of work."

"Why's it so important, anyway?"

"It's a family thing."

"Family. Ha!"

"What do you mean?"

"I don't know what's what anymore," Waldeen wails. "I've got this kid that wants to live on peanuts and sleeps with a cat—and didn't even see her daddy at Christmas. And here *you* are, talking about family. What do you know about family? You don't know the half of it."

"What's got into you lately?"

Waldeen tries to explain. "Take Colonel Sanders, for instance. He was on *I've Got a Secret* once, years ago, when nobody knew who he was? His secret was that he had a million-dollar check in his pocket for selling Kentucky Fried Chicken to John Y. Brown. *Now* look what's happened. Colonel Sanders sold it but didn't get rid of it. He couldn't escape from being Colonel Sanders. John Y. sold it too, and he can't get rid of it either. Everybody calls him

the Chicken King, even though he's governor. That's not very dignified, if you ask me."

"What in Sam Hill are you talking about? What's that got to do
with families?"

"Oh, Colonel Sanders just came to mind because C. W. and
Betty saw him. What I mean is, you can't just do something by
itself. Everything else drags along. It's all *involved*. I can't get rid of
my ex-husband just by signing a paper. Even if he *is* in Arizona and
I never lay eyes on him again."

Joe stands up, takes Waldeen by the hand, and leads her to the
couch. They sit down and he holds her tightly for a moment.
Waldeen has the strange impression that Joe is an old friend who
moved away and returned, years later, radically changed. She
doesn't understand the walking sticks, or why he would buy such
an enormous pizza.

"One of these days you'll see," says Joe, kissing her.

"See what?" Waldeen mumbles.

"One of these days you'll see. I'm not such a bad catch."

Waldeen stares at a split in the wallpaper.

"Who would cut your hair if it wasn't for me?" he asks, rum-
pling her curls. "I should have gone to beauty school."

"I don't know."

"Nobody else can do Jimmy Durante imitations like I can."

"I wouldn't brag about it."

On Saturday, Waldeen is still in bed when Joe arrives. He ap-
pears in the doorway of her bedroom, brandishing a shiny black
walking stick. It looks like a stiffened black racer snake.

"I overslept," Waldeen says, rubbing her eyes. "First I had in-
somnia. Then I had bad dreams. Then—"

"You said you'd make a picnic."

"Just a minute. I'll go make it."

"There's not time now. We've got to pick up C. W. and Betty."

Waldeen pulls on her jeans and a shirt, then runs a brush
through her hair. In the mirror she sees blue pouches under her
eyes. She catches sight of Joe in the mirror. He looks like an actor
in a vaudeville show.

They go into the kitchen, where Holly is eating granola. "She
promised me she'd make carrot cake," Holly tells Joe.

"I get blamed for everything," says Waldeen. She is rushing around, not sure why. She is hardly awake.

"How could you forget?" asks Joe. "It was your idea in the first place."

"I didn't forget. I just overslept." Waldeen opens the refrigerator. She is looking for something. She stares at a ham.

When Holly leaves the kitchen, Waldeen asks Joe, "Are you mad at me?" Joe is thumping his stick on the floor.

"No. I just want to get this show on the road."

"My ex-husband always said I was never dependable, and he was right. But _he_ was one to talk! He had his head in the clouds."

"Forget your ex-husband."

"His name is Joe. Do you want some fruit juice?" Waldeen is looking for orange juice, but she cannot find it.

"No." Joe leans on his stick. "He's over and done with. Why don't you just cross him off your list?"

"Why do you think I had bad dreams? Answer me that. I must be afraid of something."

There is no orange juice. Waldeen closes the refrigerator door. Joe is smiling at her enigmatically. What she is really afraid of, she realizes, is that he will turn out to be just like Joe Murdock. But it must be only the names, she reminds herself. She hates the thought of a string of husbands, and the idea of a stepfather is like a substitute host on a talk show. It makes her think of Johnny Carson's many substitute hosts.

"You're just afraid to do anything new, Waldeen," Joe says. "You're afraid to cross the street. Why don't you get your ears pierced? Why don't you adopt a refugee? Why don't you get a dog?"

"You're crazy. You say the weirdest things." Waldeen searches the refrigerator again. She pours a glass of Coke and watches it foam.

It is afternoon before they reach the graveyard. They had to wait for C. W. to finish painting his garage door, and Betty was in the shower. On the way, they bought a bucket of fried chicken. Joe said little on the drive into the country. When he gets quiet, Waldeen can never figure out if he is angry or calm. When he put the beer cooler in the trunk, she caught a glimpse of the geraniums in an ornate concrete pot with a handle. It looked like a petrified Easter basket. On the drive, she closed her eyes and imagined that they were in a funeral procession.

The graveyard is next to the woods on a small rise fenced in with barbed wire. A herd of Holsteins grazes in the pasture nearby, and in the distance the smokestacks of the new industrial park send up lazy swirls of smoke. Waldeen spreads out a blanket, and Betty opens beers and hands them around. Holly sits under a tree, her back to the gravestones, and opens a Vicki Barr flight stewardess novel.

Joe won't sit down to eat until he has unloaded the geraniums. He fusses over the heavy basket, trying to find a level spot. The flowers are not yet blooming.

"Wouldn't plastic flowers keep better?" asks Waldeen. "Then you wouldn't have to lug that thing back and forth." There are several bunches of plastic flowers on the graves. Most of them have fallen out of their containers.

"Plastic, yuck!" cries Holly.

"I should have known I'd say the wrong thing," says Waldeen.

"My grandmother liked geraniums," Joe says.

At the picnic, Holly eats only slaw and the crust from a drumstick. Waldeen remarks, "Mr. Spock is going to have a feast."

"You've got a treasure, Waldeen," says C. W. "Most kids just want to load up on junk."

"Wonder how long a person can survive without meat," says Waldeen, somewhat breezily. But she suddenly feels miserable about the way she treats Holly. Everything Waldeen does is so roundabout, so devious. Disgusted, Waldeen flings a chicken bone out among the graves. Once, her ex-husband wouldn't bury the dog that was hit by a car. It lay in a ditch for over a week. She remembers Joe saying several times, "Wonder if the dog is still there." He wouldn't admit that he didn't want to bury it. Waldeen wouldn't do it because he had said he would do it. It was a war of nerves. She finally called the Highway Department to pick it up. Joe McClain, she thought now, would never be that barbaric.

Joe pats Holly on the head and says, "My girl's stubborn, but she knows what she likes." He makes a Jimmy Durante face, which causes Holly to smile. Then he brings out a surprise for her, a bag of trail mix, which includes pecans and raisins. When Holly pounces on it, Waldeen notices that Holly is not wearing the Indian bracelet her father gave her. Waldeen wonders if there are vegetarians in Arizona.

Blue sky burns through the intricate spring leaves of the maples on the fence line. The light glances off the gravestones—a few thin slabs that date back to the last century and eleven sturdy blocks of marble and granite. Joe's grandmother's grave is a brown heap.

Waldeen opens another beer. She and Betty are stretched out under a maple tree and Holly is reading. Betty is talking idly about the diet she intends to go on. Waldeen feels too lazy to move. She watches the men work. While C. W. rakes leaves, Joe washes off the gravestones with water he brought in a plastic jug. He scrubs out the carvings with a brush. He seems as devoted as a man washing and polishing his car on a Saturday afternoon. Betty plays he-loves-me-he-loves-me-not with the fingers of a maple leaf. The fragments fly away in a soft breeze.

From her Sea World tote bag, Betty pulls out playing cards with Holly Hobbie pictures on them. The old-fashioned child with the bonnet hiding her face is just the opposite of Waldeen's own strange daughter. Waldeen sees Holly watching the men. They pick up their beer cans from a pink, shiny tombstone and drink a toast to Joe's great-great-grandfather, Joseph McClain, who was killed in the Civil War. His stone, almost hidden in dead grasses, says 1841–1862.

"When I die, they can burn me and dump the ashes in the lake," says C. W.

"Not me," says Joe. "I want to be buried right here."

"*Want* to be? You planning to die soon?"

Joe laughs. "No, but if it's my time, then it's my time. I wouldn't be afraid to go."

"I guess that's the right way to look at it."

Betty says to Waldeen, "He'd marry me if I'd have his kid."

"What made you decide you don't want a kid, anyhow?" Waldeen is shuffling the cards, fifty-two identical children in bonnets.

"Who says I decided? You just do whatever comes natural. Whatever's right for you." Betty drinks from her can of beer.

"Most people do just the opposite," Waldeen says. "They have kids without thinking."

"Talk about decisions," Betty goes on, "did you see _Sixty Minutes_ when they were telling about Palm Springs? And how all those rich people live? One woman had hundreds of dresses, and Morley Safer was asking her how she ever decided what on earth to wear. He was _strolling_ through her closet. He could have played _golf_ in her closet."

"Rich people don't know beans," says Waldeen. She drinks some beer, then deals out the cards for a game of hearts. Betty snatches each card eagerly. Waldeen does not look at her own cards right away. In the pasture, the cows are beginning to move. The sky is losing its blue. Holly seems lost in her book, and the men are laughing. C. W. stumbles over a footstone hidden in the grass and falls onto a grave. He rolls over, curled up with laughter.

"Y'all are going to kill yourselves," Waldeen says, calling across the graveyard.

Joe tells C. W. to shape up. "We've got work to do," he says.

Joe looks over at Waldeen and mouths something. "I love you"? She suddenly remembers a Ku Klux Klansman she saw on TV. He was being arrested at a demonstration, and as he was led away in handcuffs, he spoke to someone off-camera, ending with a solemn message, "I love you." He was acting for the camera, as if to say, "Look what a nice guy I am." He gave Waldeen the creeps. That could have been Joe Murdock, Waldeen thinks. Not Joe McClain. Maybe she is beginning to get them straight in her mind. They have different ways of trying to get through to her.

Waldeen and Betty play several hands of hearts and drink more beer. Betty is clumsy with the cards and loses three hands in a row. Waldeen cannot keep her mind on the cards either. She wins accidentally. She can't concentrate because of the graves, and Joe standing there saying "I love you." If she marries Joe, and doesn't get divorced again, they will be buried here together. She picks out a likely spot and imagines the headstone and the green carpet and the brown leaves that will someday cover the twin mounds. Joe and C. W. are bringing leaves to the center of the graveyard and piling them on the place she has chosen. Waldeen feels peculiar, as if the burial plot, not a diamond ring, symbolizes the promise of marriage. But there is something comforting about the thought, which she tries to explain to Betty.

"Ooh, that's gross," says Betty. She slaps down a heart and takes the trick.

Waldeen shuffles the cards for a long time. The pile of leaves is growing dramatically. Joe and C. W. have each claimed a side of the graveyard, and they are racing. It occurs to Waldeen that she has spent half her life watching guys named Joe show off for her. Once, when Waldeen was fourteen, she went out onto the lake with Joe Suiter in a rented pedal boat. When Waldeen sees him at the bank, where he works, she always remembers the pedal boat and how they stayed out in the silver-blue lake all afternoon, ignoring the people waving them in from the shore. When they finally returned, Joe owed ten dollars in overtime on the boat, so he worked Saturdays, mowing yards, to pay for their spree. Only recently in the bank, when they laughed together over the memory, he told her that it was worth it, for it was one of the great adventures of his life, going out in a pedal boat with Waldeen, with nothing but the lake and time.

Betty is saying, "We could have a nice bonfire and a wienie roast—what *are* you doing?"

Waldeen has pulled her shoes off. Then she is taking a long, running start, like a pole vaulter, and then with a flying leap she lands in the immense pile of leaves, up to her elbows. Leaves are flying and everyone is standing around her, forming a stern circle, and Holly, with her book closed on her fist, is saying, "Don't you know *any*thing?"

Dear Is a Greeting;
Love Is a Closing

——————————— Jill McCorkle ———————————

My friend, Marcia, describes all of her lost loves like recipes
gone bad. "Things just never jelled," she will say, or "It was going
along fine and wham, like slamming the oven door and watching
the cake fall. No amount of icing can fix it." Marcia is the dietician
at the elementary school where I teach third grade. She has ambi-
tions of opening her own catering service; I personally, prefer the
children to adults.

"God, *heaven*," she says and lifts her glass of wine. "No kids for
two months." I nod, though I'll probably miss all of the commotion of school real soon. It is the first summer I've felt alone in a
long time. "I mean, they don't appreciate anything I've prepared.
They turn up their little noses at anything green. They don't even
eat the Jell-O; they think Jell-O is to be sucked up in a straw and
sprayed on a friend." She props her feet up on my porch table and
closes her eyes. "Speaking of Jell-O," she says and laughs. "Did I
tell you about Tony Ravioli's body?"

"No, and don't tell me now," I say. His name isn't really *ravioli*,
but Marcia has named him that as of last week when they stopped
seeing each other.

"You know I felt guilty if I served anything like alfredo. I mean
he could live for a year and a half on what's stored up."

"At the time, you said he was just big boned."

"Did I?" She laughs again, and if I didn't know that she's my
age, close to thirty, I'd swear that she's a college student; straight
leg jeans, Reeboks, a thin cotton gypsy-looking blouse, her auburn
hair cut short on top and then layered to her shoulders. "Well, I
must not have known what I was saying, the same way that I must
not have known what I was doing when I went on that blind date
the other night." She reaches for the carafe, the late afternoon light
hitting the cut glass and sending small rainbows over the ceiling of
the porch. I love this time of day more than any other, the dusty
late afternoon that seems to filter everything and make it look
softer.

"It was horrible," she is saying. "Let's see. How can I give you the full picture?" She holds a strand of her hair out and it looks like copper in the light. "His name was Bob Trichinosis and he was a perfect pickled egg. He was slimey; you wouldn't want to see or touch him. You would suspect that he had been sitting in the pickling juice for years."

"Why did you go?" I ask and watch my neighbors bringing in their groceries. They walk side by side, arms filled, kiss on the doorstep.

"I thought I'd get lucky," Marcia says. "I'm about to give up, join a nunnery. I mean since my marriage, I've met no one even close. Of course, I wouldn't go back. I mean I had the Deviled Crab." I laugh, more at the picture of Marica's ex-husband that comes to my mind. I've never seen him so I always picture this man moving sideways like the kids do in side-to-side slide, and eyeballs that spring from his head like deely-boppers or whatever those things are called. They were real popular items in the third grade two years ago. Marcia's husband left her the year before she moved here; I don't even know his real name, just crab or devil. "What's so funny?" Marcia asks, and I realize that I have been staring at my neighbor's house, their clothesline filled with what look like designer sheets, pastel swirls and his and her underwear.

"The Deviled Crab," I say and watch the breeze lift the sheets like balloons, like the old parachutes we used to use for high school dances to drape off the bleachers of the gym. "I don't even know your husband's name."

"I've forgotten, too," she says, waves her hand, sips. "No, I'll tell you. Cliff Powers." She pronounces his name from the back of her throat, making it sound dull and droning. "What's Beef Stew's real name?"

"Carter Swain." Marcia is the one who named him Beef Stew. All I ever said was that he was the big football star of my hometown, the son of a farmer who wanted to stay in the business. He was big and muscular but not really interested in anything beyond high school other than cows, tobacco and soy beans.

"Or Carter Swine!" Marcia reaches for the carafe and fills us both up. "Uncooked, raw, cold in the center. It'll kill you."

"No," I shake my head and think of Carter, hair bleached by the sun with a cap pulled low on his forehead. "He's really a sweet guy. We were just too young to get married." I watch those sheets and think of the parachutes in the gym, that gym smell, the mustiness of those parachutes after being crammed in boxes in some work room closet all year until the senior prom. Carter picked me up in his daddy's pick-up truck; we left the dance early, parked there by the river while Carter drank a tall Budweiser that another boy had bought at a bootlegger's. "Sure will be glad when we're eighteen," Carter said. "We could get married, you know." Right that minute, I felt like there would never be anything else I wanted except to live in Fairview and be Carter's wife. How could I know that within 3 years I would feel like I *had* to get out, go to school, *do* something?

"Ah, your farmboy ex is boring," Marcia says. "What about Jack?" Just the sound of his name makes me jump, a short harsh sound, that breaks the softness of the dappled light hitting my neighbors' sheets. "It seemed like all of the ingredients were there." She says this as a question, eyebrows lifted and waiting for my answer. It's been six months since Jack left; six months ago, I was thinking about this time, right now, summer vacation; I was thinking that I'd be all packed up in a Mayflower and heading west to a second marriage and a new life. "What was missing?" Marcia asks, her face suddenly solemn, too much wine, my silent shrugs too serious for her.

"Let's not talk about Jack," I say, and watch my neighbors who are now in the backyard. She is wearing a large work shirt, his no doubt, cut-off jeans, flip flops while she gathers in the sheets; he is watering the small garden that I watched them dig and plant in early spring, late afternoons when I'd see them squatted side by side, staring into the rich dirt as if they could wait for things to grow. Marcia is silent now, staring out at where the sun has dropped below the roofline of the small houses. Though she has never admitted it, I can't help but think that her Cliff Powers was not an easy loss.

"Oh, let's not tarragon on such," she finally says and laughs, waits for me to join in. Marcia has made up her own language. "You know how words sound like they *mean* something else?" she had asked me one day. "Like cumin. Cumin sounds bad to me and you know so many recipes call for it."

"Sounds spicey," I had said and she waved her hand as she often does to my attempts at humor. "Laurel and Hardy" they call us at school; I'm the straight man.

"I think I'll corriander on," she finally says. "I feel saged."

"Don't curry," I say. "What's thyme?" She waves her hand, tells me she'll call tomorrow. I pour another glass of wine and wait until the last bit of light leaves the sky. It's always such a shock to leave the darkness when you have watched it come; the contrast of lamp light is so harsh and unnatural. So, I sit and try to think of a spice that would do me justice while I watch lights come on in the houses down the block. Paprika is light years away from me.

My neighbors are slow dancing in their square patch of light. It is like watching a screen, a slice of a scene where a red tablecloth and part of a refrigerator form the backdrop. They are in candle-light and their bodies, like shadows, pass back and forth, until she turns from him, briefly disappearing while he watches. It is clear from his stance, shoulders relaxed and hands on hips, that she has not gone far, perhaps just inches from the window. And now she returns, long handled spoon in one hand, and he reaches out to that very hand, his other arm around her waist and twirls in a way that makes the candles flicker. I am safely hidden by wire mesh and darkness, distanced by the length of my backyard and their silent language, silent music. They feel like there is no one else on earth; I can see it in their moves, the way she locks her arms around his neck and pulls his forehead down to meet her. I give them music; I give them Sam Cooke.

Jack was dancing, blue eyes squinted with his laugh. I turned to stir the spaghetti sauce, a dash of oregano, and then came back to him with my long handled spoon, the shade and window raised to let in the summer night, its smells of honeysuckle and lawns just mowed, it sounds of crickets and tree frogs like an echo or a back-beat to Sam Cooke. He twirled and swayed as uninhibited as a child, reminding me of my third graders who spin tirelessly like little pinwheels dotting the school grounds; drunk from spinning, they weave and sway, fall to the ground and then get up and start all over.

Marcia could not believe I met Jack at a dinosaur exhibit. She could not believe after the blind dates and dull dinners to the point

I no longer cared, that on an average Tuesday afternoon with a herd of little hellions behind me, I spotted him through the ribs of a brontosaurus. "Thank God there was no meat on those bones," she had said and tried to talk me out of feeling afraid and cautious. "Look," she said. "It sounds to me like this guy is on full boil and you are baking at high altitude. Turn up the gas." For once, I took her advice and within two months he was as much a part of this house as the base that holds it together.

Just a year ago, summer vacation, and he was standing in there in the kitchen, his loafers carelessly kicked under my bed, his clothes in my closet. The night was so warm that we took a cool shower, window open so that all could hear our singing, loud and off key, as I watched the water run from his hair to his feet and then swirl counter clockwise down the drain, *you send me,* and it was late when we stretched out on those clean white sheets, sun bleached and smelling of summer. I parted my hair with the end of a comb and Jack watched as I detangled section by section until it hung down my back like a thick wet rope.

Now he is away from her, his hands moving in a rolling gesture, quick and animiated, *loud,* I think. An argument? I hold my breath, wait, and now there is relief; she tilts back her head in laughter. One of my students, silent for two days, a plump dark haired girl who was usually chattering and giggling, broke and squatted to hug her knees when I asked what was wrong. She shook her head. Marcia was out in the hall waiting for me. I motioned for Marcia to leave without me. Thirty minutes, an hour, and finally she described what she had seen the other night when she stood outside her parents' room. "Do you think they'll divorce?" she finally asked, after fully describing the love and want that she had interpreted as hate and final. I told her that I thought everything was going to be fine and then I called her mother who said she couldn't believe she had forgotten to lock the door. I *always* lock the door, she said, and the next day after school, the girl stopped on her way outside for recess, motioned for me to bend down. "They promised that they aren't getting a divorce," she whispered and ran to catch up with the others, all problems erased with a few words. Now, he hands her a glass and they lift them, drink, move out of view.

"I have work to do," I told Jack the last night of summer last year. "School starts tomorrow," but he talked me out of it without saying a word. The next day I let my third graders make a bulletin board that looked like summer, every child, every vacation, and then I let them run like wild on the playground until they were tired, faces flushed and damp as they waited by the water fountain. Then they filed past me, socks rolled down, hair slicked back, and I followed their sweet soured smells of jungle gyms and playground dirt, into the classroom where I read about Henry Huggins and his dog Ribsy until they were exhausted from fits of laughter and put their heads on their desks, some of them sleeping like babies when the bell rang. My mind was on the night before, tonight, tomorrow night, a night in 1990, when Marcia popped her head in my classroom and interrupted my thoughts. "Hey," she said and sat in one of the small desks. "This isn't saccharine is it? It's the real thing, sweet, natural, gives you energy."

"I think so," I told her, really believing myself, feeling something that I hadn't felt since I was sitting in Carter's pick-up truck that night after the senior prom. "I really think so."

"And a lawyer," she said. "Have your cake and eat it, too. Next round I think I'll go for a higher caloric content myself." She laughed, looked so funny with her legs stretched out in front of the desk; I am used to feet that barely hit the floor. "I am happy for you," she said, a brief flash of solemn expression. "Really, I am."

I don't know my neighbors. They are college students who pass by daily with stacks of books as they run to catch the bus; they have an ease about them that makes school look like fun, like you'd want to stay there forever. I've spoken before, nodded, paused by my car with a bag of groceries as I watched them pass. They hang their clothes out to dry all year long, even when the days are so short and cold, the sun so infrequent. I started to go over one day and tell them it was raining, a cold drizzle that had just begun, but I didn't. I just stood on the porch and sipped my coffee, watched the huge oak leaves swirl and fall like slick yellow gloves, while their bed sheets lifted and fell with the wind until too drenched to move.

Jack and I used to take long walks, up the hill and through the park, a sack of bread crumbs to feed the wild ducks and gulls that gathered by the pond. He'd hold my hand as we walked and described what we wanted, what we didn't want. He felt sometimes that he needed a change of place, change of scenery. He was tired of the East, tired of the South. He would always think of Seattle as home. What if he went and found a job, a place to live? Maybe he could start the first of the year; when school got out, I could go, too.

She is in the patch of light by herself now, her back to me as she eats, but I know that he is there, across from her. I know by the way she inclines her head, the way her shoulders round as she reaches her hands across the table. A tree branch scrubs against the screen behind me, a sound like footsteps through the leaves. And now he is back in the scene; he walks behind her chair and folds his arms around her neck, nuzzles against her while she tilts her head forward, not needing to look at his face because she knows every line of it.

The last day that Jack and I walked up the hill to the park was less than six months ago, a December afternoon, all of the houses along the way lit with tiny white lights, tinseled trees that marked the windows. I saw everything I wanted in those windows, stone fireplaces and large stuffed chairs, perfect blond children standing mesmerized in front of a T.V. or crouched over homework, cats sitting on the sills, their backs arched in a stretch, tails curled. I wanted that street, the pond, the things I already knew. It was cold and I walked with my hands in my pockets, the bread bag swinging by my side. Jack had already packed his things. He was leaving the next day, had told his parents to expect him on Christmas Eve. We had pretended that the day before had been Christmas Eve, so now, it was late afternoon of the make believe holiday and I couldn't help but feel sad, the way I always do when everything is over, when the late afternoon has slipped into night. "It's just six months before you come," he said. We stood at the edge of the pond, his arms wrapped around me from behind as I leaned into him, and watched the gulls soar and circle, tried to imagine myself in a schoolroom in Seattle, to imagine all I'd leave behind. The birds knew we had brought food, and as we walked, they followed, circling our heads, begging with sharp piercing cries; they knew what they wanted and waited.

Now they are in a close embrace, barely moving from side to side; that is the way I remember my parents, will always remember my parents. I was in the kitchen pouring a glass of milk, a flannel gown reaching midcalf, and they were in the living room, a pale green room barely furnished, and they laughed about how pitiful the room looked; they talked about how it was going to look some day, and on the small record player, a 45 turned as they rocked back and forth, toe to toe, arms hugging, Ray Charles, I Can't Stop Loving You, though one of them did. But that night they were there, framed in the open doorway, swaying, swaying, until the music ended and the needle was a dull scrape against the last groove.

We threw bread to the birds; I threw pieces straight up and watched as the gulls flew straight in my direction, dipped to catch it in midair and then veered sharply to the side. It seemed they would never stop coming, a perfect maneuver clockwise above our heads. One gull tired easily and we watched as it flew so low to the ground, circled hesitantly, and finally landed belly first onto a bed of leaves. He sat, watching the others feed, broken legs tucked beneath him. He was afraid of us and so we stood a yard away and tossed pieces, some of which he got before the others descended. We moved closer, hoping to frighten the healthy ones, but instead frightened him and watched as he was forced to move again, legs limp as he searched the frozen ground for a soft spot. "He must have done it on the ice," Jack said, "must have landed wrong."

My neighbors are kissing now, long and deep, his hands locked around her hips, and I have to look away. When my parents kissed, slow and rhythmically, as Ray Charles sang, I had to look away. I was not a part of that scene, the distance lengthening, and now, before I can ever picture them in individual and separate places, each with a new partner, I see them together just as they were that night. And that night never would have happened if they had known that the house would be sold before the living room was ever furnished, if my mother had known that she would turn thirty-two and discover that she wanted something else. "We'll be okay," my dad said and turned his face from me, his profile dark and steady against the bright blue sky. "Please understand," she begged, long distance, another voice already in the background. "Things changed. You'll never know how it changed." I glance at the window and they have stopped kissing; now they are motionless, silently clinging.

The bird watched from the corner of his eye, unwilling to face us, but prepared to be roused again. The bread bag was empty and Jack was ready to walk back. It was almost dusk, freezing cold, the lights from the house shimmering from the distance. "It's my last night," he said as if I didn't know, tugged on the sleeve of my coat as I squatted there, still watching the bird. I asked for one more minute, face burning, when the others, those cruel thoughtless birds, forced him to move, again and again to land on that torn tender belly. He finally gave up and sailed yards away, up the slope of the pond and into the woods where I lost sight of him. I stood to face Jack, first glancing once more up the slope to the woods. "Don't cry," he said and wrapped his arms around me. "It's not forever." And four months later when I knew that it was, he just said, "Don't cry," a poor connection between here and Seattle, the distance lengthening. Marcia came over and did not mention Jack or food once.

Now, I wonder if Marcia has been waiting for me to speak, that night and all these nights to follow when she has come to sit on the porch; maybe she has hesitated the same way I did with my father, his dark face against that blue sky, the same way Carter did with me. I think of Carter as he helped me load boxes into a U-Haul. He was resigned to it all, accepting. "Don't you ever forget all those nights in the pickup," he said, smiled slightly before going back into the house and letting the screen door slam shut. Now, for the first time, I think of Carter in the half empty house all alone while I drove that dirt road to the highway. I see him turning out the lamps one by one while he thinks of all those nights we were together and wonders what happened. He might have even thought I'd be back.

My neighbors blow out the candles and for a second, there is darkness, then a light from another window, the other end of the house, the bedroom where the curtains are drawn but sheer. Al-

ready, I miss school, miss having lesson plans. I see them through
the sheer light like the movement of trees, against the streetlight,
one tree, two trees, their limbs intermingled. These are singular
pronouns, and these are plural. When you write in cursive, the letters all connect. When you write a letter, you should put your return address and the date. Dear is a greeting; love is a closing. It is
early to go to bed but they don't care. They turn the light off and
now the house is a dark little box. I imagine them all curled together as if they are the only people on earth. "We're going to
always be like this," one whispers now and they both believe. I
hope it's true; I want to believe people when they say, "we'll be all
right," "you will do just fine." I tell my students when bruised or
excluded or having trouble learning or watching one parent drive
away, that things will get better. They nod and believe me, take
deep breaths in preparation, never stopping once to think that I
don't _really_ know. Belief, it's what we all need.

    I go to the phone and call Marcia. "I feel like cumin," I say as soon
as she answers, and then like that student who waited two days to
break, I let it all out.
    "Cumin is a verb," she says softly, attempting a laugh. "You
know; it's something that a real pervert would do." She pauses but
I just hold the receiver tighter and look out the kitchen window to
my neighbors' dark house. "But, I guess it _can_ be a noun," she
whispers. "Either way, it's bad." She asks for a reason but I can't
give it, and now she has hung up and is on her way over. I think of
school, the playground dust, and crayon marks. I think of turning
them loose, watching their ears and noses turn pink in the winter
cold, their faces slick and shiny in the late spring. I watch them
and I hear every twist and cry as they beg to be first, beg for a
second try. And they watch me, the one who knows all of the
things that they are yet to learn, but who doesn't, most gratefully,
know everything.

Pablo Tamayo

Naomi Shihab Nye

Pablo Tamayo is moving today, to stay with his brother-in-law on Nueces Street till he can find another house. "Don't worry so much," he told me over the fence. "I'm a beat-up man, my wife is an old lady, I always told you the roof was gonna fall."

That's wrong. He never mentioned the roof. He used to call on the telephone and say in a gruff voice, "Who's there?" as if I'd called him. When I stuttered, he'd laugh and say, "This is me, I'm standing on your roof," but he never mentioned it falling.

I want to give him eggs, a flannel shirt. I want to tell him this neighborhood will be a vacuum without him. To go back to the beginning, make a catalog of his utterances since the day we met over the bamboo that divides our yards. I was standing on a ladder with clippers, trying to tell the bamboo who was boss. In the next yard he stooped over a frizzy dog, murmuring Spanish consolations. He looked like he might once have been a wrestler. "So," he said, looking up. "You're pretty tall, I guess." I told him I was his new neighbor and he said he was my old one. He pointed, "Look at how I put this eyeball back in my dog."

Once his dog had a fight with a German shepherd. Pablo came running to find the eyeball dangling on its string. He called a doctor, the doctor said twenty dollars at least. "So I do it myself. Good job, no?" The eye was now glassy white. It looked like it had been put in backwards. "My dog goes with me to Junior's Lounge," he said, giggling. You don't expect giggles from a man with tattoos. He told me Welcome to the Neighborhood, it's a Nice Neighborhood, I been here Forty, you know, Years. Throwing his head back when he spoke, like somebody proud and practiced, or kicking up dust, looking down like a kid, a brand-new kid.

Later I found myself wondering about him. What made this man act so happy? His house tilted, his wife had no teeth. We invited them for dinner, but they wouldn't come. "She don't like to chew without teeth in public." His car had not run in twenty weeks. Where was his history, what was his life?

"I was born in Mexico, like half the people in this town. They get born, they go north. Like birds or something." One night he showed me their wedding pictures. Such devastating changes the years make! From a shining silken couple, a future of roses, to a house of orange crates and dead newpapers, a shuffling duet of slippers and beans. "I love another girl first, her daddy was rich. He told her never marry a baker." His face goes dark for a moment. "Sometimes I still think of that. There was a rooster who rode on my shoulder but one day he changed, you know, he bit me on the leg." When Pablo speaks of the village in the mountains south of Monterrey, he stops smiling, as if those memories are a cathedral which can only be entered with a sober face.

The next day I ask him when he bought his house. "Aw, I never did. They wanted me to, in 1939. But I didn't like to pay so much money all at once, so I just keep payin' forty dollars a month till now." I want to shake him. Who is his landlord? "A bad, bad man. Once I had a good man but they change over the years. This guy, he won't fix the pipe, he won't paint the outside. I want to paint it, but he won't let me. What color do you think I could paint it?"

We stand back to examine the peeling boards.

"Beige."

Three days later he knocks at my door. "I just want to ask you. Is that the color of coffee with milk in it?"

His wife speaks no English and loves to wash. She wears a faded apron, veteran of a thousand washtubs. I can imagine her getting up in the mornings and going straight to her sewing machine. In a cage outside her back door lives a featherless bird named "Pobrecito." Pablo found it on Sweet Street, hobbling. She feeds its scraps of melon and bread.

Around her telephone she has pinned an arc of plastic lilies, postcards of saints, a rosary of black beads. Who is she hoping will call? If Jesus were to manifest for her in modern ways—*Buenas dias!* she would say. *Mi casita, mi perrito, mi Pobrecito, mi Jesús.* I have a garage sale and she buys my battered hiking boots. Where is she planning to go?

After much prodding, Pablo tells me they have three children.

Two are in their fifties, live in Houston or somewhere, "Naw, I don't see them, they don't see me." One is twenty. Pablo and his wife are more than seventy so that means she had the boy when she was fifty, at least. I ask him about this and he says he guesses it's true. Months later I hear another story from the widow down the street. The twenty-year-old is a grandson. She says, "Pablo lies."

When the boy comes home he turns on rock-and-roll so loud the candles quiver on our piano. His hair is longer than my hair. Pablo says, "He had bad luck. Got married too young, seventeen, something like that, to a girl born north of the border. That means she's lazy. It's true. If a Mexican is born north of the border, her husband will walk the road of tears. So they broke up. Bad luck."

Months later, after numerous references to the road of tears, I ask Pablo for details. You mean to tell me all the smooth-faced innocent-hearted Mexican girls in local high schools are going to have husbands who walk the road of tears? C'mon Pablo, find your way out of that one. He looks at me, puzzled. And then his face cracks into its goofy grin. "I got it," he says. "You get a boat."

He asks what I do, why I'm always in this house chattering away on my typing machine. "I write things down," I say.

"Like what things?"

"Like little things that happen."

He looks around, shrugs. "I don't see nothin' happenin'." Then he goes indoors to make me a perfect pie. Pablo understands pie crust, for him poetry is the fluted edge of dough. And Pablo is the only one who will ever understand the delicate grammar of the engine of his car. There was no fuel pump in the city, he said dramatically, which would fit it. So he was building a contraption of wire and soup cans, like a child's telephone. He was going to communicate with his car.

One day, after nearly a month of tinkering, I heard the engine cough, choke, exhale a huge sigh. And there was Pablo passing my house, waving madly, his one-eyed dog perched in the back window. Ten minutes later he was back. There was a problem—the car could only go as far as the amount of gas the can would hold. But it _worked_ now. That was the important thing, it worked. One night I dreamed that wings sprouted where the dented door handles were and Pablo went flying over the city, sending down lines of symbolic verse.

He said he would get another "Alamo seed" so I could have a tree like the one in his yard. He said he was tired of the mud out back, he had this plan for grass. "I used to drink more beers," he said, "than any man with a mouth." That was when he worked at the hotel, when he came home with cinnamon in his cuffs. Some days now he still journeyed out to work, dressed in a square white baker's shirt, to cafeterias or hospitals to "fill in" someone's absence. "I made 35-dozen doughnuts today," he'd say, folding his craggy hands, shaking his head. "I don't wanna be like the man who killed himself in your bathroom." This was news to me. *What man?*

Then Pablo looked worried, he'd slipped, he'd said too much. "Aw come on, I was joking, let's go hammer the fence, aye-yi-yi." He got shy sometimes, his words blurred. *What man?* And he told me his name. Howard Riley. Spoken slowly, How-ard Ri-ley, as if the name had grown longer than Pablo's head.

"He was an old man, kinda old, you know, oh what the hell, everybody's old. You're kinda old. He was old a little sooner than I was. He used to hit a golf ball in the yard, that end, this end, that end, this end. I hear this little tick, you know, like the clock, the little sound it made. But one day he went in your bathroom and shot his own head. Pow! (Finger to head.) I was at the bank. I came home with ten dollars and my wife, she said, Howard's dead. In Spanish, you know. So I went over to see him and he was gone already. They came in a car and took him. I just went to the bank! I used of think of him at night when the nuts fell on the roof. Tick, tick, tick."

"Why did he do it?"

A shrug. "I dunno. He was tired. He had nothin' else to do." Pablo stared down at his two big feet. "So let's go hammer the fence, I get the hammer, you get the nails."

Months later, on the same day I was watching him busy at work in his yard at 7 A.M., wearing a blue and white checkered jockey cap, dragging a tin pail of cilantro from one mudcrease to the next, that day his faceless landlord appeared and told him they had two weeks to get gone. After 48 years, two weeks. Pablo came to me with the same expression my father had on the day he had to fire 12 lifetime printers from his newspaper because they were being replaced by computers.

"We gotta move."

The little dog running in circles, sniffing the ground. Another fall, pecans splitting their dull-green pods in the grass. A pumpkin pie still warm in my hands. How many pies had Pablo given us? Maybe a hundred, maybe more. Lots of times we gave them away. We don't like pie too much. But we'd keep them out on the table a while, on a small pedestal, like a shrine.

"This one's good."

He'd always say it. "This one's good." Forget any other one. Pablo in the yard with a ragged tea towel on his arm, hands outstretched.

"What do you mean, move?"

His landlord wanted to build an office. I was yelling about zoning while his wife unpinned the rosary from its wall, felt the cool black beads move again in her fingers.

"You know, he might make a parking lot here where the Alamo tree is." This year the tree had had 18 leaves. From that seed Pablo found in a gutter. We joked so much when it came up, ugly stick. Not one leaf for months. Then he put small twigs around it like a barricade, tied them with string, little red flags, and it started doing things. His voodoo tree. Smack in the center of the yard.

I wanted to meet this goddamn landlord immediately. Where had he gone? What kind of office? With filing cabinets and Dictaphones and secretary's shiny legs? Obviously they wouldn't fit in this tilt-a-whirl house, they'd flatten it out, 'doze it under. Pablo's crooked stove. The ancient valentine heart tacked to the porch. From whom to whom? Gruff voice. "Me to the lady."

He stood there in his yard which was slipping out from under him, he stood there with hips cocked, plaid shirt half-buttoned, his hair still full on his head, and said, "I wanna tell you somethin'." That always meant, come a little closer, put down your groceries. "You know this world we got here?" He motioned with his arms. "Lemme tell you, this world don't love us. It don't think about us or pray for us or miss us, you know what I mean? That's what I learned when my father died. I was a young man. I got up the next day and went outside, feelin' sick, my face still fat from cryin'.

And there was the sky. Lookin' just the same. Dead or alive, it don't matter. Still the sky. So then I started lookin' around and there was still the flowers, still the bugs, I mean _the bugs,_ who cares about bugs? My father was dead and the world didn't miss him. The world didn't know his name! Ventura— Morales—Tamayo—but _I knew it._ And I say to myself, That's all we got! I know it, the barber know it, so what? This don't make me feel more bad, you know, it make me feel—better. Aw, I dunno, I gotta go find a box."

Hours later he's coming down Sheridan Street pushing a box in front of him, a giant box, like the boxes washing machines come in. He's done this before. I never knew what he did with those boxes. They went in the door and disappeared. He doesn't have a fireplace. Inside his wife is taking down the sweaters. They have the smell of sunlight in them. She's had them out on those poles and ropes so many times they're a little confused today. Now they're going someplace else. She's shufflin' around and he's shufflin' around, taking down calendars, rolling up the years. God knows where the boy is when they need him. Pablo probably rolls up his "Marijuana Boogie" poster without even reading it.

Once he said, "When you die, you die."

"Oh yeah? That's very interesting."

Then we were laughing ridiculously on our two sides of the fence.

Can I translate this great philosophy so it applies to now? "When you move, you move." Simple. Throw up the hands. Still we're very upset in our house. The sky doesn't know it, but we know it. The news comes on the television. I go out back. There is no other news.

Bluegill

———————— Jayne Anne Phillips ————————

Hello my little bluegill, little shark face. Fanged one, sucker, hermaphrodite. Rose, bloom in the fog of the body; see how the gulls arch over us, singing their raucous squalls. They bring you sweetmeats, tiny mice, spiders with clasped legs. In their old claws, claws of eons, reptilian sleep, they cradle shiny rocks and bits of glass. Boat in my blood, I dream you furred and sharp-toothed, loping in snow mist on a tundra far from the sea. I believe you are male; will I make you husband, uncle, brother? Feed you in dark movie houses of a city we haven't found? This village borders waves, roofs askew, boards vacant. I'll leave here with two suitcases and a music box, but what of you, little boot, little head with two eyes? I talk to you, bone of my coming, bone of an earnest receipt. I feel you now, steaming in the cave of the womb.

Here there are small fires. I bank a blaze in the iron stove and waken ringed in damp; how white air seeps inside the cracked houses, in the rattled doors and sills. We have arrived and settled in a house that groans, shifting its mildewed walls. The rains have come, rolling mud yards of fishermen's shacks down a dirt road to the curling surf. Crabs' claws bleach in spindled grass; dogs tear the discarded shells and drag them in rain. They fade from orange to peach to the pearl of the disembodied. Smells crouch and pull, moving in wet air. Each night crates of live crab are delivered to the smokehouse next door. They clack and crawl, a lumbering mass whose mute antennae click a filament of loss. Ocean is a ream of white meat, circles in a muscular brain. I eat these creatures; their flesh is sweet and flaky. They are voiceless, fluid in their watery dusk, trapped in nets a mile from the rocky cliffs. You are some kin to them, floating in your own dark sac.

Kelp floats a jungle by the pier, armless, legless, waving long sea hair, tresses submerged and rooty. These plants are bulbs and a nipple, rounded snouts weaving their tubular tails. Little boys find

219

them washed up on the beach, wet, rubbery, smelling of salt. They hold the globular heads between their legs and ride them like stick horses. They gallop off, long tails dragging tapered in the sand. They run along the water in groups of three or four, young centaurs with no six-guns whose tracks evoke visions of mythical reptiles. They run all the way to the point, grow bored, fight, scatter; finally one comes back alone, preoccupied, dejected, dragging the desultory tail in one hand as the foamy surf tugs it seaward. I watch him; I pretend you see him too, see it all with your X-ray vision, your soft eyes, their honeycomb facets judging the souls of all failed boys. We watch the old ones, the young ones, the boats bobbing their rummy cargoes of traps and nets and hooks.

I sit at the corner table of the one restaurant, diner near the water where fishermen drink coffee at six A.M. I arrive later, when the place is nearly empty, when the sun slants on toward noon and the coffee has aged to a pungent syrup. The waitress is the postmaster's wife; she knows I get one envelope a month, that I cash one check at MacKinsie's Market, that I rent a postbox on a six-month basis. She spots my ringless hands, the gauntness in my face, the calcium pills I pull out of my purse in a green medicinal bottle. She recognizes my aversion to eggs; she knows that blur in my pupils, blur and flare, wavering as though I'm sucked inward by a small interior flame. You breathe, adhered to a cord. Translucent astronaut, your eyes change days like a calendar watch. The fog surrounds us, drifting between craggy hills like an insubstantial blimp, whale shape that breaks up and spreads. Rock islands rise from the olive sea; they've caught seed in the wind and sit impassive, totems bristling with pine. Before long they will split and speak, revealing a long-trapped Hamlin piper and a troop of children whose bodies are musical and perfect, whose thoughts have grown pure. The children translate each wash of light on the faces of their stone capsules; they feel each nuance of sun and hear the fog as a continuous sigh, drifted breath of the one giant to whom they address their prayers. They have grown no taller and experienced no disease; they sleep in shifts. The piper has made no sound since their arrival. His inert form has become luminous and faintly furred. He is a father fit for animalistic angels whose complex mathematical games evolve with the centuries, whose hands have become transparent from constant handling of quartz pebbles and clear agates. They have no interest in talk or travel; they have developed beyond the inhabitants of countries and communicate only with the unborn. They repudiate the music that tempted them and create it now within themselves, a silent version expressed in numerals, angles, complicated slitherings. They are mobile as lizards and opaque as those small blind fish found in the still waters of caves. Immortal, they become their own children. Their memories of a long-ago journey are layered as genetics: how the sky eclipsed, how the piped melody was transformed as they walked into the sea and were submerged. The girls and smaller boys remember their dresses blousing, swirling like anemones. The music entered a new dimension, felt inside them like cool fingers, formal as a harpsichord yet buoyant, wild; they were taken up with it days at a time. . . .

Here in the diner, there is a jukebox that turns up loud. High school kids move the tables back and dance on Friday nights. They are sixteen, tough little girls who disdain makeup and smoke Turkish cigarettes, or last year's senior boys who can't leave the village. Already they're hauling net on their fathers' boats, learning a language of profanity and back-slapping, beer, odd tumescent dawns as the other boats float out of sight. They want to marry at twenty, save money, acquire protection from the weather. But the girls are like colts, skittish and lean; they've read magazines, gone to rock concerts, experimented with drugs and each other. They play truant and drive around all day in VWs, listen to AM radio in the rain and swish of the wipers, dream of graduation and San Francisco, L.A., Mexico. They go barefoot in the dead of winter and seldom eat; their faces are pale and dewy from the moist air, the continuous rains. They show up sullen-eyed for the dances and get younger as the evening progresses, drinking grocery-store mixed drinks from thermoses in boys' cars. Now they are willing to dance close and imitate their mothers. Music beats in the floor like a heart; movie-theme certainty and the simple lyric of hold-me-tight. I pause on my nightly walks and watch their silhouettes on the windows; nearby the dock pylons stand up mossy and beaten, slap of the water intimate and old. Boys sit exchanging hopeful stories, smoking dope. Sometimes they whistle. They can't see my shape in my bulky coat. Once, one of them followed me home and waited beyond the concrete porch and the woodpile;

I saw his face past the thrown ellipses of light. I imagined him in my bed, smooth-skinned and physically happy, no knowledge but intent. He would address you through my skin, nothing but question marks. Instructed to move slowly from behind, he would be careful, tentative, but forget at the end and push hard. There is no danger; you are floating, interior and protected; but it's that rhythmic lapsing of my love for you that would frighten; we have been alone so long. So I am true to you; I shut off the light and he goes away. In some manner, I am in your employ; I feed my body to feed you and buy my food with money sent me because of you. I am very nearly married to you; and it is only here, a northwestern fishing village in the rains, constant rain, that the money comes according to bargain, to an understanding conceived in your interest. I have followed you though you cannot speak, only fold, unfold. Blueprint, bone and toenail, sapphire. You must know it all from the beginning, never suffer the ignorance of boys with vestigial tails and imagined guns. I send you all these secrets in my blood; they wash through you like dialysis. You are the animal and the saint, snow-blind, begun in blindness . . . you must break free of me like a weasel or a fox, fatherless, dark as the seals that bark like haunted men from the rocks, far away, their calls magnified in the distance, in the twilight.

Ghost, my solitaire, I'll say your father was a horse, a Percheron whose rippled mane fell across my shoulders, whose tight hide glimmered, who shivered and made small winged insects rise into the air. A creature large-eyed, velvet. Long bone of the face broad as a forearm, back broad as sleep. Massive. Looking from the side of the face, a peripheral vision innocent, instinctual.

But no, there were many fathers. There was a truck, a rattling of nuts and bolts, a juggling of emergencies. Suede carpenter's apron spotted with motor oil, clothes kept in stacked crates. There were hands never quite clean and later, manicured hands. A long car with mechanical windows that _zimmed_ as they moved smoothly up and down, impenetrable as those clear shells separating the self from a dreamed desire (do you dream? of long foldings, channels, imageless dreams of fish, long turnings, echoed sounds and shading waters). In between, there were faces in many cars, road maps and laced boots, hand-printed signs held by the highway exits, threats from ex-cons, cajoling salesmen, circling patrolmen. There were counters, tables, eight-hour shifts, grease-stained menus, prices marked over three times, regulars pathetic and laughing, cheap regulation nylons, shoes with ridged soles, creamers filled early as a truck arrives with sugared doughnuts smelling of vats and heat. Men cursed in heavy accents, living in motor hum of the big dishwashers, overflowed garbage pails, ouzo at the end of the day. Then there were men across hallways, stair rails, men with offices, married men and their secretaries, empty bud vase on a desk. Men in elevators, white shirts ironed by a special Chinaman on Bleecker. Sanitary weekend joggers, movie reviewers, twenty-seventh floor, manufactured air, salon haircuts, long lunches, tablecloths and wine. Rooftop view, jets to cut swelling white slashes in the sky. And down below, below rooftops and clean charmed rhymes, the dark alleys meandered; those same alleys that crisscross a confusion of small towns. Same sideways routes and wishful arrivals, eye-level gravel, sooty perfumes, pale grass seeding in the stones. Bronzed light in casts of season: steely and blue, smoke taste of winters; the pinkish dark of any thaw; then coral falling in greens, summer mix of rot and flowers; autumn a burnt red, orange darkened to rust and scab. All of it men and faces, progression, hands come to this and you, grown inside me like one reminder.

He faced me over a café table, showed me the town on a map. No special reason, he said, he'd been here once; a quiet place, pretty, it would do. One geography was all he asked in the arrangement, the "interruption." He mentioned his obligation and its limits; he mentioned our separate paths. I don't ask here if they know him, I don't speculate. I've left him purely, as though you came to me after a voyage of years, as though you flew like a seed, saw them all and won me from them. I've lived with you all these months, grown cowish and full of you, yet I don't name you except by touch, curl, gesture. Wake and sleep, slim minnow, luminous frog. There are clues and riddles, pages in the book of the body, stones turned and turned. Each music lasts, forgetful, surfacing in the aisles of anonymous shops.

Music, addition and subtraction, Pavlovian reminder of scenes becoming, only dreamed. Evenings I listen to the radio and read fairy tales; those first lies, those promises. Directions are clear: crumbs in the woods, wolves in red hoods, the prince of temptation more believeable as an enchanted toad. He is articulate and patient; there is the music of those years in the deep well, *plunk* of moisture, *whish* of the wayward rain, and finally the face of rescue peering over the stone rim like a moon. Omens burst into bloom; each life evolved to a single moment: the ugly natural, shrunken and wise, cradled in a palm fair as camellias.

Knot of cells, where is your voice? Here there are no books of instructions. There is the planed edge of the oaken table, the blond rivulets of the wood. There is a lamp in a dirty shade and the crouched stove hunkering its blackness around a fiery warmth. All night I sit, feeling the glow from a couch pulled close to the heat. Stirring the ashes, feeding, feeding, eating the fire with my skin. The foghorn cries through the mist in the bay: *bawaah, bawaah,* weeping of an idiot sheep, steady, measured as love. At dawn I'm standing by the window and the fishing boats bob like toys across the water, swaying their toothpick masts. Perfect mirage, they glisten and fade. Morning is two hours of sun as the season turns, a dime gone silver and thin. The gnarled plants are wild in their pots, spindly and bent. Gnats sleep on the leaves, inaugurating flight from a pearly slime on the windowpane. Their waftings are broken and dreamy, looping in the cold air of the house slowly, so slowly that I clap my hands and end them. Staccato, flash: that quick chord of once-upon-a-time.

Faraway I was a child, resolute, small, these same eyes in my head sinking back by night. Always I waited for you, marauder, collector, invisible pea in the body. I called you stones hidden in corners, paper fish with secret meanings, clothespin doll. Alone in my high bed, the dark, the dark; I shook my head faster, faster, rope of long hair flying across my shoulders like a switch, a scented tail. Under the bed, beyond the frothy curtain duster, I kept a menagerie of treasures and dust: discarded metallic jewelry, glass rhinestones pried from their settings, old gabardine suitcoat from a box in the basement, lipsticks, compacts with cloudy mirrors, slippers with pompoms, a man's blue silk tie embossed with tiny golf clubs. At night I crawled under wrapped in my sheets, breathing the buried smell, rattling the bed slats with my knees. I held my breath till the whole floor moved, plethora of red slashes; saw you in guises of lightning and the captive atmosphere.

Now a storm rolls the house in its paws. Again, men are lost and a hull washes up on the rocks. All day search copters hover and sweep. Dipping low, they chop the air for survivors and flee at dusk. The bay lies capped and draggled, rolling like water sloshed in a bowl. Toward nightfall, wind taps like briers on the window-panes. We go out, down to the rocks and the shore. The forgotten hull lies breaking and splintered, only a slab of wood. The bay moves near it like a sleeper under sheets, murmuring, calling more rain. Animal in me, fish in a swim, I tell you *everything drowns.* I say *believe me if you are mine,* but you push like a fist with limbs. I feel your eyes searching, your gaze trapped in the dark like a beam of light. Then your vision transcends my skin: finally, I see them too, the lost fishermen, their faces framed in swirling hair like the heads of women. They are pale and blue, glowing, breathing with a pulse in their throats. They rise streaming tattered shirts, shining like mother-of-pearl. They rise moving toward us, round-mouthed, answering, answering the spheres of your talk. I am only witness to a language. The air is yours; it is water circling in like departure.

A Birthday Remembered

—————————— Ann Allen Shockley ——————————

"Hello—Aunt El—?"

The familiar voice came over the telephone, young, vivacious, excited—a girlish echo reminding her of the past. "Tobie—"

"Happy birthday!"

"Thank you—" Ellen felt a rush of warmth, pleased that Tobie had remembered. But hadn't Tobie always. Besides, her birthday wasn't difficult to remember, falling on Valentine's Day. *A heart born especially for me,* Jackie used to tease.

"May I come over?"

Now Tobie's voice sounded a little strained. Ellen could visualize the puckers of thin lines forming between her wide-spaced eyes. The tightness in her throat delayed an answer. Why shouldn't she? Then again, why *should* she really want to? Tobie no longer belonged to her—*them.* When Jackie died a year ago, Tobie had to go back to her father. A splintering separation, after all their years of living together, *belonging* together—Tobie, Jackie and herself.

The three of them had survived through the tumultuous stress of trying to make it, ever since Jackie walked out on Roger and came to live with her. Tobie was just five years old—too small and pale for her age, too nervous from the parental arguments.

Roger had been furious, appalled and angry at his wife's leaving him for a woman. Ellen knew it was more an affront to his male ego than losing Jackie. Particularly when it belonged to one who was striving ruthlessly to become a top business executive, amassing along the way all the exterior garnishments that were supposed to go along with it. He had purchased a large, two-story brick colonial house in the suburbs, replete with swimming pool and a paneled country squire station wagon for Jackie to do her errands. When she left him, he had tried to declare her temporarily insane.

Ellen thought that perhaps Jackie *had* been crazy to leave all of that and come to live with her in a cramped apartment on her salary. She wasn't making that much at the time as a staff writer for *Women's Homemaking* magazine's food section. But, somehow, they had made out, until Jackie got a job teaching in an elementary school. Jackie loved children, and had a way with them.

"Hey—Aunt El. You still with me?"

Tobie was waiting for an answer. One could get so involved in the past. "Of course, dear. Please *do* come over," she invited, thinking it wasn't until later she was to have dinner with Harriet. All she had to do was change from her jumpsuit to a dress.

"I'm bringing a friend who I want you to meet. Ok?"

Tobie never had an abundance of friends, only special ones who were close, for that was her way. At first, she and Jackie had mistakenly thought Tobie was ashamed of their relationship—what they were to each other. They knew Tobie was aware of it. How could she not have been. Real love can't be hidden. It inevitably is transmitted through a glance, affectionate touching, strong feelings that show.

Then there was the rainy, cold night in November, one month after Jackie had left him, when Roger came to the apartment, hurling threats, shouting obscenities. He was going to take them to court, declare them perverts, unfit to raise a child. Tobie must have heard the words flung out at them through the paper-thin walls.

"Wonderful, darling. I'll look forward to meeting your— friend."

The phone clicked and Tobie wasn't there anymore. Ellen remained seated on the couch, motionless, as if the remembrance of all that had gone by in ten years had risen like a mist to cover her in sadness. There had not been a divorce because of his man-stubbornness and Jackie's woman-fear for Tobie. When she died, he buried her. She hadn't been allowed to do this one last thing for Jackie. To *be* with her during the last rituals, to hold a fourteen-year-old who was in all but flesh, her daughter too. The next morning after the funeral, Tobie came by to be with her, to cry her tears, sustain her grief. The sorrow shared as one was their solitary entombment for her. Through the passing days, the biting cruelty of it all slowly healed, leaving only the scar tissue. Jackie had been laid to rest in her heart.

Ellen's eyes fell on the array of birthday cards on the coffee table and the vase of red roses that Harriet had sent. Meeting Harriet had helped her to get over the travail of death's cruel separation.

Incurable illnesses are like earthquakes—they swallow quickly. It wasn't too bad now. She could look back and recall without too much pain. All it takes is someone to help, someone who cares, and the eraser of time.

The living room was beginning to become shaded with dark-fingered lances of shadows. She reached over and turned on a table lamp. The day was quickly vanishing into the grayness of night. What she should do was get a drink. A good, stiff celebrating birthday martini. After all, she was forty-four years old. Six more years, if still alive, she would reach the half century mark.

She got up and went to the kitchen. There she turned on the light which brought into sharp, garish focus the ultra-modern bright chrome and copper, resembling the spacious kitchens featured in her magazine articles where various culinary talents were exhibited. Thankfully, through her writing skills, she had been able to help make their living better before Jackie passed. She had become editor of the food section and had written a cook-book. Her publisher had assured her that cookbooks always sell, and hers had.

A martini called for gin, vermouth, lemon, and an olive. She got out the glass pitcher and stirrer. Jackie preferred sunrises. She made them for her in the evenings, after the lengthy daily struggles of climbing the ladder together. Jackie had become principal of the school, a model for those beneath her, and an in-school parent for the students. Ellen marveled at how she had blossomed, learning to become independent after being a college trained housewife to Roger. _There's so much to living that I did not know before,_ Jackie had told her happily. Yes, indeed, there was a lot to living that neither had known before.

She mixed the drink in the shaker, stirred it slowly and poured some in a glass, topping it with a round green olive with a small red eye-circle. _Here's to you, Ellen Simms, on your birthday!_ She lifted the glass in a toast and the drink went down smoothly. Then the doorbell rang. Tobie must have been just around the corner. As soon as she responded, Tobie sang out cheerfully: "Happy birthday to you—happy birthday to you!"

Tobie hugged her and Ellen found her nose pressed into the cold leather of her jacket. Tobie seemed taller. _They do grow,_ she mock-

ingly reminded herself, comparing her own short stockiness to Tobie's height.

"A present for you, Aunt El—"

When Tobie thrust the gift into her arms, Ellen protested: "You
shouldn't have." The package was neatly store wrapped and tied
with a pink ribbon holding a card.

"You know I never forget your birthday, Aunt El—"

At that moment, she saw the boy standing awkwardly behind
her. He had a round, friendly face and a mass of dark brown hair
parted on the side.

"Hello—" she spoke to him.

"Aunt El—this is Warrick."

"Come in and take off your coats. Would you like some hot cocoa to warm you up? I know it's cold outside." Tobie used to love
hot cocoa with a marshmallow floating like a full-grown moon on
top. This was her favorite on Sunday mornings when they had a
leisurely breakfast together.

"Cocoa—you *know* what I like!" Tobie exclaimed, throwing off
her coat and curling up on the sofa.

Ellen watched her, noting the girlishness hadn't gone yet in the
transitional adolescent stage. She looked older. Her blonde hair was
cut short and bangs covered her forehead. Physically, she looked
more like her father with the sharp, angular face, but there was her
mother where it counted most, in her warmth and quickness of
smile. Did her father know that she was here—with her. Like visiting a widowed parent—eight years of child-rearing, child-caring,
child-loving.

"Open your present, Aunt El—"

"All right." First she read the heart shaped card with the fringed
edges about Valentine birthdays, and then the scribbled message:
To my one and only, Aunt El, with love, always. She blinked back the
tears and made a fanfare out of unwrapping the gift. It was a big,
glossy, illustrated, expensive cookbook of ancient Eastern recipes.

"Thank you, my dear." She leaned over to kiss Tobie's cheek.
"It's lovely."

"Tobie saved up a week's salary to buy it—" Warrick announced
proudly, settling in the rocker opposite the sofa. His voice was
changing, and there was an inflamed red pimple beside his nose.

On the front of his red and white pullover sweater were the words Terrence Academy. The right sleeve had a large white T.

"Warrick! Shame on you giving my secrets away," Tobie laughed, playfully chastising him.

"Where are you working?" Ellen asked, hanging their coats in the closet. She couldn't imagine Roger Ewing permitting his teen-aged daughter to work.

"I'm a library page after school at the branch near home. I like to have my _own_ money—" she added reflectively.

Ellen hesitated, wondering if she should ask. Don't forget the social amenities. Isn't that what they had taught Tobie throughout the years. "How is your—father?" she asked, the words sounding like cracked dry ice.

"Oh, Dad's ok," she shrugged, kicking off the high wooden wedge platforms with interlacing straps. "His main object in life seems to be to prove how much money he can make and _keep_."

Roger's a miser at heart; he wants every cent I spend accounted for, yet he'll go out and buy something outlandishly showy to prove he's got money, Jackie had commented about him.

Why was it that people happen to be in certain places at the right or wrong time? Like the dinner party she had been assigned to write up for the magazine to describe the elegance of the food, drinks and table setting. There seated next to her was Jackie, looking small, frail and lost among the spirited laughter and inane chitchat of the moneyed. Roger was on her other side, appearing to be thoroughly enjoying himself talking to the big bosomed woman with the glittering necklace and frosted white hair. There was the interest at first sight, hidden hormones clashing while a subtle in-tuitive knowingness flashed hidden messages above the clamor of the room. _If only we could decide our own fates, what would life then be?_

"I'll make the cocoa—" she said, retreating to the kitchen.

The martini pitcher was on the counter where she had left it. Immediately she poured another drink. She had been ruminating too much. Stop the past. Drink and be merry. Chase the haunting memories away.

"Aunt El—need any help?"

Tobie came in. She had put her shoes back on and they made a hard noise against the linoleum. The wedges looked like ancient ships, causing her to wonder if they were comfortable. The bell-bottom blue jeans billowed over them like sails. "No—nothing to making cocoa. After all the times of doing it for you—" The remainder slipped out. She wished it hadn't.

Tobie laughed, and the sound made everything all right again. "What do you think of Warrick?" she asked, reaching into the closet for cups and saucers. Everything was known to her in a place that had once been home.

"He seems like a nice—boy." Suppose it had been a girl? People choose who they want. This they had tried to instill in her in their unobtrusive way. "How does your father like him?"

"Dad hasn't met him yet," Tobie said quietly. "I wanted to get *your* opinion *first*. Anyway, Dad stays busy and away so much that we don't have much time to talk. The housekeeper takes care of the house—and me—who, I suppose, goes with the house." She gazed down at the floor, biting her lip, face clouded. "I miss Mom—don't you?"

"Yes—" she replied softly. "But we have to get used to living without loved ones. That time must inevitably come, sooner or later, for somebody."

She turned away, pretending to search the refrigerator so Tobie couldn't see her face. Do something else while waiting for the milk to warm. Prepare sandwiches. Young people were always hungry—feeding growth. She had cold chicken and potato salad left over from last night.

"I thought if *you* liked Warrick, Mom would too. He plays on the basketball team," Tobie continued, watching her slice the chicken and take out the jars of pickles and mustard from the refrigerator.

"Are you—serious, about him?" Ellen asked, praying that she wasn't. Not at this stage of youth—almost fifteen.

"Of course not! We're just friends. He's someone to go places and do things with."

"Good!" Ellen exclaimed, feeling an impending burden lifted. "There's plenty of time for the other. You have to go to college and—" she went on hurriedly about those things which normally fall in place for young lives.

Tobie smiled. "I *knew* you were going to say that, Aunt El." Then she looked directly at her, blue eyes locking Ellen's in a vise. "Anyway, someday, if I ever *do* get serious about someone, I hope it will be as wonderful and beautiful as what you and Mom had together."

God, for the first time, it was out in the open! She felt the shock of the words, unexpected, frank—a blessing. "I do too, dear. Like we had." Her hands trembled from the weight of the moment between them. A bridge had transformed Tobie from girl to woman now to her.

"Aunt El, the milk's boiling over!"

"I've lost my cocoa-making expertise," Ellen laughed, snatching the pan off the burner. The milk had boiled into a bubbling white-coated cascade of foam.

When the tray of food was ready, they went back to the living room where Warrick was watching TV. While they ate hungrily, Ellen finished her drink, feeling light, warm and happy.

When the telephone rang, it was like a rude interruption into a special cradle of time. Harriet wanted to know if she would be ready around seven-thirty for dinner. She glanced at her watch. It was just six o'clock. Besides, what was more important to her than this?

Later, Tobie said: "We'd better be going. Warrick's taking me to the movies. Thanks for the treat, Aunt El."

"And, thank *you* for the present. I'm glad you came by to make my birthday a happy one. *Both* of you."

"Nice meeting you, Miss Simms," Warrick said, extending his hand. "Tobie talks about you all the time. Now I can see why!"

She liked him. "Come back—anytime."

Tobie kissed her goodbye at the door. When they left, the tears were finally freed—in sadness and happiness too. Tobie was going to make it all right. Jackie would have been proud. They had made good parents.

Heat Lightning

———————— Lee Smith ————————

"It's not supposed to be that way."
—Willie Nelson

Geneva moves through a dream these days. Right now she sits in a straightback kitchen chair on the front porch, stringing pole beans on a newspaper on her lap and looking up every now and then at the falling-down sidetrack up on the mountain across the road, at the dusty green leaves the way they curl up in the heat, at nothing. It is real hot. The black hair on Geneva's forehead sticks to her skin and she keeps on pushing it back. She strings the beans and breaks them in two and drops them into the pot by her side without once looking down. She feels a change coming on. Geneva has known that something is up ever since last Wednesday night when she hollered out in church.

She never knew she was going to holler before she did it, she never thought of it one time. Then when she did it, she did it so loud she jumped. "Amen!" she yelled, in a hoarse carrying voice that didn't have anything to do with her at all. "Tell it!" she yelled again, about ten minutes later, and everybody was so surprised and some people turned all the way around to see who it was back there in the back making such a commotion. Her daughter, Tammy, who is nine years old and full of notions anyway, put a hymn book up in front of her face she was so embarrassed. Now there are some regular yellers in Geneva's church but they are mostly old and Geneva is not one of them. Geneva never yelled out before and she has been going to that church ten years. After prayer meeting was over Brother Deskins, the preacher, came up to Geneva outside and said he surely felt the spirit moving in that room.

Geneva pulled her mouth into a bunch. "I reckon," she said. Brother Deskins was little and scrawny and looked like a guinea hen. Geneva looked at him and he went away.

Tammy went ahead of her up the dirt road home from church, sort of bouncing and dancing in that way she had like she was too good to touch the ground. Geneva walked with her hands down at her sides and her back as straight as a board, wondering what meanness Wesley Junior had got into while she was gone. On the way home Geneva did not think once about her hollering but her mind went skitting around and around it, almost getting there a couple of times, like a fly trying to get at a piece of cake and somebody keeps swatting him off.

Now Geneva goes on stringing beans. From where she sits she can see the dirt road in front of her house beyond the fence Wesley put up when Wesley Junior was little, them not realizing then that there never was a fence that could keep Wesley Junior out or in either one, or away from anywhere he wanted to go. Wesley Junior plays in the dirt on the edge of the road and when a car or truck goes by he throws a rock at it. "You quit that," Geneva calls out sometimes, not thinking about it, knowing already he won't. There is a lot of traffic today because the James H. Drew Exposition is on up the holler, spread out like a crazy-quilt in the bottom at the fork of the road. Dust hangs in the air after every car and truck go by, hangs there solid as you please just like a curtain. This is the dryest spell anybody remembers, and Geneva's crape myrtle by the clothesline has died. She has to haul water from the well to the garden, ten or twelve buckets a day, she never thinks about it when she's doing it and it doesn't do much good.

Tammy prisses out. "I know you're going to say no," she says.

"Say no to what?" Geneva pulls out of her dream, which is about nothing really, a waiting dream.

"Well, you *are* going to say no, aren't you? You always say no. I'm not even going to say it since I know you're going to say no."

Geneva looks at the road.

"Well, aren't you going to say no?" Tammy keeps it up, pushing her face into Geneva's. Tammy has got Wesley's curly hair, his light coloring and freckles, she looks like she has been dusted all over with gold dust out of a flower. Wesley has spoiled her rotten, Geneva thinks. When she was little, all he did was give her Tootsie Rolls and throw her up in the air.

But when Wesley Junior was born, Wesley was off working on a pipeline in Ohio and nobody was there except Mrs. Goins and some neighbor women and they laid him in the bed right next to Geneva and she was almost scared to breathe he was so little. He was born a long time ahead of when she figured he was due. But Wesley Junior was dark too, as dark as Geneva herself and all her people away off in West Virgina. "Now this is _my_ baby," Geneva said to herself, and she still keeps him with her all the time and when he breaks things she hides it from Wesley. When she tells Wesley Junior no, he beats his head on a wall or the floor until it gets all bloody unless she holds him down. He is a cute little thing, though, and anyway Geneva can understand what he says just fine.

"_Mama_," Tammy says again, pushing into her shoulder. "All right, I'll tell you. You don't even care, do you? It's going to the carnival. _Why_ can't we go to the carnival? Everybody is going. Everybody I know is going. _Lois Ann_ is going," she adds.

"Well, Lois Ann hasn't got any business going," Geneva says.

"You never take us any place," Tammy is getting good and wound up now. She starts crying and then she goes in the house and Geneva can hear her in there, batting things around.

"Well," Geneva says after a while, to nobody. It's so hot that there is a fine gloss on everything and the heat pushes in on her head. Away off in the sky there is thunder but that doesn't mean anything, it thunders all the time in the mountains. Wesley Junior hits the tailgate of a blue Chevy pickup with a rock real hard and the truck slows down but then it goes on and dust hangs in the road. Geneva finishes the beans and wraps up the scraps and the newspaper in a neat pile and sits with it there in her lap.

"Lois Ann says they've got a two-headed pony and a double ferris wheel," Tammy says from behind the screen door.

Geneva gets up and goes in the house and washes out the beans and puts them on to cook with some sidemeat. Geneva is a big woman with a long white body. Her hair is long and black and she wears it pulled straight back in a ponytail low at the back of her neck. Somehow she has gotten to be twenty-eight. She washes up the sink, listening but not listening to Tammy, and Tammy goes on and on. They all talk so much, all of them—Tammy, Wesley, Wesley's Mamaw next door, Wesley's brother, Corbin, that lives with them sometimes. Geneva gets worn out listening.

Oh, there is a change coming on, all right, but Geneva doesn't know what it will be. Three times before in her life Geneva has felt it coming this way. The first time was when her pa died and she was real little, just sitting by the fire up in West Virginia and the dog started to bark outside and it hit her like a rock that her daddy was dead and sure enough, here came somebody before long to tell them and he was. The next time was the first time she saw Wesley, when she was not but sixteen years old and he came up there to work on the interstate. She was in the store buying a loaf of bread for her mama when he came in all dirty from working and that hair red-gold like a flame on his head. "Well, hel-LO there!" he spoke right up and held the door open for her, grinning, and Geneva had felt such a blush start that it went all the way down to her legs. Then he took her to the show and talked a mile a minute and then he married her three weeks later, nobody ever could see why. But when she saw him come in that door that's when she felt it, when she knew. Twelve years, now that's a long time back. The other time was about five years ago when she was carrying the baby that died, the one between Tammy and Wesley Junior, and she knew it was dead as soon as it quit moving and when Wesley took her into the clinic sure enough it was. She was about six months along at the time.

So there, Geneva sits at the table and looks at the pattern on the oil cloth, little yellow lamps in little blue squares with a blue border around them and red stripes running between. Lois Ann comes over, all dolled up, and Geneva hears them with a part of her mind but she is dreaming, then she hears them all fighting out in the front. She looks at the oilcloth and traces a square with her finger, over and over again. Nothing is worth getting up for.

"Mama! Mama!" Tammy comes in the house a while later squealing with her hair flying every which way. "Mama, Mama, come look, it's fixing to rain!"

Geneva gets up and goes to the back door and sure enough, the clouds have moved in close and it's thundering again and a little steady wind has come up and turned the leaves inside out on the shade tree in the back so their silver sides are showing, moving ever so little in the wind. Out in the back Wesley Junior whirls around and around like a top, he loves it when a storm comes up.

"You better go over to Mamaw's," Tammy says, but Geneva knows it and she is already gone out the back door and across the ditch to Wesley's Mamaw's house, a company house just like their own except that Mamaw has a TV.

"What took you so long?" Mamaw is mad as a wet hen, all wrapped up tight in the bed with everything shut down, the windows and doors and the shades pulled down. It's hot as hell and black as night in Mamaw's house. Lightning is the only thing in the world that Mamaw's scared of.

Geneva knows just what to do, she has done it so much before. She gets on the bed in the dark and holds Mamaw like a child on her lap. Mamaw is so old she has shrunk up to almost nothing and she smells like old rags and snuff and something sicky sweet that Geneva can't name. Mamaw has lived in this house in this holler all her life, near about. Geneva feels like she is going to get sick or holler out again, she can't tell which, but she never does either one in the end and she holds Mamaw tight while it thunders loud and Mamaw begins.

"Well, I wasn't but eight or nine years old and I was sitting in the front room and it was storming so hard you could see the rain coming in waves across the valley and we had this tin roof, it was making the awfulest racket you ever heard. Then all of a sudden a ball of lightning come in the attic and rolled down the stairs, rolled right through the kitchen and on down the hall and through the front room and got me where I was just a-setting in my little chair. Then it rolled on out the door and it was gone.

"I fell right out of the chair on my face and I was passed out for upwards of a hour. I turned black as a cinder, too."

"How do you know you turned black?" Geneva asks. "If you were passed out, I mean." She never has thought to ask it before.

"I turned as black as a cinder, I tell you!" Mamaw hollers out in her thin old voice and twitches around on Geneva's lap. Geneva is burning up. She listens awhile longer but the thunder has stopped and she can't hear any rain either so she puts Mamaw back down on the bed and gets up and puts up the shade to let in the light. Mamaw has little old black eyes way back in her yellow face.

"While you're over here I wisht you—" she starts, but Geneva is already gone, walked straight out the back door and over the ditch to her own house. The rain didn't amount to a thing, she sees. Thunder and heat lightning, that's about all.

Geneva goes straight in the house by the back door and won't even answer Tammy, she goes right in her room and locks the door behind her and pulls the suitcase out from under the bed and starts going through all the clothes that Anita, Corbin's wife, left here when she ran off with Bull Hopkins in such a hurry she couldn't even stop to pack her clothes. Anita was a wild thing, Geneva knows she has got halters and short shorts in here. Geneva strips down fast and leaves her own clothes lying in a pile on the floor. Then she pulls on a pair of Anita's red polyester short shorts and puts on a white halter with ruffles on it. It takes her a while to figure out how the halter works. Then Geneva goes over and stands in front of the dresser mirror and looks at herself. She has never worn shorts or a halter, either one, before, and in the mirror she is wavy and full of flesh. Her face is the same it always is, old Indian face Wesley used to say, he likes to say all kind of stuff and try to get a rise out of her.

Now Geneva takes out the sock where she keeps the money she is saving to buy curtain material. Wesley has some silver dollars in there that he has had since he was a kid and she takes those too, along with the money. Then she goes back out in the kitchen and hollers for the kids.

"What is it, Mama?" Tammy asks all big-eyed, seeing Geneva in the shorts, but Wesley Junior doesn't notice anything and he kicks at a kitchen chair until it falls over. Geneva lets it lie. Wesley Junior is small and black-headed, face like a smart little animal. Geneva leans over and kisses him hard on the face and he squirms in her arms. She straightens back up. "Come on," Geneva says. "We're going to the carnival."

Tammy and Wesley Junior both start hollering and jumping but Geneva grabs Wesley Junior tight by the hand and holds on. They go out the front door and she shuts it and looks back once where she planted the caladium bulbs she sent off for, but the dirt is dry and cracked where they never came up. "Goodbye, house," Geneva says all of a sudden, real loud.

"*Mama*," Tammy says, and looks at her funny, and then she closes her mouth but not for long. "Mama, can we take Lois Ann with us?" she says after a while.

"Sure," Geneva says. "Take Lois Ann. Go get her. Take anybody you want."

Tammy runs off and Geneva and Wesley Junior keep walking, her holding on to his hand. In a little while Tammy is back with Lois Ann. Lois Ann is wearing a tacky pink dress and she has pierced ears just like her mother who is on welfare.

A long time before they get there they can hear it, the carnival music and people talking loud, car horns, a lot of noise. Away off in the distance there is still some thunder but it's not as hot as it was. Geneva walks in her dream but when she gets there the dream is gone and all the colors are so bright they hurt her eyes. Tammy and Lois Ann are holding hands and squealing and Wesley Junior pulls first one way and then the other. They fall in with a whole raft of people moving in a steady flow across the old wooden bridge and into the bottom and Geneva loses Wesley Junior and then she grabs him again just in time to keep him from falling off. "You watch where you're going," she tells him, but he acts like he doesn't hear.

The bottom is all changed now, all different, all new. The carnival people have put up their tents everywhere and put streamers all around and set up little stalls all over the place, and the ferris wheel is so high it takes your breath away. All the rides are going. Everything in the carnival is bright and moving. None of this was here Thursday, Geneva thinks, and none of it will be here tomorrow. Every bit of this will be gone. Geneva looks back down at the creek and sees two carnival women down there with their earrings catching the sun, beating out clothes on a rock. Then they are up to the gate and Geneva pays two dollars for herself and a dollar for each of the kids. A carnival man is there just inside the gate. He is dark-faced with long curly hair like a gypsy and he has something in his hand.

"Here you go, sonny," the carnival man says, and holds out his hand to Wesley Junior, and even his voice is different and strange. Geneva thinks to stop him—you can't tell what a carnival man would have in his hand—but she can't move and Wesley Junior sticks his hand right out and gets it, a little green and red plastic snake with sequin eyes. The carnival man grins and his teeth are brown and stained, and when Geneva looks down to get away from his eyes the skin on her legs looks so white.

"Mama, Mama, can I get one of them monkeys?" Tammy grabs at Geneva's hand and points to a monkey that dances on a stick and

Geneva buys it for her and buys Lois Ann an American flag and buys Wesley Junior a plastic sword with a gold handle and a black case that hooks on to your belt.

Geneva goes over to the ticket booth and buys a roll of tickets for each kid, a quarter apiece, which doesn't sound bad until you see that each ride costs two tickets or more. Geneva doesn't care. She stares hard at the woman in the ticket booth, a woman who has dyed blond hair and a lot of makeup and shorts Geneva a dollar on change. But Geneva doesn't care. They start riding the rides and Geneva rides every one, the Tilt-A-Whirl, the roller coaster, the merry-go-round, the bumper cars. She squeals as loud as the kids and when they get dizzy and sick from riding they eat cotton candy and popcorn balls and drink warm Cokes because the ice machine broke down. While she is standing in line at the food trailer to buy the food, Geneva sees the carnival people's trailers and tents right behind the carnival, up against the tree line. That's where they live, she thinks. After they all eat, they go down the row of little tents where the games are, and everybody calls out at Geneva. Sometimes she lets the kids play and sometimes she doesn't, then she gets to throwing baseballs herself into a bushel basket and she is so close to winning so many times that the man keeps making special deals for her and finally she wins a big blue Panda bear for Tammy almost as big as Tammy herself.

"Mama." Tammy pulls at her hand. "Mama. Lois Ann has got to go to the bathroom."

"Can't you wait?" Geneva asks Lois Ann, but Lois Ann screws up her face and says she can't. Wesley Junior sets in crying because he wants to ride the silver bullet and finally Geneva says all right and buys another roll of tickets and gives him some and tells him to stay on it until she gets back, and then she takes Lois Ann and Tammy by the hand and goes off to find a bathroom. "No bathrooms!" a carnival woman says loudly, waving her hands, and Geneva backs off from her and goes to ask the old man in the food trailer. "We don't have public bathrooms," he says. "No bathrooms. I'm sorry."

Lois Ann starts crying and twisting her feet around. Geneva stares at the old man in the food trailer until he leans over and jerks a thumb back toward the mountain where the carnival people live and says, "Just go back that way. Take her somewhere back in there."

"Will you go in the bushes?" Geneva asks Lois Ann.

"_No!_" Lois Ann says, stomping her foot.

"Well, you're going to," Geneva says.

Back in the mess of trailers she sees how they live, sees their underwear strung up to dry, and when they get beyond the last one, Lois Ann squats down finally in the bushes and does it and when she straightens up she screams.

"What's the matter with you?" Tammy says.

Lois Ann puts her hand over mouth and points, and in the door of the closest trailer a man is standing, just watching them.

"Here, girls, run on now," Geneva says, handing them some tickets, and they giggle and carry on and duck their heads and run.

Geneva stands still and looks at the man. He opens the door of the trailer, an old beat-up blue Airstream, and inside the trailer Geneva can hear a dog yapping until the man comes out and shuts the door behind him. He stands on the trailer steps, squinting in the sunlight. He is the same man who was at the gate when they came into the carnival. Now he has taken off his shirt and his shoes and he is wearing some old work pants down on his hips. He stares at Geneva like he stared at her before and she stands there absolutely still and looks back. "You from around here?" he says finally, but Geneva can't talk and she nods her head yes. The man looks at her some more.

"Why don't you come on in here and visit with me awhile?" he says. "I won't bite you." He grins, a wild carnival grin that doesn't give a damn about anything, and Geneva grins back. Then she runs off as fast as she can go, without another word, and she is out of breath by the time she gets back where the rides are. But Wesley Junior is all right, he is right up there on the silver bullet like she told him, going a hundred miles a minute and screaming all the time.

I could of done that, Geneva thinks suddenly. I could of gone in that Airstream trailer and never come out. I could of moved with them wherever they are going, and stayed every night in a different town. I could of beat out my clothes on every rock in every river in the world. Geneva throws back her head and laughs until tears come up in her eyes and everybody is looking at her. Wesley Junior looks down and sees her and laughs too and his little arms flap like wings in the wind. Different, that's how Wesley Junior is, but there is something about Geneva that is like him and she might as well be up there herself right now, look at him go, like some kind of a crazy bird. Fly away, fly away. Geneva feels good. She sits down and stretches out her legs. I might as well get me some sun, she thinks.

After while Lois Ann and Tammy come along and find her and Geneva gives them two of Wesley's silver dollars to spend on gumball necklaces. Then after Wesley Junior uses up the last of the tickets they start on back. Wesley Junior runs in and out of the traffic and breaks his sword but Geneva doesn't even get after him for doing it. Lois Ann and Tammy take turns carrying the big blue panda bear and when they get close to the house Tammy gets sick. Everything Tammy throws up is pink.

Wesley is sitting in the kitchen drinking a beer. He is fit to be tied. "Where you been?" he starts in, but then he sees the panda bear and the snake and the monkey on a stick. He sits back and watches Geneva while she makes some cornbread and slices tomatoes and sets the table. Wesley Junior gets under the table and rolls around and pulls on his daddy's feet, and Geneva makes Tammy take Mamaw some cornbread.

When Geneva brings the beans over from the stove, Wesley reaches out and makes a big grab at her. "Gotcha!" he says, with his blue eyes jumping, but Geneva slips right by and puts the beans down on the table. "You all come on and eat," she says.

Indian Summer

————————— Elizabeth Spencer —————————

One of my mother's three brothers, Rex Wirth, lived about ten miles from us: he had taken over his wife's family home because her parents had needed somebody on the land to look after it.

Uncle Rex had been wild in youth, had dashed around gambling, among other things, and had not settled down until years after he married. "What Martha's gone through!" was one of Mama's oft-heard remarks. I had a wild boy friend myself back then and I used to reflect that at least Uncle Rex had married Aunt Martha. Furthermore, he did, at last, settle down.

Once stabilized, it became him to be and look like a responsible country gentleman. He was clipped and spare in appearance, scarcely as tall as his horse, and just missed being frail-looking, but he had an almost military air of authority; to me, when I thought of him, I always pictured him as approaching alone. He might be in blue work pants, he might be in a suit; his smart forward step was the same, and his crinkling smile had nothing to beg about. "How you *do?*" was his greeting to everybody, family or stranger. But the place—with its rolling, piny acreage, its big two-story house, its circular drive to the gate—was not his own. He never said this, but his brother, Uncle Hernan, who lived next door to us, said that he never had to mention it because he never forgot it for a minute. "It galls him," was Uncle Hernan's judgment. He was usually right.

The family feeling toward Uncle Rex, which was complicated but filled with reality, had to do, I believe, with his having, when a boy, fallen from a tree into a tractor disk. There was still a scar on his leg and one across his back, but the momentary threat to his manhood, the pity in that, was what gave the family its special tremor about him. If he stood safe it was still a near miss, and gave to his eyes the honest, wide openness of those of our forebears in family daguerreotypes, all the more vulnerable for having died or been killed in the Civil War and yet, at the time of the picture,

243

anyway, not knowing it, that it would happen that way, or happen at all.

To me, even stranger than the tractor disk accident and relating to no photograph of any family member whomsoever, was the time Uncle Rex almost burned alive. He had been sleepy from fox hunting, and out on the place in the afternoon had gone into an abandoned Negro house down in a little hollow with pine and camellia trees around it and built a fire in the empty chimney out of a busted chair and fallen sound asleep on an old pile of cotton—third picking, never ginned. He woke with the place blazing around him and what it came to was that he apparently, from those who saw it, walked out through a solid wall of flame. The house crashed in behind him. He was singed a little but unharmed. Well, he was precious, Mama said, and the Lord had spared him.

Over there where he lived, however, he was a captive of the McClellands; had the Lord spared him for that? A certain way of looking at it made it a predicament. It was better to speak in ordinary terms, that he'd managed the property and taken care of his wife's parents till they died, then had stayed on.

"That farm wouldn't have been anything without you, Rex," I once heard Mama pointing out. "It would have gone to rack and ruin."

"I reckon so," he would say, and brush his hand hard across the sparse hair atop his head, the color having left hold of red for sandy gray, the permanently sun-splotched scalp showing through here and there in slats and angles. "Someday I'll pick up Martha and move in with Hernan." He had as much right, certainly, to live in the old Wirth family home as Uncle Hernan had, for it belonged to all; still, he was joking when he said a thing like that, no matter how many McClellands were always visiting him, making silently clear the place was theirs.

It wouldn't have worked anyway. He was plainer by nature than Uncle Hernan, who loved his bonded whiskey and gold-trimmed porcelain, silver, table linen, and redolent cigars. Uncle Rex's wild days, even, had had nothing plush about them; his gambling had been done not in the carpeted *maisons* of New Orleans, but around and about with hunting companions; he would hunt in the coldest weather in nothing except an old briar-scratched, dog-clawed, leather jacket, standing bareheaded on deer stands through the long drizzles of winter days. Sometimes he got sick, sometimes not. "Come on, Martha," he would snort from his bed, voice muffled in cold symptoms, up to his neck in blankets, while the poor woman went off in every direction for thermometers and hot water bottles and aspirin and boiled egg and tea and the one book he wanted, which had got mislaid. "Come on! Be good for something!"

It was in the course of nature—that and pleasing the McClellands, who were strict—that Uncle Rex had given all his meanness up; he was a regular churchgoer now, first a deacon, then an elder. So all his hollering at Aunt Martha was understood as no more than prankish. Besides, Aunt Martha had been provably good for something; she'd had a son, a fine boy, so everybody said, including me; he'd gone to military academy and now he taught at one.

Once in the winter Mama and Daddy and I drove over to see Uncle Rex and found him alone. It was Sunday. Aunt Martha had gone into town to see some of her folks, who must have had some ailment, else they would have been out there.

"Come on, now," Uncle Rex said, as it was fine weather. "You want to see my filly?" He got up to get his jacket and change into some twill britches for riding in.

"How's she doing?" Daddy asked.

"She's coming on real good, a great big gal. Hope the preacher don't come. Hope Martha's not back early. Just showing a horse, Marilee," he turned to ask me, "ain't that all right on Sunday?" He fancied himself when well mounted and sat as dapper as a cavalryman. In World War I, he'd trained for that, but had never got to France.

"What's her name?" I asked him.

"Sally," he said. "How's that?" He'd put his arm across my shoulder, walking; he didn't have the mass, the complex drawing power of his brother, Uncle Hernan, but his nature was finely coiled, authentic, within him, you could tell that.

We came out to the barn all together, enwrapped (as all around us was) in the thin winter sunshine which fell without color on the smooth-worn unpainted cattle gate letting into the lot. "Mind your step," said Uncle Rex. The cows were out and grazing; two looked peacefully up; the mare was nowhere in sight. The barn stood Sunday quiet. "She must be back yonder," he said.

At the barn he reached up high to unbolt the lock on the tack room door and fling it back. The steps had rotted but a stump of wood had been upended usefully below the door jamb; if you meant business—and Uncle Rex did—about getting in, it would bear a light climbing step without toppling. Uncle Rex emerged with a bridle over his arm. The woods beyond the fenced lot were winter bare, except for some touches of oak. There were elm, pecan, and walnut, a thick stand along the bluff. Below the bluff was more pasture land, good for playing in, I remembered from childhood, handy for hunting arrowheads. It rolled pleasantly, clumped with plum bushes and one or two shade trees, down to the branch with its sandy banks.

Uncle Rex was leading the mare out now. He had found her back of the barn. He re-entered the harness room for the saddle while she stood quietly, reins flung over an iron hook set in the barn wall. Uncle Rex brushed her thick-set neck, which arched out of her shoulders in one glossy, muscular rise; he tossed on her saddle. He brought the girth under, but she spun back. "I'll hold her," Daddy said, and took the reins. "Whoa, there," he said, while Uncle Rex cinched the girth. He gathered her in then, though she wasn't sure yet that she liked it, tapped her fetlock to bring her lower for the mounting, and up he went. We stood around while he showed her off; she had a smart little singlefoot that he liked, and a long swinging walk. I still remember the straightness of his back as he rode away from us, and the jaunty swing of his elbows.

Afterward we returned to the house and there was Aunt Martha's car, back from her folks in town. She acted glad to see us: it was Uncle Rex she was cool to. The McClelland house was a country place, but it had high, white, important sides with not enough windows, like a house on a city street. The McClellands were nice people, a connection spread over two counties, yet the house was different from what we would have had. It was printed all over Aunt Martha what she was thinking; that Uncle Rex had had that horse out on Sunday. And the beast was female, too; that, I now realized, made a difference to both of them, and had all along.

Aunt Martha was pretty, with an unlined plump face, gray hair she wore curled nicely in place. She was reserved about her feelings, and if Uncle Rex had not come into her life, lighting it up for us to see it, I doubt we'd ever have thought anything about Martha McClelland. That day of the mare, she was wearing brown, but summer would see her turned out in fresh bright cotton dresses she'd made herself, trimmed in eyelet with little pleats and buttons cleverly selected. She also picked out the cars they drove; they were always green or blue. It occurred to me years after that what Aunt Martha like was owning things. Her ownership, which was not an intrusion—she wanted nothing of anybody else's—extended to all things and persons she had any claim on. When she got to Uncle Rex, then I guess she got a little bit confused; did he belong to her or not? If so, in what way? That question, I thought, would be something like Uncle Rex's own confusion over the McClelland property: he had it, but didn't actually own it. He'd certainly improved it quite a bit. But Aunt Martha also could point to improvements; Uncle Rex was so much better than he used to be. For in former days, freshly married, with promises not to still warmly throbbing in the air, he would come in at dawn, stinking of swamp mud and corn likker, having played poker all night while listening to the fox hounds running way off in the woods—some prefer Grand Opera while playing bezique, Uncle Hernan once remarked. I wondered what bezique was. Whatever it was, it wasn't for Uncle Rex.

As we drove away, Daddy said: "She's probably raising Cain about that mare."

"I don't think so," Mama said. "I don't think Martha raises Cain. Andrew is coming home at Thanksgiving. That's keeping her happy. She's proud of that boy."

"Rex is proud of him, too," said Daddy.

"Of course he is," Mama said.

Andrew was a dark-haired square-set boy, and when we used to play, as children, looking for arrowheads in the pasture, climbing through the fence to the next property where, it was said, the high bump in the ground near the old road was really an Indian mound, I would imagine him an Indian brave or somebody with Indian blood. My effort, I suppose, was to make him mysterious and hence more interesting, but the truth is there was never anything mysterious about Andrew. He was a good boy through and through, the way Aunt Martha wanted him. She would have liked him to go in the ministry but he took up history and played basketball so well he was a wonder. He wasn't so tall but he was fast and well set and had a wondrous way of guarding the ball; he knew how to dribble it and keep it safe. After graduating he got a job teaching and coaching at a military academy run by the church. This was not being a preacher but was in no way acting like his father used to act, and Aunt Martha breathed easy once he decided on it.

He was likely to be home in the summers when not working in some boys' camp.

That was all in the late 1940s, post-war. Andrew was younger than me and unlike the boys my age, he had missed the conflict. He was old enough to play basketball but not to be drafted. Somebody—a man of the town—on seeing him win a whole tournament for Port Claiborne, came up afterward to say: "Boy, it's folks like you that keeps us inter-rested here at home. Don't think you ain't doing your part." Aunt Martha was proud of that; she quoted it often and so did Uncle Rex.

With such a fine boy who'd turned out so well, a place running smoothly and yielding up its harvest year by year, a calmed-down husband with a docile wife, it seemed that Uncle Rex and Aunt Martha could sit on their porch in the summer, in their living room by the gas fire in the winter, smiling and smug and more than content with themselves because of the content they felt about Andrew. Next he would get married, no doubt, and have children, and all would be goodness and love and joy forever. But something happened before that and Aunt Martha lost, I suppose, her holy vision.

It happened like this.

One of the summers when Andrew was home sort of puttering around farming and romancing one or two girls in town and reading up for his schoolwork, he and Aunt Martha suddenly got thicker than thieves. They were always out in the family car together, either uptown or driving to Jackson, or out on the place. People leaned in the car window to tell them how much Andrew resembled her side of the family, which was true. The pity (at least to a Wirth) was how pleased they both looked about it. To start really conversing with a parent for the first time must be as strange an experience as falling in love. Daddy and Mama and I love each other but we never say very much about it. Maybe they talk to each other in an unknown tongue when I'm not around. But as for Andrew and Aunt Martha it seemed that somebody had blown up the levee of family reticence, and water and land were mingling to their mutual content.

Late that same summer, Uncle Rex and Uncle Hernan had got together and taken a train trip up to visit their third and older brother, Uncle Andrew, who had lived and worked in Chicago for years, in the law firm of Sanders, Wirth, and Pottle, but who had now retired to a farm he had bought north of Cairo. The trip had renewed the Wirth ties of blood. There is something wonderful about older-type gentlemen on trains. It brings out the good living side of them and makes them relish the table service in the diner, a highball later, and lots of well-seasoned talk. They may even have gambled a little in the club car. The visit with Uncle Andrew must have attained such a joyous and measured richness they would always preserve its privacy.

"It's the property we've looked into these last few days," young Andrew said to his father, on his return. "The possibilities are just great, what with that new highway coming through."

"I think so, too," Aunt Martha said, and served them all the new recipes she was learning. "You've just to got to listen to Andrew, Rex."

"I'm still riding the train," said Uncle Rex. "You got to wait awhile before I can listen."

Whether they let him wait awhile or not is doubtful. They were bursting with their plans and designs on the McClelland property. The new highway was coming through. Forty acres given over to real estate was something the farm would never miss. The houses, maybe a shopping center, and even a motel would all be too distant to be seen from the house, yet they glimmered full formed and visible as a mirage in Andrew's talk; and in his thoughts the large pile of money bound to result was already mounding up in the bank.

Andrew had assembled facts and figures, and had borrowed

some blueprints of suburban housing from a development firm in Vicksburg. They curled up around his ears when he talked about it all, but nobody had stopped to notice that Uncle Rex had sat the greater part of the time as stiff and straight as if his mare was under him, though the rapport he and that animal shared was not present. He listened and listened and he failed to do justice to the food, and when he couldn't stand it a minute longer he exploded like a firecracker:

"I always knew it!" he jumped up to say. "I never should have moved onto this property."

They looked up with their large brown McClelland eyes, innocent as grazing deer.

"If y'all even think," said Uncle Rex, "that you can sit here and work out all kind of plans the minute I walk out the door you can either un-think 'em or do without me. Which is it?"

"You ought to be open-minded, Father," said Andrew, exactly like he was the oldest one there. He leaned back and let the blueprints roll themselves up with a crackle. "Mother and I have gone to a lot of trouble on this."

"Just listen, Rex," Aunt Martha urged, but her new glow about life was going out like a lamp which has been switched off at the door but doesn't quite know it yet. She spoke timidly.

"I've listened enough already," said Uncle Rex.

He marched out of the room, put on his oldest, most disreputable clothes, and went off in the pickup. He eventually wound up at Uncle Hernan's. We saw him drive up, badly needing a shave. He whammed through the front door of his old home and disappeared. We didn't even dare to telephone. Something, we knew, had happened.

Aunt Martha was so stunned when Uncle Rex hit the ceiling and departed that she shook with nerves all over. She called Mama to come over there (I drove her) and sat and told Mama that everything she had belonged to Rex in her way of thinking, that the Lord had made woman subservient to man, it was put forth that way in the Bible. Did Rex think she would go against the Word of God?

"The land's all yours," Mama said, evidently aware of but not mentioning the wide gap between statements and actions. "I don't think Rex is disputing it. It just comes over him now and then. Maybe Andrew pointed it out to him."

"Andrew ought not to have mentioned it at all," said Aunt Martha. "Oh, I knew that at the time."

"I doubt his coming back to live here now, the way things are," Mama said. "They say the Wirths have got a lot of pride. Especially the men. I just don't know what to tell you. Can you move over to Hernan's with him for a while? Maybe y'all could get more chance to talk things over."

Andrew passed through, knowing everything and not stopping to talk. "He's just hardheaded," he said, in a tone of final authority, and that wasn't smart either. I recalled a saying about the McClellands, that they were so nice they didn't have to be smart. It was widely repeated.

"Hernan's got a whole empty wing," Mama said.

Aunt Martha turned red as a beet and almost cried. She kept twisting her handkerchief, knotting and unknotting it. "Do you imagine a McClelland . . . " she whispered, then she stopped. What she'd started to say was that Uncle Hernan lived with a Negro woman and everybody knew it. It was his young wife's nurse who'd come down from Tennessee with her, nursed her when she got sick and died, then stayed on to keep house. She was Melissa, a good cook—we all took her for granted. But no McClelland could be expected to be under the same roof with that! In fact, Aunt Martha may have thought of herself as sent from God to us, though Mama was also steady at the Ladies Auxiliary and of equal standing.

When we drove back home it was to learn that Uncle Rex had not only departed from Aunt Martha, he had left Uncle Hernan as well, nobody knew for where. He had gone out and loaded his mare in the horse trailer and gone off down the back road unobserved from within, while Aunt Martha was sitting there with Mama and me, crying over him. (We passed a carload of McClellands driving in as we left: at least, we, along with Uncle Rex, had escaped that.)

The next day was Sunday and a good chance for all of us over our way to get together in order to worry better.

"I'm glad I never had any children," Uncle Hernan said. Though he'd apparently had any number by Melissa, he didn't have to count them the way Uncle Rex had to count Andrew.

"I don't think for a minute Andrew and Martha calculated the effect something like this was going to have on Rex," Daddy said.

"It's just now worked to a head," Mama said, "about being on her land and all."

"Hadn't been for Rex wouldn't be much of any land to be on," Daddy said. "The McClellands make mighty poor farmers."

"He knew that," said Uncle Hernan. "He knew that everybody knows it. But the facts speak."

"Wonder where he is right now," Mama said, and from her voice I was made to recall the slight lovable man who was her brother, threatened, in her mind, in some perpetual way.

"Down in the swamp somewhere, with that pickup and that mare, living in some hunting camp," was Uncle Hernan's judgment. "I imagine he's near the river; he'll need a road for working the mare out and some free ground not to get bit to death with mosquitoes and gnats."

"This time of year?" said Mama, because fall was coming early; we were into the first cold snap.

"All times of year down in those places."

"I worry about him, I declare I do," Mama said.

"*You* worry about him. Another week of this and Martha's going to be in the hospital," Daddy said.

"That mare," said Uncle Hernan, searching his back pocket. He drew out a gigantic linen handkerchief, blew his nose in a moderate honk, and arranged his bronze mustache. "She must be getting on for ten years old."

"She was nothing but a filly that day we were over there. You remember that, Marilee?" Daddy asked.

"When was that?" Uncle Hernan asked.

"We drove over there one Sunday," said Mama. "Martha was at one of her folks in town. Rex showed off the mare—nothing would do him but for us to see her."

"Martha came back and caught him fresh out of the lot on Sunday," Daddy said.

"Lord have mercy," said Uncle Hernan. Then he said, "How are you, Marilee?"

I was not so much involved in their discussion. I was over in the
bay window reading some reports from the real estate office where
I had a job now. School teaching, after two years of it, had gone
sour on me. I said I was fine. I was keeping quietly in the background for the very good reason that the fault in all this crisis had
been partially my own. I had once suggested to Andrew, who
sometimes dropped by the office to talk to me, that the McClelland place had a gold mine in real estate if only they'd care to de-
velop it, what with the new highway laid out to run along beside
it. He'd asked me a lot of questions and had evidently got the idea
well into him, like a fish appreciative of the minnow.

I knew nobody would ever reckon me responsible, simply because I was a girl in business. A girl in business, their assumptions
went, was somebody that had no right to be and did not count in
thinking or in conversation. I could sit in the window seat reading
up on real estate not ten feet away from them, but I might as well
have been reading Jane Austen for all it was going to enter their
thinking about Uncle Rex.

A log broke in the fireplace while we all, for a most unusually
long moment, sat pondering in silence, and a spray of sparks shot
out.

"Somebody's *got* to find him," Mama said, and almost cried.

"I'd look myself," said Uncle Hernan, "but I'm down with
rheumatism and hardly able to drive, much less take a jeep into a
swamp. I might get snake bit into the bargain."

"What about Daddy?" I said, and added that I didn't want to go
into any swamp either.

"Oh, my Lord," Daddy said, which was his own admission that
the Wirth family had never given him much of a voice in their
affairs, though it stirred Mama's indignation to hear about it.
Daddy knew he certainly might be successful in any mission they
sent him on: he was Jim Summerall—a tough little farming man
and a good squirrel shot; but though you could entrust a message
to him, how could anybody be sure he'd be listened to when he
got there? A wild goose chase would be what he'd probably have
to call it, with Mama riled up besides.

"Marilee could find him," Uncle Hernan pronounced, and everybody, including myself, looked up in amazement, but didn't get
to ask him why he said it, as he picked up his walking cane and

stood up to leave. Daddy walked out with him to go down and look at where the soil conservation people were at work straightening the creek in back of ours and Uncle Hernan's properties. There was going to be a new little three-acre patch on their side to be justly divided, and a neighbor across the way to be treated with satisfaction to all. It was a nice walk.

But Uncle Hernan would have found, if not that, some other reason to leave our house. He never seemed in place there. His own house, or rather the old Wirth home where he lived, was pre-Civil War and classical in design; our was a sturdy farming house. It was within the power of architecture to let us all know that Uncle Hernan was not in his element sitting in front of our fire in the living room, in spite of Mama's antiques and her hooked rugs and all her pretty things. Then it occurred to me that, whether totally his property by deed or inheritance or purchase or not, that house in turn had claimed Uncle Hernan; that he belonged to it and they were one, and then I knew why Uncle Rex had found no peace there either and had left after two days, as restless in search as a sparrow hawk.

When Daddy got back I walked out to speak to Uncle Hernan at the fence.

"What'd you mean, I could find him?" I asked.

"Well, you've got that fella now, that surveyor," Uncle Hernan said. " 'Gully' Richard," he added, giving his nickname.

Joe Richard (pronounced in the French way, accent on the last syllable) was a man with a surveying firm over in Vicksburg whom we'd had out for a couple of jobs. He had got to calling me up lately, always at the office. For some reason, I hadn't mentioned him to anybody.

"You know how he got the name of Gully?" Uncle Hernan asked, looking at the sky.

"No, sir," I said.

"Came up to this country from down yonder in Louisiana and the first job he got to do was survey a tract was nothing but gullies. Like to never got out of there—snakes and kudzu. Says he thinks he's in there yet. Gully's not so bad, Marilee."

"No, sir," I said, and stopped. Let your family know you've seen anybody once or twice and they've already picked out the preacher and decorated the church. But Uncle Hernan wasn't like that. I thought more of him because he'd never commented on anybody I might be going with, except he did say once that the wild boy who had been my first romance could certainly put away a lot of likker. I judged if Uncle Hernan had spoken favorably of Joe Richard, it was because he esteemed him as a man, not because he was hastening to marry me off.

"What's Joe Richard got to do with Uncle Rex?" I asked, but I already knew what the connection was. He'd been surveying some bottom land over toward the river, and, furthermore, he knew people—trappers and squatters and the like. He was a tall, sunburnt, surly-looking man who kept opinions to himself. I had never liked him till I saw his humor. It was like the sun coming out. His grin showed an irregular line of teeth, attractive for some reason, and a good liveliness. He came from a distance, had the air of a divorced man, a name like a Catholic—all this, appealing to me, would be hurdles as high as a steeple to the Summeralls, the McClellands, and the Wirths (except for Uncle Hernan). But any thought that he wanted to get married at all, let alone to me, was pure speculation. Maybe what he would serve for was finding Uncle Rex.

It was a day or so before I saw him. "Will you do it?" I asked him. "Will you try?"

"Hell, he's just goofed off for a while," Joe said. "Anybody can do that. Let him come back by himself."

"He's important to us," I said, "because—" and I stopped and couldn't think of the right thing, but to Joe's credit he didn't do a thing but wait for me to finish. It came to me to put it this way, speaking with Mama's voice, I bet: "Important because he doesn't know he is."

Joe understood that, and said he'd try.

One latent truth in all this is that I was mad enough at Andrew McClelland Wirth to kill him. He'd gone about it wrong: snatching authority away from his father was what he'd obviously acted like.

During the second month of Uncle Rex's absence, with Joe Richard still reporting nothing at all, and Aunt Martha meeting with her prayer group all the time (she was sustained also by droves of McClelland relatives who were speculating on divorce), I drove up to the school where Andrew taught and got to see him between class and basketball practice. "You could have had a little more tact," I told him, when more sense was probably nearer to the point, and what I should have said. The night before I had had a dream. I had seen a little cabin in a swamp that was just catching fire, flames licking up the sides, but nobody so far, when I woke, had walked out of it. The dream was still in my head when I drove to find Andrew.

Andrew and I went to a place across the street from his little school, a conglomerate of red-brick serviceable buildings with a football field out back, a gym made out of an army-surplus aluminum airplane hangar off at the side, and a parade ground in the center, with a tall flagpole. It was a sparkling dry afternoon in the fall, chilly in shadow, hot in the sun. "If you haven't noticed anything about the Wirth pride," I continued, "you must be going through life with blinders on."

"You don't understand, Marilee," he said. "It was Mother I was trying to help. She needs something more to interest her than she's got. I thought the real estate idea you had was just about right."

"It would have been if you'd have gone through Uncle Rex."

"You may not know this, Marilee, but after a certain point I can't do a thing with Father, he just won't listen."

"You mean you tried?"

"I tried about other things. He's got an old cultivator out in back that the seat is falling off of, it's so rusty. You'd have to soak it in a swimming pool full of machine oil to get it in shape, but he won't borrow the money to buy a new one."

"He and Daddy and Uncle Hernan are going in together on one for the spring crop," I said. "It was Uncle Rex got them to do it. Didn't you know that?"

"He won't tell me anything anymore; you'd think I wasn't in the world the way he won't talk to me. I've just about quit."

I recalled that Uncle Rex had told Uncle Hernan that Aunt Martha and Andrew had got so thick he was like a stranger at his own table, but there's no use entering into family quarrels. The people themselves all tell a different tale, so how can you judge what's true?

"Promise me one thing," I said.

"What?"

"If he comes back (and you know he's bound to), glad or sad or mean or sweet or dead drunk with one ear clawed off, you go in and talk to him and tell him how it was. Don't even stop to speak to your mama. You go straight to him."

"How do you know he's bound to come back?" Andrew asked.

"I just do," I said. But I didn't; and neither did anybody else.

Andrew said: "You're bound to side with the Wirths, Marilee. You *are* one."

"Well," I said, "are you trying to break up *your* family?"

He thought it over. He was finishing his Coke because he had to go back over to the gym. He wore a coach's cap with a neat bill, a soft knit shirt, gabardine trousers, and gym shoes. He also wore white socks. All told, he looked to have stepped out of the Sears Roebuck catalogue, for he was trim as could be, but he was too regulation to be real.

"You might be right, Marilee," was his final word. "I'll try."

When I got back to Port Claiborne, Joe Richard was waiting for me. His news was that he had finally located Uncle Rex. He was living in a trapper's house down near the Mississippi River. The horse was there, and also a strange woman.

Indolent at times, in midday sun still as a turtle on a log which is stuck in the mud near some willows . . . at other times, hasty and hustling, banging away over dried-up mud roads in the pickup with a dozen or so muskrat traps in the back and the chopped bait blood-staining a sack on the floor of the seat beside him . . . at yet other times, fishing the muddy shallows of the little bayous in an old, flat-bottomed rowboat, rowing with one hand tight on a short paddle, hearing the quiet separated sounds of water dripping from paddle, pole, or line, or from the occasional bream or white perch or little mud cat he caught, lifting the string to add another: that's how it was for Rex Wirth. In spring and summer sounds run together but in the fall each is separate; I don't know why. Only insect voices mingle, choiring for a while, then dwindling into single chips of sound. The riverbanks and the bayous seem to have nothing to do with the river itself, which flows magnificently in the background, a whole horizon to itself from the banks, or glimpsed through willow fronds—the Father of Waters not minding its children.

At twilight and in the early morning hours when the dew began to sparkle, he rode the mare. He kept a smudge for her, to ward the insects off, sprayed her, too, and swabbed her with some stuff out of a bucket. The mare had nothing to worry about.

The woman was young—likely in her twenties. She came and went, sometimes with sacks of groceries. At other times she fished; sometimes a child fished with her. Another time a man came and sat talking on the porch. She had blond sunburnt hair, nothing fancy about her. Wore jeans and gingham shirts.

"A nice fanny," Joe said.

"Was it her you were studying or Uncle Rex?" I asked him.

"It's curious," he said. "I stayed longer than I meant to. I've got some good binoculars. That old guy might have found him such a paradise he ain't ever going to show up again. Ever think of that, Marilee? Some folks just looking for an excuse to leave?" I thought of it and it carried its own echo for me: Joe Richard had left Louisiana, or he wouldn't be there talking to me.

I thought that if Uncle Rex had wanted to leave forever he would have gone further than twenty miles away; he had the world to choose from, depending on which temperature and landscape he favored. There must be a reason for his choice, I thought, so I went to talk to Uncle Hernan.

"You were right," I said. "Joe Richard found him." And I told him what he'd seen.

"That would be that Bertis girl," said Uncle Hernan at once.

"Who?" I said.

"Oh, it was back before Rex was married. We all used to go down there with the Meecham brothers and Carter Bankston. It was good duck shooting in the winter and we got some deer too if you could stand the cold—cold is not too bad, but river damp goes right into your bones. Of course, we'd be pretty well fortified.

"There was a family we had, to tend camp for us, a fellow named Bertis, better than a river rat, used to work in construction in Natchez, but lost his arm in an accident, then got into a lawsuit, didn't get a cent out of it, went on relief, found him a river house, got to trapping. Well, he had a wife and a couple of kids to raise. His wife was a nice woman. Ought to have gone back to her folks. She had a college degree, if I recall correctly.

"One year, down there on the camp, Bertis came to cook and

skin for us, like he'd always done, but he was worried that year over his wife, who'd come down sick. It was Rex who decided to take her to Natchez to the hospital and let the hunt go on. Some of the bunch had invited some others—a big preacher and a senator: at this late date, I don't quite know myself who all was there. It would have been hard to carry on without Bertis and Bertis needed money, too, though I reckon we might have made up a check.

"Everybody was a little surprised at what Rex offered to take on himself. He stood straight-backed and bright-eyed when he spoke up, like a man who's volunteering for a mission and ready to salute when it's granted. Somebody ought to have offered—that was true. But there's the sort of woman, Marilee, can be around ten to a thousand men all together, and every last one of them will have the same impression of her, but not a one will mention it. So we never spoke of what crossed everybody's mind.

"The funny thing was, Bertis never stirred himself to see about his wife. He was an odd sort of fellow, not mean, but what you'd call lifesick. Some people can endure life, slowly, gradually, all that comes, but with enjoyment and good spirit; but some get lightning struck and something splits off in them. In Bertis's case it was more than an arm he'd lost; it was spirit.

"Rex stayed away and stayed away. Not till the camp was breaking up did Bertis come up to me, and I offered to drive him in. We got to the hospital but his wife wasn't there, she'd gone on to Vicksburg and it was late. The next day, on a street in Vicksburg, in an old house they'd made into apartments, we found her. She was sitting in a nice room with a coal fire burning, looking quiet and at peace. She looked more than that. She looked beautiful. Her hands had turned fine, white, delicate as a lady's in a painting, don't you know. She had an afghan over her.

"When we came in, we heard footsteps out the back hall and a door slamming. 'Hello, Mr. Bertis,' was all she said. I drove them home. As far as I recall they never asked each other's news, never exchanged a word. I put them down at the front door of that house out in the wilds, not quite in the swamps but too close to the river to be healthy, not quite a cabin but too run down to call a home— it was just a house, that was all. 'You going to be all right, Mrs. Bertis?' I asked.

" 'I reckon I can drive in a day or two,' was what she said. Bertis couldn't do much driving on account of his arm. Though she spoke, it seemed she wasn't really there; she was in a private haze. I remember how she went in the house, like a woman in a dream.

"And there was a little yellow-haired girl in the doorway, waiting for her. That's likely the one's down there now.

"Rex was gone completely for more than a month if I'm not mistaken. He took a trip out West and saw some places he'd always wanted to, though it was a strange time of year to do it, as some pointed out to him when he got back. Married Martha McClelland soon after.

"Marilee, does your mama mind your having a little touch of Bourbon now and then?"

"She minds," I said, "but she's given up."

"The next time you have some bright family ideas about real estate," said Joe Richard, "you better count to a hundred-and-two and keep your mouth shut."

"That's the truth," I said.

We were lying face down on a ridge thick in fallen leaves, side by side, taking turns with the binoculars. I had a blanket under me Joe had dug out of his car to keep me from catching a cold, he said, and I was studying my fill down through the trunks of tall trees—beech, oak, and flaming sycamore—way down to the low fronded willows near the old fishing camp with the weed-grown road and the brown flowing river beyond—and it was all there, just the way he'd said.

I had watched Uncle Rex come up from fishing and moor his boat, had watched a tow-headed child in faded blue overalls enter the field of vision to meet him, and then the blond woman, who'd stood talking in blue jeans and a sweater with the sleeves pushed up—exactly what I had on, truth to tell—taking the string of fish from him, while he walked away and the child ran after him. And I followed with the sights on them, the living field of their life brought as close as my own breath, though they didn't know it— do spirits feel as I did? When he came back, he was leading the mare. She looked well accustomed, and flicked her fine ears, which were furring over for winter, and stood while Uncle Rex lifted the child and set her in the saddle as her mother held the reins. The fish shone silvery on the string against the young woman's legs.

There is such a thing as father, daughter, and grandchild—such a thing as family that is not blood family but a chosen family: I was seeing that. Joe took the glasses out of my hand for his turn and while he looked I thought about Indian summer which isn't summer at all, but something else. There is the long hot summer, heavy and teeming, more real than life; and there is the other summer, pure as gold, as real as hope. Now, not needing glasses, or eyes, either, I saw the problem Rex Wirth must be solving and unsolving every day. If this was the place he belonged and the family that was—though not of blood—in a sense, his, why leave them ever? His life, like a tree drawn into the river and slipping by, must have felt the current pull and turn him every day. Wasn't this were he belonged? Come back, Uncle Rex!—should I run out of the woods and tell him that? No, the struggle was his own. We went away silent, never showing we were there.

Uncle Rex did come home.

It was when the weather broke in a big cold front out of the northwest. It must have come ruffling the water, thickening the afternoon sky, then sweeping across the river, a giant black cloak of a cloud, moaning and howling in the night, stripping the little trees and bushes bare of colored leaves and crashing against the willow thickets. It was like a seasonal motion, too, that Uncle Rex should decamp at that time, arrive back at Aunt Martha's with a pickup of frozen fish packed in ice and some muskrat pelts, even a few mink, the mare in her little cart bringing up the rear.

At least I thought he went home, as soon as somebody I knew out on that road called me at the office to say he'd gone by. If he'd gone to Uncle Hernan's that would have been a waste of all his motions, all to do again. I telephoned to Andrew.

"Get on out there," I said. "Don't even stop to coach basketball."

But Andrew couldn't do that. If he had started untying a knot in his shoelace when the last trump sounded, he would keep right on with it, before he turned his attention to anything new. So he started home after basketball practice.

There were giant upheavals of wind and hail and falling temperatures throughout the South, the breakup of Indian summer, but Andrew forged his way homeward, discovering along the road that the car heater needed fixing and that he hadn't got on a warm enough suit, or brought a coat.

He went straight in to Uncle Rex. It seemed to me later than anybody could program Andrew, but I guess on the other hand he'd worried about his father's absence and his mother's abandoned condition a great deal, and nobody except me had told him anything he could do about it. He had gone home a time or two to comfort her, but it hadn't worked miracles.

"I'm sorry for what I said about the land, Father," he said right out, even before he got through shivering. "You're the one ought to decide whatever we do."

Then he stopped. The big, white house was silent, emptied of McClellands, by what method God alone would ever know.

Uncle Rex and Aunt Martha were sitting alone by the gas heater. Aunt Martha had risen to greet him when he came in, but then she'd sat down again, looking subdued.

Uncle Rex rose up and approached Andrew with tears in his eyes. He placed his hands on each of his shoulders. "Son—" he said. "Son—" His face had got bearded during his long time away, grizzled, sun- and wind-burnt, veined, austere, like somebody who has had to deal with Indians and doesn't care to discuss it. His hands had split up in half a dozen places from hard use; his nails had blood and grime under them that no scrubbing would remove. "Son, this property . . . it's all coming to you someday. For now . . . "

If you looked deeply into Andrew's eyes, they did not have very much to tell. He said, "Yes, Father," which was about all that was required. When he told me about it, I could imagine both his parents' faces, how they stole glances at him, glowed with pride the same as ever, on account of his being so fine to look at and their own into the bargain. But I remembered that we are back in the bosom of the real family now—the blood one—and that blood is for spilling, among other things.

"Your mother wanted me on this place, Son," Uncle Rex went on, "and as long as she wants me here the only word that goes is mine. She can tell you now if that's so or not."

"But, Father, you left her worried sick. You never sent word to her! It's been awful!"

"That's not the point, Son," said Uncle Rex. "She wants me here."

"I want him here," Aunt Martha echoed. She looked at Andrew with all her love, but she was looking across a mighty wide river.

"You know how he's acted! You know what he did!"

"That's not the point," Aunt Martha murmured.

"Then what is the point?" Andrew asked, craving to know with as much passion as he'd ever have, I guess.

"That your father—that I want him here." She was studying her hands then—not even looking. They were speakers in a play.

As for Andrew, he said he felt as if he wasn't there anymore, that some force had moved through him and that life was not the same. Figuratively speaking, his voice had been taken from him. Literally, he was coming down with a cold. Aunt Martha gave him supper and poured hot chocolate down him, and he went to bed with nothing but the sounds of a shrieking wind and the ticking clock, in the old room he'd had from childhood on. He felt (he told me later) like nothing and nobody. Nothing . . . nobody: the clock was saying it too. There was an ache at the house's core and at some point he dreamed he rose and dressed and went out into the upstairs hall. There he saw his father's face, white, drawn, and small—a ghost face, floating above the stairwell.

"Why call me 'Son' when you don't mean it?"

There wasn't an answer, and he woke and heard the wind.

Uncle Rex—what dream did he have?

"We can't know that," said Uncle Hernan, when I talked to him. "Rex did what he had to. He settled it with those McClellands, once and for all. It was hard for Rex—remember that. Oh yes, Marilee! For Rex it was mighty hard."

Kindred Spirits

Alice Walker

Rosa could not tell her sister how scared she was or how glad she was that she had consented to come with her. Instead they made small talk on the plane, and Rosa looked out of the window at the clouds.

It was a kind of sentimental journey for Rosa, months too late, going to visit the aunt in whose house their grandfather had died. She did not even know why she must do it: she had spent the earlier part of the summer in such far-flung places as Cyprus and Greece. Jamaica. She was at a place in her life where she seemed to have no place. She'd left the brownstone in Park Slope, given up the car and cat. Her child was at camp. She was in pain. That, at least, she knew. She hardly slept. If she did sleep, her dreams were cold, desolate, and full of static. She ate spaghetti, mostly, with shrimp, from a recipe cut out from the _Times_. She listened to the jazz radio station all the time, her heart in her mouth.

"So how is Ivan?" her sister, Barbara, asked.

Barbara was still fond of her brother-in-law, and hurt that after his divorce from Rosa he'd sunk back into the white world so completely that even a Christmas card was too much trouble to send people who had come to love him.

"Oh, fine," Rosa said. "Living with a nice Jewish girl, at last." Which might have explained the absence of a Christmas card, Rosa thought, but she knew it really didn't.

"Really? What's she like?"

"Warm. Attractive. Loves him."

This was mostly guesswork on Rosa's part; she'd met Sheila only once. She hoped she had these attributes, for his sake. A week after she'd moved out of the brownstone, Sheila had moved in, and all her in-laws, especially Ivan's mother, seemed very happy. Once Rosa had "borrowed" the car (her own, which she'd left with him), and when she returned it, mother and girlfriend met her at her own front gate, barring her way into her own house, their faces flushed with the victory of finally seeing her outside where

264

she belonged. Music and laughter of many guests came from inside.

But did she care? No. She was free. She took to the sidewalk, the heels of her burgundy suede boots clicking, free. Her heart making itself still by force. _Ah,_ but then at night when she slept, it awoke, and the clicking of her heels was nothing to the rattling and crackling of her heart.

"Mama misses him," said Barbara.

Rosa knew she did. How could she even begin to understand that this son-in-law she doted on was incapable, after divorcing her daughter, of even calling on the phone to ask how she felt, as she suffered stroke after frightening and debilitating stroke? It must have seemed totally unnatural to her, a woman who had rushed to comfort the sick and shut-in all her life. It seemed unnatural even to Rosa, who about most other things was able to take a somewhat more modern view.

At last they were in sight of the Miami airport. Before they could be prevented by the stewardess, Barbara and Rosa managed to exchange seats. Barbara sat by the window because she flew very rarely and it was a treat for her to "see herself" landing. Rosa no longer cared to look down. She had traveled so much that summer. The trip to Cyprus in particular had been so long it had made her want to scream. And then, in Nicosia, the weather was abominable. One hundred twenty degrees. It hurt to breathe. And there had been days of visiting Greeks in refugee camps and listening to socialists and visiting the home of a family in which an only son— standing next to a socialist leader at a rally—was assassinated by mistake. Though it had happened over a year earlier his father still wept as he told of it, and looked with great regret at his surviving daughter and _her_ small daughter. "A man must have many sons," he said over and over, never seeming to realize that under conditions of war even a dozen sons could be killed. And not under war alone.

And then Rosa had flown to Greece, and Athens had been like New York City in late July and the Parthenon tiny. . . .

When they arrived at the Miami airport they looked about with the slightly anxious interest of travelers who still remembered segregated travel facilities. If a white person had materialized beside them and pointed out a colored section they would have attacked him or her on principle, but have been only somewhat surprised. Their formative years had been lived under racist restrictions so pervasive that wherever they traveled in the world they expected, on some level, in themselves and in whatever physical circumstances they found themselves, to encounter some, if only symbolic, racial barrier.

And there it was now: on a poster across from them a blond white woman and her dark-haired male partner danced under the stars while a black band played and a black waiter waited and a black chef beamed from the kitchen.

A striking woman, black as midnight, in a blue pastel cotton dress, tall, straight of bearing, with a firm bun of silver-white hair, bore down upon them.

It's me, thought Rosa. My old self.

"Aunt Lily!" said Barbara, smiling and throwing her arms around her.

When it was her turn to be hugged, Rosa gave herself up to it, enjoying the smells of baby shampoo, Jergens lotion, and Evening in Paris remembered from childhood embraces, which, on second sniff, she decided was Charlie. That was this aunt, full of change and contradictions, as she had known her.

Not that she ever had, really. Aunt Lily had come to visit summers, when Rosa was a child. She had been straight and black and as vibrant as fire. She was always with her husband, whose tan face seemed weak next to hers. He drove the car, but she steered it; the same seemed true of their lives.

They had moved to Florida years ago, looking for a better life "somewhere else in the South that wasn't so full of southerners." Looking at her aunt now—with her imperial bearing, directness of speech, and great height—Rosa could not imagine anyone having the nerve to condescend to her, or worse, attempt to cheat her. Once again Rosa was amazed at the white man's arrogance and racist laws. Ten years earlier this sweet-smelling, squeaky-clean aunt of hers would not have been permitted to try on a dress in local department stores. She could not have drunk at certain fountains. The main restaurants of the city would have been closed to her. The public library. The vast majority of the city's toilets.

Aunt Lily had an enormous brown station wagon, into which

Rosa and Barbara flung their light travel bags. Barbara, older than Rosa and closer to Aunt Lily, sat beside her on the front seat. Rosa sat behind them, looking out the window at the passing scenery, admiring the numerous canals—she was passionately fond of water—and yet wondering about the city's sewerage problems, of which she had heard.

How like them, really, she thought, to build canals around their pretty segregated houses—canals so polluted that to fall into one was to risk disease.

When they arrived at Aunt Lily's squat, green house, with its orange and lemon trees in the yard, far from canals and even streetlights, they were met in the narrow hall by five of her aunt's seven foster children and a young woman who had been a foster child herself but was now sharing the house and helping to look after the children with Aunt Lily. Her name was Raymyna Ann.

Aunt Lily had, a long time ago, a baby son who died. For years she had not seemed to care for children. Rosa had never felt particularly valued by her whenever Aunt Lily had come to visit. Aunt Lily acknowledged her brother's children by bringing them oranges and grapefruit packed in orange net bags, but she rarely hugged or kissed them. Well, she rarely touched these foster children, either, Rosa noticed. There were so many of them, so dark (all as black, precisely, as her aunt) and so woundedly silent. But at dinner the table was piled high with food, the little ones were encouraged to have seconds, and when they all trooped off to bed they did so in a cloud of soapy smells and dazzling linen.

Rosa lay in the tiny guest room, which had been her grandfather's room, and smoked a cigarette. Aunt Lily's face appeared at the door.

"Now, Rosa, I don't allow smoking or drinking in my house."

Rosa rose from the bed to put her cigarette out, her aunt watching her as if she were a child.

"_You_ used to smoke and drink," Rosa said, piqued at her aunt's self-righteous tone.

"Your mama told you that lie," said Aunt Lily, unsmiling. "She was always trying to say I was fast. But I never did drink. I tried to, and it made me sick. Every time she said she didn't want me laying on her freshly made-up bed drunk, I wasn't drunk, I was sick."

"Oh," said Rosa. She had the unfortunate tendency of studying people very closely when they spoke. It occurred to her for the first time that Aunt Lily didn't like her mother.

But *why* didn't Aunt Lily like her mother? The question nagged at her that night as she tried to sleep, then became lost in the many other questions that presented themselves well into the dawn.

Why, for instance, did Ivan no longer like her? And how could you live with someone for over a decade and "love" them, and then, as soon as you were no longer married, you didn't even like them?

Her marriage had been wonderful, she felt. Only the divorce was horrible.

The most horrible thing of all was losing Ivan's friendship and comradely support, which he yanked out of her reach with a vengeance that sent her reeling. Two weeks after the divorce became final, when she was in the hospital for surgery that only after the fact proved to have been minor, he neither called nor sent a note. Sheila, now his wife, wouldn't have liked it, he later (years later) explained.

The next day all the children were in school, and Barbara stood behind Aunt Lily's chair combing and braiding her long silver hair. Rosa sat on the couch looking at them. Raymyna busily vacuumed the bedroom floors, popping in occasionally to bring the mail or a glass of water. She was getting married in a couple of weeks and would be moving out to start her own family. Rosa had of course not said anything when she heard this, but her inner response was surprise. She could not easily comprehend anyone getting married, now that she no longer was, but it was impossible for her to feel happy at the prospect of yet another poor black woman marrying God knows who and starting a family. She would have thought Raymyna would have already had enough.

But who was she to talk. Miss Cynical. She had married. And enjoyed it. She had had a child, and adored it.

In the afternoon her aunt and Raymyna took them sight-seeing. As she understood matters from the local newspapers, all the water she saw—whether canal, river, or ocean—was polluted beyond recall, so that it was hard even to look at it, much less to look at admiringly. She could only gaze at it in sympathy. The beach she also found pitiable. In their attempt to hog it away from the poor, the black, and the local in general, the beachfront "developers" had erected massive boxlike hotels that blocked the view of the water for all except those rich enough to pay for rooms on the beach side of the hotels. Through the cracks between hotels Rosa saw the mostly elderly sun worshipers walking along what seemed to be a pebbly, eroded beach, stretching out their poor white necks to the sun.

Of course they cruised through Little Havana, which stretched for miles. Rosa looked at the new Cuban immigrants with interest. _Gusanos,_ Fidel called them, "worms." She was startled to see that already they seemed as a group to live better and to have more material goods than the black people. Like many Americans who supported the Cuban revolution, she found the Cubans who left Cuba somewhat less noble than the ones who stayed. Clearly the ones who left were the ones with money. Hardly anyone in Cuba could afford the houses, the cars, the clothes, the television sets, and the lawn mowers she saw.

At dinner she tried to explain why and how she had missed her grandfather's funeral. The telegram had come the evening before she left for Cyprus. As she had left her stoop the next morning she had felt herself heading in the wrong direction. But she could not stop herself. It had taken all her meager energy to plan the trip to Cyprus, with a friend who claimed it was beautiful, and she simply could not think to change her plans. Nor could she, still bearing the wounds of her separation from Ivan, face her family.

Barbara and Aunt Lily listened to her patiently. It didn't surprise her that neither knew where Cyprus was, or what its politics and history were. She told them about the man whose son was killed and how he seemed to hate his "worthless" daughter for being alive.

"Women are not valued in their culture," she explained. "In fact, the Greeks, the Turks, and the Cypriots have this one thing in common, though they fight over everything else. The father kept saying, 'A man should have many sons.' His wife flinched guiltily when he said it."

"After Ma died, I went and got my father," Aunt Lily was saying. "And I told him, 'No smoking and drinking in my house.' "

But her grandfather had always smoked. He smoked a pipe. Rosa had liked the smell of it.

"And no card playing and no noise and no complaining, because I don't want to hear it."

Others of Rosa's brothers and sister had come to see him. She had been afraid to. In the pictures she saw, he always looked happy. When he was not dead-tired or drunk, happy was how he'd looked. A deeply silent man, with those odd peaceful eyes. She did not know, and she was confident her aunt didn't, what he really thought about anything. So he had stopped smoking, her aunt thought, but Rosa's brothers had always slipped him tobacco. He had stopped drinking. That was possible. Even before his wife, Rosa's grandmother, had died, he had given up liquor. Or, as he said, it had given him up. So, no noise. Little company. No complaining. But he wasn't the complaining type, was he? He liked best of all, Rosa thought, to be left alone. And he liked baseball. She felt he had liked her too. She hoped he did. But never did he say so. And he was so stingy! In her whole life he'd only given her fifteen cents. On the other hand, he'd financed her sister Barbara's trade-school education, which her father, his son, had refused to do.

Was that what she had held against him on the flight toward the Middle East? There was no excuse, she'd known it all the time. She needed to be back there, to say goodbye to the spiritcase. For wasn't she beginning to understand the appearance of his spiritcase as her own spirit struggled and suffered?

That night, massaging Barbara's thin shoulders before turning in, she looked into her own face reflected in the bureau mirror. She was beginning to have the look her grandfather had when he was very, very tired. The look he got just before something broke in him and he went on a mind-killing drunk. It was there in her eyes. So clearly. The look of abandonment. Of having no support. Of loneliness so severe every minute was a chant against self-destruction.

She massaged Barbara, but she knew her touch was that of a stranger. At what point, she wondered, did you lose connection with the people you loved? And she remembered going to visit

Barbara when she was in college and Barbara lived a short bus ride away. And she was present when Barbara's husband beat her and called her names and once he had locked both of them out of the house overnight. And her sister called the police and they seemed nice to Rosa, so recently up from the South, but in fact they were bored and cynical as they listened to Barbara's familiar complaint. Rosa was embarrassed and couldn't believe anything so sordid could be happening to them, so respected was their family in the small town they were from. But, in any event, Barbara continued to live with her husband many more years. Rosa was so hurt and angry she wanted to kill, but most of all, she was disappointed in Barbara, who threw herself into the inevitable weekend battles with passionately vulgar language Rosa had never heard any woman, not to mention her gentle sister, use before. Her sister's spirit seemed polluted to her, so much so that the sister she had known as a child seemed gone altogether.

Was disappointment, then, the hardest thing to bear? Or was it the consciousness of being powerless to change things, to help? And certainly she had been very conscious of that. As her brother-in-law punched out her sister, Rosa had almost felt the blows on her body. But she had not flung herself between them wielding a butcher knife, as she had done once when Barbara was being at-tacked by their father, another raving madman.

Barbara had wanted to go their brother's grammar-school grad-uation. Their father had insisted that she go to the funeral of an elderly church mother instead. Barbara had tried to refuse. But *crack,* he had slapped her across the face. She was sixteen, plump, and lovely. Rosa adored her. She ran immediately to get the knife, but she was so small no one seemed to notice her, wedging herself between them. But had she been larger and stronger she might have killed him, for even as a child she was serious in all she did— and then what would her life, the life of a murderer, have been like?

Thinking of that day now, she wept. At her love, at her sister's anguish.

Barbara had been forced to go to the funeral, the print of her father's fingers hidden by powder and rouge. Rosa had been little and weak, and she did not understand what was going on anyway between her father and her sister. To her, her father acted like he was jealous. And in college later, after such a long struggle to get there, how could she stab her brother-in-law to death without killing her future, herself? And so she had lain on her narrow foldaway cot in the tiny kitchen in the stuffy apartment over the Laundromat and had listened to the cries and whispers, the pummelings, the screams and pleas. And then, still awake, she listened to the sibilant sounds of "making up," harder to bear and to understand than the fights.

She had not killed for her sister. (And one would have had to kill the mindless drunken brutalizing husband; a blow to the head might only have made him more angry.) Her guilt had soon clouded over the love, and around Barbara she retreated into a silence that she now realized was very like her grandfather's. The sign in him of disappointment hinged to powerlessness. A thoughtful black man in the racist early-twentieth-century South, he probably could have told her a thing or two about the squeaking of the hinge. But had he? No. He'd only complained about his wife, and so convincingly that for a time Rosa, like everyone else in the family, lost respect for her grandmother. It seemed her problem was that she was not mentally quick; and because she stayed with him even as he said this, Rosa and her relatives were quick to agree. Yet there was nowhere else she could have gone. Perhaps her grandfather had found the house in which they lived, but she, her grandmother, had made it a home. Once the grandmother died, the house seemed empty, though he remained behind until Aunt Lily had moved him into her house in Miami.

The day before Rosa and Barbara were to fly back north, Aunt Lily was handing out the remaining odds and ends of their grandfather's things. Barbara got the trunk, that magic repository of tobacco and candy when they were children. Rosa received a small shaving mirror with a gilt lion on its back. There were several of the large, white "twenty-five-cent hanskers" her grandfather had used. The granddaughters received half a dozen each. That left only her grandfather's hats. One brown and one gray: old, worn, none-too-clean fedoras. Rosa knew Barbara was far too fastidious to want them. She placed one on her head. She loved how she looked—she looked like him—in it.

It was killing her, how much she loved him. And he'd been so mean to her grandmother, and so stingy too. Once he had locked her grandmother out of the house because she had bought herself a penny stick of candy from the grocery money. But this was a story her parents told her, from a time before Rosa was born.

By the time she knew him he was mostly beautiful. Peaceful, mystical almost, in his silences and calm, and she realized he was imprinted on her heart just that way. It really did not seem fair.

To check her tears, she turned to Aunt Lily.

"Tell me what my father was like as a boy," she said.

Her aunt looked at her, she felt, with hatred.

"You should have asked him when he was alive."

Rosa looked about for Barbara, who had disappeared into the bathroom. By now she was weeping openly. Her aunt looking at her impassively.

"I don't want to find myself in anything you write. And you can just leave your daddy alone, too."

She could not remember whether she'd ever asked her father about his life. But surely she had, since she knew quite a lot. She turned and walked into the bathroom, forgetful that she was thirty-five, her sister forty-one, and that you can only walk in on your sister in the toilet if you are both children. But it didn't matter. Barbara had always been accessible, always protective. Rosa remembered one afternoon when she was five or six, she and Barbara and a cousin of theirs about Barbara's age set out on an errand. They were walking silently down the dusty road when a large car driven by a white man nearly ran them down. His car sent up billows of dust from the dirt road that stung their eyes and stained their clothes. Instinctively Rosa had picked up a fistful of sand from the road and thrown it after him. He stopped the car, backed it up furiously, and slammed on the brakes, getting out next to them, three black, barefoot girls who looked at him as only they could. Was he a human being? Or a devil? At any rate, he had seen Rosa throw the sand, he said, and he wanted the older girls to warn her against doing such things, "for the little nigger's own good."

Rosa would have admitted throwing the sand. After all, the man had seen her.

But "she didn't throw no sand," said Barbara, quietly, striking a heavy, womanish pose with both hands on her hips.

"She did so," said the man, his face red from heat and anger.

"She didn't," said Barbara.

The cousin simply stared at the man. After all, what was a small handful of sand compared to the billows of sand with which he'd covered them?

Cursing, the man stomped into his car, and drove off.

For a long time it had seemed to Rosa that only black people were always in danger. But there was also the sense that her big sister would know how to help them out of it.

But now, as her sister sat on the commode, Rosa saw a look on her face that she had never seen before, and she realized her sister had heard what Aunt Lily said. It was a look that said she'd got the reply she deserved. For wasn't she always snooping about the family's business and turning things about in her writing in ways that made the family shudder? There was no talking to her as you talked to regular people. The minute you opened your mouth a meter went on. Rosa could read all this on her sister's face. She didn't need to speak. And it was a lonely feeling that she had. For Barbara was right. Aunt Lily, too. And she could no more stop the meter running than she could stop her breath. An odd look across the room fifteen years ago still held the power to make her wonder about it, try to "decipher" or at least understand it. This was her curse: never to be able to forget, truly, but only to appear to forget. And then to record what she could not forget.

Suddenly, in her loneliness, she laughed.

"He was a recorder with his eyes," she said, under her breath. For it seemed to her she'd penetrated her grandfather's serenity, his frequent silences. The meter had ticked in him, too; he, too, was all attentiveness. But for him that had had to be enough. She'd rarely seen him with a pencil in his hand; she thought he'd only had one or two years of school. She imagined him "writing" stories during his long silences merely by thinking them, not embarrassing other people with them, as she did.

She had been obsessed by this old man whom she so definitely resembled. And now, perhaps, she knew why.

We were kindred spirits, she thought, as she sat, one old dusty fedora on her head, the other in her lap, on the plane home. But in a lot of ways, before I knew him, he was a jerk.

She thought of Ivan. For it was something both of them had said often about their relationship: that though he was white and she was black, they were in fact kindred spirits. And she had thought so, until the divorce, after which his spirit became as unfathomable to her as her grandfather's would have been before she knew him. But perhaps Ivan, too, was simply acting like a jerk?

She felt, as she munched the dry crackers and cheese the pert stewardess brought, in the very wreckage of her life. She had not really looked at Barbara since that moment in the toilet, when it became clear to her how her sister really perceived her. She knew she would not see Aunt Lily again and that if Aunt Lily died before she herself did, she would not go to her funeral. Nor would she ever, ever write about her. She took a huge swallow of ginger ale and tried to drown out the incessant ticking of the meter.

She stroked the soft felt of her grandfather's hat, thought of how peculiarly the human brain grows, from an almost invisible seed, and how, in this respect, it was rather similar to understanding, a process it engendered. She looked into her grandfather's shaving mirror and her eyes told her she could bear very little more. She felt herself begin to slide into the long silence in which such thoughts would be her sole companions. Maybe she would even find happiness there.

But then, just when she was almost gone, Barbara put on their grandfather's other hat and reached for her hand.

Suggestions for Further Reading

What follows is a selected list of collections of stories and novels by important contemporary southern women writers. I have confined my selections to recent titles in readily available editions. Inevitably, fine writers have been excluded, but I have tried to represent the range of southern fiction by women, both in the story and in the novel. Many of these writers are quite prolific, and I can include here only a selection of titles by each.

Adams, Alice. *Beautiful Girl: Stories.* 1979. Reprint. New York: Ballantine, 1988.

Adams, Gail Galloway. *The Purchase of Order: Stories.* Athens: University of Georgia Press, 1988.

Alther, Lisa. *Original Sins.* New York: Knopf, 1981.

Arnow, Harriette Simpson. *The Dollmaker.* Lexington: University Press of Kentucky, 1985.

Athas, Daphne. *Cora.* New York: Viking, 1978.

Bambara, Toni Cade. *Gorilla, My Love.* New York: Random House, 1981.

——— . *The Salt Eaters.* New York: Random House, 1981.

——— . *The Sea Birds Are Still Alive: Stories.* New York: Random House, 1982.

Betts, Doris. *Beasts of the Southern Wild and Other Stories.* New York: Harper & Row, 1973.

——— . *Heading West.* New York: New American Library, 1982.

Brown, Mary Ward. *Tongues of Flame.* New York: Washington Square Press, 1987.

Brown, Rita Mae. *Bingo.* New York: Bantam, 1988.

——— . *High Hearts.* New York: Bantam, 1987.

——— . *Rubyfruit Jungle.* New York: Bantam, 1988.

——— . *Sudden Death.* New York: Bantam, 1984.

Brown, Rosellen. *The Autobiography of My Mother.* New York: Ballantine, 1981.

——— . *Civil Wars: A Novel.* New York: Penguin, 1985.

——— . *Tender Mercies.* New York: Penguin, 1986.

——— . *Street Games.* New York: Ballantine, 1983.

Burroway, Janet. *Material Goods.* Tallahassee: University Presses of Florida, 1980.

————. *Opening Nights.* New York: Bantam, 1986.

————. *Raw Silk.* New York: Bantam, 1986.

Childress, Alice. *Like One of the Family: Conversations from a Domestic's Life.* Boston: Beacon Press, 1986.

————. *A Short Walk.* New York: Avon, 1981.

————. *Those Other People.* New York: Putnam, 1988.

Covington, Vicki. *Gathering Home.* New York: Simon and Schuster, 1988.

Cox, Elizabeth. *Familiar Ground.* New York: Avon, 1986.

Crone, Moira. *A Period of Confinement.* New York: Harper and Row, 1987.

————. *The Life of Lucy Fern.* New York: Cambridge Book Co., 1983.

————. *The Winnebago Mysteries and Other Stories.* New York: Fiction Collective, 1982.

Douglas, Ellen. *The Rock Cried Out.* New York: Harcourt, Brace, Jovanovich, 1979.

Durban, Pam. *All Set About with Fever Trees and Other Stories.* Boston: Godine, 1985.

Flynt, Candace. *Chasing Dad.* New York: Dial Press, 1980.

————. *Mother Love.* New York: Farrar, Straus, Giroux & Co., 1987.

————. *Sins of Omission.* New York: Random House, 1984.

Furman, Laura. *The Glass House, a Novella and Stories.* New York: Viking, 1980.

————. *The Shadow Line.* New York: Viking, 1982.

————. *Tuxedo Park.* New York: Ballantine, 1987.

————. *Watch Time Fly: Stories.* New York: Viking, 1983.

Geary, Patricia. *Living in Ether.* New York: Bantam, 1987.

————. *Strange Toys.* New York: Bantam, 1987.

Gilchrist, Ellen. *The Anna Papers: A Novel.* Boston: Little, Brown & Co., 1988.

————. *Drunk with Love: A Book of Stories.* Boston: Little, Brown & Co., 1986.

————. *In the Land of Dreamy Dreams: Short Fiction.* Boston: Little, Brown & Co., 1981.

————. *Victory Over Japan: a Book of Stories.* Boston: Little, Brown & Co., 1984.

Gingher, Marianne. *Bobby Rex's Greatest Hit.* New York: Atheneum, 1986.

——— . *Teen Angel.* New York: Atheneum, 1988.
Godwin, Gail. *Dream Children.* New York: Avon, 1983.
——— . *The Finishing School.* New York: Avon, 1986.
——— . *A Southern Family.* New York: Morrow, 1987.
——— . *Violet Clay.* New York: Penguin, 1986.
Gordon, Caroline. *The Collected Stories of Caroline Gordon.* New York: Farrar, Straus, Giroux & Co., 1981.
Grau, Shirley Ann. *Evidence of Love.* New York: Knopf, 1977.
——— . *The House on Coliseum Street.* New York: Avon, 1986.
——— . *The Keepers of the House.* New York: Avon, 1985.
——— . *Nine Women.* New York: Avon, 1987.

Hagy, Alyson Carol. *Madonna on Her Back: Stories.* S. Wright, 1986.
Hall, Martha Lacy. *Call It Living: Three Stories.* Athens, Ga.: Metamorphosis, 1982.
——— . *Music Lesson: Stories.* Urbana: University of Illinois Press, 1984.
Hardwick, Elizabeth. *The Ghostly Lover.* New York: Ecco Press, 1982.
——— . *The Simple Truth.* New York: Ecco Press, 1982.
——— . *Sleepless Nights.* New York: Vintage Books, 1980.
Hood, Mary. *And Venus Is Blue.* New York: Washington Square Press, 1987.
——— . *How Far She Went: Stories.* New York: Avon, 1986.
Hughes, Mary Gray. *The Calling: Stories.* Urbana: University of Illinois Press, 1980.
Humphreys, Josephine. *Dreams of Sleep.* New York: Penguin, 1985.
——— . *Rich in Love.* New York: Penguin, 1988.

Inness-Brown, Elizabeth. *Satin Palms: Stories.* Canton, N.Y.: Fiction International, 1981.

Jones, Gayl. *Corregidora.* Boston: Beacon Press, 1986.
——— . *Eva's Man.* Boston: Beacon Press, 1987.
——— . *White Rat.* New York: Random House, 1977.

Kornblatt, Joyce Reiser. *Breaking Bread.* New York: Dutton, 1987.
——— . *Nothing To Do With Love.* New York: Viking, 1981.
——— . *White Water.* New York: Dell, 1985.

Lowry, Beverly. *Breaking Gentle.* New York: Viking, 1988.
——— . *Come Back, Lolly Ray.* New York: Popular Library, 1978.
——— . *Daddy's Girl.* New York: Viking, 1981.
——— . *Emma Blue.* Garden City, NY: Doubleday, 1978.
——— . *The Perfect Sonya.* New York: Penguin, 1988.

Martin, Valerie. *Alexandra.* New York: Farrar, Straus, Giroux & Co., 1979.

————. *The Consolation of Nature, and Other Stories.* Boston: Houghton Mifflin, 1988.

————. *A Recent Martyr.* Boston: Houghton Mifflin, 1987.

————. *Set in Motion.* New York: Avon, 1979.

Mason, Bobbie Ann. *In Country: A Novel.* New York: Perennial Library, 1986.

————. *Shiloh and Other Stories.* New York: Perennial Library, 1985.

————. *Spence + Lila.* New York: Harper & Row, 1988.

McCorkle, Jill. *The Cheer Leader: A Novel.* New York: Penguin, 1985.

————. *July 7th: A Novel.* New York: Penguin, 1985.

————. *Tending to Virginia: A Novel.* Chapel Hill, N.C.: Algonquin Books, 1987.

Moose, Ruth. *The Wreath Ribbon Quilt and Other Stories.* Laurinburg, NC: St. Andrew's Press, 1987.

Morgan, Berry. *The Mystic Adventures of Roxie Stoner.* Boston: Houghton, Mifflin, 1974.

Norris, Gloria. *Looking for Bobby: A Novel.* New York: Knopf, 1985.

————. *Three Stories.* New York: Turnipseed Press, 1986.

Norris, Helen. *The Christmas Wife: Stories.* Urbana: University of Illinois Press, 1985.

————. *More Than Seven Watchmen.* Grand Rapids, Mich.: Zondervan, 1985.

————. *Water Into Wine.* Urbana: University of Illinois Press, 1988.

Nye, Naomi Shihab. *Yellow Glove.* Portland, Ore.: Breitenbush Books, 1986.

Osborn, Carolyn. *The Fields of Memory: Short Stories.* Bryan, Texas: Shearer Pub., 1984.

————. *A Horse of Another Color.* Urbana: University of Illinois Press, 1977.

Payne, Peggy. *Revelation.* New York: Simon & Schuster, 1988.

Petroski, Catherine. *Gravity and Other Stories.* Canton, N.Y.: Fiction International, 1981.

————. *The Summer That Lasted Forever.* Boston: Houghton Mifflin, 1984.

Phillips, Jayne Anne. *Black Tickets.* New York: Dell, 1984.

————. *Fast Lanes.* New York: Washington Square Press, 1988.

————. *Machine Dreams.* New York: Pocket Books, 1985.

Settle, Mary Lee. *Blood Tie.* New York: Signet, 1986.

Shivers, Louise. *Here to Get My Baby Out of Jail.* New York: Fawcet Crest, 1984.

Shockley, Ann Allen. *The Black and White of It.* Tallahassee, Fla.: Naiad Press, 1987.

————. *Loving Her.* Tallahassee, Fla.: Naiad Press, 1987.

————. *Say Jesus and Come to Me.* Tallahassee, Fla.: Naiad Press, 1987.

Shreve, Susan Richards. *Children of Power: A Novel.* New York: Berkley Books, 1980.

————. *Dreaming of Heroes: A Novel.* New York: Berkley Books, 1986.

————. *Miracle Play.* New York: Playboy Paperbacks, 1982.

————. *Queen of Hearts.* New York: Pocket Books, 1988.

Smith, Lee. *Black Mountain Breakdown.* New York: Ballantine, 1986.

————. *Cakewalk.* New York: Ballantine, 1983.

————. *Fair and Tender Ladies.* New York: G. P. Putnam's Sons, 1988.

————. *Family Linen.* New York: Ballantine, 1986.

————. *Fancy Strut.* New York: Ballantine, 1987.

Spencer, Elizabeth. *Fire in the Morning.* New York: Avon, 1987.

————. *Jack of Diamonds and Other Stories.* New York: Viking, 1988.

————. *The Stories of Elizabeth Spencer.* New York: Penguin, 1983.

————. *The Voice at the Back Door.* New York: Avon, 1986.

Taylor, Sheila Ortiz. *Faultline: A Novel.* Tallahassee, Fla.: Naiad Press, 1982.

————. *Spring Forward/Fall Back: A Novel.* Tallahassee, Fla.: Naiad Press, 1985.

Tyler, Anne. *The Accidental Tourist.* New York: Penguin, 1986.

————. *Breathing Lessons.* New York: Knopf, 1988.

————. *Celestial Navigation.* New York: Berkley Books, 1984.

————. *Dinner at the Homesick Restaurant.* New York: Berkley Books, 1983.

Walker, Alice. *The Color Purple.* New York: Pocket Books, 1985.

————. *Meridian.* New York: Pocket Books, 1986.

————. *The Third Life of Grange Copeland.* New York: Pocket Books, 1988.

————. *You Can't Keep a Good Woman Down: Stories.* New York: Harcourt Brace Jovanovich, 1982.

Williams, Joan. *Country Woman.* Boston: Atlantic-Little, Brown, 1983.

————. *Pariah and Other Stories.* Boston: Atlantic-Little, Brown, 1983.

Williams, Joy. *Breaking and Entering.* New York: Vintage, 1988.

————. *The Changeling.* Garden City, N.J.: Doubleday, 1978.

—————— . *State of Grace.* New York: Charles Scribner's Sons, 1986.
—————— . *Taking Care: Short Stories.* New York: Vintage, 1985.
Wilson, Leigh Allison. *From the Bottom Up: Stories.* New York: Penguin, 1984.
—————— . *Wind Stories.* New York: Morrow, 1989.

Notes on Contributors

Alice Adams was born in 1926 in Fredericksburg, Virginia. She received her B.A. from Radcliffe College and has published a number of novels and short story collections. Her most recent novel *Second Chances* was published by Knopf in 1988. Her short story collections include *Beautiful Girl* (1979) and *Return Trips* (1984). Her stories have appeared in *The New Yorker*, *Atlantic*, *Paris Review*, and *Redbook*. She lives in California.

Toni Cade Bambara was born in New York City, but she nows lives with her daughter in Atlanta, where she has been writer in residence at Spelman College since 1977. She holds a B.A. from Queens College and an M.A. from the City College of the City University of New York. Her collections of short fiction include *The Black Woman* (1980), *Gorilla, My Love* (1972), and *The Sea Birds Are Still Alive* (1977). Her novel *The Salt Eaters* was published by Vintage Books in 1981.

Sallie Bingham was born in 1937 in Louisville, Kentucky. She received her B.A.
from Radcliffe College and has published
widely in such journals as the *Atlantic, Redbook, Shenandoah,* and *Greensboro Review.*
She has received an O. Henry Award, the
Greensboro Review Fiction Award, and has
held fellowships at Yaddo, the McDowell
Colony, and the Virginia Center for the
Creative Arts. Her novels and short story
collections include *After Such Knowledge*
(1959), *Touching Hand* (1968), and *The Way
It Is Now* (1972). She is also a playwright;
her work has been produced by the American Place Theater in New York and the
Actor's Theater of Louisville, among others. Her autobiography, *Passion and Preju-
dice,* was published by Knopf in 1989. She
lives in Prospect, Kentucky.

Jane Bradley teaches writing and wom-
en's studies at Virginia Polytechnic Institute
and State University in Blacksburg. Her
stories have appeared in the *North American
Review, Virginia Quarterly Review,* and *Kan-
sas Quarterly.* Her collection of stories,
Power Lines, is being published by the University of Arkansas Press. She is currently
working on a novel, *The Importance of
Things.* Bradley is also a playwright; her
work has been produced in Syracuse, N.Y.,
and she has recently completed a play on
the life of Kathe Kollwitz.

Mary Ward Brown was reared on a farm in the Black Belt of Alabama where she still lives. In addition to her collection *Tongues of Flame* (1986), she has published stories in *Prairie Schooner, McCall's, U.S. Catholic,* and *New Stories from the South: The Year's Best, 1986.*

Moira Crone was born and grew up in the tobacco country of Eastern North Carolina. She attended Smith College and The Johns Hopkins University in the 1970s. Her early stories are collected in *The Winnebago Mysteries* (Fiction Collective, 1982). Her fiction has appeared in *The New Yorker, Mademoiselle, Ohio Review, Southern Review,* and *American Voice.* Her first novel, *A Period of Confinement* appeared in 1986. In 1987–88 she was a fellow at The Bunting Institute of Radcliffe College, where she worked on a new novel. She teaches at Louisiana State University.

Pam Durban was born in South Carolina in 1947. She holds a B.A. from the University of North Carolina at Greensboro and an M.F.A. from the University of Iowa. In 1985 her first collection of stories, *All Set About with Fever Trees,* was published by Godine. Her stories have appeared in the *Georgia Review, Crazyhorse, Tri Quarterly,* and *New Writers of the South.* She has received a James Michener Fellowship, a *Crazyhorse* Fiction Award, and the Mary Roberts Rhinehart Award. She teaches at Georgia State University in Atlanta where she is at work on a novel.

Ellen Gilchrist was born in 1935 in Vicksburg, Mississippi. She received her B.A. from Millsaps College and attended the University of Arkansas. In addition to her books of short stories, _Drunk With Love, In the Land of Dreamy Dreams,_ and _Victory Over Japan,_ she has published a collection of poetry and two novels. Her novel _The Anna Papers_ appeared in 1988. Gilchrist has received a fellowship from the National Endowment for the Arts and won the American Book Award for Fiction for _Victory Over Japan._ She won a national scriptwriting competition from the National Educational Television Network for "A Season of Dreams," based on stories by Eudora Welty. She lives in Fayetteville, Arkansas.

Marianne Gingher was born in Guam and grew up in Greensboro, North Carolina, where she was educated in the public schools. She holds degrees in art and in English, and in 1974 received an M.F.A. in creative writing from the University of North Carolina at Greensboro. Her short fiction has appeared in _Greensboro Review, Carolina Quarterly, South Carolina Review, North American Review, Redbook, McCall's,_ and _Seventeen._ A collection of short fiction, _Teen Angel,_ was published by Atheneum in 1988. Her novel _Bobby Rex's Greatest Hit_ (Atheneum, 1986) won the Sir Walter Raleigh Award for fiction and was cited as a Best Book for 1986 by the American Library Association. Other awards include a Bread Loaf Fellowship and a P.E.N. Syndicated Fiction Prize. Gingher lives in Greensboro and teaches writing and literature at the University of North Carolina at Chapel Hill.

Gail Godwin was born in 1937 in Birmingham, Alabama, and grew up in Asheville, North Carolina. She holds a B.A. from the University of North Carolina at Chapel Hill and M.A. and Ph.D. degrees from the University of Iowa. She has published numerous novels and collections of stories, most recently *The Finishing School* (1985) and *A Southern Family* (1988). She also writes libretti, including the libretti to "Anna Margarita's Will" and other works by Robert Starer. Godwin has received fellowships from the National Endowment for the Arts and the Guggenheim Foundation and a literature award from the American Institute and Academy for Arts and Letters. She lives in Woodstock, New York.

Shirley Ann Grau was born in 1929 in New Orleans, Louisiana. She holds a B.A. from Tulane University. She has published eight books of fiction, most recently a collection of stories, *Nine Women* (1985). Her two previous collections of stories are *The Black Prince* (1955) and *The Wind Shifting West* (1973). In 1965 she received the Pulitzer Prize in Fiction for *Keepers of the House*. Other novels include *The House On Coliseum Street* (1961), *The Condor Passes* (1971), and *Evidence of Love* (1977). She divides her time between Metairie, Louisiana, and Martha'a Vineyard.

Mary Hood is a native of coastal Georgia and currently lives and writes in Woodstock in the north Georgia foothills. Her short stories and essays have appeared in *Georgia Review*, *Harper's*, *Kenyon Review*, *Best American Short Stories 1984*, and *North American Review*. She has published two collections of short fiction, *How Far She Went* (1983) and *And Venus Is Blue* (1986), and she has recently completed a novel. She is the recipient of a Pushcart Prize, the 1983 Flannery O'Connor Award for Short fiction, and the *Southern Review*/Louisiana State University Short Fiction Award.

Gayl Jones was born in 1949 in Lexington, Kentucky. She received a B.A. from Connecticut College and B.A. and D.A. degrees from Brown University. She has published two novels, *Corregidora* (1975), and *Eva's Man* (1976), and a collection of stories, *White Rat* (1977). Recently she has written narrative poems including *Song for Anninho* and *Xarque* (Lotus Press, 1981, 1985). Jones has received fellowships from the National Endowment for the Arts, the Michigan Society of Fellows and a Howard Foundation Award. She last taught at the University of Michigan, Ann Arbor.

Bobbie Ann Mason was born in 1940 in Mayfield, Kentucky. She received her B.A. from the University of Kentucky, an M.A. from the State University of New York at Binghamton, and a Ph.D. from the University of Connecticut. She has published in *The New Yorker, Atlantic, Redbook,* and other magazines. Her stories have been collected in *Shiloh and Other Stories* (1982); and she has published two novels, *In Country* (1985) and *Spence + Lila* (1988). For *Shiloh and Other Stories* she received a Hemingway Foundation Award in 1983, and she has been awarded fellowships from the National Endowment for the Arts and the Guggenheim Foundation. She lives in Pennsylvania.

Jill McCorkle was born in 1958 in Lumberton, North Carolina. She received a B.A. from the University of North Carolina at Chapel Hill and an M.A. from Hollins College. In 1984 Algonquin Books published her novels *The Cheerleader* and *July 7.* Her most recent novel, *Tending to Virgina,* appeared in 1987. She lives in Boston.

Naomi Shihab Nye was born in St. Louis, Missouri, in 1952. She holds a B.A. from Trinity University in San Antonio, Texas. Her books of poetry are *Different Ways to Pray, Hugging the Jukebox* (National Poetry Series), and *Yellow Glove,* all available from Breitenbush Books, Portland, Oregon. For *Hugging the Jukebox* she was the co-winner of the Texas Institute of Letters poetry award in 1982. The story printed here was cited among the year's best in the 1984 Pushcart Prize anthology. Nye lives in San Antonio.

Jayne Anne Phillips was born in 1952 in Buckhannon, West Virginia. She received her B.A. from the University of West Virginia and her M.A. from the University of Iowa. She has contributed to *Iowa Review, Fiction International, Ploughshares,* and *Atlantic.* Among her collections of short stories are *Black Tickets* (1979) and *Fast Lanes* (1987). Her novel *Machine Dreams* appeared in 1984. Phillips has received numerous awards including a National Endowment for the Arts Fellowship, the Sue Kaufman Award for First Fiction from the American Academy of Arts and Letters, and a Bunting Institute Fellowship from Radcliffe College. She lives in Boston.

Ann Allen Shockley was born in 1927 in Louisville, Kentucky. She received her B.A. from Fisk University and her M.S.L.S. from Case Western Reserve University. She has published three works of fiction, *Loving Her* (1974), *The Black and White of It* (1980), and *Say Jesus and Come to Me* (1982). Her stories have appeared in *New Letters, Black World, Essence, Liberator,* and *Sinister Wisdom.* In addition she has written numerous nonfiction works on black American writers, including *Living Black American Authors* (with Sue P. Chandler). She is special collections librarian at Fisk University in Nashville, Tennessee.

Lee Smith was born in Grundy, Virginia. She received her B.A. from Hollins College and attended the Sorbonne. She has published one collection of stories, *Cakewalk* (1979), and seven novels including *Oral History* (1983), *Family Linen* (1985), and most recently *Fair and Tender Ladies* (1988). She received a Book-of-the-Month Club fellowship for her first novel, *The Last Day the Dogbushes Bloomed,* and her other honors include two O. Henry Awards, a Sir Walter Raleigh Award, and the North Carolina Award for Literature. She teaches at North Carolina State University in Raleigh.

Elizabeth Spencer was born in 1921 in Carrollton, Mississippi, and received the B.A. from Belhaven College in Jackson, Mississippi. Her M.A. is from Vanderbilt University. She has published numerous novels and collections of stories, including *Fire in the Morning* (1948), *The Light in the Piazza* (1960), *Ship Island and Other Stories* (1969), *The Snare* (1972), *The Collected Stories* (1981), and most recently *Jack of Diamonds* (1988). In 1988 she was one of three writers to receive an award from the National Endowment for the Arts for her "extraordinary contribution" to American literature. She lived for many years in Montreal, Canada, and has recently moved to Chapel Hill, North Carolina, where she teaches at the University of North Carolina.

Alice Walker was born in 1944 in Eatonton, Georgia. She received her B.A. from Sarah Lawrence College. She has published numerous essays, fiction, and poetry, including *In Search of Our Mother's Gardens: Womanist Prose* (1983); story collections *In Love and Trouble* (1973) and *You Can't Keep a Good Woman Down* (1981); and the novels *Meridian* (1976) and *The Color Purple* (1982). She has received an award from the American Academy and Institute of Arts and Letters, the Lillian Smith Award of the Southern Regional Council, and a Guggenheim Fellowship. *The Color Purple* was awarded the 1983 Pulitzer Prize for Fiction and the American Book Award for fiction. Walker lives in San Francisco.